HERITAGE

Country
Harvest

C O O K B O O K

OVER 700 FAVORITE RECIPES FROM THE
AMISH IN NORTHERN INDIANA

Ray and Malinda Yutzy
1545 W 450 N
Howe, IN 46746

First Printing April 2001, 5M
Second Printing September 2001, 7.5M
Third Printing October 2002, 7.5M
Fourth Printing August 2003, 7.5M
Fifth Printing March 2004, 7.5M

ISBN 1-890050-45-8 (Spiral)

2673 TR 421
Sugarcreek, OH 44681

Carlisle Printing
WALNUT CREEK

Contents

Acknowledgments

We wish to thank everyone from the northern Indiana Amish community that helped with this cookbook. Many of these recipes are used daily and are quite delicious! We hope you will enjoy them. We invite you to visit our farms, wood shops and country stores.

Sincerely,

The Raymond & Malinda Yutzy Family

1545 W 450 N

Howe, IN 46746

Amish Roots

Who are the Amish? This is a question often asked by newcomers who never saw the horse and buggy folks of nothern Indiana.

As an introduction we will try to answer this question. They are only ordinary folks who try to live a godly life in a world full of uncertainties. They try to live a simple life and as close to nature as possible in a rural setting. In the past, most were farmers, but in recent years they need to adapt some, while still trying to keep the faith of their forefathers. The New Testament teachings of Jesus Christ are the center of their faith.

We need to go back in time about 475 years. In 1525 a small group of Christian believers in Europe no longer felt comfortable with the Roman Catholic Church, which was the state church at the time. They felt church and state should be separate, (The Amish still adhere to this teaching).

For hundreds of years the State Church controlled almost all aspects of the general population's lives. The group felt uncomfortable with infant baptism that automatically made every child a member of the State Church. They also felt it wasn't right to serve in the military or go to war.

Because of this and numerous other reasons the Swiss Brethren, as they were first called, started a new congregation. At the first service they baptized each other on the confession of Jesus Christ as their personal Saviour. They were called Anabaptists meaning re-baptizers since they had also been baptized as infants. The Swiss Brethren did not believe an infant could understand the seriousness of baptism and the plan of salvation at such a young age.

The Anabaptist movement grew throughout Europe in the 1500s and 1600s even under relentless persecution from the State Church. Many were burned at the stake for their faith. Some were drowned in rivers, some sent to the galleys, beheaded, etc. to try to make them recant.

About 1536 an influential Roman Catholic priest also left the State Church and came to the Anabaptist camp. Menno Simons, a Holland Dutchman was a very powerful preacher and writer and was hunted like an animal after he joined the movement. His writings very much strengthened the Anabaptist churches in western Europe at the time and still have much influence in Christian circles. The Anabaptists were now also called Mennonites.

More than 150 years later, in 1693, a young Mennonite bishop by the name of Jacob Amman became concerned that the church was losing out in simplicity. He felt some New Testament teachings were also being neglected. Amman formed his own group of the more conservative-minded Mennonites and broke away from the mainstream. This group is referred to as the Amish.

In general this group of hardworking farmers and day laborers lived in western Germany, Switzerland, and eastern France. Many Amish worked for rich landlords and became well known for working with the soil, building up the sometimes wartorn farmsteads. Some became excellent horsemen and good animal husbandmen. Family ties were very important.

In the early 1700s the pressures of military conscription in Europe, along with promise of a better life in America, the Amish also were caught up in the immigration movements. Many crossed the wide, dangerous ocean to the promised land of freedom in William Penn's colony in Pennsylvania. After the Revolutionary War many more Amish came to America from Europe. As the States opened up for settlement, the Amish started moving into the frontier; to Ohio, Indiana, and west, along with the "English" pioneers.

In 1841 the first Amish settlers moved into the LaGrange-Elkhart community. The first four families came from Somerset County, Pennsylvania. Starting from this little group there are now over 100 church districts with about 3,000 families.

With so many families (with 5–6 children or more) it takes a great deal of food and food preparation if we wish to live simply and within our means. Along with preserving our spiritual heritage we also wish to preserve hardworking ethics of raising and preserving our own home-grown foods. The Amish however are not exempt from buying from the Aldi and Wal-Mart stores of our day.

FOOD FOR THEIR FAMILIES

Since their beginning, the Amish have believed in strong family ties. A family unit works together for a common cause, whether it is a barn raising, a husking bee for an unfortunate farmer or raising foods in the home garden. Putting up hay and milking cows are also part of the food system along with butchering our own meat. Last but not least, are the ideas of preparing the healthy, delicious meals in the family kitchen.

Most Amish plow their gardens in the spring, but some do in the fall on heavy soils. It needs to be decided how big the garden needs to be to provide enough food for the winter. A plot about 100 feet square will usually be enough space to grow most vegetables and strawber-ries for a family of 6–10.

A typical farm family has enough chores for everyone who is old enough and able to help in the morning and again in the evening. This teaches responsibility and working together for the benefit of all. Amish families on a farm sit around the table each day for three deli-cious, filling meals, and happy conversation and communication. Sel-dom will you find an "It's so-o boring!" attitude. This, along with the hard work in the field and gardens makes for good-sized, well earned appetites.

To satisfy the appetites of these hungry, hard working men, women, and children keeps the cooks busy. Canning, drying, and preserving foods, not to mention all the sewing and mending that goes with a family.

The food traditions handed down from our ancestors in Europe were brought over the ocean and of course blended with what foods were available in the New World. Handed down from mother to daughter, etc. the recipes were preserved in handwritten collections at the time. As printing became more common these were put together, sometimes into cookbooks. Even at that, sometimes a recipe would be lost, never to be found.

The need to ever keep making new cookbooks with newly tried or recently discovered recipes is an ongoing tradition among the Amish. We, in the northern Indiana community have decided to assemble our own unique, new cookbook to keep those precious handed down recipes and newer ones from getting lost or discarded. We think they are from some of the best cooks in the world. Now you may enjoy the HERITAGE COUNTRY HARVEST COOKBOOK that is in your hands. Happy Eating!

J.M. S.M.

Be the Best of Whatever You Are

If you can't be a pine on the top of the hill,
Be a scrub in the valley—but be
The best little scrub by the side of the rill;
Be a bush if you can't be a tree.

We can't all be captains, we've got to be crew,
There's something for all of us here,
There's big work to do, and there's lesser to do,
And the task you must do is near.

If you can't be a highway then just be a trail,
If you can't be the sun be a star;
It isn't by size that you win or you fail—
Be the best of whatever you are.

This Book

This book is now completed
For loved ones far and near
We wish you many blessings
From the recipes in here.

The tips, the hints and sayings
Some humorous, some wise
Are all a part of this good book
And bring sparkle to the eyes.

Good luck to friends and neighbors
As you read this book today
It was only with our trust in God
This book was sent its way.

—LSY

Breakfast
Foods

PANCAKES

Sara Whetstone

1¹/4 c. flour	1 egg
1 Tbsp. sugar	2 Tbsp. oil
3 tsp. baking powder	1¹/4 c. milk
¹/4 tsp. salt	

Mix dry ingredients together then add eggs, oil and milk. Fry.

PANCAKES

Anna Fern Hochstetler

2 eggs (well beaten)	$^1/_2$ c. sugar
5 Tbsp. salad oil or melted butter	1 tsp. salt
	2$^1/_4$ c. flour
2 c. milk	3 scant Tbsp. baking powder

Mix milk, oil, eggs, salt and sugar. Beat well. Stir in flour and baking powder. Stir till most lumps are gone.

FLUFFY PANCAKES

Mrs. Glen (Alma) Whetstone

1 c. flour	$^3/_4$ c. milk
1 Tbsp. sugar	1 egg
2 tsp. baking powder	$^1/_4$ c. vegetable oil
$^1/_2$ tsp. salt	

Mix flour, sugar, baking powder and salt. Then add milk, egg and oil. Stir well.

DELICIOUS PANCAKES

Mrs. Ervin (Edna) Borntrager

2 c. all purpose flour	2 c. milk
4 tsp. baking powder	$^1/_3$ c. vegetable oil
1 tsp. salt	2 eggs
2 Tbsp. sugar	

Mix flour, baking powder, salt and sugar in bowl. Beat eggs and add milk and oil. Add to flour mixture.

POTATO PANCAKES

Mrs. Jr. (Barbara) Yoder

3 c. finely shredded potatoes
1¹/₂ Tbsp. flour
¹/₈ tsp. baking powder
¹/₂–1 tsp. salt
¹/₂ tsp. grated onion
2 eggs (beaten)

Combine potatoes and eggs. Mix dry ingredients and onions. Mix well and drop by tablespoon onto greased skillet. Brown lightly on both sides.

OAT PANCAKES

Mrs. Enos Hilty
Mrs. Daniel Lee Mishler

1 c. oatmeal
1 c. whole wheat flour
2 Tbsp. sugar
2 tsp. baking powder
1 tsp. salt
2 eggs (lightly beaten)
1¹/₂ scant c. milk
¹/₄ c. vegetable oil
1 tsp. lemon juice

Combine oatmeal, flour, sugar, baking powder and salt in bowl. Make a well. Combine eggs, milk, oil and lemon juice. Pour into well and stir until moistened. Pour on lightly greased griddle. Grease only the first time. Makes 6 servings.

OATMEAL PANCAKES

Mrs. Freeman Edna Mishler
Treva Miller

1¹/₂ c. quick oats
2 c. buttermilk
1 tsp. salt
2 eggs (beaten)
1 tsp. soda
1 Tbsp. maple syrup
³/₄ c. whole wheat flour

Soak oatmeal in buttermilk a short time. Beat eggs, add to oatmeal mixture. Add rest of ingredients; mix well. Fry on greased frying pan. Serves 6.

BROWN SUGAR OATMEAL PANCAKES

Mrs. Floyd Bontrager
Mrs. Kenny (Ruby) Schrock

2 eggs (beaten)
4 Tbsp. vegetable oil
2 c. buttermilk (or milk)
1 c. whole wheat flour
1 c. all purpose flour

1 tsp. soda
1 tsp. salt
$^2/_3$ c. brown sugar
$1^1/_4$ c. quick oatmeal

WHOLE WHEAT PANCAKES

Mrs. Ray (Malinda) Yutzy

2 c. whole wheat flour
1 c. oatmeal
4 tsp. baking powder
$^1/_2$ tsp. salt

2 Tbsp. honey
$^1/_4$ c. oil
2 eggs
$1^3/_4$–2 c. milk

Mix together dry ingredients. Add honey, oil and eggs. Stir. Add milk $^1/_2$ cup at a time, beating well each time. Let stand several minutes before frying. Fresh ground flour works best.

JOHNNY CAKE

Lillian Mast

$1^1/_2$ c. cornmeal
$^1/_2$ c. flour
1 egg
1 tsp. salt

1 tsp. soda
1 Tbsp. molasses (optional)
milk

Mix all ingredients and add milk to make consistency of pancake batter. Fry on hot griddle.

WAFFLES

Mrs. Floyd (Loretta) Lehman
Mrs. Leland H. Lambright

4 eggs (separated)   1 rounded c. flour
1 c. milk   2 Tbsp. vanilla
4 Tbsp. butter (melted) $1/2$ tsp. salt

Beat the egg whites till nice and stiff; set aside. Beat remaining ingredients then mix with egg whites using a wire whisk. Bake in waffle iron. Makes about 3 big waffles.

WAFFLES

Marvin and Ruby Hochstetler

3 c. flour $1/2$ c. butter (melted)
1 tsp. salt   2 c. milk
2 tsp. sugar   4 eggs (separated)

Beat egg yolks, add milk and beat for 1 min. Add dry ingredients and melted butter and beat again. Fold in stiffly beaten egg whites. Bake on hot waffle iron.

PANCAKE SYRUP

Mary Esther Whetstone

$1^1/4$ c. brown sugar $1/3$ c. light Karo
$3/4$ c. white sugar   1 c. water

Bring to boil, stirring constantly. Simmer for 5 min. Add 1 tsp. vanilla. White sugar can be omitted and more Karo added for a thicker syrup. Maple flavor may also be added.

SCRAMBLED EGG CASSEROLE
Delilah Yoder

CHEESE SAUCE:

1 Tbsp. butter	$^1/_4$ tsp. salt
2$^1/_2$ Tbsp. flour	$^1/_8$ tsp. pepper
1 c. milk	$^1/_2$ c. American cheese (shredded)

Melt butter, blend in flour and cook for 1 min. Gradually stir in milk. Cook until thick. Add salt, pepper and cheese. Stir until cheese melts.

1 c. ham	$^1/_4$ c. green onion (chopped)
1 (4 oz.) can mushrooms (drained)	1 doz. eggs (beaten)

TOPPING:

$^1/_4$ c. butter (melted)	2$^1/_4$ c. soft bread crumbs

Sauté ham and green onion in butter until onion is tender. Add eggs and cook over med. heat until eggs are set. Stir in mushrooms and cheese sauce. Put eggs in 9" x 13" pan. Put bread crumbs mixed with melted butter over top. Bake at 350° for 30 min.

BREAKFAST CASSEROLE
Mrs. Christy Yoder

5 eggs	12 slices bread (cubed and buttered)
$^1/_2$ tsp. salt	
2$^1/_2$ c. milk	1 lb. sausage (cooked, may
2 c. grated American cheese	also use ham or bacon)
$^1/_4$ tsp. pepper	

Arrange bread cubes in bottom of greased pan. Pour the eggs, which have been beaten, along with the milk, salt and pepper over the bread crumbs. Put meat over this and sprinkle with cheese. Prepare and refrigerate overnight if desired. Bake at 350° for 45 min.

CHEESE SOUFFLE

Anna Fern Hochstetler
Mrs. Amos Yoder

8 slices bread, cubed
1 lb. cheese, grated
6 eggs (beaten)
2 c. milk

$^1/_4$ c. margarine (melted)
1 Tbsp. onion salt
salt and pepper to taste
cubed ham, bacon or sausage

Layer bread, cheese and meat in baking pan. Mix eggs, milk, melted butter and seasonings. Pour over rest of ingredients. Refrigerate overnight. Bake at 325° for 45 min.

BRUNCH BREAKFAST

Mrs. Alvin (Wilma) Beechy

2 c. toasted bread crumbs
1 c. cheddar cheese (grated)
4 eggs
2 c. milk

$^1/_2$ tsp. salt
$^1/_4$ tsp. dry mustard
$^1/_8$ tsp. onion salt
bacon or sausage

Grease 11" x 17" casserole dish. Beat egg, milk and seasonings. Crumble bacon or sausage into egg mixture. Put bread croutons on bottom of dish, next the grated cheese, pour the egg mixture over it. Bake at 325° for 50 min.

BREAKFAST CASSEROLE

Katie Irene Miller

6 qt. potatoes
1 can cream of mushroom
   soup
$1^1/_4$ c. milk

grated cheese
3 lb. sausage
1 lb. bacon
$1^1/_2$ doz. lg. eggs

Cook, grate and fry the potatoes. Mix together soup and milk. Fry bacon and sausage. Scramble the eggs with $^1/_2$ amount of fried bacon. Stir in cheese just as the eggs are about done. May add some minced onion. Put together hot, in order given in casserole dish. Bake at 250° for $^1/_2$ hour. Very delicious!

BREAKFAST CASSEROLE

Mrs. Amos L. Miller

2 (12 oz.) pkgs. link sausage
  or ham
8 slices bread
2 c. grated cheese

8 eggs (beaten with 2 c. milk)
1 tsp. dry mustard
1 tsp. salt
1 can cream of mushroom soup

Brown sausage and cut in 1/4" pieces. Cube bread and spread into 9" x 13" pan. Spread sausage and cheese over bread. Pour eggs over all. Cover with soup; refrigerate overnight. Bake at 325° for 1 hr.

BREAKFAST PIZZA

Mrs. David Eash

1 lb. sausage
1 c. hash browns (optional)
1 c. shredded cheese

1 pkg. (8) crescent rolls
  or homemade pizza dough

5 or 6 eggs, beaten with 1/4 c. milk, 1/2 tsp. salt, 1/8 tsp. pepper

Place dough in 12" pizza pan. Brown sausage and spoon on crust. Sprinkle with potatoes, top with cheese and pour egg mixture over all. Bake at 375° for 25–30 min. Serves 6–8. You may use any kind of meat you desire.

---— ❖ —---

Write down any number, add the next larger number, add 9, divide by 2, subtract the first number. Is your answer 5?

---— ❖ —---

What a wonderful life I've had! If only I'd realized it sooner.

BREAKFAST BURRITOS
Mrs. Amos Yoder

12 eggs (scrambled)
1 lb. pork sausage
$^1/_2$ c. chopped onions
burrito shells
$^1/_2$ c. chopped peppers
5 med. potatoes
cheese

Scramble the eggs with milk and seasonings. Fry the sausage with salt, pepper, onions and chopped peppers. Put potatoes through shredder; fry with seasoning until soft. Mix potatoes, eggs and sausage together, and spoon into burritos. Prepare sausage gravy before hand and put small amount in bottom of baking pan. Next put in burritos and then the rest of gravy. If you use cheese put it with the eggs or on top of burritos before adding last gravy. Bake at 350° for 15–20 min. or until heated through.

GRANOLA CEREAL
Mrs. William (Luella) Schrock

12 c. oatmeal
2 c. brown sugar
2 c. wheat germ
1 c. oleo (melted)
1 Tbsp. vanilla
1 tsp. maple flavoring
1 c. sunflower seeds or nuts
1 lb. graham crackers (crushed)
1 c. toasted coconut (optional)

Toast for 1 hr. at 250°–300°. Honey may be substituted for brown sugar.

GRANOLA
Mrs. Mervin (Ella) Schrock

12 c. quick oats
3 c. coconut
3 c. brown sugar
2 c. wheat flour
3 tsp. salt
$1^1/_2$ c. oleo
1 Tbsp. maple flavoring
1 Tbsp. vanilla

Melt oleo; add flavoring. Mix all dry ingredients. Mix in melted oleo. Toast in slow oven, stirring occasionally.

GRANOLA

Marietta Miller

12 c. oatmeal	3 c. brown sugar
3 c. wheat germ	1 Tbsp. salt
1 c. sunflower seeds	1 c. vegetable oil
3 c. coconut	

Toast in 300° oven stirring every 15 min.

GRANOLA CEREAL

Mrs. William Troyer

$^1/_4$ c. butter	$1^1/_2$ c. oatmeal (rolled)
$^1/_3$ c. honey	1 c. coconut
3 c. Cheerios	1 c. raisins

Heat oven to 350°. In 13" x 9" baking pan melt butter, stir in honey, add remaining ingredients, except raisins, adding them when done baking. Bake 15–20 min., stirring after 10 min. Cool store in tight container.

GRANOLA

Freeman (Edna Ellen) Mishler

4 c. rolled oats	1 tsp. vanilla extract
1 c. oat bran	$^1/_4$ c. Canola oil
1 c. sesame seeds	$^3/_4$ c. maple syrup

Mix well. Toast in slow oven at 250°–300° till done, stirring often. Remove from oven and add variations:

> 1 c. chopped peanuts
> $^1/_2$ c. raisins
> $^1/_2$ c. carob chips

———— ❖ ————

*When God measures men He puts the tape
around the heart, not the head.*

GRANOLA

Mrs. Kenny (Ruby) Schrock

8 c. oatmeal	$1/2$ c. margarine
2 c. coconut	$1/2$ c. brown sugar
1 c. wheat germ	$1/3$ c. vegetable oil
$1/2$ c. sunflower seeds	$1/2$ c. sorghum
dash of salt	$1/3$ c. honey
2 tsp. cinnamon	$1/4$ c. peanut butter
$3/4$ c. nuts	1 tsp. vanilla

Mix first 7 ingredients and set aside. Melt margarine and brown sugar. Add next 5 ingredients. Stir until peanut butter is melted. Pour over oatmeal and stir thoroughly. Toast in 300°–350° oven until golden brown. Stir every 10–15 min. Cool and break up into small pieces.

GRANOLA CEREAL

Mrs. William A. Miller

3 pkgs. graham crackers (fine) or $3/4$ box vanilla wafers	1 c. pecans (optional)
8 c. oatmeal (uncooked)	1 c. maple syrup
2 c. coconut (med.)	1 c. sunflower seeds
$1^1/2$ c. brown sugar	2 c. chocolate chips (optional)
2 tsp. soda	$1/2$ c. wheat germ
1 tsp. salt	4 sticks oleo

Mix dry ingredients except chocolate chips. Melt oleo and syrup and mix well with dry ingredients. The syrup is what makes it good. Bake until golden brown at 300° for 2 hrs. Cool and add chips if you so desire.

———— ❖ ————

If we pause to think, we'll have reason to thank.

APPLESAUCE GRANOLA
Mrs. Daniel (Martha) Miller

3 lb. oatmeal
1 lb. coconut
3/4 lb. oat bran or wheat germ
2 c. brown sugar
1 lb. sunflower seeds
1 Tbsp. cinnamon
1 Tbsp. salt
1 c. vegetable oil
1 qt. applesauce

Mix all dry ingredients well with oil then add applesauce. Toast in oven on low heat till golden, stirring every 15 min.

GRAPE NUTS
Mrs. Elmer Hochstetler

1 c. oleo (melted)
4 c. sour milk
2 tsp. salt
2 tsp. baking powder
2 tsp. vanilla
3 c. brown sugar
5 c. wheat flour
3 c. oatmeal

GRAPE NUTS
Orpha Schrock

5 lb. brown sugar
8 lb. whole wheat flour
1 1/4 Tbsp. salt
1 1/2 c. oleo (melted)
1 1/2 tsp. maple flavor
2 Tbsp. vanilla
2 1/2 qt. buttermilk or sour milk
4 tsp. soda

Put in pans and bake. Put through screen when cooled and toast in slow oven. Makes about 15 lbs.

———— ❖ ————

Acknowledge your own sins—not your neighbor's.

BROWN SUGAR GRAPENUTS

Mrs. Harley H. Lambright
Mrs. Howard Miller

4 c. brown sugar
2 qts. sour milk
4 tsp. salt
4 tsp. baking soda

14 c. whole wheat flour
$^1/_2$ lb. butter (melted)
4 tsp. vanilla flavoring
2 tsp. maple flavoring

Bake at 350° until done. Crumble and dry. This is always our winter cereal!

CORN CRUNCH CEREAL

Mrs. Raymond (Malinda) Yutzy

1 qt. buttermilk or sour milk
4 c. cornmeal
4 c. whole wheat flour
2 c. brown sugar
2 tsp. salt

2 tsp. baking powder
2 tsp. soda
1 stick butter or margarine
   (melted)

Mix all dry ingredients together. Stir in milk and butter. Spread into cake pans. Bake at 350°. Put through screen or Salad Master and toast in slow oven, stirring every 15 min. Same as for grapenuts.

COLD CEREAL

Mrs. Wilbur (Norma) Borntrager

4 c. graham flour
4 c. quick oats
2 c. brown sugar
$^3/_4$ c. sunflower seeds

1 c. margarine (softened)
2 tsp. salt
2 tsp. soda

Mix all ingredients together. Bake on cookie sheet for 20 min. at 325°. Stir often for even roasting. Cool. Add chocolate chips and raisins, if you prefer. Serve with milk.

CEREAL CAKE

Mrs. Howard Miller

4 c. oatmeal
1¹/₂ c. brown sugar
1¹/₂ c. milk, or sour milk,
  or buttermilk

2 c. flour
2 tsp. soda
¹/₂ tsp. salt

Mix and bake like a cake. Serve with milk.

CEREAL CAKE

Mrs. Andrew (Carrie) Hochstetler
Mrs. Perry (Melinda) Lambright

4 c. oatmeal
2 c. wheat flour
1¹/₂ c. sugar
2 tsp. soda
1 tsp. salt

¹/₂ c. shortening or vegetable oil
1³/₄ c. milk
vanilla or maple flavoring
3/4 c. coconut (optional)

Mix all ingredients. Add coconut, dates, raisins, or nuts, etc. for a more granola type cereal. Cake may be crumbled and toasted as grapenuts. Cake is especially good when served warm.

CEREAL CAKE

Mrs. Perry Troyer

¹/₂ c. coconut
4 c. oatmeal
2 c. whole wheat flower
1¹/₂ c. brown sugar
3 tsp. soda

2 tsp. baking powder
1 tsp. salt
2 tsp. cinnamon
¹/₂ c. shortening
2 c. milk

Mix dry ingredients, cut in shortening, add milk and flavoring. Bake in moderate oven.

————— ❖ —————

A happy marriage is a union of two good forgivers.

CEREAL COOKIES
Miss Elsie Mae Miller

2 c. whole wheat flour
2 c. oatmeal
$1/2$ c. vegetable oil
$1/2$ c. brown sugar or sorghum

2 c. milk
1 tsp. soda
$1/2$ tsp. salt
$1^1/2$ tsp. cinnamon

Mix like any cookie dough. Stir these up before breakfast and bake in a Kitchen Queen oven which has preheated all night. Crumble in your bowl and add milk. Also good with chopped apples baked in.

BAKED OATMEAL
Mrs. William A. Miller

1 c. vegetable oil
$1^1/2$ c. sugar
4 lg. eggs
6 c. oatmeal

4 tsp. baking powder
1 tsp. salt
1 tsp. cinnamon
2 c. milk

Mix oil, eggs and sugar together until glossy and yellow. Add remaining ingredients and beat. Bake at 400° for 30–40 min. May serve with brown sugar and raisins.

BAKED OATMEAL
Mrs. Raymond (Malinda) Yutzy

1 c. brown sugar
$1/2$ c. butter (melted)
2 eggs (beaten)
3 c. oatmeal

1 tsp. salt
2 tsp. baking powder
1 c. milk

Mix all together. Pour in small cake pan. Bake at 350° for 30–40 min. Variations: Add **1 c. chocolate chips, M & Ms, nuts, or** $1/2$ **c. peanut butter.**

Just a Housewife

They call me 'just a housewife'
And I'm glad to bear the name.
You will never see me listed
On the 'Honor Roll of Fame.'
Career women look with pity
At my apron, broom and mop,
But I wouldn't trade them places
For things their money bought.
They call me 'just a housewife'
And I'm surely glad indeed
That God thought I would be useful
In this work of love and need.
As I wash the floor and windows,
Stylish ladies pity me,
But I wouldn't trade them places
If their mansions were all free!
Some folks are quite successful,
'Kings of Finance,' so they say,
And they seem to find their glory,
Gathering gold along the way.
Let them have their golden moments;
I'm not jealous of their life;
Tho' I may work hard at trying
To be a more considerate wife.
Yes, they call me 'just a housewife,'
But I'm more—much more you see,
I am keeper of a household
Which is 'Home Sweet Home' to me;
I am rich in love and loved ones,
I work hard in this life.
I'm so glad God thought me useful,
Being 'just a plain housewife.'

Breads, Rolls, Biscuits & Muffins

General Breadmaking Directions

After mixing ingredients as directed in recipe, grease hands and knead dough vigorously about 5–10 minutes. You may wish to place dough on floured table top for kneading. Place dough in greased bowl and grease top of dough. Cover and set in warm place, out of draft, and let rise until double. Knead lightly and let rise again until double in size. Repeat until dough has risen 2 or 3 times (whatever recipe calls for).

Divide into given portions and form into loaves. Bang each loaf hard with the palm of the hand to get rid of air bubbles. Place into greased loaf pan with smooth-side up. Prick with fork to release air bubbles. Let rise until double in size. Bake as directed. Grease top and sides of loaf with butter after removing from pans. Cool on racks.

HINTS:
- Sealing bread in plastic bags before it is completely cooled off will keep crust nice and soft.
- For finer textured bread, try letting dough rise in a place cooler than room temperature.
- Using milk instead of other liquid usually gives a softer crust which becomes a richer brown when baked.
- If your loaves get flat instead of nice and round, try making a stiffer dough.
- Bread is better when worked down twice, or more often.
- If bread is baked before it rises to double in size, it will not crumble so easily.

❖

Before you begin to give someone a piece of your mind,
consider carefully whether you can spare any.

BREAD

Mrs. Duane Bontrager

**10^1/$_2$ c. Robin Hood flour
(sifted)
6 Tbsp. sugar
2 Tbsp. salt**

**^{1}/$_2$ c. Wesson oil
3^1/$_4$ c. hot water
2 Tbsp. instant yeast**

Stir well to dissolve sugar and salt with oil and water. Beat in 2 c. flour (from the 10^1/$_2$ c.) and yeast with beater. Gradually beat in more flour until too thick to beat. Use hands for rest of flour. Turn on table and cover with bowl for 10–15 min. Now knead 1 or 2 min. If dough is sticky add a little more flour. Grease bowl and dough. Cover with plastic. Put in warm place. Let rise 1 hr. Punch down, flip dough. Let rise ^{1}/$_2$ hr. Now put on table, cut into 4 parts. Take rolling pin, roll ^{1}/$_2$" thick. Roll up forming your loaf, place in greased pan, also grease top of loaf. Stick with fork about 6 times. Cover with plastic, let rise 2–3 hrs. Bake at 350° for 30 min. For brown bread use 2 cups whole wheat flour and 8 cups white flour.

BREAD

Mrs. David (Marlene) Miller

**1 c. warm water
^{1}/$_3$ tsp. sugar
Let stand.**

1 Tbsp. yeast

**1 c. hot water
^{1}/$_4$ c. Crisco oil
^{1}/$_4$ c. sugar**

**1 tsp. salt
6 c. flour**

When making brown bread add: 1 c. whole wheat flour. May use lard instead of Crisco oil. Makes 2 loaves. Bake at 350° for 20–25 min.

———— ❁ ————

Happiness is an inside job.

WHITE BREAD SPEEDY SUPPER BREAD

Lydiann Stutzman

PART 1:

1 pkg. yeast
1 1/2 c. flour
2 Tbsp. sugar
1 tsp. salt
pinch of thyme, marjoram
   and oregano (optional)

2 eggs
mixture of 1/2 c. hot milk and
   1/4 c. butter

GROUND BEEF FILLING:

2 Tbsp. chopped onions
1 lb. ground beef
1/2 tsp. salt

pinch of pepper
1 c. pizza sauce
1/2 tsp. sugar

Fry onions and ground beef in 10" round skillet. Stir in remaining ingredients. Simmer while preparing bread. To prepare bread, place yeast in bowl soaked in a little warm water. Mix together part 1 in order given. Beat at med. speed for 3 min. Spoon part 1 over hot ground beef mixture. Brush with 1 Tbsp. melted butter. Sprinkle generously with grated Parmesan cheese. Let stand in warm place for 30 min. Bake at 350° for 25–30 min. Serve hot. Note: May be baked in 9" sq. pan.

WHITE BREAD

Mrs. Paul Whetstone

1 c. warm water
2 Tbsp. yeast
1/3 c. honey, Karo, or
   sorghum
1 c. milk

1/4 c. oil
2 tsp. salt
5 1/2–6 c. flour
2 eggs

Put in half of flour. Let stand for 45 min. Beat and add the rest. Makes 3 loaves.

BREAD

Lydia Sue Yoder

2 c. flour
2 Tbsp. yeast
2 c. warm water
$^1/_3$ c. oil
$^1/_3$ c. sugar

1 Tbsp. salt
1 c. lukewarm milk
$^1/_2$ c. mashed potatoes
Approx. 6 c. flour

Mix 2 c. flour and yeast. Add sugar, salt, and warm water; mix and add oil. Soften potatoes in milk before adding. Use flour as needed.

BREAD

Mrs. Glen (Ida Mae) Beechy
Ruby Mullet

1 Tbsp. salt
$^1/_3$ c. lard
$^1/_2$ c. sugar

2 Tbsp. yeast
4 c. lukewarm water
10 c. Seal of Minnesota flour

Mix in order given, add 5 c. flour and really beat then add rest of flour. Makes 4 loaves. Let rise 1 time, put in pan then let it rise a little or it will get holes. Bake at 350° for 30–35 min.

BREAD

Mrs. Mervin C. Miller

2 Tbsp. instant yeast
4 c. warm water
1 c. sugar or $^3/_4$ c. honey
2 Tbsp. lard or $^1/_2$ c. oil

1 Tbsp. salt
13–14 c. flour (May use Seal of Minnesota)

Mix warm water, lard, salt, and sugar together. Put in yeast and add flour. Use beater for about 10 min. Then put in more flour until dough is stiff. For brown bread add $^3/_4$ c. per loaf of bread and don't use so much white flour. Yield: 4 loaves.

HILLBILLY BREAD

Mrs. Christy Yoder

4 c. warm water
3 Tbsp. yeast
1 c. warm water
1 c. oil

4 c. whole wheat flour
6 tsp. salt
1 c. brown sugar
$3^1/_2$ lbs. (10 or 11 c.) white flour

Mix together 4 c. warm water, brown sugar, yeast, whole wheat flour and salt. Let stand 1 hr.; then add the rest of ingredients, mixing only until flour is all mixed in. Grease bowl and dough. Cover. Let set for 30 min. Knead dough. Let rise again 1 hr. Put in pans. Let rise until double in bulk. Bake at 350° for 30 min.

BREAD

Mrs. Leroy (Betty) Yoder

$^1/_3$ c. vegetable oil
$^1/_3$ c. sugar
1 Tbsp. salt
1 qt. warm water

2 c. whole wheat flour
2 Tbsp. instant yeast
4 c. Seal of Minnesota flour
4 c. bread flour

Stir first 4 ingredients together until dissolved then add whole wheat flour, instant yeast, and Seal of Minnesota flour. Stir until well mixed then add 4 c. bread flour. Let rise until double in size; punch down; let rise another 20 min. Work out and shape in 4 loaves. Let rise again and bake at 350° for 25 min.

The Bashful Boy

Two ladies gay, met a boy one day,
His legs were briar scratched,
His clothes were blue, but a nut brown hue
Marked the place where his pants were patched.
They bubbled with joy, at this blue-brown boy
With his patch of nut brown hue
"Why don't you patch with a color to match,"
They chuckled, "Why not blue?
Come, don't be coy, my blue-brown boy,
Speak out," and they laughed with glee.
And he blushed rose red, as he bashfully said,
"Dat hin't no patch, dat's me!" —Author Unknown

WHOLE WHEAT BREAD   *Suanna Miller*

Soften:

2 Tbsp. yeast in 2 c. warm water

Add: **4 tsp. salt**   **2 c. white flour**

        1 Tbsp. sugar

    Let stand till double in size (approx. 45 min.).

In another bowl mix:

$^1/_2$ c. brown sugar   **$^1/_2$ c. hot water**

$^1/_2$ c. vegetable oil   **1 c. whole wheat flour**

    Add to first mixture then add:

1 c. whole wheat flour   **3 c. white flour** (or until it can
easily be kneaded with hands).

    Let the dough rise in a covered bowl 2 times. Form into loaves the second time. Bake at 325° for $^1/_2$ hr.

WHOLE WHEAT BREAD   *Mrs. Tobie E. Miller*

3$^1/_2$ c. warm water   **2 Tbsp. yeast**

$^1/_8$ c. black strapped molasses **1 c. warm water**

1$^1/_2$ Tbsp. salt   **4 c. whole wheat flour**

$^1/_2$ c. sugar   **7$^1/_2$–8 c. Seal of Minnesota flour**

$^3/_4$ c. peanut oil

    Dissolve yeast in 1 c. warm water. Mix 3$^1/_2$ c. warm water in lg. bowl. Add molasses, sugar, salt and peanut oil. Stir well and add wheat flour and gradually add white flour. Knead well. Let rise 10 min. Punch down. Let rise 1 hr. Punch down and let rise again in warm place, preferably close to stove. Put in pans and rise 1 hr. Bake at 325° (very important) for 35–40 min. Too hot stove tends to make dry bread. This bread stays moist for a week.

———— ❖ ————

Better to eat a dry crust of bread with peace of mind than have a banquet in a house full of trouble. Proverbs 17:1 (TEV)

BROWN BREAD

Fanny Mae Bontrager

1 c. quick oats
$^1/_3$ c. brown sugar
2 tsp. salt
2 Tbsp. lard, shortening
   or oil
2 c. hot water (not boiling)

2 c. fine ground whole
   wheat flour
1 pkg. yeast
300 mg. ascorbic acid pill
   (crushed, optional)
2 c. Seal of Minnesota flour

Combine in bowl: oats, sugar, salt, lard, and hot water. Stir till lard is melted. Add whole wheat flour, yeast and ascorbic acid. Mix thoroughly then beat vigorously (100 strokes) with spoon. Cover and set in warm place for 20 min. Gradually add white flour working in with hand. Knead well, using more or less flour to make smooth elastic dough. Cover and let rise in warm place. When light, work out into loaves and place in greased pans. Let rise. Bake at 375° till top of loaves lose their shine. Reduce heat to 350° till done. Yield: 2 small loaves.

100% WHOLE WHEAT BREAD

Mrs. Daniel Lee Mishler

3$^1/_2$ c. water
1 Tbsp. lecithin (optional)
$^1/_2$ c. Canola oil
$^1/_2$ c. honey or brown sugar
1 Tbsp. gluten (optional)

1 Tbsp. salt
1 egg
2 Tbsp. yeast
1 tablet vitamin C (optional)
flour

Dissolve lecithin in warm water. Add the rest of ingredients and flour to the right consistency (around 10 c. fresh ground). Knead 3 times at about 15 min. intervals. Put in 3 med. pans. Bake at 350° for 30 min. May take a little experience to get the dough the right consistency.

OATMEAL BREAD
Mrs. Mervin C. Miller

2¹/₄ c. boiling water
1 Tbsp. oleo
2 tsp. salt
¹/₂ c. sugar
1 c. rolled oats

2 Tbsp. instant yeast
¹/₄ c. molasses
¹/₄ c. brown sugar
6–6¹/₂ c. flour

In a fix-n-mix bowl, combine boiling water, butter, salt and sugar. Stir in oats; cool to lukewarm. In another bowl dissolve yeast in warm water. Stir in molasses, brown sugar and 1 c. flour. Beat until smooth. Add to oats mixture and enough remaining flour to make a stiff dough. If you use instant yeast just wait until oats mixture is a little cooled and put in there instead of into another bowl. Makes 2 loaves.

CORN BREAD
Pollyanna Schrock

³/₄ c. sugar
1 c. shortening
2 eggs
1 c. sour milk
2 tsp. cream of tartar

2 c. cornmeal
2 c. flour
2 tsp. soda
2 tsp. salt

Mix all ingredients and pour into greased pan. Bake at 400° for 20–25 min.

CORN BREAD
Mrs. Howard Miller

2 c. cornmeal
2 c. flour
¹/₂ c. sugar
8 tsp. baking powder

1 tsp. salt
3 eggs
2 c. milk
¹/₂ c. lard (melted) or oil

Sift together dry ingredients. Add milk, eggs and oil. Bake in greased pan 20–25 min. at 400°.

CORN BREAD

Mrs. Glen Hershberger

1 c. cornmeal	$^1/_2$ tsp. salt
1 c. flour	1 or 2 eggs
$^1/_4$ c. sugar	1 c. milk
4 tsp. baking powder	$^1/_4$ c. shortening (melted)

Sift together dry ingredients. Add milk, well beaten eggs and shortening. Bake in greased pan 20–25 min. at 400°.

VERY GOOD CORN BREAD

Mrs. Alvin (Wilma) Beechy

1 c. cornmeal	1 c. milk
2 c. Bisquick mix	2 eggs (slightly beaten)
(the homemade)	

Put the Bisquick mix into a bowl, add cornmeal. Mix with milk and eggs. Then pour into greased and floured pan. Bake at 350° for 30 min.

CORN PONE

Mrs. David I. Bontrager

$^1/_2$ c. rich milk	pinch of salt
1 egg	2 tsp. baking powder
$^1/_2$ c. cornmeal	$^1/_2$ c. sugar
1 c. flour	$^1/_2$ c. melted butter

Beat egg; add dry ingredients. Stir in milk, then add butter last.

❖

Practice makes perfect, so be careful what you practice.

ZUCCHINI BREAD

Christina Miller
Wilma Beechy

2 c. flour	1 c. vegetable oil
2 c. sugar	2 c. zucchini (peeled and grated)
1 tsp. soda	$1/2$ c. nuts
1 tsp. baking powder	3 eggs
1 tsp. salt	2 tsp. vanilla

Mix dry ingredients, and then the rest; mix well. Bake in moderate oven for 1 hr. or until done.

ZUCCHINI BREAD

Marietta Miller

3 eggs	1 tsp. cinnamon
2 c. sugar	3 c. flour
1 c. salad oil	1 tsp. salt
2 c. shredded zucchini	1 tsp. soda
3 tsp. vanilla	1 c. nuts

Bake at 350° for 35–40 min. or until done.

BANANA BREAD

Mrs. Harry Wayne Miller

$1/2$ c. shortening	$1/4$ tsp. nutmeg
1 c. sugar	2 c. flour
2 eggs	1 tsp. soda
2 bananas (mashed)	1 tsp. salt

Cream shortening and sugar. Add eggs, bananas, spices and flour. Place in loaf pan. Bake at 350° for 50–60 min. This is good to eat fresh or can be frozen.

❖

Brown sugar will heal proud flesh.

BANANA NUT BREAD
Mrs. William J. Troyer

1$^1/_2$ c. sugar
$^1/_2$ c. shortening
2 eggs
1 tsp. vanilla
$^1/_2$ tsp. salt

2 c. flour
1 tsp. soda in 5 Tbsp. sour milk
1 c. bananas (mashed)
nuts (optional)

Cream together sugar, shortening, eggs and vanilla. Combine dry ingredients and add sour milk with soda and bananas. Can put in round tin cans or bread pans. Bake at 350° for 30 min.

WHOLE WHEAT BANANA BREAD
Ruby Yutzy

2 c. whole wheat flour
1 Tbsp. wheat germ (optional)
1 tsp. baking soda
$^1/_2$ tsp. salt
2 eggs
2 c. mashed ripe bananas

$^1/_2$ c. honey
$^1/_4$ c. vegetable oil
1 Tbsp. lemon juice
$^1/_2$ tsp. vanilla
1 c. chopped walnuts

Measure flour, wheat germ, soda and salt into lg. bowl. Stir to blend. Combine eggs, bananas, honey, veg. oil, lemon juice and vanilla until well blended. Pour over flour mixture. Add walnuts. Stir just until blended. Pour into a greased and floured 8" x 5" x 3" loaf pan. Bake at 350° until sides pull away from pan, and pick inserted in center comes out clean, (45–55 min.). Cool in rack before removing from pan. Makes 1 loaf.

❖

One of the great arts of living is the art of forgiving.

PUMPKIN BREAD

Mrs. Eli H. Hochstetler

3 c. granulated sugar
1 c. vegetable oil
4 eggs (beaten)
2 c. canned pumpkin
3 1/2 c. flour
2 tsp. soda

1 1/2 tsp. salt
1/2 tsp. ground cloves
1 tsp. each–cinnamon, allspice,
   nutmeg
2/3 c. water

Mix sugar, oil and eggs; add pumpkin. Sift together dry ingredients and add to sugar mixture. Add water and stir just until mixed. Pour into 2 greased and floured 9" x 5" loaf pans. Bake at 350° for 1 hr.

AUTUMN BREAD

Anna Fern Hochstetler

2/3 c. vegetable oil
3 c. sugar
4 eggs (well beaten)
1 3/4 c. pumpkin or squash
2/3 c. water
3 1/2 c. flour

1/2 tsp. salt
1/2 tsp. nutmeg
1/2 tsp. cloves
1 tsp. cinnamon
1/2 tsp. baking powder
2 tsp. baking soda

Mix all together. Bake at 350° for 1 hr. in greased tin cans. Let cool 10 min. Remove from cans and roll in sugar.

MONKEY BREAD

Suanna Miller

4 pkg. buttermilk biscuits
1 1/4 c. white sugar
2 tsp. cinnamon
1 c. brown sugar

2 tsp. cinnamon
3/4 c. butter
nuts

Cut each bisuit in 4 pieces. In a bag, mix white sugar and 2 tsp. cinnamon. Coat each piece and drop in 9" x 13" pan. Melt together brown sugar, cinnamon, and butter. Stir and bring to a boil. Pour over biscuits in pan. Sprinkle with nuts. Bake at 350° for 35–40 min.

PLUCK-IT BREAD
Fanny Mae Bontrager

2 c. scalded milk
$^1/_2$ c. shortening or butter
2 tsp. salt
$^1/_2$ c. brown sugar
1 c. oatmeal
2 eggs
$^1/_2$ c. cold water
1$^1/_2$ c. fine ground whole
wheat flour

1 c. Seal of Minnesota flour
  (or similiar)
2 env. yeast
3 c. Seal of Minnesota flour
cinnamon and sugar
melted butter

Mix first 5 ingredients into 6 qt. mixing bowl. Beat eggs and water and add into bowl. Add 2 flours and yeast. Blend; beat 100 strokes. Cover; let set in warm place 20 min. Beat in 2 or more cups flour. Knead in more flour until dough is smooth and elastic. Let rise until light. Pinch off 1–1$^1/_2$" balls of dough. Dip into melted butter then in cinnmon and sugar mix. Place sugared side down in greased tube cake pan. Alternate 3 rings of balls in each pan. Extra dough may be formed into rolls. Let rise. Bake at 375° for 15 min. Reduce heat to 350° till rolls are done.

SUSAN'S DOUGHNUTS
Lillian Mast

2$^1/_2$ c. warm milk
$^1/_2$ c. water
1$^1/_2$ Tbsp. yeast
$^1/_2$ c. mashed potatoes
$^1/_2$ c. oleo

1 c. sugar
1$^1/_2$ tsp. salt
3 eggs
flour

Mix together milk, water, melted oleo, sugar and salt. Sprinkle yeast over the top and let set for 5 min. Add beaten eggs and mashed potatoes; mix thoroughly. Add enough flour to make a soft, yet manageable dough. Let rise until double in size. Punch down and work out into doughnuts. Let rise and fry in deep fat.

LIGHT-AS-A-FEATHER DOUGHNUTS

Mrs. Ray (Malinda) Yutzy

³/₄ c. milk
¹/₄ c. sugar
1 tsp. salt
¹/₄ c. margarine

¹/₄ c. warm water
1 pkg. yeast
1 egg (beaten)
3¹/₄ c. flour

Scald milk; stir in sugar, salt and margarine. Cool to lukewarm. Measure warm water into lg. bowl. Sprinkle in yeast; stir until dissolved. Add lukewarm mixture, egg, and half the flour. Beat until smooth. Stir in enough additional flour to make a soft dough. Turn dough out onto a lightly floured board. Knead until smooth and elastic, about 10 min. Place in bowl, cover and let rise until double. Punch down, roll out about ¹/₂" thick and cut. Place on floured sheet pans. Let rise until double in size. Fry in Wesson oil. Dip in glaze: **2 c. powdered sugar, ¹/₃ c. milk** and **1 tsp. vanilla**.

GLAZED DOUGHNUTS

Wilma Miller

2 Tbsp. yeast
¹/₂ c. warm water
1 tsp. sugar
³/₄ c. sugar
2 tsp. salt

¹/₂ c. Crisco
2 c. scalded milk
2 eggs (well beaten)
7¹/₂ c. Robin Hood flour

Soak yeast in warm water; add the teaspoon of sugar. Put ³/₄ c. sugar, salt and Crisco in bowl. Pour scalded milk over Crisco mixture. When cooled add eggs and yeast mixture. Add flour mixture. Mix together and let rise until double in size then roll out and cut. Lay on floured board and let rise again. Fry in deep fat (360°) until brown. Always flip your donuts. Fry top side first.

GLAZE FOR DOUGHNUTS:

2 tsp. white Karo
1¹/₂ c. powdered sugar

1 tsp. vanilla
2 or 3 Tbsp. hot water

Roll doughnuts in glaze.

DONUTS

Mrs. Mary Kay Graber

1 c. shortening
$^1/_2$ c. sugar
2 tsp. salt
6 egg yolks
13 c. flour (Gold Medal)

$^1/_2$ tsp. nutmeg
1 c. mashed potatoes
3 pkg. dry yeast (in 1$^1/_2$ c. lukewarm water)

Beat egg yolks, put in potatoes, scald milk to lukewarm. Put in shortening, sugar and salt. Then put in egg mixture, flour and yeast. Let rise 90 min., roll, and let rise again. Cook in vegetable oil.

GLAZE:

Mix **2 Tbsp. white Karo,** $^3/_4$ **c. sugar,** and **1 c. water;** bring to a boil. Add enough **powdered sugar** to make a paste, then add more syrup until it's right to glaze. Add **1 tsp. vanilla.**

MOUNT MARY COLLEGE DOUGHNUTS

Ida Lambright

1 c. lard
1 c. mashed potatoes
1 c. sugar
6 egg yolks
1 Tbsp. salt

3 pkg. yeast
Approx. 14 c. flour
4$^1/_2$ c. skim milk (scalded and
cooled)

GLAZE:

2 lb. powdered sugar   1 tsp. vanilla
1 rounded tsp. unflavored gelatin (soaked in a little cold water then dissolved in part of hot sugar syrup)

Put together like rolls. Let set 1 hr., roll out and cut. Let rise 1$^1/_2$–2 hrs. in warm place, then fry. Glaze doughnut while still hot.

For glaze: To moisten powdered sugar use a light syrup instead of water to keep the shine in glaze. Also use **1**$^1/_2$ **Tbsp. Karo** if you want to make glaze about the consistency of cream.

FILLED DONUTS
Wilma Beechy

2 pkg. yeast
1 c. lukewarm water
1 tsp. sugar
1 c. milk (scalded then cooled)
7 c. Robin Hood flour (sifted)

$^2/_3$ c. sugar
$1^1/_2$ tsp. salt
2 eggs or 4 egg yolks
$^1/_2$ c. oleo

Stir yeast and water together, add tsp. sugar and stir. Let set. Cream together oleo, sugar, salt; add well beaten eggs; stir and then add milk, yeast mixture and flour; mix to a soft dough. Let rise until double in size, then roll out and cut into strips as you like. Let rise until light and fry in deep fat. When cooled, cut in slit for frosting.

FROSTING:

2 egg whites (beaten)
1 Tbsp. flour
4 Tbsp. milk

$^3/_4$ c. Crisco
2 tsp. vanilla
2 c. powdered sugar

Stir together milk and flour, then add Crisco, vanilla and 1 c. powdered sugar; beat together, then add beaten egg whites, 2 or more c. powdered sugar. Optional: add **8 oz. cream cheese.**

CREAM STICKS
Vera Mae Miller

2 pkgs. yeast
1 c. lukewarm water
1 c. milk (scalded)
$^1/_2$ c. oleo
$^2/_3$ c. sugar

2 eggs (beaten)
$^1/_2$ tsp. salt
1 tsp. vanilla
6 c. flour

Stir sugar, salt and oleo into scalded milk. Cool to lukewarm. Put yeast in lukewarm water; stir to dissolve. Add milk mixture, eggs and vanilla; then add flour. Mix and knead well. Let dough rise until double in size. Knead and roll; form into sticks and let rise again. Deep fat fry.

CINNAMON ROLLS

Leah Mishler

1 c. mashed potatoes
1 c. potato water
²/₃ c. shortening
²/₃ c. sugar
2 beaten eggs

1 c. milk (scalded)
1 scant Tbsp. salt
1 pkg. or 1 Tbsp. dry yeast
flour (enough to make soft
    dough easy to handle)

Cook and mash potatoes and add remaining ingredients except yeast and flour. Dissolve yeast in ¹/₄ c. **warm water**, and add **1 tsp. sugar**. Let set 5 min. Add to other mixture and work in flour to a soft dough consistency. Let rise in a warm place until double in bulk. Work down and let rise again (about 1 hr.) Divide dough in 3 parts and roll out in rectangle shape. Spread with oleo and sprinkle with brown sugar and cinnamon. Roll up and cut in 1" pieces and lay cut side down in greased pan. Let rise until double and bake at 350° or until golden.

FOUNDATION SWEET ROLLS

Mrs. Glen Hershberger

1 c. milk (scalded)
¹/₂ c. sugar
1¹/₂ tsp. salt
¹/₂ c. shortening
2 cakes yeast

1 c. water (lukewarm)
2 eggs (beaten)
¹/₂ tsp. nutmeg
7 c. flour

Pour scalded milk over sugar, salt and shortening. Dissolve yeast in lukewarm water. Add yeast and eggs. Beat well; add flour gradually, beating well. Knead lightly, working in just enough flour so that dough can be handled. Place dough in a greased bowl; cover and let rise about 2 hrs. (double in size). Make into cinnamon butterscotch rolls, by dividing into 2 portions. Roll into oblong pieces ¹/₄" thick. Brush with **6 Tbsp. butter** and sprinkle with **1¹/₂ c. brown sugar**, and **1 Tbsp. cinnamon**. Roll and cut in 1" thick slices. Let rise until light (about 1 hr.). Bake in moderate oven. Frost with powdered sugar frosting.

CINNAMON ROLLS
Ruby Mullet

2 c. sugar
1²/₃ c. Crisco oil
4 eggs (beaten)
4 pkg. dry yeast

5 c. warm water
12 c. flour
4 tsp. salt

Mix sugar, oil, eggs and salt. Put yeast in warm water and let set 5 min; add to first mixture. Gradually add flour until well mixed. Let rise till double in size. Punch down and rise again. Roll out flat. Coat with melted butter, brown sugar, and cinnamon. Roll up, cut, put in pans and let rise. Bake at 350°. Makes 11–12" pie pans. They freeze well!

ROLLS
Mrs. Glen (Alma) Whetstone

2 pkgs. (2 Tbsp.) yeast
¹/₃ c. water
1 Tbsp. sugar
1¹/₂ c. milk (scalded)
2 eggs (beaten)

1 c. sugar
²/₃ c. lard
1 tsp. salt
1 c. mashed potatoes
6¹/₂ c. flour

Mix yeast, water, and 1 Tbsp. sugar together; set aside. Mix milk, lard, sugar and salt. Add yeast mixture, then flour. Work down twice. Roll out and spread butter, sugar, and cinnamon on. Bake at 350°.

———— ❖ ————

Adding a pinch of baking powder to powdered sugar icing will help it stay moist and not crack.

———— ❖ ————

The optimist sees the doughnut; the pessimist sees the hole.

CINNAMON ROLLS

Mrs. Christy Yoder

1¹/₂ c. water
2 tsp. salt
¹/₂ c. sugar
¹/₂ c. oleo or butter

2 pkgs. dry yeast
¹/₂ c. warm water
3 egg yolks (beaten)
6 c. flour

Put yeast in ¹/₂ c. warm water. Let set for 5 min. Scald milk, then add sugar, salt and oleo or butter. Then add yeast. Add eggs and 3 c. flour. Mix and add 3 more c. flour. Let rise till double. Roll out and spread with melted butter and sugar. Roll up, cut in ³/₄"–1" slices and let rise. Bake at 325°–350° for 20 min. or until brown.

REFRIGERATOR CINNAMON ROLLS

Mrs. Floyd (Loretta) Lehman
Viola Bontrager

2 pkgs. yeast
2 eggs
³/₄ c. sugar
³/₄ c. Crisco

2¹/₂ tsp. salt
2¹/₂ c. warm water
7–7¹/₂ c. flour

Put Crisco, sugar, eggs and salt in lg. bowl; mix well. Add 4 c. flour mixed with yeast, add water and mix well; then add rest of flour. Let rise in a bowl at least 8 hrs. in refrigerator. Roll out as usual and let rise 1 hr. Bake at 325° for 15–20 min. Makes 2 big cookie sheets.

---- ❖ ----

To cut cinnamon rolls:
Simply place 10" section of thread or dental floss under the roll where you want it cut. Bring ends of thread together and crisscross so that the thread cuts through dough. A neat treat!

QUICK BUTTERMILK SWEET ROLLS

Mrs. Harley H. Lambright

2 Tbsp. dry yeast	2 eggs
$1/2$ c. buttermilk	$1/2$ c. sugar
$5^1/2$–6 c. flour	2 tsp. baking powder
$1/2$ c. butter or oleo	2 tsp. salt

In lg. bowl dissolve yeast in water; add buttermilk, eggs, $2^1/2$ c. flour, butter, sugar, baking powder and salt. Blend $1/2$ min. on low speed scraping bowl constantly. Beat 2 min. on med. speed; stir in enough remaining flour to make dough easy to handle. Dough should remain soft and sticky. Turn dough onto well floured board. Knead 5 min. or about 500 turns. No need to let it rise. Shape dough immediately into desired rolls or coffee cakes. Cover; let rise in warm place about 1 hr. Dough is ready if impression is made. Bake at 350°.

OATMEAL ROLLS

Sarah Yoder

2 c. water	$1/3$ c. brown sugar
1 c. quick cooking oats	1 Tbsp. sugar
3 Tbsp. butter	$1^1/2$ tsp. salt
1 pkg. yeast with $1/3$ c. warm water	$4^3/4$–$5^1/4$ c. flour

Boil water, add oatmeal, butter and salt. When boiling add brown sugar. Cool; add $1/2$ flour, yeast, rest of flour. Let rise 1 hr. Roll out, spinkle with cinnamon and roll up. Let rise 45 min. Bake at 350° for 25 min.

———— ❖ ————

The recipe for a good speech includes shortening.

APPLE ROLLS

Mrs. Mary Kay Graber

$^1/_3$ c. milk	2 Tbsp. sugar
$^1/_2$ tsp. salt	4 tsp. baking powder
2 c. flour	3 Tbsp. shortening

Make soft dough. Roll, then spread with butter, cinnamon and apples. Make into a roll. Bake until almost done. Pour syrup, which has been cooked, over it and finish baking.

SYRUP:

1 Tbsp. flour	1 c. boiling water
$1^1/_2$ c. sugar	1 Tbsp. butter
$^1/_2$ tsp. salt	

CORNMEAL ROLLS

Lydiann Stutzman

$^1/_3$ c. cornmeal	2 eggs (beaten)
$^1/_2$ c. sugar	1 pkg. yeast
1 tsp. salt	$^1/_4$ c. lukewarm water
$^1/_2$ c. shortening (melted)	4 c. flour
2 c. milk	

Combine cornmeal, sugar, salt, shortening and milk in double boiler. Cook until thick, stirring often. Cool to lukewarm. Add eggs and yeast dissolved in warm water. Beat well. Let rise in bowl 2 hrs. Roll out, cut, brush with oleo and place in oiled pans or sheets. Let rise 1 hr. Bake at 375° for 15 min.

--------------- ❖ ---------------

Gather crumbs of happiness and they will make you a loaf of contentment.

JELLY ROLL

Mrs. Perry Schrock

1 egg	$^1/_4$ c. brown sugar
4 egg yolks	4 Tbsp. flour
$^1/_4$ tsp. salt	$^1/_4$ tsp. salt
$^3/_4$ c. flour	$^2/_3$ c. cold water
$^3/_4$ c. white sugar	4 Tbsp. butter
1 tsp. baking powder	$^1/_2$ tsp. maple flavoring
4 egg whites	$^1/_4$ c. cream (whipped)
$^1/_4$ tsp. cream of tartar	

Beat 1 whole egg, 4 yolks and salt till light colored. Sift together flour, sugar and baking powder and beat gradually into eggs. Add vanilla and stiffly beaten egg whites with cream of tartar. Bake as jelly roll. Roll in damp towel and cool. Filling: cook next four ingredients till thick in double boiler. Add butter and maple flavoring. Cool; blend in whipped cream. Spread on roll and reroll.

DANISH BRAID

Mrs. Freeman J. Yoder
Mary Esther Yoder

5 c. Robin Hood flour	1 c. oleo
$^1/_2$ tsp. salt	
$^1/_4$ c. warm water	1 Tbsp. yeast
3 eggs	$^1/_2$ c. white sugar
1 c. warm water	

Mix first 3 ingredients together till crumbly, then the next 2 ingredients and then the last 3. Mix and stir all together, then let it set overnight. Divide the dough in 4 parts. Roll in oblong strips, 4" x 10" long. Put slits in side 1" apart, 1" long. Put orange glaze or put cinnamon, sugar and oleo in middle. Put in greased sheet. Bake 20 min. at 350°. Drizzle frosting on top after it's baked.

STICKIE QUICKIE BUNS
Mrs. Marlin Miller

Heat: 3/4 c. milk
  1/2 c. water
  1/4 oleo

1/4 c. sugar
1 tsp. salt

Mix: 1 1/2 c. **Robin Hood flour** 1 1/2 **Tbsp. yeast**

TOPPING:

3/4 c. oleo
1 c. brown sugar
1 tsp. cinnamon

3/4 c. nuts
1 Tbsp. Karo
1 Tbsp. water

Pour the warm liquid above, into flour and yeast and mix; add: **1 egg**, beaten, stir in 1 3/4 **c. flour** by hand. Cover and let rise until melted. Pour topping into a 9" x 13" cake pan. Stir batter down and drop by Tbsp. into the "topping". Bake at 375° for 15 min. Cover with cookie sheet and invert.

SWEET BUNS
Mary Miller

1 c. milk (scalded)
1/2 c. white sugar
1/2 c. lard
2 eggs (beaten)
1 c. lukewarm water

1 tsp. sugar
2 pkg. (2 Tbsp.) dry yeast
1 Tbsp. salt
6–7 c. bread flour

Scald milk and cool. Dissolve yeast in 1 tsp. sugar and 1 c. warm water. Cream sugar, eggs, lard and salt together. Add milk and yeast mixture, then flour. Let rise 1 hr. or until double. Roll out to 3/4" thick. Cut to bun shape and let rise. Bake at 400° for 10–15 min.

———— ❖ ————

Any housewife, no matter how large her family, can always get some time alone by doing the dishes.

BUTTER HORNS

Emma Bontrager

Cream together:

1 pkg. yeast	**3 eggs (beaten)**
1 Tbsp. sugar	**1 c. lukewarm water**

Let stand to rise 15 min.

Add:

$1/2$ c. sugar	**$1/2$ c. shortening**
$1/2$ tsp. salt	**5 c. flour**

Knead well. Put in refrigerator overnight. In the morning, take out and make 2 parts. Use oil to roll out in 12" circles. Cut each circle in 12 wedges. Beginning at the wide side roll each wedge toward point. Place on greased baking sheet, with point on underside. Let rise 3–4 hrs. Bake at 400° for 10–15 min.

BISCUITS SUPREME

Mrs. Harry Wayne Miller

2 c. flour	**$1/2$ tsp. salt**
2 tsp. sugar	**4 tsp. baking powder**
$1/2$ c. shortening or lard	**$1/2$ tsp. cream of tartar**
$2/3$ c. milk	

Sift dry ingredients together. Cut in shortening until mixture resembles coarse crumbs. Add milk all at once and stir until dough follows fork around bowl. Roll $1/2$" thick. Cut with biscuit cutter. Place on ungreased cookie sheet. Bake at 450° for 10–12 min. Makes approx. 16 biscuits.

❖

When cleaning your gas range, use baking soda and a wet cloth.
Never use a choreball as it scratches the enamel.

SOUTHERN GAL BISCUITS

Christina Miller

2 c. sifted flour
4 tsp. baking powder
$^1/_2$ tsp. salt
$^1/_2$ tsp. cream of tartar

2 Tbsp. sugar
$^1/_2$ c. shortening
1 egg (unbeaten)
$^2/_3$ c. milk

Sift flour, baking powder, salt, sugar and cream of tartar into bowl. Add shortening, blend until consistency of cornmeal. Pour milk into mixture slowly, add egg and stir to a stiff dough. Bake on cookie sheet 10–15 min. at 450°. Quick, easy, and alway delicious.

DUTCH SQUASH BISCUITS

Mrs. William Schrock

4 c. bread flour
1 Tbsp. yeast
$^1/_2$ c. lukewarm water
1 c. milk (scalded)

$^1/_2$ tsp. salt
4 Tbsp. butter (melted)
$^1/_4$ c. sugar
$1^1/_4$ c. sifted squash

Dissolve yeast in lukewarm water. Mix a sponge. Let rise $^3/_4$ hr. Then mix all ingredients to make a soft batter. Put into baking pan. Let rise till light. Bake 25 min. at 420°. Remove from oven and butter tops.

TOMMY LOMIES BISCUITS

Marvin and Ruby Hochstetler

2 c. flour
4 tsp. baking powder
4 Tbsp. shortening

$^3/_4$ c. milk
$1^1/_2$ Tbsp. sugar

Mix and knead. Roll out and cut or just drop on cookie sheet. Bake at 400° for 20 min.

CLOUD BISCUITS

Mrs. Dorothy Yoder

4 c. flour
8 tsp. baking powder
1 tsp. salt
2 Tbsp. sugar

1 c. shortening
2 eggs (beaten)
1²/₃ c. milk

Rub together first 5 ingredients to resemble crumbs. Combine beaten egg and milk then add all at once. Knead gently, 20 strokes. Bake at 450° for 10–20 min.

GOLDEN MORNING MUFFINS

2 c. flour
1 c. cornmeal
5 tsp. baking powder
1 tsp. salt
¹/₂ c. sugar
¹/₂ c. vegetable oil

2 eggs
¹/₂ c. orange juice concentrate
1 c. skim milk
1 - 7 oz. can crushed pineapple
   (drained well)
¹/₂ c. carrrots (freshly grated)

Preheat oven to 425°. In a mixing bowl combine first 4 ingredients, mixing well. In another mixing bowl beat sugar, oil, eggs, orange juice concentrate, and milk until smooth. Make a well in the dry ingredients and pour in egg and oil mixture. Stir just until moist. Gently fold in drained pineapple and grated carrots. Line muffin tins with paper liners. Divide batter in 24 cups. Bake for 20–25 min.

———— ❖ ————

If you want to be blue, be bright blue.

———— ❖ ————

*There is something better than understanding God
and that is trusting Him.*

BRAN MUFFINS
Emma Bontrager

2 c. boiling water
2 c. 100% Bran cereal
 Let cool then add:
3 c. brown sugar
4 eggs
1 qt. buttermilk
5 c. flour

1 c. oleo

5 tsp. soda
1 tsp. salt
4 c. oatmeal

Bake at 400° for 15 min. or until done. These freeze well.

NUTTY APPLE MUFFINS
Mary Miller

$1^1/_2$ c. flour
$1^1/_2$ tsp. baking soda
$^3/_4$ tsp. salt
$^1/_2$ tsp. nutmeg
2 eggs

1 c. sugar
$^1/_3$ c. vegetable oil
2 c. apples (diced and peeled)
$1^1/_2$ c. chopped nuts

In lg. bowl combine sugar and oil. Beat in eggs and salt. Add soda and nutmeg; stir well. Stir in flour, apples and nuts. Fill 18 greased muffin cups $^3/_4$ full. Bake at 350° for 25–30 min.

OATMEAL MUFFINS
Anna Marie Miller

2 c. flour
$^3/_4$ c. sugar
$4^1/_2$ tsp. baking powder
$^1/_2$ tsp. baking soda
$^1/_2$ tsp. salt

$1^1/_2$ c. oatmeal
2 eggs (beaten)
2 Tbsp. butter (melted)
1 c. water

Cream butter and sugar. Beat in eggs and salt. Add baking powder, soda and water; stir well and add remaining ingredients. Pour into a 9" greased loaf pan or paper-lined muffin tins. Bake at 350° for 45–55 min. for loaf; 30 min. for muffins.

BLUEBERRY MUFFINS
Mrs. Ray Yutzy

4 c. flour
6 tsp. baking powder
1 tsp. salt
1/2 c. sugar
2 eggs

2 c. milk
3/4 c. oil
2 c. blueberries
2 Tbsp. sugar

Sift together flour, baking powder, salt and 1/2 c. sugar. Combine eggs, milk and oil. Add all at once to flour mixture. Stir until dry ingredients are moist, but still lumpy. Fold in blueberries. Fill greased muffin pans 2/3 full. Sprinkle with 2 Tbsp. sugar. Bake in 400° oven for 25 min.

BANANA MUFFINS
Mrs. Perry Troyer

1 c. all purpose flour
1 tsp. baking powder
1/2 tsp. salt
3/4 c. sugar
1 1/2 c. mashed bananas
   (3–4 bananas)

3/4 c. raisins (optional)
1/2 c. oatmeal
1 tsp. soda
1 egg
1/3 c. shortening

Fill muffin cups 3/4 full. Bake at 375° for 20–25 min. or until top springs back when lightly touched. Makes about 12 muffins.

———— ❖ ————

Yesterday is like a canceled check—it's gone.
Tomorrow is a promissory note—not here yet.
Today is cash—use it wisely and prepare to meet your God.

PIZZA CRUST OR BREADSTICKS

Mrs. Richard (Helen) Miller

1 c. warm water	1 tsp. salt
1 Tbsp. yeast	2 Tbsp. oil
1 tsp. sugar	Approx. 3$^1/_2$ c. flour

Dough should be as soft as biscuit dough. Cover and let rise until double in bulk (about 45 min.). Punch down and press into 2 pans, or roll out and cut in sticks and let rise for 10–15 min., then bake. When baked put butter on while still hot. Sprinkle with pizza seasoning or garlic.

WHEAT PIZZA CRUST

Mrs. Harry Wayne Miller

1 pkg. ($^1/_4$ oz.) active dry yeast	1$^1/_4$ c. whole wheat flour
1$^1/_2$ c. warm water	2 Tbsp. sugar
2 Tbsp. vegetable oil	$^1/_2$ tsp. salt
	1$^3/_4$–2 c. all purpose flour

In a bowl dissolve yeast in water; add oil. Combine whole wheat flour, sugar and salt. Add to yeast mixture and stir till smooth. Stir in enough all purpose flour to form a soft dough. Knead until smooth. Cover and let rise for 15–20 min. Bake at 350° with pizza toppings.

❖

Add a tablespoon of vinegar to each loaf of bread you are making. It will keep it soft longer and keep it from smelling strong so soon.

THICK CRUST PIZZA DOUGH
Wilma Miller

3 c. warm water
3 Tbsp. yeast
2 Tbsp. sugar

$7^1/_2$ c. flour
6 Tbsp. veg. oil
2 tsp. salt

Combine warm water, yeast and sugar. Let set 10 min. Add flour, oil, and salt; mix well. Let rise 10–15 min. Spread out on 4 lg. cookie sheets. Add your favorite toppings. Bake at 400° for 15–20 min.

PIZZA HUT PIZZA DOUGH
Delilah Yoder

2 pkg. yeast
2 tsp. sugar
$^2/_3$ c. warm water
2 c. cold water
2 Tbsp. sugar

$^1/_4$ tsp. garlic salt or powder
3 Tbsp. oil
1 scant Tbsp. salt
$^1/_2$ tsp. oregano
$6^1/_2$ c. flour

Mix warm water, yeast and 2 tsp. sugar. Let stand 5 min. until bubbly. In another bowl, mix cold water, 2 Tbsp. sugar, garlic powder, oil, salt, oregano and 3 c. flour; beat until smooth. Add yeast mixture. Add rest of flour. Work until elastic. Let rise until double. Press $^1/_2$ of dough on a greased pan. Let rise 5–10 min. Repeat with other half. Add sauce. Bake at 400° for 10–15 min. Then add your meats, etc. Put back in oven until hot and cheese is bubbly.

PIZZA CRUST
Edna Fern Schrock

1 Tbsp. yeast
1 tsp. sugar
2 Tbsp. vegetable oil
1 c. warm water

1 tsp. salt
Approx. $2^1/_2$ c. flour
dash of garlic powder
dash of oregano

Mix all together and let set for 5 min. Makes 2 pans.

PIZZA DOUGH

Mrs. Sherman (LuElla) Miller

3 Tbsp. white sugar
1 Tbsp. salt
2 1/4 c. water (lukewarm)
2 pkgs. (2 Tbsp.) dry yeast

1 Tbsp. oregano
2 Tbsp. shortening or oil
7 scant c. flour

Dissolve yeast in water, add sugar, salt, shortening or oil and oregano. Mix well and add 1/2 of flour and beat until no lumps. Gradually add remaining flour. Knead until elastic. Let rise till doubled. This is enough for 2 sheets.

PIZZA DOUGH

Mrs. Amos Beechy

1 c. warm water
2 pkg. active dry yeast
1 tsp. salt

1 tsp. sugar
2 Tbsp. cooking oil
3 c. sifted Robin Hood flour

Dissolve yeast and sugar in warm water. Stir in salt and oil. Add flour and knead until it forms a smooth ball. Let rise in a greased, covered bowl in a warm place until doubled. Put dough in greased 11" x 17" pizza pan. Add your own toppings!

PIZZA DOUGH

Treva Miller

2 1/2 c. bisquick mix
1 Tbsp. yeast

3/4 c. warm water

--- ❖ ---

In all things give thanks.

Favorite Recipes

Cookies—Enjoyed By All

"Hey, the cookie jar is empty,"
My small brothers and sisters cry.
"The empty jar must be filled,"
That cry never fails to make me sigh.

So after dinner I begin—
Roll up my sleeves and plunge right in.
And amid the clutter of dough
The baking crew at last does win.

Soon the aroma of fresh baked cookies
Fill the beautiful summer air
And I am rewarded at last
By my brother's pleased smile, so fair.

Father comes from the dairy barn,
Mother comes briskly down the stairs
Small siblings come from everywhere—
Grab a cookie and flop on a chair.

So, as you can plainly see
Cookie making has joys its own.
So the very best thing to do—
Do it, without a moan or groan.

—Regina Coblentz

Cookies, Brownies & Bars

SOFT OATMEAL COOKIES

Mrs. Perry (Melinda) Lambright

2 c. brown sugar
3/4 c. lard
2 eggs
1 c. sour milk
1 tsp. soda
1 Tbsp. vanilla

1/2 tsp. salt
3 c. flour
3 c. oatmeal
raisins, chocolate chips, and
    nuts (optional)

Mix in order given. Bake in medium oven until browned.

OATMEAL COOKIES

Mrs. Freeman E. Yoder

2 c. brown sugar
1 c. Crisco
2 eggs
1 tsp. soda
1/2 tsp. salt

1 tsp. baking powder
1 tsp. vanilla
3 c. oatmeal
1 1/2 c. flour
3/4 c. chocolate chips

Cream together sugar and Crisco. Add next 5 ingredients. Beat well, then add the rest. Mix well, then make ball-sized of walnuts and roll in powdered sugar until well coated. Bake at 350°–375°. Do not overbake. Makes about 30 cookies.

CHEWY OATMEAL COOKIES

Loretta Kuhns

2 c. butter (melted)
3 c. brown sugar
4 eggs
1 tsp. salt
1/2 c. peanut butter
1/2 c. coconut

1 box vanilla pudding
2 tsp. baking soda
3 c. flour
3 c. oatmeal
1 1/2 c. chocolate chips

Mix all together real well. Chill. Bake at 350° for 15 min. or until done.

MOM'S SOFT BANANA OATMEAL COOKIES

Sara Mae Yoder

5 pk. Nutra Sweet
1 c. mashed bananas
2 eggs (beaten)
$^3/_4$ c. shortening
2 c. oatmeal
1 c. whole wheat flour

$^1/_2$ c. oat bran
$^1/_2$ tsp. soda
$^1/_2$ tsp. baking powder
$^1/_2$ tsp. salt
$^1/_4$ tsp. nutmeg
$^3/_4$ tsp. cinnamon

Nuts may also be put in if you wish. These cookies are good for people who need to watch their diet.

PEANUT BUTTER OATMEAL COOKIES

Mrs. Daniel (Martha) Miller

1 c. lard
1 c. peanut butter
$1^1/_2$ c. sugar
2 c. brown sugar
$^1/_2$ c. Karo
$^1/_2$ c. coconut
4 eggs
1 tsp. salt

1 Tbsp. vanilla flavoring
1 Tbsp. coconut flavoring
$^1/_2$ c. hot water mixed with
   1 tsp. soda
4 c. flour
1 Tbsp. baking powder
3 c. oatmeal

Mix in lg. bowl in order given. Bake at 375°. Makes $4^1/_2$ doz.

———— ❀ ————

*Colored Coconut: When baking cookies or cakes
for special events, tinting coconut gives an added touch.
To color, just place the flakes in glass jar, sprinkle with
a few drops food coloring; cover jar and shake well.*

MONSTER COOKIES

Mrs. Perry Schrock

1 lb. butter	1 Tbsp. vanilla
4 c. sugar	11 c. oatmeal
1 doz. eggs	6 c. flour
3 lbs. peanut butter	1 lb. chocolate chips
2 lbs. brown sugar	1 lb. M & Ms
8 tsp. baking soda	2 c. nuts

Combine above ingredients, drop by teaspoonful onto lightly greased cookie sheets and bake at 350° 10–15 min. Makes about 200 cookies.

MONSTER COOKIES

Velda Kuhns
Mrs. Ezra (Elsie) Hochstetler

3 eggs	1¹/₂ c. peanut butter
1 c. brown sugar	4¹/₂ c. oatmeal
1 c. white sugar	¹/₂ c. chocolate chips
1 Tbsp. Karo	¹/₂ c. M & Ms
2 tsp. soda	1 tsp. vanilla
¹/₂ c. oleo	

Mix everything together and bake at 350° for 12 min.

———————— ❁ ————————

Sticky Situation: When a recipe requires honey or molasses, keep them from sticking to the measuring cup by greasing it. If the recipe also calls for oil, just measure that first.

———————— ❁ ————————

A well-read Bible makes a well-fed soul.

OATMEAL CHOCOLATE CHIP COOKIES

Mrs. Perry Troyer

2 c. butter
2 c. brown sugar
2 c. white sugar
4 eggs
1 tsp. salt
24 oz. chocolate chips
1 - 8 oz. Hershey bar with almonds

5 c. oat flour
4 c. flour
2 tsp. baking powder
2 tsp. soda
2 tsp. vanilla

Refrigerate dough a half hour before baking. Bake at 375°. Do not use too much flour! Do not overbake.

OATMEAL COOKIES

Viola Bontrager

1 c. margarine
2 c. brown sugar (packed)
2 eggs (beaten)
1 tsp. vanilla
2 c. flour

1 tsp. salt
1 tsp. baking powder
1 tsp. soda
3 c. quick oats

Form into balls and roll in powdered sugar and flatten a little. Bake at 350° for 12–15 min.

GRANDMA'S OATMEAL COOKIES

Mary Miller

1 c. white sugar
1 c. brown sugar
3/4 c. lard
2 eggs
1/4 c. water
2 c. flour
1/2 tsp. salt

1 tsp. soda
1 tsp. baking powder
1 tsp. vanilla
1 c. coconut or chocolate chips
3 c. quick rolled oats
1/2 c. chopped nuts (optional)

Blend sugar and shortening with eggs and water. Sift together dry ingredients and add to first mixture. Stir in vanilla, oats and coconut. Drop by teaspoonfuls on greased cookie sheet. Flatten with bottom of glass. Bake at 375° until light brown. Do not over bake!

PRIDE OF IOWA COOKIES *Mrs. Jonas Yoder*

1 c. brown sugar
1 c. white sugar
1 c. shortening
2 eggs
2 c. flour
$^1/_2$ tsp. salt

1 tsp. soda
1 tsp. baking powder
1 tsp. vanilla
1 c. coconut or chocolate chips
3 c. quick rolled oats
$^1/_2$ c. nuts

Blend sugar and shortening. Add beaten eggs. Sift together dry ingredients and add to first mixture. Stir in vanilla, coconut or chocolate chips, oats and nuts; mix well. Drop by teaspoonful onto greased cookie sheet. Flatten with bottom of glass. Bake at 375° until light brown. Do not overbake.

BANANA OATMEAL COOKIES

Mrs. David (Marlene) Miller

$1^1/_2$ c. sifted flour
1 c. sugar
$^1/_2$ tsp. soda
1 tsp. salt
$^1/_4$ tsp. nutmeg
$^3/_4$ tsp. cinnamon

$^3/_4$ c. shortening
1 egg (beaten)
1 c. ripe bananas (mashed)
$1^3/_4$ c. rolled oats
$^1/_2$ chopped nuts

Sift together dry ingredients. Cut in shortening. Add egg, banana, oats and nuts. Drop by teaspoonful onto ungreased cookie sheets. Bake at 400° about 15 min. Do not overbake.

———— ❖ ————

*Store your flour, cornmeal, etc. in glass container
then take spearmint or doublemint gum out of the wrappers
and put in with the flour to keep them from getting
"mealy bugs" during the summer months.*

NEVER FAIL SOFT SUGAR COOKIES

Treva Miller

3 c. Wesson oil
2 c. white sugar
1 c. brown sugar
4 eggs
2 c. buttermilk
2 tsp. soda

6 tsp. baking powder
5 tsp. vanilla
6 c. flour
1 box vanilla pudding
1 tsp. maple flavoring

Beat oil, sugar, instant pudding and eggs; then add soda to buttermilk. Add flour and rest of ingredients. Sprinkle with sugar. Bake at 425°.

SUGAR COOKIES

Mrs. Sherman (LuElla) Miller

6 eggs (well beaten)
5 c. white sugar
2$^{1}/_{2}$ c. oil
3 tsp. soda
6 tsp. baking powder
1 tsp. salt

2 tsp. vanilla
2 tsp. lemon
3 c. milk
12–13 c. flour (or less)
1 box instant vanilla pudding
(optional)

Sprinkle sugar on top and bake at 350°. May omit the sugar sprinkling and frost with Crisco frosting or brown sugar frosting.

BROWN SUGAR FROSTING:

$^{1}/_{4}$ c. butter (melted)
1 c. brown sugar

$^{1}/_{4}$ c. milk

Boil for 2 min. then cool and add powdered sugar.

——— ❀ ———

It can be done, it will be done,
It shall be done;
Tomorrow!

SUGAR COOKIES
Mrs. Paul Whetstone

3 eggs
2^1/$_2$ c. white sugar
1^1/$_2$ c. milk
1^1/$_4$ c. oil
1 tsp. vanilla flavoring

1 tsp. lemon flavoring
1^1/$_2$ tsp. soda
3 tsp. baking powder
6–7 c. flour

Mix in order given. Bake. Fills a Fix 'n Mix. Good and soft.

SUGAR COOKIES
Delilah Yoder

1 c. lard
2^1/$_2$ c. white sugar
3 eggs
2 tsp. soda
3 tsp. baking powder

1 tsp. salt
2 c. milk
6 c. flour
vanilla flavoring
lemon flavoring

Cream lard and sugar. Add eggs and flavoring. Alternate dry ingredients with milk into the lard, sugar and egg mixture. Roll out and sprinkle with sugar. Bake at 350°.

SPICY SUGAR COOKIES
Loretta Kuhns

1^1/$_2$ c. shortening
2 c. sugar
2 eggs
^{1}/$_2$ c. honey or sorghum
^{1}/$_4$ c. milk

2 tsp. vanilla
1^1/$_2$ tsp. salt
2 tsp. cinnamon
3 tsp. baking soda
5 c. flour

Mix well. Chill. Roll in sugar and bake at 350° for 15 min. A good chewy cookie.

————— ❖ —————

^{1}/$_2$ teaspoon baking powder equals 1 egg.

CHRISTMAS SUGAR COOKIES
Mrs. David Eash

2 eggs
2 c. sugar
1 c. soft butter
1 c. Milnot or milk

2 tsp. baking powder
1 tsp. soda in hot water
2 tsp. vanilla
5 c. flour

FROSTING:
powdered sugar
soft butter

milk
food coloring

Mix eggs, sugar, butter, Milnot, soda and vanilla. Add flour and baking powder. Refrigerate overnight. Roll on floured surface about 3/4" thick. Cut shapes. Handle dough as little as possible. Bake at 350° about 5 min. Test like cake for spring-back if done. Use this recipe for drop cookies.

CHURCH COOKIES
Mrs. Freeman (Lydia Sue) Yoder

1 c. white sugar
3 c. brown sugar
2 c. lard (melted)
2 c. sour milk
1 c. cream
4 eggs (beaten)

4 tsp. baking powder
2 tsp. soda
1 Tbsp. vanilla
1/2 tsp. salt
1/2 tsp. lemon flavoring
8 c. flour

———— ❖ ————

A cheerful heart makes its own blue sky.

———— ❖ ————

He who indulgeth, bulgeth!

SOUR CREAM COOKIES   *Mrs. Ervin (Edna) Bontrager*

$1^3/_4$ c. shortening
3 c. white sugar
4 eggs
1 tsp. salt
2 tsp. soda
4 tsp. baking powder
1 Tbsp. vanilla
$6^1/_2$ c. Robin Hood flour
2 c. sour cream

Cream together first 3 ingredients. Add rest of ingredients and mix well. Bake at 350°.

ICING:
1 stick butter or oleo
   (melted)
1 lb. powdered sugar
water

Spread while still warm.

BUTTERMILK COOKIES   *Mrs. Eli Glick*

1 c. shortening
3 eggs
2 tsp. baking powder
2 c. white sugar
1 tsp. soda
1 c. buttermilk or sour cream
4 c. flour
1 tsp. salt
1 tsp. vanilla and lemon

Mix sugar, shortening, add eggs; mix well. Add vanilla and buttermilk. Add dry ingredients. Bake at 350° for 15 min. or till slightly browned.

FROSTING:
1 egg (beaten)
1 box powdered sugar
4 Tbsp. butter
2 tsp. cream or evaporated milk

Mix together and frost.

———————— ❖ ————————

Love is like a rose;
it buds, it blooms, it grows . . .

BUTTERMILK COOKIES (TO CUT)

Mrs. William (Velda) Miller

4^1/$_2$ c. sugar
3 sticks oleo
1^1/$_2$ c. shortening
1^1/$_2$ Tbsp. soda
1^1/$_2$ tsp. salt
7 eggs

2 c. buttermilk or 1 Tbsp.
   vinegar to 1^1/$_2$ c. milk
1^1/$_2$ Tbsp. flavoring
14^1/$_2$ c. flour
1^1/$_2$ Tbsp. baking powder

Cream together sugar, oleo, shortening, soda and salt. Add rest of ingredients. Chill overnight. Roll out on floured board and cut.

BROWN BUTTER ICING:

^{1}/$_4$ c. butter
2 c. powdered sugar

^{1}/$_2$ tsp. vanilla

Brown butter and pour over powdered sugar. Add vanilla. Mix till smooth and spread on cookies. Take icing recipe times 5 if you want enough for all the cookies.

ANDY POLLY COOKIES (ROLL COOKIES)

Mrs. Devon (Ruby) Miller

1^1/$_2$ c. shortening
^{1}/$_2$ c. butter or margarine
2 c. white sugar
2 c. brown sugar
4 eggs (beaten)
2 tsp. lemon flavoring
1 Tbsp. vanilla flavoring

9 c. flour
4 tsp. soda
4 tsp. baking powder
1 tsp. salt
^{1}/$_2$ tsp. nutmeg
2 c. milk or cream

Beat eggs in large mixing bowl. Add sugars and shortening, mix well, add flavorings. Add sifted dry ingredients, alternate with milk, stir well. Let set in cool place 4 hrs. or overnight. Bake at 375°–400°.

OLD FASHIONED COOKIES *Mrs. Harry Wayne Miller*

1 c. brown sugar
1 c. white sugar
1 c. Wesson oil
3 eggs
pinch of salt
1 c. milk

2 tsp. vanilla or lemon flavoring
2 tsp. soda
2 tsp. baking powder
flour (approx. 5 c.; enough to roll)

May be dropped. Press down with glass bottom dipped in jello mixed with sugar. Chocolate chips may be added.

CHOCOLATE CHIP COOKIES *Marietta Miller*

$6^2/_3$ c. flour
3 tsp. baking soda
1 c. Crisco
1 c. oil
2 c. brown sugar
1 c. sugar

1 box instant vanilla pudding
3 tsp. vanilla
6 eggs
2 c. chocolate chips
$1^1/_2$ tsp. baking powder

Mix all together. Bake at 350°.

---— ❖ ——---

Yesterday is only a dream
and tomorrow is only a vision
but today—well lived
makes every yesterday
a dream of happiness;
and every tomorrow a vision of hope . . .

CHOCOLATE CHIP PUDDING COOKIES

Mrs. John (Edith) Hochstetler

$2^1/_4$ c. unsifted flour
1 tsp. soda
$^1/_2$ c. butter or margarine
   (softened)
$^1/_4$ c. sugar
$^3/_4$ c. brown sugar (firmly
   packed)

1 tsp. vanilla
1 pkg. chocolate or vanilla
   instant pudding
2 eggs
1 pkg. (12 oz.) chocolate chips
1 c. nuts (optional)

Combine flour and soda. Beat until creamy: butter, sugar, vanilla and pudding mix. Add eggs; gradually add flour. Stir in chips and nuts. Batter will be stiff. Drop by teaspoonful onto cookie sheets. Bake at 375° for 8–10 min. Note: to get two colors make one batch with chocolate pudding and one batch with vanilla pudding. Put a dab of each together to make a cookie. Vanilla chips may also be used.

CHOCOLATE CHIP COOKIES   *Mrs. Floyd Bontrager*

3 c. flour
1 tsp. soda
1 tsp. salt
1 c. shortening
$^3/_4$ c. brown sugar

$^3/_4$ c. white sugar
1 tsp. vanilla
2 eggs
$^1/_2$ c. nuts
$^3/_4$ c. chocolate chips

Sift together: flour, soda and salt; set aside. Blend together shortening, sugars, vanilla and eggs. Add flour mixture and mix well. Stir in nuts and chocolate chips. Bake at 375° for 10–12 min. Do not overbake.

———— ❀ ————

*Cookies will stay moist in the jar if a slice of
bread is placed in the jar.*

CHOCOLATE CHIP COOKIES   *Mrs. Freeman E. Yoder*

4 eggs
3 c. lard (may use 1 stick
  oleo instead of all lard)
5 c. brown sugar
2 tsp. salt
3 c. sour milk or buttermilk

12 c. pastry flour
6 tsp. baking powder
6 tsp. soda
2 Tbsp. maple flavoring
1 c. chocolate chips

Cream together first 4 ingredients till light and fluffy. Put soda in the milk. Sift baking powder with flour. Add milk to creamed mixture, but do not stir until flour is added. Add flavoring and chocolate chips. Drop onto floured pans. Pat cookies down with floured spoon. Bake at 425° for about 8 min.

CHOCOLATE CHIP PUDDING COOKIES

Mrs. Harry Wayne Miller
Wilma Beechy

3 c. flour (unsifted)
1 tsp. baking powder
1 c. butter or oleo (softened)
1/4 c. sugar
3/4 c. light brown sugar
  (firmly packed)
1 pkg. (4 serving size) Jello
  chocolate or vanilla instant
  pudding

1 tsp. vanilla
2 eggs
1 pkg. (12 oz.) chocolate chips
1 c. nuts (optional)

Mix flour with baking soda. Combine butter, sugar, brown sugar, pudding mix and vanilla in lg. bowl. Beat until smooth and creamy. Add eggs. Gradually add flour mixture. Stir in chocolate chips and nuts. Batter will be stiff. Drop by rounded measuring teaspoon onto ungreased cookie sheet. Bake at 375° for 8–10 min. Makes 7 dozen.

CAROB CHIP COOKIES

Mrs. Freeman (Edna Ellen) Mishler

$^1/_3$ c. Canola oil
$^1/_2$ c. maple syrup
1 tsp. vanilla
1 egg

$1^3/_4$ c. oat or brown rice flour
1 tsp. soda
$^1/_2$ c. unsweetened carob chips
dash of allspice (optional)

Mix, drop by teaspoonful onto cookie sheet. Bake at 350° for 8–10 min. or until done.

SOFT CHOCOLATE CHIP COOKIES

Mrs. William (Velda) Miller

1 tsp. vanilla
2 sticks butter
$^3/_4$ c. brown sugar

$^1/_4$ c. white sugar
1 sm. box instant vanilla
    pudding

Mix all together. Then add **2 eggs**. Mix and add:

$2^1/_4$ c. flour

1 tsp. soda

Then mix everything together. Bake at 375° for 8–10 min. Remove from oven while middle is still soft, then let stand a few min. before taking from pan. May also use this to make a *big* pan full of bars.

———— ❖ ————

Friends are the chocolate chips in the cookie of life.

———— ❖ ————

Thought for the day:
What encourages you to be faithful to God?

PUMPKIN OATMEAL CHOCOLATE CHIP COOKIES

Mrs. Lester A. Beechy
Mary H. Hochstetler

1¹/₂ c. butter or shortening
2 c. brown sugar
1 c. white sugar
1 egg
1 tsp. vanilla
1 pt. pumpkin
3 c. oatmeal

4 c. flour
1 tsp. salt
2 tsp. cinnamon
2 tsp. soda
1¹/₂ c. chocolate chips and/or
   raisins

Cream butter and sugar; add egg and vanilla, then stir in pumpkin; add dry ingredients. Then add chocolate chips or raisins. Bake at 350° for 10 min.

CHOCOLATE CHIP ZUCCHINI COOKIES

Mrs. Amos L. Miller

2¹/₂ c. flour
1¹/₂ tsp. baking powder
1 tsp. cinnamon
³/₄ tsp. salt
1 c. brown sugar
1 c. chocolate chips
¹/₂ c. white sugar

³/₄ c. margarine
1 egg
1 tsp. vanilla
1¹/₂ c. grated zucchini
   (unpared)
³/₄ c. nuts

Cream sugar and margarine. Beat in egg and vanilla. Add dry ingredients alternately with zucchini. Add chocolate chips and nuts. Bake at 375°.

❖

Remember the banana—when it left the bunch it got skinned.

MOLLY'S COOKIES

Mrs. Paul Whetstone

1 c. butter	2 c. flour
1 c. brown sugar	1 tsp. soda
1 c. white sugar	1 tsp. baking powder
2 eggs	2 c. oatmeal
1 tsp. cinnamon	1 c. chocolate chips

Mix in order given. Bake at 350° for 10–12 min. Delicious!

CHOCOLATE CHIP COOKIES

Wanda Yoder

$1/4$ c. white sugar	1 tsp. vanilla
$3/4$ c. brown sugar	1 c. chocolate chips
1 box vanilla instant pudding	2 eggs (beaten)
1 c. margarine (softened)	3 c. all purpose flour
1 tsp. soda (dissolved in a little hot water)	

Mix first 5 ingredients then stir, add remaining ingredients. Batter will be stiff. Drop on ungreased cookie sheet. Bake at 350° for 8–10 min. For chocolate cookies, use chocolate pudding. Very good and soft!

SPECIAL CHOCOLATE CHIP COOKIES

Sara Mae Yoder
Mrs. Freeman (Edna Ellen) Mishler

2 c. vegetable oil	2 c. oatmeal
4 eggs	9 c. flour
5 c. brown sugar	4 tsp. salt
$1/2$ c. milk	2 scant tsp. soda
4 Tbsp. vanilla	$1^1/2$ Tbsp. baking powder
1 Tbsp. vanilla (butter and nut)	3–4 c. chocolate chips

Bake at 375° for 8–10 min. for chewy cookies. Cookies will appear moist. DO NOT OVER BAKE. Makes a little more than a Fix 'n Mix bowl full.

OUTRAGEOUS CHOCOLATE CHIP COOKIES

Mrs. Mervin (Ella) Schrock

1 c. sugar	2 c. flour
$^2/_3$ c. brown sugar (packed)	1 c. quick oats
1 c. margarine (softened)	2 tsp. soda
1 c. peanut butter	$^1/_2$ tsp. salt
1 tsp. vanilla	1 (12 oz.) pkg. chocolate chips
2 eggs	

Heat oven to 350°. Beat sugars, margarine, peanut butter, vanilla, and eggs until well blended. Add dry ingredients. Stir in chips. Drop by teaspoonful 2" apart on ungreased cookie sheets. Bake 10–12 min. Cool 1 min. before removing from cookie sheet. Yield: 4 doz. cookies.

ULTIMATE CHOCOLATE CHIP COOKIES

Loretta Kuhns

1$^1/_2$ c. Crisco	2 tsp. salt
2$^1/_2$ c. brown sugar	2 Tbsp. vanilla
$^1/_4$ c. milk	3$^1/_2$ c. flour
1$^1/_2$ tsp. soda	2 c. chocolate chips
2 eggs	

Dissolve baking soda in milk. Bake at 350° for 15 min.

❖

The reason volunteers aren't paid isn't because they are worthless—but because they're priceless.

❖

The modern definition of coffee: "break fluid."

CHOCOLATE CHIP COOKIES
Ruby Yutzy

$^2/_3$ c. white sugar
$2^1/_2$ c. brown sugar
4 eggs
$1^1/_2$ c. margarine
2 tsp. salt

5 c. flour
2 tsp. baking soda
2 tsp. vanilla
1 pkg. (12 oz.) chocolate chips
1 c. nuts (optional)

Cream together sugars and margarine. Add eggs and vanilla. Stir flour, salt and soda together and add to mixture. Add chocolate chips and nuts. Bake at 350° for 10–12 min. Makes about 8 doz.

CHOCOLATE BIT COOKIES
Suvilla Graber
Mrs. Perry Schrock

2 c. brown sugar
1 c. white sugar
2 c. shortening
6 eggs
1 Tbsp. vanilla

2 tsp. salt
4 tsp. soda
4 tsp. cream of tartar
7 c. sifted flour
2 (3 oz.) pkg. chocolate bits

Mix well in order given. Drop by teaspoonful onto cookie sheet. Bake at 375° for 10–12 min. Nuts may be added.

CHOCOLATE CHIP PEANUT BUTTER COOKIES
Mrs. Paul Whetstone

1 stick butter
$^1/_2$ c. sugar
$^1/_2$ c. brown sugar
1 egg

$^1/_2$ c. peanut butter
1 c. flour
1 tsp. baking soda
1 c. chocolate chips

Bake at 375° for 10–12 min.

APPLESAUCE COOKIES

Ida Lambright

1 c. applesauce
1 c. seedless raisins
1 c. white sugar
1 egg (unbeaten)
2 c. sifted all purpose flour
1 tsp. salt
1 tsp. baking powder

1 tsp. cinnamon
$^1/_2$ tsp. soda
$^1/_2$ tsp. nutmeg
$^1/_2$ tsp. cloves
1 c. chopped nuts
$^1/_2$ c. shortening

Mix applesauce and raisins; set aside. Combine sugar, shortening and egg in mixing bowl; beat until fluffy. Stir in applesauce and raisins. Sift flour with salt, baking powder, soda and spices; add and mix well. Stir in nuts. Drop soft dough by teaspoonful 2" apart onto greased baking sheets. Bake at 375° for 12–15 min. Makes 4–5 doz. soft cookies. Perfect for snacks.

COFFEE COOKIES

Mrs. Richard (Helen) Miller

4 c. brown sugar
2 c. Crisco
4 eggs
2 Tbsp. vanilla

2 tsp. soda
6 tsp. baking powder
2 c. coffee (brewed)
8 c. all purpose flour

These may be dropped or rolled and cut. Bake at 350°.

FROSTING:

1 c. powdered sugar
pinch of salt

$1^1/_2$ Tbsp. Crisco
$^1/_2$ tsp. vanilla

———— ❖ ————

Housework: something you do that no one notices unless you don't do it!

DELICIOUS RAISIN COOKIES

Katie Mast

2 c. white sugar	8 c. flour
2 c. brown sugar	2 tsp. soda
1 lb. oleo	4 tsp. baking powder
4 eggs	1 1/2 tsp. salt
2 tsp. vanilla	1 box raisins

Cook raisins in 2 c. water till water is gone. Cool, add last. Mix eggs, melted oleo, sugar and vanilla. Add flour, soda, baking powder and salt. Mix and form in balls and roll in powdered sugar. Bake at 325° for 10 min. or till done.

CHOCOLATE NUT COOKIES

Mrs. Mervin C. Miller

1 c. sugar	1/4 lb. chocolate
1/2 c. milk	2 c. flour
1/4 lb. butter	1/3 tsp. salt
2 eggs	2 tsp. baking powder
1/2 tsp. flavoring	3/4 c. nut meats (optional)

CHINESE CHEWS

Mrs. John Hochstetler

1/2 c. oleo	2 eggs
2 Tbsp. white sugar	1/4 c. coconut
1 c. flour	3/4 c. nuts
1 1/2 c. brown sugar	2 Tbsp. flour
1 tsp. vanilla	

Mix together the oleo, white sugar, 1 c. flour and press into 9" x 9" pan; bake at 350° for 15 min. Second part: Mix eggs, coconut, nuts, brown sugar, flour and vanilla and place over the above baked part. Bake again at 350° for 25 min.

BUTTERSCOTCH COOKIES

Mrs. Glen (Ida Mae) Beechy

2 c. brown sugar	1 tsp. cream of tartar
1 c. butter and lard (mixed)	1 tsp. vanilla
2 eggs (well beaten)	4 c. flour
1 tsp. soda	$1/2$ c. crushed peanuts (optional)

Mix everything well; shape in roll and let stand overnight in a cool place. Slice and bake in floured pan.

COCOA MINT DOLLARS

Mrs. John Hochstetler

$1/3$ c. butter or oleo	$1/2$ tsp. baking soda
$1/3$ c. shortening	$1/2$ tsp. salt
1 c. white sugar	$3/4$ c. cocoa
1 egg	$1/4$ c. milk
$1 1/2$ tsp. baking powder	2 c. sifted flour

Cream together oleo, shortening and sugar until light and fluffy. Beat in egg. Stir in dry ingredients alternately with milk. Form in 4 rolls, 1" in diameter. Chill until firm enough to slice easily. Cut into $1/8$" slices. Bake at 350° about 10 min. Put together with milk filling.

Mix together:

3 c. powdered sugar	3–4 Tbsp. cream
$1/4$ tsp. mint extract	$1/4$ tsp. salt
4 drops green food coloring	

———— ❖ ————

Happiness is contagious . . . why not be a carrier.

PIZZA COOKIES
Mrs. Harvey (Marie) Hochstetler

$^1/_2$ c. white sugar
$^1/_3$ c. brown sugar
$^1/_2$ stick oleo

1 egg
$^1/_2$ c. peanut butter
1 tsp. vanilla

Mix the above ingredients. Add **1**$^1/_2$ **c. flour**. Press or roll dough on pizza pan (15" size). Roll dough to edge of pan. Bake at 375° for 10 min. Remove from oven. Add **1 c. chocolate chips, 2 c. miniature marshmallows and M & Ms** if desired. Return to oven for 5–10 min. Cut when cool.

CHEWY CHOCOLATE COOKIES
Vera Miller

1$^1/_4$ **c. butter or margarine**
  (softened)
1$^3/_4$**–2 c. sugar**
2 eggs
2 tsp. vanilla

2 c. all purpose flour
$^3/_4$ **c. unsweetened cocoa**
1 tsp. baking soda
dash of salt
1 c. chopped nuts

Cream butter or margarine and sugar in large bowl. Add eggs and vanilla; blend well. Combine flour, cocoa, soda and salt; gradually blend into creamed mixture. Stir in nuts. Drop by teaspoonful onto ungreased cookie sheet. Bake at 350° for 8–9 min. Do not overbake! Cookies will be soft. Cool on sheets until set, about 1 min. Remove to wire rack to cool completely. Store in airtight container. Yield: about 4$^1/_2$ doz.

❖
---

*Remember that if the outlook may not be bright
at times, the uplook always is.*

CHOCOLATE CRINKLES

Mrs. Eli (Mary Etta) Miller
Suanna Miller

1 c. cocoa	2 c. flour
$^1/_2$ c. vegetable oil	2 tsp. baking powder
1 c. white sugar	2 tsp. vanilla
4 eggs	$^1/_2$ tsp. salt

Mix oil, cocoa and sugar. Blend in eggs one at a time. Add vanilla, flour, baking powder and salt. Chill dough several hrs. or overnight. Drop by spoonfuls or make balls; roll in powdered sugar then in white sugar. Bake in 350° oven very slowly. Will easily burn at bottom if oven is too hot.

CHOCOLATE PEANUT BUTTER COOKIES

Freeda Lehman

1 c. lard	1 tsp. soda
1 c. peanut butter	$^1/_2$ tsp. nutmeg
2 c. brown sugar	1 tsp. cinnamon
4 eggs	1 c. water
3 c. flour	2 c. oatmeal
1 tsp. salt	chocolate chips

Cream together shortening, peanut butter and egg. Add remaining ingredients. Bake at 350°.

❖

To prevent clothes from sticking to the wash line on a cold day,
wipe the line with a cloth moistened with vinegar.

HOLSTEIN COOKIES

Mrs. Mary Ann Lambright
Mrs. Amos Yoder

2¹/₂ c. Robin Hood flour
1 tsp. baking soda
¹/₂ c. margarine (softened)
¹/₄ c. sugar
¹/₂ tsp. salt

³/₄ c. brown sugar
1 tsp. vanilla
2 eggs
1 (4 oz.) pkg. or ³/₄ c. vanilla
    instant pudding

To make the 2 color cookies make 1 batch of dough with vanilla instant pudding and one batch with chocolate instant pudding, then take a little of each and roll it together. Roll in white sugar before baking. Bake at 350°. Do not overbake!

OLD-FASHIONED BUTTER COOKIES

Mrs. William Schmucker

3 c. sifted all purpose flour
1 tsp. baking powder
¹/₂ tsp. salt
1 c. butter (softened)
³/₄ c. sugar

1 egg
2 Tbsp. cream or milk
1¹/₂ tsp. vanilla extract
cookie decorators

Sift flour with baking powder and salt. Cream butter. Gradually add sugar, cream well. Stir in egg, cream and vanilla. Add dry ingredients gradually; mix well. Chill if necessary. Roll out, ¹/₃ at a time, on floured surface to ¹/₈" thickness. Cut in desired shapes. Place on ungreased cookie sheets. Bake at 400° for 5–8 min. until delicately browned. Cool and decorate. Makes about 6–7 doz.

❖

The father is the head of the house.
The mother is the heart of the house.

SPICY COOKIES
Suanna Miller

1 c. lard
2 c. brown sugar
3 eggs (beaten)
1 c. plus 4 Tbsp. milk
4 c. flour (or more)
2 tsp. baking soda
2 tsp. baking powder
2 tsp. cinnamon
$^1/_4$ tsp. cloves
1 tsp. nutmeg
1 tsp. vanilla

Cream together the first 3 ingredients then add the remaining ingredients in order given.

ICING:
6 Tbsp. butter or margarine
3 Tbsp. hot water
1 Tbsp. vanilla
2 c. powdered sugar

Melt butter then add rest in order.

WHOOPIE PIES
Dorothy Yoder
Mrs. Daniel Lee Mishler

4 c. flour
2 c. sugar
2 tsp. soda
$^1/_2$ tsp. salt
1 c. shortening
1 c. cocoa
2 eggs
2 tsp. vanilla
1 c. sour milk
1 c. cold water

Cream together sugar, salt, shortening, vanilla and eggs. Sift together flour, soda and cocoa. Add this to the first mixture alternately with water and sour milk. Add slightly more flour if milk is not thick.

FILLING:
2 eggs (beaten)
2 c. sugar
1 Tbsp. vanilla
$1^1/_2$ c. Crisco

Beat eggs, sugar and vanilla well. Add Crisco and continue beating until smooth. Spread this between 2 cookies.

CORA BYLER'S WHOOPIE PIE FILLING

Mrs. Katie Hochstetler

1 egg white or one whole
  egg (beaten)
1 Tbsp. vanilla
2 Tbsp. flour
  Add **marshmallow cream.**

2 Tbsp. milk
2 c. powdered sugar (or as
  needed)
$^3/_4$ c. **Crisco**

PEANUT BUTTER WHOOPIE PIES

Mrs. Ezra (Elsie) Hochstetler

4 c. brown sugar
$^2/_3$ c. peanut butter
$^2/_3$ c. margarine
4 eggs
4 c. flour

1 c. whole wheat flour
1 tsp. salt
2 tsp. baking powder
4 tsp. soda (dissolved in 6 Tbsp.
  boiling water)

Cream sugar, margarine, peanut butter and eggs together. Add flour, salt and baking powder. Then add soda water and beat. Bake at 350° for 8–10 min.

FROSTING:

3 c. powdered sugar
$^1/_3$ c. milk
$^1/_2$ tsp. salt

$^1/_3$ c. peanut butter
1 Tbsp. hot water

Mix all together and spread between 2 cookies.

——————— ❖ ———————

The richest person is one who finds pleasure in everyday duties.

——————— ❖ ———————

There aren't enough crutches in the world for all the lame excuses.

PUMPKIN WHOOPIE PIES

Mrs. Fernandis Graber
Mrs. Perry Schrock

2 c. brown sugar
1 c. vegetable oil
1¹/₂ c. pumpkin (cooked
   and mashed)
2 eggs
3 c. flour
1 tsp. salt

1 tsp. baking powder
1 tsp. soda
1 tsp. vanilla
1 tsp. cinnamon
¹/₂ tsp. ginger
¹/₂ tsp. cloves

Cream sugar and oil. Add pumpkin and eggs; cream again. Add rest of ingredients. Mix well. Drop by teaspoonful onto greased cookie sheet. Bake at 350° for 10–12 min.

PUMPKIN WHOOPIE PIES

Mrs. Eli Miller

¹/₂ c. oil
1 c. brown sugar
2 eggs (beaten)
1 c. mashed pumpkin
³/₄–1 c. all purpose flour
³/₄ c. whole wheat flour

4 tsp. baking powder
2¹/₂ tsp. cinnamon
¹/₄ tsp. ginger
¹/₂ tsp. nutmeg
1 c. raisins
1 c. chopped nuts

Beat first 4 ingredients with egg beater then add dry ingredients. Add raisins and nuts last. Bake at 350° for 15 min.

Variations: Shredded zucchini may be used instead of pumpkin. Add last with raisins and nuts.

———— ❖ ————

Bee Stings: make a paste of baking soda and water
and put on sting or put on mud.

LITTLE DEBBIE COOKIES

Ida Hochstetler
Esther Eash

$1/2$ c. butter or oleo
$1/2$ c. lard
3 c. brown sugar
4 eggs
3 c. quick oats
2 tsp. vanilla

1 tsp. salt
2–3 c. flour
2 tsp. flour
2 tsp. cinnamon
1 tsp. soda
$1^1/2$ tsp. nutmeg (optional)

Cream together brown sugar and shortening. Add eggs and beat well; add vanilla and dry ingredients. Bake at 350°.

FILLING:

3 egg whites
2 tsp. vanilla
4 c. powdered sugar

$1^1/2$ c. Crisco (creamed)
5 Tbsp. flour
4 Tbsp. milk

Beat egg whites; then stir in vanilla and milk. Add powdered sugar, Crisco and flour; beat well. Put filling between cookies while warm.

SARA'S SQUASH SWEETS

Sara Mae Yoder

2 c. vegetable oil
4 c. squash (canned or cooked)
4 c. sugar
$6^1/2$ c. sifted flour
2 c. oatmeal

4 tsp. soda
4 tsp. baking powder
4 tsp. cinnamon
1 c. walnuts
1 tsp. salt

Frost with **1 pkg. cream cheese, 1 tsp. vanilla, 3–4 Tbsp. milk and powdered sugar** until the right consistency. Put frosting between 2 cookies. Very soft. Bake at 350°.

BUTTERNUT SQUASH COOKIES

Mrs. Perry A. Bontrager

1 egg
1 c. sugar
1/2 c. shortening
1 c. squash (cooked, mashed
   and cooled, or canned)

1 tsp. baking powder
1 tsp. soda
2 c. flour
1/2 tsp. vanilla
pinch of salt

Dough need not be as stiff as other cookie dough. Beat eggs. Cream in sugar and shortening. Add squash, then sift in dry ingredients. Bake at 400°.

FROSTING:
1 c. powdered sugar
vanilla

1 Tbsp. Crisco

Add boiling water a little at a time until it's the right consistency. These are very moist cookies! You may also choose the frosting of your choice.

PUMPKIN COOKIES

Mrs. Freeman Schmucker

1 c. shortening
1 c. pumpkin
1 tsp. cinnamon
1 tsp. baking powder
nuts (optional)

1 egg
1 c. brown sugar
2 c. flour
1 tsp. soda
1/2 tsp. salt

ICING:
1 Tbsp. milk

1/4 c. pumpkin

Add powdered sugar till it's right to spread.

❀
---

1 lemon = 3–4 tablespoons lemon juice
1 orange = 6–8 tablespoons orange juice

MOLASSES CRINKLES

Miss Alice Miller

1¹/₂ c. shortening (softened)
2 c. brown sugar
2 eggs
¹/₂ tsp. salt
¹/₂ c. molasses

4 tsp. soda
4¹/₂ c. flour
1 tsp. cloves
2 tsp. cinnamon
2 tsp. ginger

Cream together shortening, sugar, eggs, salt, molasses and soda. Then add sifted dry ingredients. Dough may be chilled or may be used right away. Roll into balls. Dip into water and then sugar. Bake just until set but not hard. Makes 3 doz.

GINGER SNAP COOKIES

Christina Miller
Vera Mae Yoder

³/₄ c. shortening
1 c. brown sugar (packed)
1 egg
2¹/₄ c. flour
¹/₄ c. molasses
1 tsp. cinnamon

¹/₂ tsp. cloves
2 tsp. soda
1 tsp. ginger
¹/₄ tsp. salt
white sugar

Mix throughly, shortening, brown sugar, egg and molasses. Blend in remaining ingredients, except white sugar. Cover, chill 1 hr. Heat oven to 375°. Shape dough into balls and dip tops into white sugar. Place balls, sugared side up, on lightly greased baking sheets. Bake 10–12 min. or just until set. Immediately removef from baking sheet. Makes 4 doz. cookies.

---------- ❖ ----------

Baking powder will remove tea or coffee stains
from china pots and cups.

HONEY SUGAR SNAPS
Mrs. Sherman (LuElla) Miller

2 c. white sugar	2 c. precreamed shortening
2 c. brown sugar	1 c. honey
4 eggs	2 tsp. nutmeg
6 tsp. soda	1 tsp. salt
9 c. flour	1 c. sugar
1 c. butter or oleo (softened)	2 tsp. cinnamon

In a large bowl combine sugars and shortenings. Add eggs and beat well. Add honey and dry ingredients. If mixture is too dry to mix with the spoon, mix with hands. In a small bowl combine the 1 cup sugar and cinnamon. Shape dough into balls and roll into sugar and cinnamon mixture and bake at 350° until golden brown and crinkly on top when down.

WHEAT GERM CRUNCHIES
Mrs. John (Edith) Hochstetler

3 c. oatmeal	3 eggs
2 c. whole wheat flour	3 tsp. baking powder
2 c. brown sugar	2 tsp. cinnamon
1 c. coconut	$1^1/_2$ tsp. vanilla
$1^1/_2$ c. oleo	$1^1/_2$ tsp. maple flavoring
1 c. wheat germ	1 tsp. salt
1 c. wheat bran	

Mix altogether and bake in cookie sheets for 15–20 min. Crumble and dry. Cool and seal in container.

———— ❁ ————

An old toothbrush works fine to clean combs.

SPEEDY BROWNIES

Mrs. William J. Troyer
Mrs. Harvey (Marie) Hochstetler

1³/₄ c. all purpose flour	5 eggs
2 c. sugar	1 c. vegetable oil
¹/₂ c. baking cocoa	1 tsp. vanilla
1 tsp. salt	1 c. semi sweet chocolate chips

In a mixing bowl combine everything except the chocolate chips. Beat until smooth. Pour into a greased 9" x 13" baking pan. Sprinkle with chocolate chips. Bake at 350° for 30 min. or until a toothpick inserted near the center comes out clean. Cool in pan on wire rack.

CREAM CHEESE BROWNIES

Mrs. Lester A. Beechy

1 chocolate cake mix	¹/₂ c. sugar
8 oz. cream cheese	chocolate chips
1 egg	

Mix cake mix according to directions. Pour into cookie sheet with sides. Beat cream cheese, egg, and sugar well. Put in lines on top of cake mix batter and swirl with knife for marble effect. Put chocolate chips on top. Bake at 350° until done. Best if not over-baked.

CHOCOLATE CHIP BROWNIES

Mrs. Amos Yoder

1 c. brown sugar	1 tsp. soda
1 c. white sugar	1 tsp. salt
1 c. oil	¹/₄ c. milk (optional)
2 eggs (beaten)	1 c. chocolate chips
3 c. all purpose flour	¹/₂ c. nuts (optional)

Cream together the sugars and oil. Add beaten eggs and mix. Add dry ingredients. Spread on baking sheet and sprinkle chocolate chips and nuts on top. Bake at 325° for 20 min.

CHEWY FUDGE SQUARES

Sara Whetstone

1 chocolate cake mix	2 c. miniature marshmallows
2 eggs	1 c. nuts or chocolate chips
$1/2$ c. butter (melted)	2 Tbsp. vegetable oil

Stir together cake mix, eggs and butter. Add vegetable oil, stir in marshmallows, nuts, chocolate chips.

Bake at 350° for 30–35 min. or until set in center.

OLD FASHIONED BROWNIES

Suella Miller

1 c. oil	1 c. white sugar
4 eggs (beaten)	2 c. flour
1 tsp. vanilla	$1/2$ c. cocoa
1 tsp. salt	1 tsp. baking powder
1 c. brown sugar	$1/2$ c. walnuts (coarsely broken)

Preheat oven to 350°. Beat together oil, eggs, vanilla, salt and brown sugar in large bowl. Combine white sugar, flour, cocoa and baking powder in smaller bowl. Dump dry mix to wet mixture. Stir thoroughly. Spread into a large cookie sheet. Sprinkle nuts on top. Bake for 30 min. or until center is done.

CHOCOLATE CHIP SQUARES

Mrs. Ezra A. Schrock

3 eggs	1 tsp. soda
$3/4$ c. white sugar	$1/2$ tsp. salt
$3/4$ c. brown sugar	3 c. flour
1 stick oleo (melted)	chocolate chips
1 tsp. vanilla	

Mix together in order as given.

BUTTERSCOTCH BROWNIES
Christina Miller

1/4 c. butter
1 c. brown sugar
1 egg
1 c. flour

1 tsp. vanilla
1/2 tsp. salt
1 tsp. baking powder
1/2 c. chopped nuts

Melt butter; stir in sugar; add eggs, flour, vanilla, salt, and baking powder. Add nuts last. Sprinkle sugar over top. Bake in square loaf pan at 350° for 30 min. Remove from pan immediately. This is a must!

COOKIE DOUGH BROWNIES
LaVerda Yoder

2 c. sugar
1 1/2 c. flour
1/2 tsp. salt
1 c. vegetable oil

4 eggs
2 tsp. vanilla
1/2 c. chopped walnuts
1/2 c. cocoa

FILLING:

1/2 c. butter (softened)
1/2 c. brown sugar
1/4 c. sugar

2 tsp. milk
1 tsp. vanilla
1 c. flour

GLAZE:

1 c. semi-sweet chocolate chips
3/4 c. chopped walnuts

1 Tbsp. shortening

Mix together the top ingredients and bake at 350°. When done put the filling on top; when that is hard enough pour the glaze on top of it.

———— ❖ ————

Birthdays are good for you! Statistics show that the people who have the most, live the longest.

BROWNIES

Ruby Yutzy

2 c. sugar
³/₄ c. butter and lard
  (combined)
4 eggs
1 c. flour
¹/₂ tsp. salt
¹/₂ c. cocoa
1 tsp. vanilla
¹/₂ c. nutmeats

Cream together sugar and butter. Add eggs. Sift together flour, salt, and cocoa and add to mixture. Stir in vanilla and nutmeats. Pour into greased and floured 9" x 13" cake pan. Bake at 350° about 45 min. or until pick inserted in center comes out clean. May drizzle chocolate icing over top when cooled.

TEXAS BROWNIES

Mrs. Elmer Hochstetler

2 c. all purpose flour
2 c. white sugar
¹/₂ c. butter or margarine
¹/₂ c. shortening
1 c. water
¹/₄ c. dark, unsweetened cocoa
¹/₂ c. buttermilk
2 eggs
1 tsp. baking soda
1 tsp. vanilla

FROSTING:

¹/₂ c. butter or margarine
2 Tbsp. dark cocoa
¹/₄ c. milk
3¹/₂ c. unsifted powdered sugar
1 tsp. vanilla

In a heavy saucepan combine butter, shortening, water and co-coa; stir and heat to boiling. Pour boiling mixture over the flour and sugar mixture. Add buttermilk, eggs, baking soda and vanilla. Pour in a well buttered 17¹/₂" x 11" jelly roll pan. Bake at 400° for 20 min. While brownies bake, prepare the frosting. In a saucepan combine the butter, cocoa and milk. Heat to boiling, stirring constantly. Mix in powdered sugar and vanilla. Put on brownies while still warm.

TWINKIES

Mrs. Amos L. Miller

1 box yellow cake mix
1 box instant vanilla pudding
1 c. water

4 eggs
1/2 c. Wesson oil

Bake in 2 flat cookie sheets.

FILLING:

3 egg whites
3 tsp. vanilla
1 1/2 c. Crisco
3 Tbsp. flour

5 Tbsp. milk
3 c. powdered sugar (or as
needed)

Mix all ingredients together and beat until smooth. Then put on 1 cake and put the other on top.

TWINKIES

Mrs. Glen (Alma) Whetstone

1 yellow cake mix
1 c. water

4 eggs
1/2 c. vegetable oil

FILLING:

1/4 c. water
1/2 c. sugar
4 2/3 c. powdered sugar
1/2 tsp. salt

2 egg whites (beaten stiff)
2 tsp. vanilla
1 c. Crisco

Mix cake mix, water, oil and eggs. Put on 2 cookies sheets and bake at 350° until done.

For filling: boil water and sugar together for 1 min. Cool completely before adding powdered sugar, salt, beaten egg whites, vanilla and Crisco. Spread on one cake and put the other cake on top.

———— ❀ ————

If there's room in your heart,
there's always room in your house.

RHUBARB DELIGHT SQUARES

Fanny Mae Bontrager

1 c. flour
1 tsp. baking powder
$^1/_2$ tsp. salt
4 Tbsp. butter
1 egg (beaten)
2 Tbsp. milk

2 c. finely cut rhubarb
3 oz. pkg. red jello
$^1/_2$ c. flour
1 c. sugar
$^1/_4$ c. butter (melted)

Mix together first 6 ingredients. Pat a thin layer in bottom of 9" x 9" pan. Sprinkle evenly with rhubarb and jello. Make crumbs with last three ingredients. Spread over rhubarb and jello. Bake at 350° until crust is light golden brown.

RHUBARB DREAM BARS

Mary Miller
Mrs. Sam (Wilma) Whetstone

2 c. flour
$^3/_4$ c. powdered sugar

1 c. butter

FILLING:
4 eggs
2 c. sugar
4 c. rhubarb (diced)

$^1/_2$ c. flour
$^1/_2$ tsp. salt

Mix crust ingredients until crumbs form. Press into bottom of a 9" x 13" pan. Bake at 350° for 15 min. Blend eggs, sugar, flour and salt until smooth, fold in rhubarb, spread over crust and bake until the middle is a little firm.

———— ❖ ————

Some people are like a wheelbarrow, no good unless pushed.

BLUEBERRY BARS

Mary Miller

1 c. flour
1 c. quick oats
1 c. brown sugar
$^1/_2$ tsp. salt
$^1/_2$ c. shortening
$2^1/_2$ c. blueberries

Mix all together except blueberries. Press half the mixture in a greased 8" x 8" pan. Spread blueberries over crust. Cover with remaining oatmeal mixture. Bake at 350° for 30–40 min.

APPLE BARS

Mrs. Tobie (Esther) Miller

$1^3/_4$ c. white sugar
1 c. vegetable oil
3 eggs
2 c. all purpose flour
$^1/_2$ tsp. salt
$^1/_2$ tsp. cinnamon
1 tsp. baking powder
2 c. chopped apples

Combine sugar, vegetable oil and eggs. Beat well, then add the rest of the ingredients. Bake at 350° in a lightly greased jelly roll pan. Cool and cut into bars. Yield: 24 bars.

CHERRY CAKE BARS

LaVerda Yoder
Ruby Yutzy

1 c. oleo (softened)
4 eggs
$1^3/_4$ c. sugar
3 c. flour
$^1/_2$ tsp. salt
$1^1/_2$ tsp. baking powder
1 tsp. vanilla
1 can cherry pie filling

Cream together oleo, eggs and sugar. Mix together flour, salt, baking powder, vanilla and filling. Combine dry ingredients and creamed mixture and spread half of batter in greased sheet pan. Pour 1 can filling over this. Drop rest of batter by spoonfuls over filling. Bake at 350° for 40 min. Cool and glaze.

GLAZE:

2 tsp. white Karo
1 tsp. vanilla
$1^1/_2$ c. powdered sugar
2 or 3 Tbsp. hot water

MOLASSES BARS
Mary Esther Whetstone

4 c. white sugar
14 c. flour
1 tsp. salt
2 c. oleo
2 c. Brer Rabbit Molasses (mild)

5 eggs (beaten)
3 Tbsp. soda
$^1/_2$ c. boiling water
12 oz. chocolate chips

In a large bowl mix flour, sugar and salt. Work in oleo with a pastry blender. Make a well and add molasses, then hot water mixed with soda. Add eggs and chocolate chips and mix well. Take a handful of dough and form a roll, 1" thick. Place on greased and floured pan; 3 on pan lengthwise. Brush top with beaten egg for a glaze. Bake at 375° for 13 min. or until you think they are barely done. Then cut each roll into 4 bars.

SPICY MOLASSES BARS
Fanny Mae Bontrager

1 lb. butter
4 c. white sugar
5 eggs
1 tsp. salt
$^1/_2$ c. boiling water
2 c. sorghum molasses

3 Tbsp. soda
14 c. flour
4 tsp. ginger
4 tsp. cinnamon
2 tsp. cloves

Cream butter and sugar; add eggs and salt and beat. Combine water, molasses and soda. Add to butter mix. Sift flour and spices. Mix in with rest of ingredients. Shape into 1" dia. logs, 4" apart on baking sheets. Brush tops with beaten egg. Bake at 375° for 13 min. Do not overbake! Cut logs at 3" or 4" intervals immediately after removing from oven.

❖

Those who can't laugh at themselves, leave the job to others.

PUMPKIN BARS

Mrs. Perry Troyer

1 c. oil or $^3/_4$ c. lard
4 eggs (beaten)
2 c. sugar
2 c. pumpkin
$^1/_2$ tsp. salt
$^1/_2$ tsp. cloves

2 c. flour
2 tsp. baking powder
1 tsp. soda
2 tsp. cinnamon
$^1/_2$ tsp. ginger
$^1/_2$ tsp. nutmeg

Mix together and bake on cookie sheet. Frost and sprinkle with chopped nuts.

ZUCCHINI BARS

Mrs. Mervin (Ella) Schrock

2 c. grated zucchini
1 c. white sugar
1 c. brown sugar
2 c. flour
3 eggs

1 c. vegetable oil
3 tsp. cinnamon
1 tsp. salt
2 tsp. baking soda
1 tsp. baking powder

Slightly beat eggs, add sugars and oil; mix well. Add zucchini alternately with sifted dry ingredients. Mix well. Bake on greased cookie sheet or loaf pan at 350° for 30 min.

FROSTING:

4 oz. cream cheese
$^1/_2$ c. soft butter

2 c. powdered sugar
1 tsp. vanilla

Mix well and spread on cooled zucchini bars. Sprinkle chopped nuts on top. Very good!

❖

---

*In making others happy, you will be happy too, for the
happiness you give away, returns to "shine on you".*

LUNCH BOX DATE BARS

Emma Hochstetler

6 eggs
1 1/2 c. brown sugar (firmly packed)
1 tsp. vanilla
1 1/2 c. graham crackers (finely crushed)
1 tsp. baking powder
1/2 tsp. salt
1 c. ground walnuts or pecans
1 1/2 c. pitted dates

Beat eggs until thick and lemon colored, beat in sugar and vanilla. Stir together the cracker crumbs, baking powder and salt. Mix and add nuts and dates. Turn into a buttered 9" x 13" baking pan. Bake at 350° for 30–35 min. or until set. Let cool and cut into squares.

CHOCOLATE CREAM BARS

Katie Bontrager

3/4 c. water
1/2 c. butter
1 1/2 sq. unsweetened chocolate
2 c. flour
1 1/2 c. brown sugar (packed)
2 eggs
1 tsp. salt
1/2 c. sour cream
1 tsp. soda
8 oz. pkg. cream cheese (softened, and mixed with 1/3 c. sugar)
1 egg (beaten and mixed with 1 tsp. vanilla)
1 c. (6 oz.) chocolate chips

In a small saucepan combine water, butter and chocolate. Cook and stir over low heat until smooth. Combine flour and sugar in bowl. Add eggs, salt, sour cream and soda. Beat until smooth. Stir in chocolate mixture. In another bowl beat until smooth the next 5 ingredients. Spread chocolate batter in greased 15" x 10" x 1" pan. Drop cream cheese mixture by tablespoon over batter. Cut through the batter with a knife to swirl. Sprinkle with chocolate chips. Bake at 375° for 20–25 min. or until a toothpick inserted near the center comes out clean. Cut into bars.

CHOCOLATE CHIP CREAM CHEESE BARS

Mrs. Marlin Miller

1 yellow cake mix	1 egg
$1/3$ c. vegetable oil	

Mix ingredients together and press in cake pan (all but one cup). Bake for 15 min. at 350°. Top with bottom ingredients and sprinkle the 1 cup of reserved crumbs on top and bake for another 15 min.

8 oz. cream cheese	1 egg
$1/3$ c. sugar	1 c. chocolate chips

CAN'T LEAVE ALONE BARS   *Mrs. Leroy (Betty) Yoder*

1 box yellow cake mix	$3/4$ c. chocolate chips
2 eggs	$1/4$ c. peanut butter chips
$1/3$ c. vegetable oil	1 can Eagle Brand milk
$1/4$ c. butter	

Mix cake mix, eggs, and oil and put half of mixture in bottom of a greased cake pan. Melt next 4 ingredients together. You may use 1 cup chocolate chips instead of chocolate and peanut butter chips. Put on top of cake mix and crumble rest of cake mix on top. Bake at 350° for 30 min. You may use chocolate cake mix then use $1/4$ cup chocolate chips and $3/4$ cup peanut butter.

MARBLE SQUARES   *Mrs. Clayton Yoder*

1 c. butter (melted)	1 tsp. soda
$3/4$ c. sugar	1 tsp. vanilla
$2/3$ c. brown sugar	$2^1/4$ c. flour
2 eggs	1 c. chocolate chips
$1/2$ tsp. salt	M & Ms

Mix all ingredients except M & Ms. Bake 3 min., then swirl and put M & Ms on top. Bake another 25 min. or until done at 350°.

CHOCOLATE REVEL BARS

Mrs. Marlin Miller
Loretta Kuhns

1 c. butter (softened)	3 c. quick cooking oats
2 c. brown sugar	1 c. (6 oz.) chocolate chips
2 eggs	1 (14 oz.) can sweetened con-
2 tsp. vanilla	densed milk
2$^{1}/_{2}$ c. sifted flour	2 Tbsp. butter
1 tsp. salt	$^{1}/_{2}$ tsp. salt
1 tsp. baking soda	2 tsp. vanilla

Cream together: softened butter and brown sugar in large mixing bowl. Add eggs, vanilla, flour, salt and baking soda. Stir in oats; mix well. Spread $^{2}/_{3}$ of mixture on a 15" x 10" x 1" in lightly greased jelly roll pan. Melt together chocolate chips, sweetened condensed milk, butter and salt, stirring constantly over low heat. Blend in vanilla. Spread over mixture in pan. Dot with remaining dough. Bake for 30 min. at 350°. Do not overbake.

M & M DREAM BARS

Mrs. Jr. (Barbara) Yoder

2 c. oatmeal	1 c. oleo (melted)
1 tsp. soda	2 cans Eagle Brand milk
1$^{1}/_{2}$ c. flour	$^{1}/_{2}$ c. peanut butter
1 c. brown sugar	1 c. M & Ms or chocolate chips

Mix oatmeal, flour, brown sugar, soda and oleo until creamy. Press crumbs in cookie sheet (reserving 1$^{1}/_{2}$ cup). Bake 12 min. at 350°. Mix milk and peanut butter; spread on top of partly baked crust. Top with remaining crumbs and M & Ms or chocolate chips. Bake 12–15 min. at 350°.

———————— ❖ ————————

Salt dissolved in alcohol will often remove grease spots
from clothing, when all else fails.

SALTED NUT BARS

Mrs. Kenny (Ruby) Schrock

1¹/₂ c. flour

¹/₂ tsp. baking powder

¹/₄ tsp. soda

¹/₂ c. sugar

¹/₂ c. butter

²/₃ c. brown sugar

2 eggs

¹/₂ tsp. salt

TOPPING:

²/₃ c. Karo

¹/₂ c. butter

12 oz. pkg. peanut butter chips

2 tsp. vanilla

2 c. Rice Krispies

2 c. salted peanuts

Mix together, pat into a 10" x 15" cookie sheet. Bake 12–15 min. at 350°. When done, sprinkle 4 cups miniature marshmallows on top and return to oven till marshmallows are puffy. Cool. Heat Karo, butter, chips and vanilla till blended. Stir in Rice Krispies and salted peanuts. Spread evenly on top. Cut when cool.

TEN MINUTE COOKIE BARS

Mrs. Mervin E. (Katie Fern) Miller

1 c. butter

1 c. sugar

4 c. quick oats

Melt butter. Pour over brown sugar and oats. Mix well. Press into a 13" x 9" x 2" baking pan. Bake at 400° for 10 min.

FROSTING:

1 c. chocolate chips

1¹/₂ c. peanut butter

Melt together in saucepan. Spread over baked layer. Chill. Cut in 36 bars.

———— ❖ ————

Silence can be beautiful and impressive;
don't break it unless you can improve it.

O HENRY BARS

Mrs. Perry Schrock

4 c. quick oatmeal   1 c. butter
1 c. brown sugar $^1/_2$ c. white sugar
    Mix together and put in 10" x 15" pan. Bake at 350° for 12 min.

FROSTING:
1 c. chocolate chips   1 c. peanut butter
    Melt together and frost. Cut while still warm.

CHOCOLATE CHIP BARS

Inez Yutzy

2 block margarine (melted)   2 tsp. salt
$^1/_2$ c. salad oil   2 tsp. baking soda
$1^1/_2$ c. brown sugar   1 tsp. baking powder
$1^1/_2$ c. white sugar $4^1/_2$ c. flour
4 eggs   1 pkg. chocolate chips
    Mix all together. Put in 2 greased 13" x 9" x 2" pans. Bake at
350° for 20–25 min.

--------- ❖ ---------

*There is so much good in the worst of us
and so much bad in the best of us
that it behooves all of us
not to talk about the rest of us.*

—Robert Louis Stevenson

--------- ❖ ---------

*Friendship, like a young tree, must be planted in rich soil,
watered properly with common sense to establish
deep roots and then grow in sunshine of time.*

TOFFEE TOPPED BARS
Mrs. William Schmucker

2 c. brown sugar (firmly packed)
2 c. all purpose flour
$^1/_2$ c. butter or margarine (softened)
1 tsp. baking powder
$^1/_2$ tsp. salt
1 tsp. vanilla extract
1 c. milk
1 egg
1 c. chocolate chips
$^1/_2$ c. chopped pecans or walnuts
$^1/_4$ c. flaked coconut (optional)

In a large mixing bowl, mix together brown sugar and flour. Cut in the butter until mixture resembles coarse crumbs. Remove 1 cup of mixture and set aside. To mixture in large bowl, add baking powder and salt. Using a fork, lightly beat in vanilla, milk and egg. Continue beating until a smooth batter forms. Pour batter in greased 9" x 13" baking pan. Sprinkle reserved crumbs on top. Sprinkle the chocolate chips, nuts, and coconut evenly on top. Bake at 350° for 35 min. or until toothpick inserted in center comes out clean. Makes 24 bars.

CRUNCH BARS
Sara Whetstone

$^1/_2$ c. oleo (softened)
$^2/_3$ c. sugar
2 eggs (beaten)
1 tsp. vanilla
$^3/_4$ c. flour
$^1/_2$ tsp. baking powder
$^1/_4$ tsp. salt
1 Tbsp. cocoa
$^1/_2$ c. nuts
marshmallows
1 c. chocolate chips
1 c. peanut butter
$1^1/_2$ c. Rice Krispies

Mix everything together except the last 4 ingredients. Then bake in 9" x 13" pan at 350° for 15–20 min. Remove from oven and top with marshmallows to cover well. Return to oven for about 3 min. Cool. Melt together chocolate chips and peanut butter. Then stir in Rice Krispies and put on top; chill and cut in squares.

DOUBLE CHOCOLATE CRUMBLE BARS

Vera Miller

$^1/_2$ c. butter
$^3/_4$ c. sugar
2 eggs
1 tsp. vanilla
$^3/_4$ c. all purpose flour

$^1/_2$ c. chopped pecans
2 Tbsp. unsweetened cocoa
$^1/_4$ tsp. baking powder
$^1/_4$ tsp. salt

TOPPING:
2 c. miniature marshmallows
1 (6 oz.) pkg. semi-sweet
chocolate chips

1 c. creamy peanut butter
$1^1/_2$ c. Crisp Rice cereal

Cream butter and sugar; beat in eggs and vanilla. Set aside. Stir together flour, chopped nuts, cocoa, baking powder and salt; stir into egg mixture. Spread in bottom of greased 13" x 9" x 2" baking pan. Bake at 350° for 15–20 min. or until bars test done. Sprinkle marshmallows evenly on top; bake 3 minutes more. Cool. In small saucepan combine chocolate chips and peanut butter; cook and stir over low heat until chocolate is melted. Stir in cereal. Spread mixture on top of cooked bars. Chill; cut in bars. Refrigerate. Yield: 3–4 doz. bars.

WHOLE WHEAT OATMEAL BARS

Mrs. Amos L. Miller

$^3/_4$ c. margarine or lard
$1^1/_2$ c. brown sugar
$1^3/_4$ c. whole wheat flour
1 c. small marshmallows
$^1/_2$ tsp. soda

$^1/_2$ tsp. salt
1 c. oatmeal
1 egg
1 tsp. vanilla

Mix margarine, brown sugar, egg and vanilla until creamy. Then add the rest of ingredients. Spread in greased 9" x 13" pan and sprinkle with chocolate or butterscotch chips over top. Bake at 350° for 20 min. Do not over bake.

CHEWY OATMEAL BARS

Viola Bontrager

1 c. butter or margarine
2 eggs
1 tsp. soda
2 tsp. vanilla
2 c. brown sugar

2 c. flour
$^1/_2$ tsp. salt
$^1/_2$ c. chopped nuts
2 c. oatmeal
6 oz. chocolate chips

Set oven at 350°. Put batter in 13" x 9" pan. Sprinkle with M & Ms and bake. Do not overbake!

GRANOLA BARS

Mrs. Ray Yutzy

$^3/_4$ c. peanut butter
1 c. Karo
$^1/_4$ c. brown sugar
2 tsp. vanilla or maple
   flavoring

2 sticks butter or oleo (melted)
2 c. Rice Krispies
2 c. chocolate chips
1 c. coconut
5 c. oatmeal

Mix together first 5 ingredients; mix well. Add the rest in order given; mix well. Mixture will be crumbly. Press hard into 2 buttered 9" x 13" cake pans. Bake at 325° for 30–40 min. or until golden brown on top. Cut when cold. Store in airtight container.

———— ❖ ————

The only time people really care about which side their bread is buttered on is when they drop it on the floor.

To Make a Cake

TURN ON THE OVEN, get out bowl, spoons and ingredients, grease pan and crack nuts. Remove 18 blocks and seven toy cars from kitchen table. Measure 2 cups flour, salt and baking powder in sifter. Remove boy's hands from flour, measure 1 more cup of flour and add to bowl. Get dustpan and brush up pieces of bowl which boy knocks on floor. Get another bowl. Answer doorbell! Return to kitchen. Remove boy's hands from bowl. Wash boy. Get out eggs. Answer questions. Return to kitchen. Take out grease. Remove one fourth inch salt from it which boy added. Get another pan and grease it. Tie dog up! Return to kitchen and find boy and wash all ingredients off of him. Take up greased pan and remove nut shells from it. Head for boy, who flees knocking bowl off from table. Wash kitchen floor, table and walls. Call baker and lie down.

Cakes &
Frostings

GOOD COFFEE CAKE

Mrs. Katie Hochstetler
Dorothy Yoder

¹/₄ lb. butter or oleo
1 c. sugar
3 eggs (beaten)
2 c. flour
¹/₄ tsp. salt
1 tsp. baking powder

1 tsp. baking soda
1 c. sour cream
1 tsp. vanilla
¹/₂ c. chopped nuts
¹/₂ c. sugar
1 tsp. cinnamon

Cream butter and sugar. Add eggs and blend well. Sift together flour, salt, baking powder and soda. Add dry ingredients to cream mixture alternately with sour cream to which vanilla has been added. Mix just to blend: nuts, sugar and cinnamon. Pour $1/2$ of dough into 9" tube pan. Sprinkle $1/2$ of nut mixture over this. Pour rest of batter and top with remaining nut mixture. Bake at 350° for 45 min.

COFFEE CAKE

Mrs. Sherman (LuElla) Miller

2 c. brown sugar
2 c. flour
¹/₂ tsp. salt
³/₄ c. butter

1 c. brewed coffee
1 tsp. soda (dissolved in coffee)
1 egg (beaten)

Mix brown sugar, flour, salt and butter until crumbly. Reserve 1 cup crumbs. Add coffee with soda and egg; stir until smooth. Pour into greased cake pan. Sprinkle the 1 cup crumbs over top. Bake at 350°. Chocolate chips and nuts may also be added on top.

———— ❖ ————

For baking, it's best to use medium to large eggs;
extra large eggs may cause cakes to fall when cooled.

APPLE CINNAMON COFFEE CAKE

Mrs. Kenny (Ruby) Schrock

2 c. Apple-Cinnamon Toasted
Oats cereal (coarsely crushed)
$^1/_2$ c. brown sugar (packed)
$^1/_4$ c. butter or margarine
(melted)

2 Tbsp. all purpose flour
1 tsp. cinnamon

CAKE:

1$^1/_2$ c. sugar
1 c. vegetable oil
2 eggs
$^1/_4$ tsp. salt
1 tsp. vanilla
2 c. all purpose flour

1 c. Apple-Cinnamon Cheerios
(finely crushed)
1 tsp. baking soda
4 c. apples (cored, peeled and
chopped)

Heat oven to 350°. Combine all topping ingredients; set aside. In a large bowl beat sugar, oil, eggs, salt and vanilla until light and fluffy. Slowly add flour, crushed cereal and soda, mix well. Stir in apples. Spread batter into 13" x 9" greased pan. Sprinkle topping over batter. Bake for 50–55 min. or until toothpick inserted comes out clean. Yield: 16 servings.

DOUBLE DELIGHT COFFEE CAKE

Mrs. Elmer Miller

2 c. flour
2 tsp. baking powder
1 tsp. salt
1 c. sugar
2 eggs

1 c. water
$^3/_4$ c. vegetable oil
2 (3$^1/_2$ oz.) pkgs. instant vanilla
pudding

Mix all ingredients together. Pour into pan. Top with mixture of **1 c. brown sugar, 2 tsp. cinnamon**, and **1 c. nuts** (optional). Bake at 350° for 25–30 min. May also be drizzled with caramel frosting.

RHUBARB COFFEE CAKE
Mrs. Mervin C. Miller

1¹/₂ c. brown sugar (packed)
¹/₂ c. shortening
1 egg
2 c. all purpose flour

1 tsp. soda
¹/₂ tsp. salt
1 c. sour cream
1¹/₂ c. chopped rhubarb

In a mixing bowl, cream sugar and shortening; add egg. Combine flour, soda and salt; add alternately with the sour cream to first mixture. Fold in rhubarb. Spread in a greased 13" x 9" baking pan. Combine topping ingredients; sprinkle over batter. Bake at 350° for 40–45 min.

TOPPING:

¹/₄ c. brown sugar
¹/₄ c. brown sugar (packed)
¹/₂ c. pecans or walnuts

1 Tbsp. oleo
1 tsp. cinnamon

APPLE COFFEE CAKE
Mrs. Amos L. Miller

Sift:
1 c. white sugar
1¹/₂ c. flour

¹/₄ tsp. salt
1 tsp. soda

Add:
¹/₂ c. shortening

Mix like pie dough—then add to batter:
1 egg (beaten)
1 tsp. vanilla

¹/₂ c. milk
2 apples (finely chopped)

Pour into 8" x 12" pan. Sprinkle topping on top. Bake at 350°.

TOPPING:
2 Tbsp. butter
1 tsp. cinnamon
¹/₂ c. brown sugar

2 Tbsp. flour
¹/₂ c. nuts

CREAM FILLED COFFEE CAKE

Mrs. Ezra A. Schrock

1 c. milk	2 eggs (beaten)
1 stick oleo	1 Tbsp. yeast
$^1/_2$ c. sugar	$^1/_4$ c. warm water
1 tsp. salt	$3^1/_2$ c. flour

CRUMBS:

3 Tbsp. oleo	$^1/_2$ c. flour
$^1/_2$ c. brown sugar	

Scald milk; add oleo, sugar and salt; add to beaten eggs. Dissolve yeast in warm water and add to other ingredients. Add flour. Let rise; work out and divide into 3 pie pans. Spread crumbs on top. Let rise again. Bake at 350° for 30 min. Cool and split each cake and fill with filling.

FILLING:

$^1/_2$ c. sugar	1 egg
4 Tbsp. water	2 tsp. vanilla
$^1/_2$ c. Crisco	$4^3/_4$ c. powdered sugar
$^1/_2$ c. oleo	

Boil together sugar and water for 3 min. or until syrupy. Add Crisco, oleo, egg and vanilla. Stir in powdered sugar.

----------- ❖ -----------

*Everytime you bake a cake put a teaspoon of baking powder
in. If it doesn't ask for it, put it in; you will be surprised.*

----------- ❖ -----------

*Little deeds of kindness
done in a quiet way
Reach both deep and wide
and always bring their pay.*

CREAM FILLED COFFEE CAKE

Mrs. Eli (Mary Etta) Miller

1¹/₂ Tbsp. yeast
¹/₂ c. warm water
³/₄ c. milk
1 stick oleo

1¹/₂ tsp. salt
¹/₂ c. white sugar
2 eggs
3¹/₂–4 c. flour

CRUMBS:

¹/₂ c. brown sugar
a little cinnamon and oleo

¹/₄ c. flour

Dissolve yeast in warm water. Heat the milk, melt the butter. Add salt, white sugar and the milk. Cool this to lukewarm. Add beaten egg and the yeast. Mix all together and add flour as needed, enough to make a nice dough. Let rise 1 hr. Work out in 4 pie pans. Put crumbs on top and let rise again. Bake at 400° for 10–15 min. When cakes are cool, cut off the tops and spread the filling on.

FILLING:

4 Tbsp. water
¹/₂ c. white sugar
4²/₃ c. powdered sugar
2 egg whites (beaten)

³/₄ c. Crisco
2 tsp. vanilla
¹/₂ tsp. salt

Boil water and sugar for 1 min. Mix the powdered sugar, Crisco, salt and vanilla together. Then add sugar and water, then fold in egg whites.

———— ❖ ————

When recipe calls for adding raw eggs to hot mixture,
always begin by adding a small amount of mixture
to the beaten eggs slowly to avoid curdling.

COFFEE CAKE

Suanna Miller
Mrs. Ervin (Edna) Bontrager

1 yellow cake mix
3 oz. instant vanilla pudding
3 oz. instant butterscotch
  pudding (optional)

1 c. vegetable oil
4 eggs
1 c. water

CRUMBS:
1 c. brown sugar
1 Tbsp. cinnamon

1 c. (or more or less) nuts

Put half of cake batter in 9" x 13" pan. Put half of crumbs on top. Then rest of cake batter, then rest of crumbs. Bake at 350° for 45–60 min. Drizzle with glaze of powdered sugar and water.

———— ❖ ————

Recipe for a Happy Family

1 husband
1 wife and children
1 Bible for each
1 home
1 package of work
1 tablespoon patience
1 tablespoon understanding
1 cup of kisses
1 package of play together
generous portions of prayer
1 small puddle
3 cups of love
2 tablespoons forgiveness

Mix thoroughly and sprinkle with awareness. Bake in moderate oven of everyday life, using all grudges as fuel. Cool, turn onto platter of cheerfulness. Garnish with tears and laughter and in large helpings serve God, country and community.

CHOCOLATE CREAM CAKE

Malinda Yutzy

3 lg. eggs (separated)
1 tsp. vanilla
1/2 c. sugar

pinch of salt
3/4 c. cake flour

FILLING:

1/2 c. sugar
1/4 c. flour
1 1/2 c. milk

6 egg yolks
2 tsp. vanilla
pinch of salt

GLAZE:

1/2 c. sugar
3 Tbsp. corn syrup

2 Tbsp. water
1/2 c. chocolate chips

Beat together egg yolks and vanilla until blended. Beat in half of sugar until pale and thick. Beat together egg whites and salt until peaks form. Gradually beat in remaining sugar until stiff peaks form. Fold yolk mixture into egg whites. Sift flour over mixture and fold in gently. Do not over mix. Pour batter into a greased 9" round cake pan lined with waxed paper. Bake at 350° for 25 min. Invert cake onto wire rack and remove pan. Leave wax paper on cake and turn right side up. Cool. To prepare filling, mix together sugar and flour in saucepan. Gradually whisk in milk, then egg yolks, vanilla and salt. Bring to boil; boil for 1 min., whisking constantly. Chill for 30 min. with plastic wrap pressed on surface. Cut cake in half horizontally. Remove waxed paper. Place bottom layer on serving plate. Spread evenly with filling. Top with remaining cake layer. To prepare glaze, bring sugar, corn syrup and water to a boil in saucepan, stirring constantly until sugar has dissolved. Remove from heat. Add chocolate chips; stir until smooth. Pour glaze over cake, allowing it to drip down sides. Let glaze set before serving.

❖

Take time to be friendly—it is the road to happiness.

ANGEL FOOD CAKE
Mrs. David Bontrager

2 c. egg whites
1 tsp. vanilla
1 tsp. salt
1½ tsp. cream of tartar

1 c. sugar
1 c. pastry flour
1 c. powdered sugar

Beat first three ingredients together until foamy, add cream of tartar, beat; add sugar then beat until stiff. Fold in flour and powdered sugar which has been sifted together. Bake at 350° for 30–40 min. or until toothpick inserted comes out clean.

ANGEL FOOD CAKE
Mrs. David (Katie) Bontrager

1³/₄ c. egg whites
¼ c. cold water
½ tsp. salt
2 tsp. cream of tartar

2½ c. sugar
2 tsp. vanilla
2 c. pastry flour

Add salt and cream of tartar to egg whites. Beat until it stands in peaks. Sift sugar, add to egg whites 1 cup at a time. Fold smooth after each addition. Sift flour and add 1 cup at a time. Fold until smooth. Add vanilla. Run cold water over tube pan, shake out excess. Pour batter into pan. Bake at 350° for 1 hr. or until done. For chocolate cake, omit ¼ c. flour and add ¼ c. cocoa. Various flavored cakes can be made by decreasing 2 Tbsp. sugar and adding 2 Tbsp. jello.

———— ❖ ————

Smile a little, smile a little as you go along,
not alone when life is pleasant, but when things go wrong.

ANGEL FOOD CAKE

Emma Bontrager

1¹/₂ c. egg whites
1¹/₂ c. white sugar
1¹/₂ tsp. cream of tartar
3 Tbsp. jello (optional)

1 c. cake flour
¹/₂ tsp. salt
1 tsp. almond flavoring

Sift together $^3/_4$ c. of sugar and flour 3 times; set aside. Beat egg whites until frothy, add salt and cream of tartar. Beat until it stands in peaks. Add $^3/_4$ c. sugar, about 3 Tbsp. at a time, beating well with egg beater. Lightly fold in sugar and flour mixture, add flavoring. Bake at 375° for about 35–40 min. or until done.

CHOCOLATE ANGEL FOOD CAKE

Mrs. Ezra (Elsie) Hochstetler

2 c. egg whites
2 tsp. cream of tartar
¹/₂ tsp. salt
2 c. sugar

2 tsp. vanilla
1 c. plus 5 Tbsp. cake flour
3 Tbsp. cocoa

Add cream of tartar, salt and vanilla to egg whites and beat till foamy. Then gradually add 1 cup sugar and beat till stiff peaks. Sift flour, cocoa and 1 c. sugar together twice; then fold into stiff egg whites. For white cake omit the cocoa and add 3 Tbsp. more flour.

———— ❖ ————

When Grandma uses a pinch of that and a pinch of this,
Her cake turns out just de-lish;
But let a new bride try a dash of this and a pinch of that,
You never saw a cake so flat!

ORANGE CHIFFON CAKE
Betty Yoder

2 c. flour
1¹/₂ c. sugar
Mix well and add:
¹/₂ c. oil
7 egg yolks (unbeaten)
Stir until smooth:
1 c. egg whites (7 or 8 eggs)

3 tsp. baking powder
1 tsp. salt

³/₄ c. cold water
3 Tbsp. grated orange rind

¹/₂ tsp. cream of tartar

Beat egg whites until they hold stiff peaks. Pour egg yoke mixture gradually over beaten egg whites, gently folding with rubber scraper. Pour into ungreased pan. Bake at 350° till top springs back when lightly touched.

FROSTING:

¹/₃ c. butter (softened)
3 c. powdered sugar

1¹/₂ Tbsp. grated orange rind
a little orange juice

MARBLE CHIFFON CAKE
Betty Yoder

¹/₃ c. unsweetened cocoa
2 Tbsp. sugar
¹/₄ c. water
2 Tbsp. vegetable oil
2 c. flour
1¹/₂ c. sugar
3 tsp. baking powder

1 tsp. salt
¹/₂ c. vegetable oil
7 eggs (separated)
³/₄ c. cold water
2 tsp. vanilla
¹/₂ tsp. cream of tartar

Cream cocoa, 2 Tbsp. sugar, ¹/₄ c. cold water and 2 Tbsp. oil in a small bowl; stir until smooth; set aside. Combine flour, 1¹/₂ c. sugar, baking powder and salt in large mixer bowl; add in order: ¹/₂ c. vegetable oil, egg yolks, ³/₄ c. cold water, and vanilla. Beat at low speed until combined, then at high speed for 5 min. Beat egg whites in large mixer bowl with cream of tartar until stiff. Pour batter in slowly; fold in lightly by hand. Remove ¹/₃ of batter to a separate bowl; fold in chocolate mixture. Pour half of light mixture in 10" tube pan, top with dark mixture. Repeat layers; with narrow spatula swirl gently through batters to marble. Bake at 325° for 65–70 min. or until done.

LEMON CHIFFON CAKE
Mrs. William Troyer

2 c. all-purpose flour, or
  2¹/₄ c. cake flour
1¹/₂ c. sugar
3 tsp. baking powder
1 tsp. salt
¹/₂ c. vegetable oil
7 egg yolks (with all purpose
  flour) or 5 yolks (with cake flour)

³/₄ c. cold water
2 Tbsp. lemon juice
1 tsp. lemon flavoring
1 c. egg whites (about 8 eggs)
¹/₂ tsp. cream of tartar

Heat oven to 325°; mix flour, baking powder and salt. Beat in oil, egg yolks, water, lemon flavoring and juice with spoon until smooth. Beat egg whites and cream of tartar in large mixing bowl until stiff peaks form. Pour egg yolk mixture gradually over beaten egg whites folding with rubber spatula just until blended. Pour into ungreased 4" x 10" tube pan. Bake until top springs back with touched lightly (about 1¹/₄ hrs.). Invert pan until cake is cold.

FLUFFY FROSTING:
1 egg white
²/₃ c. white sugar
¹/₄ c. Karo

2 Tbsp. water
¹/₈ tsp. cream of tartar
¹/₈ tsp. salt

Put in double boiler. Beat until mixture stands in peaks. Remove from heat; add ¹/₂ **tsp. vanilla.** Spread on top of cake.

SPONGE CAKE
Fanny Mae Bontrager

4 eggs (separated)
salt
1 tsp. lemon flavoring

1 c. sugar
1 c. flour

Place egg yolks, dash of salt and lemon into small bowl and egg whites and dash of salt into a larger bowl. Beat egg whites stiff; continue beating while gradually adding ³/₄ c. sugar. Now beat egg yolks, gradually adding remaining ¹/₄ c. sugar. Fold yolks into whites. Sift flour in small amounts over eggs. Fold in after each addition. Mix only until flour is thoroughly blended in. Bake in ungreased 9" x 12" loaf cake pan at 350° till top is light golden brown. Serve with strawberries.

STRAWBERRY SHORTCAKE   *Mrs. Daniel Lee Mishler*

1 c. sugar	$^1/_8$ tsp. salt
4 Tbsp. lard or oleo	1 c. milk
1 egg	1 tsp. vanilla
2 c. flour	strawberries
3 tsp. baking powder	

Cream sugar and shortening. Add eggs and sift dry ingredients alternately with milk. Add flavoring and pour in greased pan and bake in moderate oven. Serve with strawberries and milk.

SHORTCAKE   *Mrs. Freeman E. Yoder*

$1^1/_2$ c. sugar	$^1/_2$ tsp. salt
$^1/_2$ c. shortening	4 tsp. baking powder
2 eggs	3 c. flour
1 c. milk	1 tsp. vanilla

Cream together sugar, shortening and eggs. Add milk and vanilla but don't stir until you've added the dry ingredients. Place in 9" x 13" pan. Bake at 350° until done.

EASY SHORTCAKE   *Mrs. Harvey (Marie) Hochstetler*

2 c. New Rinkle flour	$^1/_2$ c. butter or oleo
$^1/_3$ c. sugar	1 egg (well beaten)
4 tsp. baking powder	$^1/_3$ c. milk
$^1/_2$ tsp. salt	

Sift together flour, sugar, baking powder and salt. Cut in butter. Add egg and milk. Blend well. Bake at 450° for 15 min.

STRAWBERRY LONG CAKE   *Mrs. Devon (Ruby) Miller*

2 c. flour (sifted)
6 Tbsp. sugar
3 tsp. baking powder
$^3/_4$ tsp. salt

$^1/_3$ c. shortening
1 lg. egg (beaten)
$^2/_3$ c. milk

CRUMBS:
$^1/_4$ c. butter
$^1/_4$ c. brown sugar

3 Tbsp. flour

Sift together flour, sugar, baking powder and salt; mixing in shortening, egg and milk. Spread in a greased 9" x 9" baking dish. Cream together butter, brown sugar and flour. Drop this on top of first mixture. Bake at 400°. Serve warm with fruit and milk.

FILLED SHORTCAKE   *Mrs. Daniel (Martha) Miller*

$^1/_2$ c. lard
2 c. sugar
1 egg
1 tsp. salt

$1^1/_2$ c. milk
3 c. flour
2 tsp. baking powder
$1^1/_2$ pt. pie filling

Cream together lard, sugar, egg and salt. Add dry ingredients. Pour half of batter in cake pan; cover with pie filling. Pour on rest of batter. Top with crumbs.

CRUMBS:
$^1/_2$ c. oatmeal
$^1/_2$ c. brown sugar

$^1/_2$ c. flour
$^1/_4$ c. butter or lard

———— ❖ ————

The reason a dog has so many friends:
He wags his tail instead of his tongue!

CARROT CAKE
Mrs. Harley H. Lambright

2 c. white sugar
1¹/₂ c. Wesson oil
4 egg (beaten)
2 c. flour (sifted)
1 tsp. cinnamon

2 tsp. soda
1 tsp. salt
3 c. finely grated carrots
¹/₂ c. chopped nuts (optional)

Combine sugar and cooking oil. Add eggs and mix well. Mix in flour which has been sifted with cinnamon, salt and soda. Slowly mix in carrots and nuts. Pour into greased and floured pan. Bake at 300° for 30–40 min. or until done.

ICING:
8 oz. cream cheese
2 c. powdered sugar

2 tsp. vanilla
¹/₄ lb. butter

Soften cream cheese, blend in butter. Then add all other ingredients.

APPLE DAPPLE
Mrs. Freeman (Edna Ellen) Mishler

2 eggs
2 c. white sugar
1 c. cooking oil
2³/₄ c. flour
¹/₂ tsp. salt

1 tsp. soda
3 c. chopped apples
2 tsp. vanilla
¹/₂ c. nuts

Sift together dry ingredients and add to eggs, sugar and oil mixture. Next add apples, vanilla and nuts; mix well. Pour into greased cake pan. Bake for 45 min. at 350° or until done.

ICING:
1 c. brown sugar
2 Tbsp. butter

¹/₄ c. milk

Cook 2¹/₂ min. Stir a little after removing from stove, but do not beat! Drizzle over cake while icing and cake are still hot.

WALNUT APPLE CAKE
Emma Hochstetler

2 eggs

2 c. sugar

$^1/_2$ c. vegetable oil

2 tsp. vanilla extract

2 c. all purpose flour

$2^1/_2$ tsp. cinnamon

2 tsp. soda

1 tsp. salt

$^1/_4$ tsp. nutmeg

4 c. peeled, chopped tart apples

1 c. chopped walnuts

In a mixing bowl, combine eggs, sugar and vanilla; mix well. Combine dry ingredients, add to the egg mixture and mix well (batter will be stiff). Stir in apples and walnuts. Spread into a greased 13" x 9" pan. Bake at 350° for 45–50 min. or until toothpick inserted comes out clean. For the sauce, combine sugar, flour, milk and butter in a saucepan. Bring to a boil over med. heat, boil and stir for 2 min. Remove from heat, stir in vanilla, cut cake into squares. Top with warm sauce. Put walnut on top if desired.

BUTTER SAUCE:

$^3/_4$ c. sugar

3 Tbsp. all purpose flour

1 c. milk

2 Tbsp. butter (no substitute)

walnut halves on top (optional)

---- ❖ ----

The best and most beautiful things in the world
cannot be seen or even touched.
They must be felt with the heart.

—Helen Keller

HONEY NUT APPLE CAKE *Mrs. Tobie (Esther) Miller*

2 c. sugar
1 c. vegetable oil
2 eggs
1 tsp. vanilla
2 c. all purpose flour
1 tsp. baking soda

1 tsp. cinnamon
$^1/_4$ tsp. salt
3 c. apples (peeled and finely chopped)
1 c. chopped nuts
1 c. raisins

Heat oven to 350°. In a med. bowl combine all topping ingredients; set aside. In a large bowl combine sugar, oil, eggs, and vanilla; beat until well mixed. Add flour, baking soda, cinnamon and salt; mix well. Stir in apples, nuts and raisins. Spread batttter into greased 13" x 9" pan. Sprinkle topping onto batter, pressing firmly. Bake for 45 min. or until apples are tender. Serve warm.

TOPPING:

$^3/_4$ c. quick oats
$^1/_2$ c. brown sugar
$^1/_4$ c. butter or margarine (melted)

2 Tbsp. all purpose flour
$^1/_2$ tsp. cinnamon

SWEET APPLE CAKE *Mrs. William (Luella) Schrock*

6 or more apples (peeled and sliced)
2 c. sugar
1 tsp. cinnamon
2 Tbsp. butter
2 eggs
$^1/_2$ c. lard

1$^1/_4$ c. milk
3 c. flour
1 tsp. cream of tartar
3 tsp. baking powder
$^1/_2$ tsp. salt
1 tsp. vanilla

Place a layer of apples in bottom of a greased 9" x 13" pan. Sprinkle $^1/_2$ c. of the sugar and cinnamon over them. Add butter in chunks over apples. Mix the cake batter by creaming rest of sugar and lard, then add eggs and beat well. Add milk alternately with sifted dry ingredients. Pour over apples. Bake at 350° for 30 min. or until apples are done. Serve warm with milk.

RAW APPLE CAKE
Mrs. Ora Mast

1 c. white sugar
1 c. brown sugar
1 c. shortening
2 eggs (beaten)
  Mix and add:
2 1/2 c. flour
  Last add:
4 c. diced apples

1 Tbsp. cinnamon
1 tsp. salt
2 tsp. soda (dissolved in 1/4 c.
  hot water)

1/2 c. nuts (optional)

Bake at 350° for 45 min.–1 hr. Makes a very delicious moist cake. Can also be used as date pudding.

BANANA NUT CAKE
Mrs. Eli H. Hochstetler

3 c. all purpose flour
2 c. sugar
1 tsp. baking powder
1 tsp. baking soda
1 tsp. salt
1 tsp. ground cinnamon
1 tsp. nutmeg
4 eggs (lightly beaten)

1 1/3 c. vegetable oil
1 1/2 tsp. vanilla extract
1 (8 oz.) can crushed
  pineapple (undrained)
2 c. mashed, ripe bananas
  (3–4 med.)
1 1/2 c. chopped walnuts
confectioner's sugar

In a mixing bowl, combine dry ingredients. Beat in eggs, oil and vanilla. Fold in pineapple, bananas and nuts. Pour into a well greased 10" tube pan. Bake at 350° for 60–65 min. or until cake tests done. Cool in pan 15 min. before removing to a wire rack. When completely cooled, dust with confectioner's sugar. Yield: 12–16 servings.

PINEAPPLE WEDDING CAKE
Sarah Yoder

2 c. flour
2 c. sugar
2 eggs
1 tsp. soda

1 can crushed pineapple with
   syrup
$^1/_4$ tsp. salt
1 c. nuts

Mix well. Bake in 9" x 13" pan at 350° for 30–40 min. Top with cream cheese frosting.

CREAM CHEESE FROSTING:

1 stick oleo
8 oz. cream cheese
1 tsp. vanilla

4 Tbsp. milk
enough powdered sugar to
   thicken

DELICIOUS WHITE CAKE
Mrs. Andrew (Carrie) Hochstetler

2 c. sugar
$^1/_2$ c. shortening
1 c. milk
3 c. cake flour

3 tsp. baking powder
1 tsp. vanilla
6 egg whites (beaten till fluffy)

Cream together sugar and shortening. Add alternately milk, cake flour, baking powder and vanilla. Last add egg whites.

❀

Ideas are funny little things,
they don't work unless you do.

PUMPKIN SPICE CAKE

2 c. flour	2 tsp. cinnamon
2 c. sugar	2 c. pumpkin
2 tsp. baking powder	4 eggs
2 tsp. soda	1 c. salad oil
1/2 tsp. salt	1 c. nuts (optional)

Sift flour with sugar, baking powder, soda, salt and cinnamon. Add remaining ingredients except nuts. Beat until smooth. Add nuts. Pour into 9" x 13" pan. Bake at 350° for 45 min. Can be baked in bundt or angel food cake pan.

FROSTING:

1 stick butter or margarine	1 box powdered sugar (or till
8 oz. cream cheese	right consistency)
1 tsp. vanilla	

Cream butter and cream cheese. Add vanilla and powdered sugar. Mix until smooth. May be glazed with sugar and water glaze.

AUNT SARAH'S BUTTERMILK CAKE

Fanny Mae Bontrager

3/4 c. butter or lard	4 c. flour
2 c. sugar	1 tsp. cinnamon
2 eggs	1 tsp. allspice
pinch of salt	1/2 tsp. cloves
2 c. buttermilk	2 Tbsp. cocoa
1 tsp. soda	1 c. raisins

Cream butter or lard, sugar and eggs. Add buttermilk and soda. Sift together flour, spices and cocoa. Mix into first mixture and beat well. Add raisins. Bake in moderate oven 45–50 min. in 10" x 15" pan. Note: This is an old cake recipe.

PIG-PICKIN CAKE

Anna Fern Hochstetler

1 box yellow cake mix
$^{1}/_{2}$ c. vegetable oil

1 can mandarin oranges with juice

ICING:

1 lg. can crushed pineapple
1 sm. box instant vanilla
   pudding

1 lg. Cool Whip

Mix cake mix, oil and oranges. Bake at 350° for 30–35 min. For icing: mix dry pudding and pineapple together. Then add Cool Whip. Put on cake and refrigerate. A moist and good cake!

MARBLE CAKE

Ruby Mullet

1 c. sugar
1 egg
$^{1}/_{4}$ c. butter
1 c. sweet milk

1 tsp. cinnamon
2 tsp. baking powder
1 tsp. allspice
$1^{1}/_{2}$ c. flour

Mix all together except spices. Put half of batter in pan. Put spices in leftover batter then twirl into batter in pan.

CINNAMON SUPPER CAKE

Wilma Beechy

$1^{1}/_{2}$ c. white sugar
$^{1}/_{2}$ c. shortening
2 eggs
3 c. flour

3 tsp. baking powder
$^{1}/_{2}$ tsp. salt
1 c. milk

Bake at 375° for 20–25 min.

TOPPING:

6 scant Tbsp. powdered
   sugar

2 tsp. cinnamon
2 Tbsp. butter (melted)

Spread on cake.

FRUIT CAKE (CHRISTMAS)   *Mrs. Naomi Miller*

2 c. raisins, chopped   2 c. water
2 c. dates, chopped
  Cook together.
  Add to raisin mixture while still warm:
2 c. brown sugar   2 tsp. cinnamon
1 c. lard $1/2$ tsp. salt
2 eggs   2 c. jelly candy (cut in half)
2 c. mixed nuts $1/2$ tsp. cloves
2 tsp. soda   4 c. flour
  Bake at 300°–350 for 1 hr. or more.

PUMPKIN CAKE   *Mrs. Enos Hilty*

4 c. pumpkin (cooked and   2 c. white sugar
  mashed)   4 eggs
  Sift and add:
5 c. flour   4 tsp. soda
1 tsp. cloves $1/2$ tsp. salt
1 tsp. cinnamon   1 c. Canola oil
  Mix well. Grease and flour pan. Bake at 350° for 1 hr. This makes a large cake. This cake is extra good when you use $1/2$ whole wheat flour.

FEATHER CAKE   *Ida Lambright*

$1/2$ c. shortening   3 c. flour
2 c. sugar   3 tsp. baking powder
3 whole eggs or 5 egg whites $1/2$ tsp. salt
1 c. milk   1 tsp. vanilla
  Cream shortening, add sugar and beat again. Add milk and flour alternately with baking powder and vanilla. Last add the eggs. Mix and bake in pans of your choice.

COWBOY CAKE

Mrs. Glen Hershberger

2 c. brown sugar $^1/_2$ c. shortening
2 c. unsifted flour

Combine together and crumble. Reserve $^3/_4$ cup of crumbs then add the following ingredients to the rest:

1 c. sour milk or buttermilk 1 tsp. soda
1 egg 2 tsp. vanilla
$^1/_2$ tsp. salt

Pour in baking pan, then put remaining curmbs on top before baking.

HUMMINGBIRD CAKE

Mrs. Amos L. Miller

3 c. flour $1^1/_2$ c. cooking oil
3 c. sugar $1^1/_2$ tsp. vanilla
1 tsp. salt 8 oz. can crushed pineapple
1 tsp. soda (undrained)
1 tsp. cinnamon 2 c. chopped pecans
3 eggs (beaten) 2 c. mashed bananas

Combine dry ingredients in large bowl; add eggs and oil until moistened. Do not beat. Stir in vanilla, pineapple, pecans and bananas. Spoon batter in one 13" x 9" pan or tube pan. Bake at 350°.

ICING:

2 (8 oz.) pkgs. cream cheese 2 (16 oz.) pkgs. powdered sugar
1 c. oleo (softened) 2 tsp. vanilla

Cut the recipe in half for a long or tube pan.

———— ❖ ————

Moisten a bar of soap and rub it on a mosquito bite. It will stop itching and acts as a disinfectant to prevent infection.

INCREDIBLE CAKE

Mary Miller

1 box yellow cake mix
2 eggs

1 sm. box instant butterscotch pudding mix, (prepared as directed)

TOPPING:
$^1/_4$ c. chopped pecans $^1/_2$ c. butterscotch chips

Mix cake mix, eggs and prepared pudding. Pour into greased 13" x 9" cake pan. Sprinkle toppings over cake and bake at 350° for 25–30 min.

CAKE MIX

Mrs. Daniel (Martha) Miller

8 c. flour
6 c. sugar
$^1/_4$ c. baking powder

1$^1/_2$ tsp. salt
1$^1/_2$ c. vegetable oil

Mix dry ingredients in a large bowl, cut in oil until evenly distributed. Store in an airtight container in a cool dry place. Use within 10–12 weeks. Makes about 16 cups of mix. This mix can be used in recipes that ask for cake mixes such as dump cakes, friendship cakes and others. Use 3$^1/_3$ cups mix for 1 cake.

———— ❖ ————

Keep several mothballs in your mailbox to prevent wasps from building nests in it.

OATMEAL CAKE

Mrs. William Schmucker

1^1/$_4$ c. boiling water	1^1/$_2$ c. flour
1 c. quick oats	1 tsp. soda
^{1}/$_2$ c. lard	^{1}/$_2$ tsp. vanilla
1 c. granulated sugar	^{1}/$_2$ tsp. salt
1 c. brown sugar	^{1}/$_2$ tsp. cinnamon
2 eggs (beaten)	^{1}/$_2$ c. nuts

Pour boiling water over oats. Cool. Cream lard and sugars. Add beaten eggs, then add oatmeal, flour, and rest of ingredients. Bake at 350° for 30 min.

TOPPING:

2 Tbsp. butter (melted)	^{3}/$_4$ c. brown sugar
^{1}/$_2$ c. milk	^{1}/$_2$ tsp. vanilla
^{1}/$_2$ c. chopped nuts	

Mix together and cook 3 min. Spread on cake as soon as removed from oven.

❈

Picnic Pointer: fill clean plastic jugs ^{3}/$_4$ full of water and freeze. They'll keep cold foods cold and as the ice melts it can be used for drinking, or rinsing hands and faces.

❈

A few years ago it was the baby calling that would wake me up in the middle of the night; sigh . . . these days it's nature calling!

WHOLE WHEAT OATMEAL CAKE *Mrs. Enos Hilty*

1¹/₄ c. boiling water   1 c. oatmeal
1 sq. butter
  Soak for 20 min. Set aside to cool.

  Cream:
1 c. brown sugar   2 eggs
1 c. white sugar

  Mix together:
1 ¹/₃ c. whole wheat flour   ¹/₂ tsp. nutmeg
1 tsp. soda   ¹/₂ tsp. salt
1 tsp. cinnamon
  Add mush mixture to creamed sugar mixture. Then add flour and dry ingredients. Bake in 9" x 13" greased cake pan. Bake at 350° for 50 min.

TOPPING: Combine:
1 c. chopped nuts   1 tsp. vanilla
¹/₂ c. sugar   6 Tbsp. butter
1 c. coconut   ¹/₄ c. milk
  At end of baking time, remove hot cake, sprinkle at once with topping and return to 400° oven for about 7 min. to bubble topping. Be careful not to overbrown coconut in topping.

---------- ❖ ----------

To rid your house of flies, put a sponge in a saucer and saturate with oil of lavender, using one to each room.

---------- ❖ ----------

Drinking warm jello water will oftentimes settle an upset stomach.

RUBY VELVET CAKE
Katie Irene Miller

2 c. flour
1/2 c. cocoa
1 tsp. salt
1/2 c. shortening
1 3/4 c. sugar

1 1/4 tsp. soda
1/2 tsp. baking powder
1 c. milk
3 eggs
1 tsp. vanilla

FROSTING:
8 oz. cream cheese (softened)
1/2 c. butter or margarine
   (softened)

1 tsp. vanilla
3 c. powdered sugar

Heat oven to 350°. Grease and flour 2 - 8" round cake pans. Sift dry ingredients into a bowl. Add shortening, milk and vanilla. Beat well. Add eggs and mix thoroughly. Bake for 35–40 min. or until toothpick inserted comes out clean. For frosting: cream butter and cream cheese until well blended. Add sugar and vanilla. Beat until light and fluffy. Makes about 4 cups frosting.

EARTHQUAKE CAKE
Lillian Mast

1 c. chopped pecans
1 c. shredded coconut
1 box Pillsbury Plus
   chocolate cake mix

1/2 c. margarine (melted)
8 oz. cream cheese (softened)
3 1/2 c. powdered sugar

Sprinkle pecans and coconut on bottom of 9" x 13" pan. Mix cake mix as directed on box; pour over pecans and coconut. Combine margarine and cream cheese. Add powdered sugar. Drop by dollops over top of cake. Bake at 350° for 45–55 min. Top crust will crack. Do not frost.

———— ❖ ————

A great many open minds should be closed for repairs.

COCOA EGGLESS CAKE
Sarah Rose Miller (Grade 4)

2 c. brown sugar	3 tsp. soda
3 c. flour	2 c. sour milk
1/4 c. cocoa	1/2 c. lard (melted)

Preheat oven to 350°. In large bowl measure sugar, flour, cocoa and soda. Mix until blended; now make a hole in center to pour in sour milk. Stir briskly until smooth; and melted lard last. Continue to stir speedily to creamy stage. Pour into greased and floured 13" x 9" x 2" cake pan. Top with fluff frosting when baked and cooled. Chocolate Cake Hint: Add a ripe banana to a chocolate cake; only keeps the cake moist, but also gives it a good flavor.

FLUFF FROSTING:

3 c. powdered sugar	1/2 tsp. vanilla
1/4 c. milk	2 Tbsp. shortening

In med. bowl measure powdered sugar. Add milk and vanilla. Stir until smooth. Add shortening last. Vigorously stir until fluffy-like. Makes 1 1/4 cups (plenty for 1 cake). Use remaining for graham cracker sandwiches or apply to an apple pie. For chocolate flavor, add 2 Tbsp. cocoa to powdered sugar plus 1 Tbsp. more milk.

HAPPY VALLEY CHOCOLATE CAKE
Mrs. Perry Troyer
Mrs. Katie Hochstetler

3 c. flour	2 c. cold water
2 c. white sugar	2 tsp. vanilla
2 tsp. baking soda	2 tsp. vinegar
4 heaping tsp. cocoa	1/2 c. vegetable oil
1 tsp. salt	

Mix dry ingredients, add remaining ingredients. Bake at 375° for 35 min. or until done. More cocoa may be added.

SALAD DRESSING CAKE

Mary Miller
Mrs. Glen Hershberger

1 c. sugar
2 c. flour
4 Tbsp. cocoa
2 tsp. soda

$^1/_4$ tsp. salt
1 c. salad dressing
1 c. water
1 tsp. vanilla

BAKED ON FROSTING:
$^1/_8$ c. white sugar
$^1/_4$ c. brown sugar

$^1/_2$ c. chocolate chips

Sift together dry ingredients. Add salad dressing, water and vanilla. Pour into greased 13" x 9" cake pan. For frosting: mix the sugars and sprinkle over unbaked cake. Sprinkle chocolate chips over this. Bake at 350° for 35–40 min.

GOOD SALAD DRESSING CAKE

Mrs. Ervin (Edna) Bontrager

1 c. white sugar
1 c. hot water
1 c. salad dressing

2 Tbsp. cocoa
2 tsp. soda
2 c. cake flour

Mix together and bake at 350° for 35 min. My favorite recipe for cake. Very simple.

MIDNIGHT CAKE

Lillian Mast

$1^1/_4$ c. sugar
$1^1/_2$ c. flour
1 tsp. baking powder
3 Tbsp. cocoa
$^1/_2$ tsp. salt

1 tsp. soda
1 c. hot water
$^1/_2$ c. shortening
1 tsp. vanilla
2 eggs

Combine dry ingredients, then add shortening and hot water. Mix well. Beat in eggs, one at a time. Bake at 350° for 25–30 min.

SUPREME CHOCOLATE CAKE
Suanna Miller

1 box chocolate cake mix
1 (3 oz.) box vanilla instant pudding
1 (3 oz.) box chocolate instant pudding
1 c. vegetable oil
1 c. water
4 eggs
1 (11.5 oz.) pkg. chocolate chips

Stir half of chocolate chips into cake batter. Pour batter into a 9" x 13" pan. Sprinkle rest of chips on top. Bake at 350° for 45 min. or till done.

JIFFY CHOCOLATE CAKE
Mrs. Howard Miller

2 eggs
$^3/_4$ c. cocoa
2 c. sugar
1 c. lard or oil
3 c. flour
1 c. milk with 1 tsp. vinegar
2 tsp. soda
2 tsp. vanilla
1 tsp. salt
1 c. hot water

Put all ingredients together in one bowl before mixing in order given. Mix well. Bake in 350° oven for 30 min. or until done.

———— ❖ ————

*When a man is carried away with his own importance,
he seldom has a search party looking for him.*

———— ❖ ————

The recipe for a happy family includes a heaping cup of patience.

CHOCOLATE MARSHMALLOW CAKE

Freeman (Edna Ellen) Mishler

$^1/_2$ c. butter (no substitutes)
6 Tbsp. cocoa
2 Tbsp. shortening
$^1/_2$ tsp. baking powder
$^1/_4$ tsp. salt
$^1/_4$ tsp. baking soda

2 eggs
1 c. sugar
$^1/_2$ c. unsweetened applesauce
1 tsp. vanilla extract
1 pkg. sm. marshmallow
   (divided)

In a saucepan melt butter, cocoa and shortening. Cool for 10 min. Combine flour, baking powder, soda and salt; set aside. In another bowl beat eggs, sugar, applesauce and vanilla. Stir in dry ingredients; mix well. Bake at 350° for 20–30 min. Set aside $^1/_2$ c. marshmallows for glaze. Sprinkle remaining marshmallows over cake. Return to oven for 2 min.

GLAZE:

$^1/_2$ c. sugar
2 Tbsp. milk
2 Tbsp. butter

$^1/_2$ c. semi-sweet chocolate
   chips
$^1/_2$ c. marshmallows

Boil sugar, milk and butter for $1^1/_2$ min. Remove from heat and stir in chocolate chips and marshmallows.

CAROB CAKE

Freeman (Edna Ellen) Mishler

$2^1/_2$ c. flour
$1^1/_2$ c. sugar
3/4 c. carob
2 tsp. soda
1 tsp. baking powder

1 tsp. salt
2 eggs
1 c. sour milk or buttermilk
1/2 c. vegetable oil
1 tsp. vanilla

Mix dry ingredients in large bowl. Add liquids. Beat well. Pour into 9" x 13" pan. Bake at 350° for 35–40 min.

TURTLE CAKE

Katie Irene Miller

1 German chocolate cake mix
1 can (13 oz.) Eagle Brand milk

14–16 oz. caramels
1 stick oleo
1 c. chopped nuts, optional
1 c. chocolate chips

Make the cake mix as directed. Put half in a loaf pan and bake at 350° for 15 min. While this is baking melt together: Eagle Brand milk, caramels, and oleo. Take cake out of oven and pour caramel mixture over hot cake. Sprinkle nuts over caramel. Pour the rest of cake batter over the top. Sprinkle with the chocolate chips. Bake again for 15 min. Note: This can also be baked in cookie sheet pan as bars.

3 HOLE CAKE

Marietta Miller
Mrs. Leland H. Lambright

3 c. flour
2 c. sugar
1/3 c. cocoa
1 tsp. salt

2 tsp. soda
2 Tbsp. vinegar
2 c. water
2/3 c. oil

Bake at 350° for 30 min.

BLACK MAGIC CAKE

Freeda Lehman

2 c. flour
2 c. sugar
3 Tbsp. cococa
2 tsp. soda
1 tsp. baking powder
1 tsp. salt

2 eggs
1 c. strong coffee
1 c. buttermilk
1/2 c. vegetable oil
1 tsp. vanilla

Combine dry ingredients, then add the rest. Beat at med. speed for 2 min. Batter will be thin. Bake at 350° for 35–40 min. in oblong pan. Moist!

MOIST CHOCOLATE CAKE

Freeda Lehman

2 c. all purpose flour
1 tsp. salt
1 tsp. baking powder
2 tsp. soda
³/₄ c. cocoa
2 c. sugar

1 c. vegetable oil
1 c. hot coffeee
1 c. milk
1 tsp. vanilla extract
2 eggs

Sift together dry ingredients in a mixing bowl. Add oil, coffee and milk, then stir. Add eggs and vanilla; beat 2 min. Batter will be thin. Bake at 325° for 25–30 min.

ICING:

1 c. milk
5 Tbsp. flour
¹/₂ c. butter (softened)

¹/₂ c. shortening
1 c. sugar
1 tsp. vanilla

Combine the milk and flour in a saucepan; cook until thick, cover and cool. In a mixing bowl beat butter, shortening, sugar and vanilla until creamy. Add chilled milk and flour mixture and beat for 10 min.

DARK MOIST CAKE

Mrs. David Eash

2 c. Robin Hood flour
2 c. sugar
¹/₂ c. cocoa
¹/₂ tsp. salt
2 tsp. baking powder

1 c. oil
1 c. sour milk
1 egg
1 c. boiling water
1 tsp. vanilla

Mix together flour, sugar, cocoa, salt and soda. Stir in oil, milk and egg. Add water and vanilla. Bake at 350° for 45–50 min.

FROSTING:

¹/₂ c. white shortening
3 Tbsp. cocoa

1 tsp. vanilla
1 box powdered sugar

Add **1 Tbsp. milk** at a time (enough to moisten). Mixture should be creamy and spread easily.

FROSTING FOR ANGEL FOOD CAKE

Emma Bontrager

8 oz. cream cheese (softened) 2 c. Cool Whip
2 c. powdered sugar

Mix cream cheese and powdered sugar; gradually blend in Cool Whip. Frost cake and top with your favorite glaze.

SEAFOAM FROSTING

Mrs. Eli (Mary Etta) Miller

2 egg whites ($^1/_4$ c.)
$1^1/_2$ c. light brown sugar
  (packed)
$^1/_3$ c. water

1 Tbsp. light corn syrup, or
  $^1/_4$ tsp. cream of tartar
1 tsp. vanilla extract

In top of double boiler, combine egg whites, brown sugar, corn syrup and $^1/_3$ c. water. With portable electric mixer or rotary beater beat about 1 min. to combine ingredients. Cook over rapidly boiling water (water in bottom should not touch top of double boiler), beating constantly, about 7 min., or until stiff peaks form when beater is raised. Remove from boiling water. Add vanilla; continue beating until frosting is thick enough to spread, about 2 min.

Makes enough to fill and frost an 8" or 9" two-layer cake; or to frost a 13" x 9" x 2" cake.

COCONUT PECAN FROSTING

Lillian Mast

1 c. cream
$^1/_2$ c. butter or margarine
1 c. sugar
3 egg yolks

1 tsp. vanilla
$1^1/_3$ c. coconut
1 c. chopped pecans

Cook and stir over med. heat: cream, margarine, egg yolks and vanilla, until thickened. Add the coconut and pecans. Beat until thick enough to spread.

CHOCOLATE FROSTING
Mrs. Katie Hochstetler

1 c. sugar
2 heaping Tbsp. cornstarch
Cook together. Then add:
1 tsp. vanilla

1 Tbsp. cocoa
1 c. hot water

1 Tbsp. butter

PENUCHE ICING
Mrs. Daniel (Martha) Miller

$^1/_2$ c. butter
1 c. brown sugar

$^1/_4$ c. milk
2 c. powdered sugar

Melt butter in saucepan. Stir in brown sugar. Boil and stir in milk. Boil, stirring constantly. Cool to lukewarm. Gradually add powdered sugar.

CREAM CHEESE FROSTING
Loretta Kuhns

8 oz. cream cheese
1 stick oleo
Mix all together.

$2^1/_2$ c. powdered sugar

CARAMEL FROSTING
Loretta Kuhns

1 stick butter (not oleo)
1 c. brown sugar

$^1/_4$ c. milk
$2^1/_2$–3 c. powdered sugar

Boil at rolling boil for 2 min. Cool. Add powdered sugar till spreading consistency.

QUICK ICING
Mrs. Glen Hershberger

5 Tbsp. brown sugar
3 Tbsp. milk

2 Tbsp. butter or oleo

Warm and mix. Cool and add **1 tsp. vanilla** and **powdered sugar**.

FLUFFY WHITE FROSTING

Harvey (Marie) Hochstetler

³/₄ c. Crisco   3 c. powdered sugar
¹/₄ c. milk   vanilla

Mix together and spread on cake.

WHITE FLUFFY FROSTING

Lydiann Stutzman

1 c. white sugar   5 Tbsp. boiling water
¹/₄ tsp. cream of tartar   2 egg whites
¹/₂ tsp. cornstarch   vanilla
pinch of salt

Boil together sugar, cream of tartar, cornstarch, salt and water for 1 or 2 min. Then beat in partly beaten egg whites; beat till stiff. Add vanilla. A not so rich frosting.

---- ❖ ----

Happiness is not having what you want, but wanting what you have.

---- ❖ ----

Kind hearts are the gardens;
Kind thoughts are the roots;
Kind works are the flowers;
Kind deeds are the fruits.

Favorite Recipes

Sunshine Pie

A pound of patience you must find
Mixed well with loving words so kind;
Drop in two pounds of helpful deeds
And thoughts of other people's needs.

A pack of smiles to make the crust,
Then stir and bake it well you must.
And now I ask that you may try
The recipe of this Sunshine Pie.

Pies

NO BAKE CREAM PIE
Mrs. Perry (Melinda) Lambright

2^1/$_4$ c. milk
^{3}/$_4$ c. white sugar
^{1}/$_4$ c. brown sugar
^{1}/$_4$ c. cornstarch

^{1}/$_4$ tsp. salt
1 tsp. vanilla
1 stick oleo

Use ^{1}/$_4$ cup of the milk to make thickening with cornstarch. Cook together and pour hot into baked shell. Sprinkle with nutmeg. Makes 1 pie.

NO BAKE CREAM PIE
Mrs. Ervin (Edna) Bontrager

2^1/$_4$ c. milk
^{3}/$_4$ c. sugar
^{1}/$_4$ c. cornstarch

pinch of salt
^{1}/$_4$ c. butter or oleo

Cook and put in baked pie crust. Sprinkle with cinnamon.

CREAM PIE
Wilma Beechy

1 heaping Tbsp. flour
^{2}/$_3$ c. white sugar
^{1}/$_3$ c. brown sugar
2 eggs (separated)

pinch of salt
vanilla
1^1/$_2$ c. milk

Fold in stiff beaten egg whites last. Bake at 400° for 10 min. Then reduce oven to 350° until done.

———— ❖ ————

Moisten a bee or wasp sting with Clorox, pain is soon gone.

CREAM PIE

Mrs. Enos Hilty

2 egg yolks
$^1/_3$ c. white sugar
$^2/_3$ c. brown sugar
1 tsp. vanilla

2 c. milk
pinch of salt
2 heaping Tbsp. flour
2 egg whites (beaten)

Mix all ingredients except egg whites. Beat egg whites and fold in. Pour in unbaked pie shell and bake at 400° for 15 min. then reduce heat to 325° until done.

OLD FASHIONED CREAM PIE

Christina Miller

$^1/_3$ c. flour
2 c. whipping cream
(unwhipped)

$^1/_2$ c. butter (melted)
1 unbaked 9" pie shell
1 c. brown sugar

Blend flour into melted butter. Add brown sugar. Mix thoroughly. Add cream and stir until well blended. Pour into unbaked pie shell. Bake at 375° for 50–55 min. Cool before serving.

OLD FASHIONED CREAM PIE

Mrs. Ervin (Edna) Bontrager

2 c. cream (heated)
1 c. brown sugar
2 Tbsp. flour

$^1/_2$ c. sugar
1 tsp. vanilla
3 egg whites (beaten)

Mix everything together except egg whites. When mixed well, fold in egg whites. Put in 9" unbaked pie shell. Bake at 400° til golden brown. Reduce heat to 325° until done.

ICE CREAM PIE

Mary Esther Yoder

2 Tbsp. butter   2$^1/_2$ c. Rice Krispies cereal
$^3/_4$ c. Marshmallow Creme or $^1/_2$ pkg. marshmallows

Melt butter, then add marshmallows or Marshmallow Creme.
Mix in Rice Krispies and press into pan. Cool. Fill with **ice cream**
and top with **strawberries, peanuts** or whatever you wish.

ICE CREAM PIE

Mrs. Roy E. Miller

$^1/_2$ c. peanut butter   2 c. Rice Krispies cereal
$^1/_2$ c. corn syrup   1 qt. vanilla ice cream

Combine peanut butter, corn syrup and cereal and press into
pan. Chill until firm then add ice cream. Makes 1 pie.

OUR FAVORITE" PUMPKIN PIE

Mrs. Fernandis R. Graber

1 c. pumpkin $^1/_4$ tsp. salt
1 rounded Tbsp. flour $^1/_4$ tsp. cinnamon
1 scant c. sugar $^1/_4$ tsp. ginger (scant)
2 eggs (separated) $^1/_4$ tsp. nutmeg
1$^1/_3$ c. milk

Heat pumpkin. Remove from heat and add flour. Stir well. Add
dry ingredients. Beat and add egg yolks and milk. Beat egg whites
and add last. Fold into mixture.

Pour into unbaked pie shell and bake at 400° for 20 min., then
reduce heat to 350° and bake until mixture becomes firm, approx.
25 min. longer.

PUMPKIN PIES

Katie Mast

6 eggs
6 c. brown and white sugar
6 Tbsp. flour (level)
$^1/_2$ tsp. ginger
2 tsp. salt

6 tsp. cinnamon
6 c. pumpkin (cooked and
    mashed)
5 c. milk
2 c. cream

Mix together in order given. Bake at 375°.

PUMPKIN PIE

Ruby Yutzy

Stir **1 Tbsp. flour** into **1 c. pumpkin**.
Then add:

1 c. sugar
2 egg yolks
$^1/_4$ tsp. salt

$^1/_4$ tsp. cinnamon
$^1/_4$ tsp. ginger
$^1/_4$ tsp. nutmeg

Mix well, then add **1$^1/_2$ c. milk**. Beat **2 egg whites** and add to mixture. Pour into **unbaked pie crust**. Bake at 350° about 50 min. or until set.

PUMPKIN PIE

Mrs. David Bontrager

$^1/_2$ c. pumpkin or squash
    (cooked)
$^2/_3$ c. sugar
2 Tbsp. flour
1 egg

pinch of salt
$^1/_2$ tsp. cinnamon
$^1/_4$ tsp. ginger
1 pt. milk

Separate egg, then beat egg white and add to rest of ingredients mixed together. Bake at 400° for 10 min. Reduce heat to 350° and bake until done. Makes 1 pie.

PUMPKIN PIE

Mrs. Perry A. Bontrager

1 egg

$^1/_2$ c. white sugar

$^1/_2$ c. pumpkin

1 Tbsp. flour

1 c. milk

$^1/_2$ tsp. cinnamon

pinch of salt

Double for 1 big pie. Sift flour, cinnamon and sugar into bowl, add enough milk to make a thick paste. Add egg yolks and stir well. Add remaining milk which has been heated to the boiling point. Beat well before adding egg white which has been beaten. Try to keep egg white on top of mixture with beater so as to form a meringue. May only add $^3/_4$ tsp. cinnamon per 1 big pie instead of 1 tsp. Bake at 400° for 10 min. Reduce to 350° and bake till set. May use butternut squash instead of the pumpkin and call it Squash Pie.

BUTTERNUT PIE

Mrs. Howard Miller

5 c. sugar (or less)

6 eggs

6 c. butternut squash
   (mashed)

6 c. cream or milk

1$^1/_2$ tsp. salt

3 tsp. vanilla

6 Tbsp. flour

Mix all ingredients. Beat well. Pour into 4 large unbaked pie shells. Sprinkle with cinnamon. Bake at 450° for 10 min. Reduce oven to 325° and bake till set.

After dinner rest awhile, after supper walk a mile.

PUMPKIN CUSTARD PIE
Mrs. Kenny (Ruby) Schrock

3 egg yolks (beaten)
$^3/_4$ c. brown sugar
1 Tbsp. flour
1 tsp. cinnamon
$^1/_2$ c. pumpkin
$^1/_4$ c. white sugar

$^1/_4$ tsp. salt
1 tsp. vanilla
dash of nutmeg
2 c. rich milk
3 egg whites (beaten)

Heat milk to boiling point. Add to rest of ingredients. Fold in egg whites last. Bake at 400° for 15 min. Reduce heat to 325° until pie is done. Makes 1 (9") pie.

LEMON SPONGE PIE
Fanny Mae Bontrager

1 c. sugar
1 Tbsp. butter
2 Tbsp. flour
juice of $^1/_2$ lemon

3 egg yolks
1 c. milk
3 egg whites (beaten stiff)

Mix sugar, butter and flour. Add lemon juice, egg yolks and milk. Beat well. Fold in beaten egg whites. Pour into unbaked pie shell. Bake at 375° until outside half is set. Center may seem a bit soft.

--- ❖ ---

A quiet answer quiets anger, but a harsh one stirs it up. Proverbs 15:11

LEMON MERINGUE PIE

Mary Miller

1 c. sugar
3 Tbsp. cornstarch
1 1/2 c. cold water
3 egg yolks (slightly beaten)
1 tsp. lemon flavoring

1/4 c. lemon juice
1 Tbsp. margarine
1 (9") baked pastry shell
3 egg whites
1/3 c. sugar

In a 2 qt. saucepan, stir together 1 c. sugar and cornstarch. Gradually stir in water until smooth. Stir in egg yolks. Stirring constantly, bring to a boil over med. heat. Stir in next 3 ingredients. Cool. Turn into pastry shell. In a small bowl beat egg whites until foamy. Gradually beat in 1/3 c. sugar; continue beating until stiff peaks form. Spread some meringue on edge of filling first, touching crust all around, then fill in center. Bake at 350° for 15–20 min. or until lightly browned. Cool. Serves 6–8.

CHOCOLATE WHIP PIE

Vera Mae Miller

CRUST:

1 c. graham cracker crumbs
3 Tbsp. sugar

3 Tbsp. butter (melted)

Mix and press in pie pan.

FILLING:

1 c. milk chocolate chips
8 lg. marshmallows

1/4 c. milk
dash of salt

Melt filling ingredients together in double boiler; keep water in double boiler hot, but not boiling. Stir until smooth. Cool. Fold in **1 c. heavy cream (whipped).** Pour into crust. Chill 2 hrs. This is also good frozen.

———— ❖ ————

Of all my wife's relatives, I like myself the best.

CHOCOLATE PIE

Mrs. David Eash

1$^1/_2$ c. water
1 Tbsp. butter
$^3/_4$ c. sugar
3 heaping Tbsp. flour

1 Tbsp. cocoa
2 tsp. vanilla
$^3/_4$ c. cream or milk

Put water and butter in saucepan over low heat. Mix rest of ingredients, add to water and bring to boil. Enough for 1 pie.

CHOCOLATE PIE

Mrs. Freeman J. Yoder

2 c. water
2 c. milk
4 rounded Tbsp. flour
1$^1/_2$ c. sugar

1 heaping Tbsp. cocoa
2 eggs
pinch of salt
1 tsp. vanilla

Heat water and milk to a boil. Keep $^1/_2$ c. of milk to mix dry ingredients, then stir it in. Don't stir more than you have to, but make it boil. Add flavoring when done. Chill and put in baked pie shells. Makes 2 pies.

AMISH VANILLA PIE

Mrs. Enos Hilty

$^1/_2$ c. brown sugar
1 Tbsp. flour
$^1/_4$ c. dark corn syrup
1$^1/_2$ tsp. vanilla
1 egg (beaten)
1 c. water

1 c. unsifted flour
$^1/_2$ tsp. cream of tartar
$^1/_8$ tsp. salt
$^1/_2$ c. brown sugar
$^1/_2$ tsp. soda
$^1/_4$ c. butter

Mix first six ingredients and cook until thickened. Make crumbs with the last six ingredients. Pour syrup into unbaked pie shell. Top with the crumbs and bake. Makes 1 pie.

VANILLA CRUMB PIE
Christina Miller

CRUMBS: Mix:

2 c. flour

1/2 c. sugar

1 tsp. cream of tartar

1/2 c. lard

1 tsp. soda

FILLING FOR PIE:

4 c. milk

4 Tbsp flour

2 c. brown sugar

1 1/2 c. dark syrup

2 eggs (beaten)

Boil together, then add vanilla. Divide filling into 3 unbaked pie crusts. Top with crumbs and bake in hot oven.

LANCASTER SHOO FLY PIE
Velda Kuhns

FILLING:

1/2 c. molasses

1 c. hot water

3/8 c. brown sugar

1/2 tsp. soda

1 egg (beaten)

1/8 tsp. salt

CRUMBS:

1 c. flour

1/3 c. margarine

1/3 c. brown sugar

1/4 tsp. soda

1/3 tsp. cream of tartar

Pour liquid mixture in unbaked crust. Put crumbs on top. Bake slow until done. Good, but better with whipped cream.

———— ❖ ————

Some people treat God like a lawyer, they only go to Him when they are in trouble.

COTTAGE PIE

Mrs. Alvin (Wilma) Beechy

2 c. molasses
2 c. sugar
4 c. cold water

2 eggs
2 Tbsp. flour

1¹/₂ c. flour
1 c. white sugar
¹/₂ c. butter

³/₄ c. milk
1 tsp. baking powder
1 egg

Mix first 5 ingredients and pour into 3 unbaked pie shells. Then mix rest of ingredients together as cake and pour over liquid mixture. Bake.

EGGNOG PIE

Vera Mae Yoder

CRUST:

¹/₂ c. butter
¹/₄ c. brown sugar

1 c. flour

Heat oven to 400°. Mix all ingredients with hands. Spread in 2 pie pans. Bake this 5 min.

FILLING:

1 env. Knox gelatine
¹/₄ c. cold water
1 c. sugar
¹/₂ tsp. salt
2 Tbsp. cornstarch
1³/₄ c. scalded milk

5 egg yolks
vanilla
butter
1 c. whipped cream
nutmeg

Dissolve gelatine in cold water and set aside. Then mix sugar, salt, and cornstarch with a little milk and pour in the 1³/₄ c. scalded milk; cook this till thick and smooth. Then stir this mixture to egg yolks. Return to boil and cook a few min. Add vanilla, butter and gelatine. Let cool; then fold in whipped cream. Sprinkle with nutmeg.

KATIE MOMMY'S CUSTARD PIE

Mrs. Daniel (Martha) Miller

2 c. hot milk
3 eggs (separated)
1 tsp. vanilla

$^1/_2$ tsp. salt
$^1/_3$ c. brown sugar
2 Tbsp. white sugar

Mix together egg yolks, vanilla, salt and brown sugar. Add to milk. Beat egg whites and white sugar. Mix altogether and pour into unbaked pie shell. Sprinkle with nutmeg or cinnamon. Bake at 375°. Remove from oven while custard is still soft and jiggly in center.

CUSTARD PIE

Mrs. Elmer Hochstetler

$2^1/_2$ c. milk (heated)
$^3/_4$ c. white sugar
1 Tbsp. flour

3 eggs
salt
vanilla

Separate eggs, beat whites till foamy. Mix sugar and flour, add milk, egg yolks and vanilla. Then last of all add egg whites. Bake at 400° for 10–15 min., then reduce heat.

BOB ANDY PIE

Mrs. Mervin (Katie Fern) Miller

2 c. sugar
4 rounded Tbsp. flour
1 tsp. cinnamon
$^1/_2$ tsp. cloves

pinch of salt
1 heaping Tbsp. butter
4 eggs
4 c. milk

Mix together dry ingredients. Add butter, beaten egg yolks and milk. Then fold in beaten egg whites and pour into 2 unbaked pie shells. Bake in moderate oven until nice and brown.

BOB ANDY PIE

Sara Mae Yoder

2 c. sugar
3 heaping Tbsp. flour
1 tsp. cinnamon
$^1/_2$ tsp. cloves

1 heaping Tbsp. butter
3 egg yolks (beaten)
3 c. sweet milk

Beat egg separately. Make paste with dry ingredients, yolks and some milk. Fold in whites. Makes 2 pies.

COCONUT MACAROON PIE

Christina Miller

$1^1/_2$ c. sugar
2 eggs
$^1/_2$ tsp. salt
$^1/_2$ c. butter or oleo

$^1/_2$ c. milk
$^1/_4$ c. flour
$1^1/_2$ c. shredded coconut
1 (9") unbaked pie shell

Beat eggs, sugar and salt until mixture is lemon colored. Add soft butter and flour. Blend well. Add milk. Fold in 1 c. coconut. Pour into pie shell. Top with remaining coconut. Bake until set.

BLACK WALNUT PIE

Mrs. Andrew (Carrie) Hochstetler

1 c. brown sugar
5 eggs
$2^1/_2$ Tbsp. flour
2 c. Karo

2 Tbsp. oleo (softened)
3 c. milk
$2^1/_2$ c. walnuts

Heat milk for quicker baking. Makes 3 pies.

———— ❖ ————

Pray earnestly; you can't expect a thousand dollar answer to a ten cent prayer.

BLACK WALNUT PIE

Mrs. Elmer Hochstetler

1^1/$_4$ c. brown sugar
5 eggs
2^1/$_2$ Tbsp. flour
2 c. white syrup
  Makes 3 pies.

5 Tbsp. oleo (softened)
3 c. milk
2^1/$_2$ c. walnuts

OATMEAL PIE

Mrs. William J. Troyer

8 eggs
3 c. brown sugar
^{3}/$_4$ c. margarine (melted)

3 c. Karo
3 c. rolled oatmeal
2 c. coconut and nutmeats

Cream first 3 ingredients together. Add Karo and rest of ingredients. Mix well. Bake in slow oven. Makes 3 pies.

OATMEAL PIE

Wilma Miller

3 eggs (well beaten)
^{2}/$_3$ c. white sugar
1 c. brown sugar
2 Tbsp. butter

^{2}/$_3$ c. quick oats
^{2}/$_3$ c. coconut
1 tsp. vanilla
1 c. milk

Blend all ingredients and pour into unbaked pie crust. Bake at 350° for 30–35 min.

OATMEAL PIE

Mrs. Howard Miller

1 c. brown sugar
1 c. oatmeal
1 c. coconut
1 c. light Karo

2 eggs
3 Tbsp. milk
^{1}/$_2$ c. oleo

Mix all together. Pour in unbaked pie shell. Bake at 350° until done.

OATMEAL PECAN PIE

Mrs. Tobie E. Miller

8 eggs (beaten)
2 c. brown sugar
1 lb. butter
3 c. Karo

3 c. rolled oats
2 c. coconut (unsweetened)
2 c. nuts (pecans)
1 c. evaporated milk

Melt butter; cream sugar, butter and eggs together. Add Karo and rest of ingredients, and mix. Bake in slow oven for 40–45 min. Makes 4 pies.

ALMOST PECAN PIE

Ida Lambright
Mrs. Perry (Melinda) Lambright

3 eggs
$^3/_4$ c. dark corn syrup
$^1/_4$ c. butter or oleo (melted)
$^1/_4$ tsp. salt

$^3/_4$ c. milk (optional)
1 c. quick oats
$^1/_2$ c. sugar
$^1/_3$ c. chopped pecans

Beat eggs until foamy, add syrup, sugar, salt, milk and butter. Stir in oats and nutmeats. Pour in pie shell.

PECAN PIE

Mrs. David (Katie) Bontrager

3 eggs (beaten)
$^3/_4$ c. brown sugar
$^3/_4$ c. Karo
1 Tbsp. flour (slightly rounded)

$^1/_2$ c. milk
1 tsp. vanilla
dash of salt
1 c. pecans

Beat eggs and flour together. Add rest of ingredients, except pecans. Put pecans in unbaked pie crust and pour mixture on top. Bake in slow oven, as they brown easily. Bake until center has set.

(NOT SO SWEET) PECAN PIE
Katie Bontrager

3 eggs
1$^1/_2$ c. Karo
2 Tbsp. butter (melted)

1 tsp. vanilla
1$^1/_2$ c. pecans

Beat eggs well, add syrup, beat. Add butter, vanilla and pecans. Pour into unbaked pie shell (1 pie). *It's not so sweet, but still good!*

CREAM CHEESE PECAN PIE
Mrs. Cristy Eash

8 oz. cream cheese
$^1/_2$ c. sugar
1 egg (beaten)
$^1/_2$ tsp. salt
1 tsp. vanilla

3 eggs
$^1/_4$ c. sugar
1 c. light corn syrup
1 tsp. vanilla
1 c. pecans

Mix first 5 ingredients; spread into bottom of 10" unbaked pie shell. Mix the rest of ingredients; pour on top of cream cheese mixture. Bake at 35–45 min. until golden brown.

PECAN CREME PIE
Mrs. Jonas Yoder

2 c. milk
1 c. sugar
1 Tbsp. cornstarch

1 Tbsp. flour
2 eggs

Cook as for vanilla pudding. When cold put in pie crust. Sprinkle with pecans. Garnish with whipped cream. Sprinkle with pecans on top.

———— ❖ ————

A gentleman is a gentle man.

APPLE PIE

Mrs. Jonas Yoder

4 c. apples (cut up)
   Cook and stir in:

2 Tbsp. butter	**2 rounded Tbsp. clear jel**
1 c. sugar	**¹/₂ tsp. cinnamon**
¹/₂ tsp. salt	**1 tsp. lemon juice**

APPLE PIE

Katie Irene Miller

1 heaping Tbsp. clear jel	**a little butter**
1 c. water	**dash of salt**
1 c. white sugar	**³/₄ qt. apples (finely chopped)**
³/₄ tsp. cinnamon	

CRUMBS:

1 c. flour	**¹/₂ tsp. soda**
¹/₄ c. brown sugar	**¹/₂ tsp. cream of tartar**
¹/₄ c. butter	

Cook first 3 ingredients till thick. Add cinnamon, butter and salt. Stir in apples. Makes 1 pie.

❖

If Tupperware is sticky or has stains, soak with dishwasher detergent for several hours. This usually removes most stains if not set too hard.

APPLE PIE
Mary Miller

6 c. chopped apples (pared)   1 tsp. cinnamon
3 Tbsp. cornstarch $^1/_2$ tsp. salt
1$^1/_2$ c. sugar   2 c. water

CRUMBS:
1 c. brown sugar   1$^1/_2$ c. flour
$^2/_3$ c. margarine

Mix cornstarch, sugar, cinnamon and salt in large saucepan. Gradually add water. Bring to a boil; boil 1 min. Add apples and cook till apples are soft. Divide apple filling into 2 unbaked pie shells, add top crust and bake in 350° oven until pie filling bubbles. This is also good with a crumb topping or whipped cream instead of a top crust. For crumb topping, mix sugar and flour, rub in margarine till crumbs form. Sprinkle over pies. Bake as directed for top crust.

APPLE CRUMB PIE
Mrs. Eli (MaryEtta) Miller

4 c. apples (sliced)   pinch of salt
1$^1/_2$ c. water $^1/_2$ c. brown sugar
2 Tbsp. clear jel $^3/_4$ c. flour
1 c. sugar   2 Tbsp. butter
1 tsp. cinnamon

Put apples, sugar, cinnamon, 1 c. water and salt in saucepan. Cook until apples are half cooked. Combine clear jel with $^1/_2$ c. water and stir in apple mixture. Cook just long enough to cook clear jel. Pour into unbaked pie shell. Combine remaining ingredients and put on top of pie. Bake at 425° until nice and brown.

---- ❖ ----

To be without some of the things you want is an indispensible part of happiness.

—Bertrand Russell

APPLE PIE
Mrs. Sherman (LuElla) Miller

2 c. hot water (divided) pinch of salt
2 c. sugar 2 Tbsp. butter
6 Tbsp. clear jel or cornstarch 6 c. apples (sliced)

Cook apples and $1^1/_2$ c. water, sugar and salt together until apples are almost done. Then mix $^1/_2$ c. water with clear jel and add to apple mixture. Cook for 2 min., stirring constantly. Add butter. This makes 2 (8" or 9") pies. Pour into unbaked pie shell and sprinkle cinnamon on top of filling before putting on the top crust. Bake at 400° for 30–35 min.

ONE APPLE PIE
Mrs. Ora Mast

2 c. apples (diced) 2 eggs (beaten)
2 Tbsp. flour 1 Tbsp. butter (melted)
$^3/_4$ c. white sugar 5 Tbsp. water
$^3/_4$ c. brown sugar cinnamon on top

Mix all together and put in unbaked pie crust. Do not overbake.

SOUR CREAM APPLE PIE
Mrs. Tobie (Esther) Miller

6 lg. apples (peeled and $^1/_3$ c. flour
  chopped) 1 egg (beaten)
$1^2/_3$ c. sour cream 2 tsp. vanilla
1 c. sugar $^1/_4$ tsp. salt

CRUMBS:
$^1/_2$ c. walnuts (chopped) 1 tsp. cinnamon
$^1/_2$ c. flour $^1/_2$ c. butter
$^1/_3$ c. white sugar pinch of salt
$^1/_3$ c. brown sugar

Mix together filling ingredients and put into pie shell. Bake at 450° for 10 min., then at 350° for 30 min. Prepare crumbs by combining the ingredients until crumbly. Remove pie from oven and immediately put crumbs on top. Return to oven and bake another 15 min. until lightly browned.

APPLE PIE

Mrs. Leroy (Betty) Yoder

Cook:

3 c. white sugar	4 c. water
1/2 c. brown sugar	

Thicken with:

4 Tbsp. clear jel and a little water

Remove from stove and add:

5¹/₂ c. apples (sliced)	a little butter
1/2 tsp. cinnamon	

Pour into 3 unbaked pie shells, put crust on top and bake.

SHOESTRING APPLE PIE

Mrs. Ezra (Elsie) Hochstetler

2¹/₂ c. white sugar	pinch of salt
2 Tbsp. flour	4 Tbsp. water
3 eggs (well beaten)	4 c. shoestring apples

Mix all together and put in 2 unbaked pie shells. Sprinkle cinnamon on top. Bake at 325° until done.

PINEAPPLE PIE

Mary Esther Whetstone

2 c. water	2 Tbsp. flour
2 c. sugar	2 Tbsp. cornstarch
1 lump butter	1 c. water
2 eggs	1¹/₂ c. crushed pineapple

Bring to boil 2 cups water, sugar and butter. Beat together eggs, flour, cornstarch and 1 cup water. Bring to a boil again. Remove from heat and add pineapple. Cool a bit and pour in baked pie crust. Cool completely and top with whipped cream. Serve.

PINEAPPLE PIE

Mrs. Eli Miller

1 pie:	3 pies:	
8$^1/_2$ oz.	2$^1/_2$ c.	pineapple
1 c.	3 c.	sugar
1 Tbsp.	2 Tbsp.	minute tapioca
1 c.	5 c.	water
1 Tbsp.	3 Tbsp.	clear jel (rounded)
		pinch of salt

Boil until thick.

RHUBARB CUSTARD PIE

Mary Esther Whetstone

2 c. rhubarb (diced) $^3/_4$ c. sugar
1 c. milk   2 Tbsp. flour
2 egg yolks   2 Tbsp. butter

MERINGUE:
2 egg whites   3 Tbsp. powdered sugar
pinch of salt

Scald the milk and add the butter. Beat egg yolks and add sugar and flour. When butter is melted stir the milk in egg mixture. Line an 8" or 9" pie pan with pastry and spread rhubarb over pastry. Cover with egg and milk mixture and bake at 425° for 20 min., then set oven at 325° and bake another 25 min. or until set. Put beaten egg whites on top and brown. Delicious!

---------------- ❖ ----------------

I not only use all the brains I have, but all I can borrow.

—Woodrow Wilson

RHUBARB PIE

Mrs. Ray (Mary Alice) Yoder
Mrs. Perry (Melinda) Lambright

4 c. rhubarb
4 c. sugar
   Cook until tender. Mix:
$^1/_2$ c. sugar
$^3/_4$ c. cornstarch
$^1/_2$ tsp. salt

$^1/_4$ c. butter
2 c. water

6 egg yolks
1 c. cream, milk, or Milnot

Bring to boil; cool. Top with **Cool Whip**. Can be made with $^1/_2$ cup more sugar and 2 more egg yolks.

RHUBARB CUSTARD PIE

Mrs. Freeman Schmucker

1 heaping c. rhubarb
$^3/_4$ c. sugar
1 c. milk
2 eggs (separated)

1 Tbsp. flour
1 Tbsp. butter (melted)
pinch of salt

Cut rhubarb fine; mix sugar, flour, salt, beaten egg yolks, milk and melted butter. Pour over rhubarb which has been placed in unbaked pie shell. Bake until firm. Cover with meringue, made of beaten egg whites and **2 Tbsp. sugar**. Brown.

RHUBARB CUSTARD PIE

Mrs. Howard Miller

2 c. rhubarb
2 eggs (beaten)
1 rounded Tbsp. flour

$1^1/_4$ c. (or less) sugar
$^1/_2$ c. cream
$^1/_2$ c. water

Cut rhubarb in small pieces. Mix rest of ingredients and pour over rhubarb and sprinkle top with **cinnamon**. Bake at 400° for 10 min. then at 325° till set.

RHUBARB PIE
Emma Bontrager

1¹/₂ c. rhubarb
2 Tbsp. flour
2 egg yolks

1¹/₄ c. sugar
³/₄ c. cream

Beat egg whites and stir in last. Soak rhubarb overnight.

STRAWBERRY PIE
Mrs. Harley H. Lambright

1¹/₄ c. water
2 Tbsp. cornstarch
³/₄ c. white sugar

¹/₂ c. strawberry jello
1 c. mashed strawberries

Cook together sugar, water and cornstarch until clear. Add jello. Cool and add strawberries. Pour in baked pie shell. Top with whipped cream.

STRAWBERRY PIE
Mrs. Glen (Ida Mae) Beechy

3 c. sugar
3 heaping Tbsp. clear jel

4¹/₂ c. water
6 oz. strawberry jello

Cook together, add mashed strawberries and put into crusts. Makes 3 pies.

---------- ❀ ----------

Next time a plastic bread wrapper melts onto the toaster or the coffeepot, try this: rub some petroleum jelly on the spot, reheat the appliance and use a paper towel to rub off the plastic and the printing.

STRAWBERRY PIE

Mrs. Elmer Hochstetler

3³/₄ Tbsp. cornstarch
1¹/₄ c. sugar
1¹/₂ c. water
3 Tbsp. light corn syrup
1 sm. pkg. strawberry gelatin
3 drops red food coloring (optional

1 qt. fresh strawberries (whole or sliced)
2 (8") pie shells
whipped topping

Mix cornstarch and sugar until smooth. Add water and corn syrup. Cook until thick; add gelatin and food coloring; cool. Add strawberries and pour into pie shells. Top with whipped topping.

FRESH PEACH PIE

Mary Miller

1 pie:	4 pies:	
3 c.	12 c.	fresh peaches (peeled and sliced)
1 tsp.	4 tsp.	lemon juice
1 c.	4 c.	granulated sugar
¹/₄ c.	1 c.	flour
¹/₄ tsp.	1 tsp.	cinnamon
¹/₂ tsp.	2 tsp.	salt

CRUMB TOPPING:

¹/₂ c.	2 c.	brown sugar
¹/₃ c.	1¹/₃ c.	butter or margarine
³/₄ c.	3 c.	flour

In a lg. mixing bowl, combine peach slices and lemon juice. In another bowl, combine flour, sugar, cinnamon and salt. Combine sugar mixture with fruit mixture. Turn into pastry lined pan. For crumb topping, combine sguar and flour. Add butter and rub together until crumbs are formed. Sprinkle fine crumbs over peaches. Bake at 425° for 10 min. and then reduce oven to 350°. Bake 35 min. longer or until pie puffs up.

CHERRY PIE FILLING
Mrs. Daniel (Martha) Miller

1 qt. cherries
2 c. sugar
$2^1/_2$ c. water (divided)
$^1/_2$ c. clear jel

$^1/_2$ tsp. salt
1 tsp. almond flavoring
cherry jello

Bring to boil: juice of cherries, sugar and 2 c. water. Thicken with clear jel and $^1/_2$ c. water. Bring to a full boil, stirring well for a few min. Remove from heat. Add salt, flavoring and enough jello for a good color. Add cherries. Makes 2 pies. Bake at 400° for 10–15 min. Reduce to 350° till done.

BLUEBERRY PIE
Mrs. Leroy (Betty) Yoder

1 c. sugar
1 c. water
3 Tbsp. clear jel

3 Tbsp. lemon jello
1 Tbsp. lemon juice
$2^1/_2$ c. fresh blueberries

Boil together sugar, water and clear jel until thick. Add lemon jello and lemon juice. Chill. When cold add blueberries. Pour into baked pie crust. Top with whipped topping.

RAISIN CRUMB PIE
Mrs. Freeman E. Yoder

$^1/_2$ c. raisins
1 c. brown sugar
2 Tbsp. cornstarch

2 c. water
1 Tbsp. vinegar
salt

CRUMBS FOR TOP:
1 c. flour
$^1/_4$ c. shortening (oleo)

$^1/_2$ c. brown sugar
$^1/_2$ tsp. soda

Place all in saucepan except the ingredients, for crumbs. Bring to a boil, thicken and cool. Put in unbaked pie shell. Let filling cool a little before putting crumbs on top. Makes 1 pie.

RAISIN PIE

Mrs. Eli Miller

2 c. raisins
2 c. water
1/2 c. brown sugar
2 Tbsp. cornstarch

1 tsp. cinnamon
1/8 tsp. salt
1 Tbsp. vinegar
1 Tbsp. butter

Boil raisins in 1 3/4 c. water for 5 min. Combine brown sugar, cornstarch, cinnamon and salt. Moisten with remaining 1/4 c. water; add this to the raisins. Remove from heat, add butter and vinegar. Makes 1 (2-crust) pie.

RAISIN CREAM PIE

Wilma Beechy

2 egg yolks
1 1/2 c. milk
1/2 c. raisins
1/2 c. water
3/4 c. sugar

1 level Tbsp. cornstarch
1 rounded Tbsp. flour
1 tsp. vanilla
1/2 tsp. salt

Cook raisins and water together. Makes 1 pie.

RAISIN CREAM PIE

Mrs. Alvin (Wilma) Beechy

1 c. sugar
2 c. milk
4 egg yolks
2 rounded Tbsp. flour
1 stick butter or oleo
1 c. raisins (cooked in sm.
  amount of water)

1 tsp. vanilla
1/4 tsp. salt
egg whites (well beaten)
sugar
whipped cream

Mix sugar, flour and salt; add egg yolks and enough milk to form a smooth paste or mixture. Then add to milk which was heated in a double boiler. Stir constantly until it boils. Add a little more milk if it is too thick. Remove from heat and add vanilla, butter and raisins. Cool, then pour in baked pie shells. Top with well beaten egg whites and small amount of sugar or whipped cream.

PIE CRUSTS

Mrs. Daniel (Martha) Miller

5 c. flour
1 tsp. salt
2 c. lard

1 egg
milk or water

Mix flour, salt and lard together till crumbly. Put egg in 1 cup and fill with milk or water. Mix all together. Makes several pie crusts.

PIE CRUST

Mrs. Paul Whetstone

3 c. flour
1 tsp. salt
1 c. lard

$^1/_4$ c. oil
$^1/_4$ c. milk
$^1/_4$ c. water

PIE CRUST

Mrs. John Hochstetler

4 c. pastry flour
1 Tbsp. sugar
2 tsp. salt
1$^3/_4$ c. Crisco

1 tsp. vinegar
1 egg
$^1/_2$ c. water

Mix flour, sugar and salt. Add Crisco; mix until crumbly. Beat in a bowl: vinegar, egg and water; add to flour mixture. Chill for $^1/_2$ hr. Yield: 6 single crusts.

PIE CRUST

Mrs. Ervin (Edna) Bontrager

5 c. flour
2 tsp. salt
1 tsp. baking powder
2 c. Crisco or precreamed
   shortening

1 egg
1 tsp. vinegar
water

Mix flour, salt, baking powder and shortening. Beat egg in 1 cup measuring cup, add vinegar and enough water to make 1 cup mix.

NEVER FAIL PIE DOUGH
Mrs. Roy E. Miller

1 c. lard
1/2 c. water

3 c. flour
1 tsp. salt

Mix in order given until well mixed. Makes 4 crusts. This dough always turns out nice for me.

PIE CRUST
Mrs. Devon (Ruby) Miller

7 1/2 c. New Rinkle flour
3/4 tsp. baking powder
1 tsp. salt

2 c. lard or good brand vegetable shortening
1 c. cold water

Sift flour, baking powder and salt. Cut in lard; add cold water and work together with hands. Makes 5 crusts.

————— ❖ —————

*If you can't sleep because a cricket's come calling, here's
a sure cure. Put a wet washcloth in your kitchen
or bathroom sink at night and you'll find your
"noisy neighbor" hiding there in the morning.*

————— ❖ —————

*My interest is in the future because I'm going to spend
the rest of my life there.*

—Charles F. Kettering

Favorite Recipes

Desserts

CORNSTARCH PUDDING
Mrs. Devon (Ruby) Miller

4 c. milk
2 eggs (beaten)
3 Tbsp. flour
1 Tbsp. cornstarch

1 c. sugar
2 Tbsp. milk
1 Tbsp. vanilla

1 c. Rich's Topping

8 graham crackers (crushed)

Preheat milk in 3 qt. saucepan. In small mixing bowl beat the eggs, add sugar and stir well; add the flour and cornstarch; stir; add 2 Tbsp. milk. After milk is scalded stir into milk, stirring constantly until it cooks. Remove from heat, add vanilla; cool. When cooled, whip 1 cup Rich's Topping and add to pudding. Put in layers with crushed graham crackers. This recipe may be used for "dirt pudding," adding 8 oz. cream cheese while pudding is hot and substituting Oreo cookies for crackers. Makes 1 oblong Tupperware pan.

BAVARIAN CREAM PUDDING
Laura Yutzy

1 env. plain gelatin
$1/3$ c. cold water
$3/4$ c. milk
2 eggs (separated)
$1/2$ c. sugar

1 c. cream (whipped)
16 graham crackers
3 Tbsp. brown sugar
3 Tbsp. butter (melted)

Dissolve gelatin in cold water; let set. Heat milk, beat egg yolks with sugar and add to hot milk. Cook 1 min. or until custard consistency and add gelatin. Let cool until it starts to set. Beat egg whites; whip cream and mix together. Add your above custard pudding and mix together. Crush graham crackers; add brown sugar and butter. Press half of crumbs in cake pan; pour pudding on top of crumbs and top with remaining crumbs and let set. Serves 10–12.

BUTTERSCOTCH PUDDING   *Mrs. Elmer Hochstetler*

2 c. brown sugar
$^1/_2$ tsp. soda
$3^1/_2$ c. boiling water
1 tsp. vanilla
$^1/_2$ c. butter

3 eggs
$^1/_3$ c. white sugar
3 c. milk
1 c. flour

Boil together first 5 ingredients. Mix rest of ingredients and add to boiling mixture. Cook until thick.

CARAMEL BUTTERSCOTCH PIE OR PUDDING
Viola Bontrager

Boil to a syrup:
$^1/_4$ c. butter or margarine
1 c. brown sugar
Mix:
3 Tbsp. flour
1 Tbsp. cornstarch
pinch of salt

1 c. water

1 or 2 egg yolks (beaten)
$1^1/_2$ c. milk

Mix flour, cornstarch, salt and a little milk to make a smooth paste, gradually add rest of milk and beaten egg yolks. Add to boiling syrup and cook until thickened.

CREAMY BUTTERSCOTCH PUDDING
Mrs. Cristy Eash

1 can sweetened condensed
  milk
$1^1/_2$ c. cold water
1 sm. box instant butterscotch
  pudding

2 c. Rich's Topping
36 vanilla wafer cookies

Mix condensed milk and water, then add pudding and chill 5 min. Beat Rich's Topping and mix with pudding. Put half of crushed cookies on bottom and half on top of pudding.

MYSTERY PUDDING

Polly Farmwald

1¹/₄ c. flour
1 c. sugar
1 egg (beaten)
1 (17 oz.) can fruit cocktail
  (undrained)
¹/₂ c. brown sugar
1 tsp. soda
¹/₄ tsp. salt
1 tsp. vanilla
¹/₂ c. nuts

Combine flour, sugar, soda and salt in mixing bowl. Combine beaten eggs, fruit cocktail and vanilla. Add to dry ingredients and mix to dampen. Pour into greased 8" sq. pan. Mix together brown sugar and nuts; sprinkle over batter. Bake at 350° for 45 min. Top with **whipped cream** before serving.

SWEETHEART PUDDING

Mary Esther Whetstone

CRUMBS:

2 c. graham crackers
  (crushed)
¹/₃ c. sugar
²/₃ c. butter (melted)

Mix and reserve 1 cup of mixture. Line pan with remaining crumbs like pie crust and add cooled pudding.

PUDDING:

4 c. milk
3 egg yolks
1 c. sugar
3 Tbsp. flour
1 tsp. vanilla

Heat milk to boiling. Mix egg yolks, sugar and flour and add to milk. Cook until thick and add vanilla.

TOPPING:

3 eggs whites   3 Tbsp. sugar

Beat egg whites until stiff; add sugar. Put on top of pudding and sprinkle with the reserved crumbs. May use whipped cream instead of egg whites on top and cook egg whites in pudding.

OHIO FOOD PUDDING
Mrs. Mervin Ella Schrock

20 graham crackers (rolled
   fine)
1 tsp. flour

$^1/_2$ c. butter or lard
$^1/_4$ c. white sugar

Mix as for pie crust and pack into pan. Reserve some cracker crumbs to put on top.

CUSTARD FILLING:

3 egg yolks
$^1/_4$ c. sugar
pinch of salt
$2^1/_2$ c. milk

2 Tbsp. flour
vanilla
egg whites
sugar

Cook first 5 ingredients until thick; add vanilla, pour in pan over cracker crumbs. Whip egg whites and add a little sugar then put on top of custard. Put reserved crackers on top.

SIMPLE PUDDING
Mrs. Ervin J. (Edna) Bontrager

3 c. Rich's Topping
3 c. water

3 (3 oz.) boxes instant pudding
1 can Eagle Brand milk

CRUST:

2 c. graham crackers
   (crushed)

1 Tbsp. sugar
$^1/_2$ c. margarine (melted)

Beat topping. Mix pudding with water. Put all together and mix. Put graham crackers in bottom of pan. Keep a little to put on top. This is not so rich!

———— ❖ ————

May you live all the days of your life.

—Jonathan Swift

DIRT PUDDING

Katie Irene Miller

2¹/₂ c. instant vanilla
  pudding
6 c. milk

6 c. whipped topping
4 oz. cream cheese (softened)
2 pkg. Oreo cookies

Heat milk, then cool. Crush cookies and put in bottom of 2 (9" x 13") pans. After milk is cooled beat together pudding mix, milk, whipped topping and cream cheese. Put in pans and cover with cookie crumbs. This is very delicious when frozen 2 or 3 days before serving!

DIRT PUDDING

Leanna Yutzy

2 boxes instant vanilla
  pudding
3 c. cold milk (2% works best)

2 c. cream (whipped)
35–40 Oreo cookies (crushed)
8 oz. cream cheese

Mix together pudding and milk. Whip cream and mix softened cream cheese to it. Whip together pudding and cream cheese mixture. Press layer of cookie crumbs in dish. Add pudding on top then add another layer of cookies and another layer of pudding. Save enough cookies to put on last.

DIRT PUDDING

Lillian Mast

¹/₂ stick oleo (softened)
1 c. powdered sugar
8 oz. cream cheese
3¹/₂ c. 2% milk (or you can
  boil the milk)

2 (3¹/₂ oz.) pkgs. instant vanilla
  pudding
12 oz. whipped topping
1 (20 oz.) pkg. Oreo cookies

Cream together oleo, cream cheese and powdered sugar. In another bowl mix milk, pudding and whipped topping. Combine the 2 mixtures. Crush cookies and put half on the bottom of a pan or bowl. Then add the pudding and then the rest of the crushed cookies on top.

DATE PUDDING
Wima Beechy

2 c. brown sugar | 3 c. hot water
1 Tbsp. butter

Boil this 3 min. and put in a pan. Drop batter in and bake.

BATTER:
1 c. brown sugar | 4 tsp. baking powder
3 Tbsp. butter | 1 c. dates
1 c. sweet milk | $^1/_2$ c. nuts
2 c. flour

Serve with whipped cream.

DATE PUDDING
Freeda Lehman

1 c. dates (cut fine) | 1 egg (beaten)
1 tsp. soda | 1 c. nuts (optional)
1 tsp. butter | 1 c. flour
1 c. boiling water | whipped cram or Rich's Topping
1 c. sugar

Pour boiling water over dates and soda. Add butter, sugar, egg, flour and nuts. Bake in 350° oven until done (do not overbake). When cold, cut into small squares and alternate layers of whipped cream, caramel sauce and date cake.

CARAMEL SAUCE:
1 c. brown sugar | butter
3 Tbsp. flour | 1 tsp. vanilla
1 c. boiling water | 1 tsp. maple flavoring

Mix sugar and flour in saucepan. Pour water over this; add butter, vanilla and flavoring. Cook until clear, then cool.

APPLE DANISH

Mrs. Kenny (Ruby) Schrock
Mrs. Sam (Wilma) Whetstone

PASTRY:
3 c. all purpose flour
$^1/_2$ tsp. salt
1 c. shortening

1 egg yolk
$^1/_2$ c. milk

FILLING:
6 c. apples (sliced and peeled)
$1^1/_2$ c. sugar
$^1/_4$ c. butter or margarine
  (melted)

2 Tbsp. all purpose flour
1 tsp. ground cinnamon

GLAZE:
1 egg white (lightly beaten)
$^1/_2$ c. confectioner's sugar

2–3 tsp. water

In mixing bowl combine pastry ingredients. Stir just until dough clings together. On lightly floured surface, roll half of dough into 15" x 10" rectangular pan. Transfer to 15" x 10" x 1" cookie sheet; set aside. In a bowl mix filling. Spoon over pastry in pan. Roll out remaining dough to equalize and place over filling. Brush with egg white. Bake at 375° for 40 min. Combine confectioner's sugar and enough water to achieve a drizzling consistency. Drizzle over warm pastry. Yield: 20–24 servings.

APPLE GOODIE

Mary Miller

$^3/_4$ c. granulated sugar
2 Tbsp. flour
$^1/_2$ tsp. salt

1 tsp. cinnamon
4 c. apples (peeled and sliced)

TOPPING CRUMBS:
1 c. oatmeal
1 c. brown sugar
1 c. flour

$^1/_4$ tsp. soda
$^1/_4$ tsp. baking powder
$^1/_2$ c. margarine

Sift together sugar, salt, flour and cinnamon. Combine with apples. Place in greased 13" x 9" cake pan. Mix oatmeal, brown sugar, flour, soda, baking powder; cut in margarine. Spread crumbs over apple mixture and bake at 375° for 35–40 min.

APPLE CRISPETT

Mrs. Glen Hershberger

1 qt. apples (sliced)	$^3/_4$ c. brown sugar
$^1/_2$ c. water	1 c. flour
$^3/_4$ c. sugar	5 Tbsp. butter

Peel and slice the apples and pour the water over them. Mix the other ingredients as for pie crust and pour over the apples and water. Do not stir together. Bake in a shallow pan for 45 min. When cool, cut in squares and serve with ice cream or whipped cream.

APPLE DUMPLINGS

Mary Esther Whetstone

2 c. flour	$^7/_8$ c. milk
2 tsp. baking powder	butter (melted)
$^1/_2$ tsp. salt	apples (sliced)
2 Tbsp. lard	brown sugar
1 Tbsp. butter	cinnamon

Sift flour, baking powder and salt. Cut in lard and butter; add milk and mix well into a dough. Roll dough out to a rectangle $^1/_4$" thick. Spread with melted butter and apples. Sprinkle with brown sugar and cinnamon. Roll up and cut (like cinnamon rolls) into slices about 2" wide, and place in pan cut-side up. Cover with sauce. Bake in moderate oven and serve warm with milk.

SAUCE:

1 scant c. sugar	$^1/_4$ tsp. salt
1 Tbsp. flour	1 or more c. hot water

Mix sugar, flour and salt. Add hot water and boil for 3 minutes. Pour over dumplings before baking.

❖

Glue fine sandpaper on your quilt patterns to prevent the pattern from slipping over the material.

FRUIT COBBLER

Mrs. Raymond Yutzy

1 qt. fruit pie filling
$^3/_4$ c. flour
$^3/_4$ c. sugar
1 tsp. baking powder
$^1/_4$ tsp. salt
3 Tbsp. butter (softened)
2 eggs

Pour pie filling in 10" pie pan. Mix together flour, sugar, baking powder, salt, butter and eggs. Spoon over fruit filling. Bake in 400° oven for 30 min. or until top is lightly golden. Serve warm with milk or whipped cream.

PLUM WHIRLIGIGS

Mary Miller

FILLING:

2 qt. canned plums
   (chopped)
1 c. clear jel
$^3/_4$ c. sugar (adjust to your taste)
1 c. water

WHIRLIGIG:

2 c. flour
4 tsp. baking powder
1 tsp. salt
4 Tbsp. shortening
4 Tbsp. milk
2 eggs (slightly beaten)
$^1/_2$ c. butter or margarine
1 c. butter or margarine
1 c. sugar
$^1/_2$ tsp. cinnamon

Drain off plum juice, measure into saucepan and add enough water to make 6 cups liquid; bring to a boil. Meanwhile, make a thickening of clear jel and sugar, gradually adding the water. Stir thickening into the boiling plum juice. Return to boil, stirring constantly. Boil gently 1 min. Remove from heat and add chopped plums. Pour into greased 13" x 9" x 2" cake pan; set aside. To make whirligigs combine flour, baking powder and salt in a bowl. Cut in shortening until soft crumbs form. In another bowl, mix eggs and milk. Add to flour mixture; mix to make a smooth dough. Knead for several min. Divide dough into two parts. Roll each part into a 12" x 8" rectangle. Spread with sugar, dot with butter, sprinkle with cinnamon. Starting at long end, roll up; seal edges. Cut into slices. Place slices over plum mixture. Bake at 400° for 22–25 min. or until golden brown.

CHERRY POT PIE

Mrs. Sam (Wilma) Whetstone

1 egg
1 c. sugar
1 c. milk

3 tsp. baking powder
3 c. flour
2 Tbsp. butter

2 c. fruit
1 c. sugar

$^1/_2$ c. fruit juice

Mix fruit, sugar and fruit juice and put in bottom of pan. Cream together egg, sugar and butter until smooth, add the rest. Bake at 350°. Serve with milk, warm or cold.

EASY FRUIT COBBLER

Mrs. Howard Miller

fresh or canned fruit, or berries
Place in the bottom of a well greased and fairly deep baking/serving dish.
Mix together:

1$^1/_2$ c. sugar
3 c. flour
6 tsp. baking powder

$^2/_3$ tsp. salt
1$^1/_2$ c. milk

Pour thin batter evenly over the fruit. Sprinkle sugar over the top and pour 1 c. hot water over all. Do not stir. Bake till top is crusty and brown (about 1 hr.). Serve warm with milk.

PEACH COBBLER

Mrs. Mahlon (Mary) Miller

4 c. fresh peaches (sliced) or fresh blueberries; add **1 c. sugar**; let set. Melt **1 stick oleo** in a baking dish.
Mix:

1 c. flour
$^1/_2$ c. sugar
1$^1/_2$ tsp. baking powder

1 tsp. salt
$^3/_4$ c. milk

Mix and pour over melted oleo (do not mix). Spoon peaches over batter. Bake at 375° for 40–45 min. Good with ice cream or milk.

CARAMEL DUMPLINGS
Fanny Mae Bontrager

1 c. sugar
2 c. boiling water

1 Tbsp. butter

1 Tbsp. butter
pinch of salt
$^1/_2$ c. sugar
$^1/_2$ tsp. vanilla

1 c. flour
3 tsp. baking powder
$^1/_2$ c. milk

In heavy pan caramelize sugar, stirring constantly. As soon as sugar is light brown add boiling water. Keep on stirring till sugar is dissolved; add butter. Make batter with the rest of the ingredients. Drop by tablespoonful into boiling syrup. Batter will slide off spoon smoothly if spoon is first dipped into hot syrup. After dumplings are all in syrup allow to come to boil then cover tightly and lower heat for 10–15 min. or until dumplings are done. May be served warm with milk.

CINNAMON PUFF
Edna Fern Schrock

2 c. sugar
2 Tbsp. lard
4 c. flour

4 tsp. baking powder
2 c. milk

Mix all all together and sprinkle with brown sugar and cinnamon. Delicious cold but better hot!

FRUIT SLUSH
Anna Fern Hochstetler
Katie Bontrager

1 qt. peaches (chopped)
6 oz. frozen orange juice
1 c. crushed pineapple
3 bananas (smashed or sliced)

2 c. water
2 c. sugar (use less when using canned peaches)

Mix well and freeze.

CIRCUS PEANUT JELLO

Mary Miller
Mrs. Wilbur (Norma) Bontrager

2 lg. boxes orange jello
1/2 lb. or 40 circus peanuts
1 can crushed pineapple

1 1/2 c. liquid Rich's Topping
2 pkg. graham crackers (optional)

Put orange jello in a bowl. Follow directions on box, but use all hot water. Put in circus peanuts in hot jello and let dissolve. When cool and partly set, add pineapple and Rich's Topping; mix altogether. Crush graham crackers, press half in bottom of pan, then pour jello mixture on top, and then another layer of cracker crumbs. Chill for 1 hr. before serving.

ORANGE SALAD

Mrs. Floyd (Loretta) Lehman

1 sm. box tapioca pudding
1 sm. pkg. instant vanilla pudding

1 sm. pkg. orange jello
2 c. hot water

1 can mandarin oranges

1 c. Rich's Topping

Mix puddings and jello together, then add the hot water. Boil for about 3–5 min. Then cool and add the oranges and whipped topping.

COTTAGE CHEESE PUDDING

Wilma Miller

Mix together:

1 sm. box green, orange, or lemon jello with 1 c. water
1 c. cream (whipped)

1 box cottage cheese
1 sm. can crushed pineapple
sugar and salt to taste

May add **miniature marshmallows** when ready to eat.

MESSY PINK STUFF
Mrs. Wilbur (Norma) Bontrager

1 can condensed milk
8 oz. cream cheese
1 can pie filling

1 can crushed pineapple
1^1/$_2$ c. Rich's Topping (whipped)

Mix together and chill. Serve.

ORANGE FLUFF
Mrs. David Eash

3 oz. orange jello

1 c. hot water

^{3}/$_4$ c. sugar
8 oz. cream cheese

1 c. Rich's Topping

Mix together jello and hot water. Let set till jelly stage. Stir together sugar, cream cheese and Rich's topping and add to first 2 ingredients. Line dish with graham crackers then pour in pudding and put graham crackers on top.

ORANGE DESSERT
Fanny Mae Bontrager

1 (6 oz.) pkg. orange jello
2 c. boiling water
1 Tbsp. lemon juice
2 c. cold milk

2 oranges (sliced crosswise and
    pulled apart)
^{1}/$_2$ c. cream (whipped)

Dissolve gelatin in boiling water. Chill, stirring frequently. Mix in lemon juice and milk. Chill and stir frequently till mixture begins to thicken; fold in orange sections and whipped cream. Pour into glass bowl and chill till firmly set. Ready to serve.

ORANGE DANISH
Mrs. David (Marlene) Miller

1 qt. water
1 c. sugar
1¹/₄ c. sugar

¹/₂ c. clear jel
1 pkg. Wyler's orange drink mix
choice of fruit

Bring water and 1 cup sugar to a boil. Mix 1¹/₄ cup sugar and clear jel with enough boiling water to make a paste. Stir into boiling water and bring to boil. Add drink mix. Cool and add fruit.

RHUBARB DESSERT
Polly Farmwald

2 c. rhubarb (cut)
¹/₄ c. minute tapioca
   (softened in ¹/₄ c. cold water)

1 c. sugar
2 c. water

Cook all together until rhubarb is soft, stirring often. When done add **any flavor jello**. Serve with cream, milk or plain. This is also good with ice cream.

RHUBARB DESSERT
Mrs. Mervin C. Miller

5 c. fresh rhubarb
3 c. sugar
1 tsp. salt
5 c. water

1 c. minute tapioca (if using
   baby pearl use 1¹/₂ c.)
jello to suit your taste

Cook water and rhubarb to boiling. Add tapioca. When tapioca is done add rest of ingredients. Before serving, adding strawberries or pineapple is also very good.

RHUBARB DESSERT

Mary H. Hochstetler

2 c. rhubarb (chopped)
1 box yellow cake mix
   (sprinkle over rhubarb)

1 c. sugar
2 c. water
1 (3 oz.) box strawberry jello

Put in cake pan in order given. Do not stir. Bake at 350° for 45 min.

STRAWBERRY RHUBARB DESSERT

Mrs. Wilbur (Norma) Bontrager

10 c. sugar
1 (20 oz.) can crushed
   pineapple
3 (3 oz.) pkg. strawberry jello

$1^1/_2$ c. sugar
4 Tbsp. clear jel
5 c. rhubarb (cubed)

Cook rhubarb and pineapple together then add dry ingredients and cook 2 min. Cool and serve. This is good frozen too.

———— ❖ ————

This cleanup trick works while you sleep! Lay your dirty barbecue grill rack on the lawn overnight—the dew will combine with the enzymes in the grass to loosen any burned on grease. Try it with messy oven racks too!

STRAWBERRY PIZZA

Mrs. Mervin (Ella) Schrock

1¹/₂ c. flour   ¹/₂ c. sugar
1¹/₂ tsp. baking powder   ¹/₂ c. butter
1¹/₂ tsp. vanilla   1¹/₂ Tbsp. milk

Mix like pie crust and press into a pizza pan. Bake at 350° for 10 min. Cool.

FILLING:

8 oz. cream cheese   1 c. powdered sugar
1 sm. box instant pudding   ¹/₂ c. milk (heat and cool be-
1 c. Rich's Topping (whipped)   fore using)

Mix cream cheese, powdered sugar, milk and pudding mix. Add whipped topping and spread over cooled crust.

Top with fruit: **diced apples, bananas, pineapple, grapes, oranges** or whatever you wish.

GLAZE:

1 c. water   1 Tbsp. clear jel
2 Tbsp. sugar   2 Tbsp. strawberry jello

Cook until thickened; cool and pour over fruit.

———— ❖ ————

Blend 1 cup of love and ¹/₂ cup of kindness; add alternately in small portions, 1 cup of appreciation and 3 cups of pleasant companionship into which has been sifted 3 teaspoons of deserving praise.
Flavor with teaspoon carefully chosen advise.
Lightly fold in 1 cup of cheerfulness to which has been added a pinch of sorrow. Pour with tender care into small clean hearts and let bake until well matured. Turn out on the surface of society. Humbly invoke God's blessing and it will serve all mankind.

FRUIT PIZZA

Christina Miller

CRUST:
1½ c. flour
½ c. powdered sugar

¾ c. cold butter or margarine

Spread over crust:
1 c. powdered sugar
8 oz. cream cheese

1 c. whipped topping

PINEAPPLE GLAZE:
1 c. pineapple juice
2 c. water
½ tsp. salt

¾ c. sugar
3 Tbsp. clear jel

Bake crust to a golden brown, cool. Top with cream cheese mixture. Top with your favorite fruits. Cook glaze till clear. Cool, drizzle over fruits. Chill.

FRUIT PIZZA

Pollyanna Schrock

CRUST:
2 c. Bisquick
⅓ c. sugar

⅓ c. oleo
1 egg

Spread over crust:
1 c. powdered sugar
1 c. Cool Whip

8 oz. cream cheese

Bake crust at 350° for 20 min. or until crust is brown. Put on your favorite fruit and cover with pineapple glaze (recipe above). Cool the glaze before putting on top of fruit pizza.

———— ❖ ————

When you cease to make a contribution you begin to die.

—*Eleanor Roosevelt*

FRUIT PIZZA

Mrs. Eli Miller

1¹/₃ c. flour
1 tsp. baking powder
¹/₂ c. butter or oleo

¹/₂ c. brown sugar
1 egg
pinch of salt

Cream together butter, brown sugar, egg, flour, baking powder and salt. Place in greased pizza or cookie sheet. Bake in 375° oven for 10 min. or until light brown. Cool.

Cream together:
8 oz. cream cheese
³/₄ c. powdered sugar

1 Tbsp. milk
1 tsp. vanilla

Spread this over cooled crust and arrange any kind of fruit on top. Combine pineapple juice or any kind of fruit juice and enough water to make 2 cups.

Add:
¹/₂ c. white sugar

1 heaping Tbsp. clear jel

Cook till clear, cool and spread over arranged fruit.

TAPIOCA

Mrs. William Schrock

¹/₂ c. tapioca

1 qt. milk

1¹/₄ c. sugar
2 eggs
1 level Tbsp. cornstarch

pinch of salt
1 tsp. vanilla

1 can crushed pineapple

1 c. whipped topping

Bring tapioca and milk to a boil and keep stirring until it cooks, then cook till clear (over low heat). Then add sugar, eggs, cornstarch, salt and vanilla. Stir till it thickens; when cold add pineapple or candy bars and whipped topping.

(MILK) TAPIOCA PUDDING

Mrs. John Hochstetler

4 c. milk
1¹/₂ c. sugar
2 egg yolks

1 tsp. vanilla
¹/₂ c. tapioca
Cool Whip

Heat milk to boiling with ³/₄ c. sugar, add tapioca, stirring. Bring to boil again, turn heat down, simmer 5–10 min. Stirring, add rest of sugar, egg yolks and vanilla. Add to tapioca, cook 2 more min., cool, then add Cool Whip. If desired add candy bars.

BUTTERSCOTCH TAPIOCA

Mrs. David (Katie) Bontrager

6 c. boiling water
1 tsp. salt
Cook for 15 min.

1¹/₂ c. tapioca (sm. pearl)

Add:
2 c. brown sugar
Cook until done, stirring often.

Mix together and add:
2 eggs (beaten)
Cook until it bubbles.

¹/₂ c. white sugar

Add:
1 stick butter (melted and browned)
Serve with **whipped cream** and **candy bars**.

1 tsp. vanilla

———— ❖ ————

Be careful what you think; your thoughts are heard in heaven.

CREAMY TAPIOCA PUDDING

Fanny Mae Bontrager

1 qt. milk
²/₃ c. baby pearl tapioca
¹/₂ c. sugar
3 egg yolks
¹/₄ tsp. salt

1 c. milk
3 egg whites
¹/₄ tsp. salt
1 tsp. vanilla
¹/₂ c. sugar

Bring milk to a boil; add tapioca. Cook over med. heat, stirring frequently. Continue cooking until most of pearls turn clear when held on a spoon a few seconds. Beat together egg yolks, salt, milk and sugar. Add to hot tapioca, stirring constantly. Remove from heat as soon as yolks are cooked. Leaving on heat too long will curdle yolks. In large bowl make meringue with egg whites, salt, vanilla and sugar. When stiff slowly pour in hot tapioca mixture, beating vigorously. Continue beating about a min. This is good served slightly warm with fresh Rhubarb Delight Squares.

FLUFFY TAPIOCA

Mary Esther Whetstone

2 c. milk
1 egg yolk

3 Tbsp. minute tapioca
5 Tbsp. sugar

Heat milk to boiling. Mix together egg yolk, minute tapioca and sugar. Stir into boiling milk and bring to boil again. Beat egg white till stiff and pour hot mixture over egg white and stir until well blended. Stir occasionally while cooking. Can also add **bananas** when ready to serve.

ORANGE TAPIOCA PUDDING

Katie Irene Miller

1 box or 3¹/₂ oz. tapioca
  pudding
1¹/₂ box orange jello

1 box French vanilla pudding
3 c. water

Cook all together, then cool. Beat **2 c. Rich's Topping** then mix in well with mandarin oranges and pineapple. Mix in cooled mixture.

TAPIOCA PUDDING

Mrs. Harry Wayne Miller

5 c. hot water
1 c. tapioca
$^1/_2$ c. cold water
1 c. brown sugar
$^3/_4$ c. white sugar
2 eggs (beaten)
1 Tbsp. butter (melted)
1 tsp. vanilla

Mix tapioca with water and cook till clear. Mix together cold water, the sugars and beaten eggs. Add to tapioca. Add butter and vanilla. When cool add about 2 cups whipped topping, pineapple and/or candybars.

BLACK CHERRY TAPIOCA

Mrs. Andrew (Carrie) Hochstetler

2 qt. boiling water and/or
  cherry juice
1 c. baby pearl tapioca
1 c. sugar
1 (3 oz.) box black cherry jello
1 pkg. black cherry Kool-Aid
1 pt. pitted black cherries
  (canned or frozen)
2 c. whipped topping mix

Heat water to boiling. Add tapioca. Boil 5 min. or until almost clear. Add sugar, jello and Kool-Aid. Before serving add cherries and whipped topping.

TAPIOCA

Esther E. Eash

5 qt. boiling water
$2^1/_2$ c. baby pearl tapioca
1 tsp. salt
  Cook until almost clear. Add:
1 lg. box jello (raspberry)
4 c. sugar
1 qt. crushed pineapple
1 qt. fruit cocktail

JELLO TAPIOCA

$^1/_2$ c. baby pearl tapioca   1 sm. pkg. gelatin (any flavor)
4 c. boiling water $^3/_4$ c. sugar

Place water in heavy saucepan, bring to boil. Add tapioca; stir. Bring back to boil, then simmer, keeping the lid on. Stir once or twice. Cook till most of tapioca shows clear when held on a spoon for a few minutes. Remove from heat. Add gelatin and sugar, stirring well after each addition till completely dissolved. As tapioca cools, stir occasionally till tapioca no longer shows a tendency to settle to the bottom. Chill. Add your favorite fruit.

GRAPE (FRUIT)   *Mary Sue Yoder*

4 qt. grape juice $2^1/_2$ c. Mira-Clear or Perma Flo
2 qt. water   2 c. water
$2^1/_2$ c. sugar

Mix first 3 ingredients; set aside. Mix Mira-Clear or Perma Flo and water. Then mix to first 3 ingredients until thick. Eat with fresh cake. Canned blueberries can also be done like this instead of grape juice and adding berries when thick. Note: If using Perma Flo use $^1/_4$ c. to 1 qt. water.

FRUIT BASE   *Malinda Yutzy*

3 c. water   1 (3 oz.) pkg. jello powder
$^1/_2$ c. clear jel $^3/_4$ c. sugar
1 c. cold water

Bring water to a boil. Mix clear jel with cold water. Stir into boiling water; boil several minutes, stirring constantly. Remove from heat. Add jello powder and sugar. Cool. Add any fruit.

KOOL-AID DESSERT

Mrs. Wilbur (Norma) Bontrager
Mrs. Glen (Ida Mae) Beachy

2 qt. water
2 c. sugar

1 c. clear jel
2 pkg. Kool-Aid

Bring water to a boil then add the rest ingredients; then boil till thick. Add fruit when cooled off.

EAGLE BRAND DESSERT

Mrs. Glen (Alma) Whetstone
Marlene Miller

1 box vanilla instant
  pudding
1/2 box instant butterscotch
  pudding

1^1/2 c. water
1 can Eagle Brand milk
2 c. Rich's Topping
graham crackers (crushed)

Mix the puddings, water and milk together. Add whipped Rich's Topping. Put cracker crumbs in bottom of pan, then pudding, then sprinkle crumbs on top of pudding.

QUICK AND EASY DESSERT

Mrs. Raymond Yutzy

1 pack crackers (crushed)
1/4 c. butter (melted)
1/4 c. brown sugar

2 c. cold milk
3/4 c. instant pudding mix
1 qt. fruit pie filling

Mix together cracker crumbs, butter and sugar. Press into a small cake pan; set aside. Beat together milk and pudding; mix 2 min. and pour onto cracker crust. Let pudding set several min. then top with pie filling. Graham, soda, or Ritz crackers can be used. This is handy for unexpected company.

PARADISE DESSERT
Mrs. Leroy (Karen) Miller

¹/₄ c. butter	1 c. fruit
1 c. powdered sugar	1 pkg. cream cheese
1 egg	1 tsp. vanilla
graham crackers	pinch of salt
1 c. cream	¹/₄ c. chopped nuts

Cream together melted butter, powdered sugar and egg. Put graham crackers in bottom of dish then pour in butter mixture. Whip cream and add cream cheese, fruit, vanilla and salt. Pour this on top of butter mixture, then spread graham crackers on top with nuts.

MISSISSIPPI MUD
Sarah Yoder

¹/₃ c. cocoa	1¹/₂ c. flour
2 c. sugar	¹/₄ tsp. salt

Mix and add:

2 sticks oleo (melted)	4 eggs (beaten)
1 tsp. vanilla	1¹/₂ c. chopped nuts

Mix well; grease and flour 15" x 13" cookie sheet and pour mixture into pan. Bake at 350° for 20 min. Remove from oven and put on a layer of small marshmallows. Place in oven again (just to melt marshmallows, not brown). Cool. Spread with icing.

ICING:

1 box powdered sugar	1 tsp. vanilla
¹/₃ c. cocoa	1 stick oleo
¹/₃ c. milk	

Cream well and spoon on cooled cookies, cut in bars.

———— ❖ ————

A little nonsense now and then is relished by the wisest of men.

CHOCOLATE ECLAIR
Mrs. William (Velda) Miller

2 boxes instant vanilla
  pudding
3 c. milk

8 oz. cream cheese
1 c. Rich's Topping
1 box graham crackers

Heat milk to scalding. Cool and mix with pudding. Mix cream cheese to whipped topping and mix into pudding. Line rectangular Tupperware pan with whole graham crackers. Put half of pudding on top of crackers, then another layer of crackers, then pudding and then crackers on top again. Top with frosting. Note: $1^1/_2$ c. evaporated milk with $1^1/_2$ c. water can be used instead of whole milk.

FROSTING:

3 Tbsp. cocoa
3 Tbsp. vegetable oil
3 Tbsp. butter
1 tsp. vanilla

2 Tbsp. Karo
3 Tbsp. milk
$1^1/_2$ c. powdered sugar

Cook together all ingredients except powdered sugar, until melted. Cool and add powdered sugar and drizzle over graham crackers.

HEATH BAR DESSERT
Loretta Kuhns

2 c. Ritz crackers (crushed)
1 Tbsp. sugar
$^1/_2$ c. oleo (softened)
2 pkg. vanilla instant
  pudding

4 c. vanilla ice cream (softened)
1 c. whipped topping
2 Heath bars (crushed)

Mix Ritz crackers, sugar and oleo. Press into cake pan. Mix pudding and milk; let set; add ice cream. Spread on top of crust. Cover with whipped topping. Sprinkle with crushed Heath bars.

NUTTY DESSERT

Mrs. Edith B. Knepp

In 9" x 13" cake pan, layer in order given:

2 lg. cans cherry pie filling   **nuts to cover**
1 cherry chip cake mix (dry)   **1 stick butter (cut up)**

Bake in 350° oven for 45 min.

RHUBARB BUTTER CRUNCH

Mrs. Devon (Ruby) Miller

3 c. rhubarb (fresh or frozen)
1 c. white sugar   **3 Tbsp. flour**

TOPPING:
1 c. brown sugar   **$^1/_2$ c. butter or margarine**
1 c. rolled oats   **$^1/_2$ c. shortening**
1$^1/_2$ c. flour

Combine rhubarb, sugar and flour. Place in 9" x 9" greased baking dish. Combine brown sugar, oats and flour; cut in butter and shortening; sprinkle over rhubarb mixture. Bake at 375° for 40 min. Serve warm with milk or ice cream.

GRAPE DELIGHT

Fanny Mae Bontrager

1 pkg. graham crackers   **$^1/_4$ c. sugar**
$^1/_4$ stick butter   **1$^1/_2$ c. grape puree**
$^1/_4$ c. sugar   **2 Tbsp. unflavored gelatin**
8 oz. cream cheese   **1 c. hot water**
1 c. cream (whipped)   **$^1/_2$ c. sugar**

Make crumbs with graham crackers, butter and sugar. Mix cream cheese with sugar and whipped cream. Sprinkle gelatin on grape puree and stir. Add hot water to dissolve gelatin and add sugar. Cool the grape mixture. Make layer of crumbs in glass bowl. Top with cream cheese; add grape last.

FROZEN CHERRY DELIGHT

Loretta Kuhns

1 can cherry pie filling

1 can crushed pineapple

1 can Eagle Brand milk

16 oz. Cool Whip

Mix well and pour in cake pan. Set in freezer.

CHERRY CHEESECAKE

Mrs. Tobie (Esther) Miller

16 graham cracker halves

$^3/_4$ c. white sugar

$^1/_2$ stick butter (melted)

2 eggs

2 (8 oz.) cream cheese

1 c. white sugar

1 tsp. vanilla

cherry pie filling

whipped cream

Crush crackers. Add sugar and melted butter. Press into 9" x 13" pan. Mix eggs, cream cheese, sugar and vanilla. Pour onto cracker crumb mixture. Bake at 350° for 12 min. Cool. Pour on cherry pie filling and top with whipped cream.

LEMON CRUNCH

Sarah Yoder

$^2/_3$ c. oleo (melted)

2 c. flour

$^1/_3$ c. brown sugar

2 c. pecans

$2^1/_2$ c. powdered sugar

2 (8 oz.) cream cheese (softened)

2 c. Rich's Topping (whipped)

instant lemon pudding or fruit pie filling

Mix oleo, flour, brown sugar and pecans. Spread in cake pan and bake at 325°. Stir often. Remove from oven when light brown and spread evenly; cool. Blend powdered sugar, cream cheese and whipped topping. Spread over crunch. Top with lemon pudding or pie filling. Chill.

RHUBARB DESSERT
Mary Miller

FILLING:

4 c. rhubarb (finely chopped)
1 c. sugar
1¹/₂ c. water

1 box (3 oz.) cherry jello
6 Tbsp. clear jel
³/₄ c. water

BOTTOM CRUST:

¹/₂ c. margarine
1 c. flour

CREAM CHEESE FILLING:

8 oz. cream cheese
1 c. powdered sugar

2 c. Cool Whip

Mix crust ingredients, press into 13" x 9" cake pan. Bake at 375° for 15 min. Cool. Mix cream cheese, powdered sugar and Cool Whip and place on top of cooled crust. Combine rhubarb, sugar and water and boil well. Add a thickening of clear jel and water. Return to boil and boil 1 min. Remove from heat and add cherry jello. Chill and place on cream cheese layer.

PUMPKIN TORTE
Pollyanna Schrock

24 graham crackers
¹/₂ c. margarine

¹/₃ c. sugar

Press in 9" x 13" pan. Add:

2 eggs (beaten)
8 oz. cream cheese

³/₄ c. sugar

Mix and pour over graham crackers. Bake at 350° for 20 min. Cook till thickened:

2 c. pumpkin
1 Tbsp. cornstarch
3 egg yolks
¹/₂ c. sugar

¹/₂ c. milk
¹/₂ tsp. salt
2 tsp. cinnamon

Add **1 pkg. Knox gelatin** dissolved in ¹/₄ **c. cold water**. Add **3 beaten egg whites**, fold into cooled mixture.

SODA CRACKER DELIGHT

Ida Hochstetler

6 egg whites   **³/₄ tsp. cream of tartar**
   Beat together, then add:
2 c. sugar   **2 tsp. vanilla**
   Fold in:
2 c. soda crackers (crushed)
   Spread in cake pan and bake at 350° for 15 min. or until brown. Cool and put one can **cherry pie filling** on top. If desired, top with **whipped cream** before serving.

RHUBARB TORTE

Mrs. Perry (Melinda) Lambright

1 c. butter   **4 Tbsp. sugar**
2 c. flour
   Mix until crumbly. Pat into 9" x 13" pan. Bake at 350° for 10 min.

5 c. rhubarb (cut fine)   **¹/₄ tsp. salt**
6 egg yolks   **1 c. cream**
2 c. sugar   **1 tsp. vanilla**
7 Tbsp. flour
   Mix these ingredients together, pour over crust and bake at 350° for 45 min. until custard is set.

MERINGUE:
6 egg whites   **¹/₄ tsp. salt**
³/₄ c. sugar   **¹/₄ tsp. cream of tartar**
   Beat egg whites stiff, gradually add sugar, salt and cream of tartar; spread over torte. Bake at 350° for 15 min.

---- ❖ ----

*I'm a great believer in luck, I find the harder I work,
the more I have of it.*

—*Stephen Leacock*

PINEAPPLE DELIGHT

Anna Fern Hochstetler

2 sm. boxes lemon jello
3 c. boiling water
12 marshmallows (quartered)
1 c. red grapes (halved)
1 can crushed pineapple
  (drained)
1 c. pineapple juice (add
  water if necessary)
$^1/_2$ c. sugar
1$^1/_2$ Tbsp. flour
1 egg (beaten)
1 c. Rich's Topping
  pudding
County Line cheese (finely
  shredded)

Melt marshmallows in hot jello, then add pineapple and grapes. Pour in pan and let set. Cook juice, sugar, flour and egg till thick. Cool. Whip Rich's Topping and mix with pudding. Spread on top of jello. When ready to serve, put County Line cheese on top.

CHEESECAKE

Anna Fern Hochstetler

8 oz. cream cheese
1 c. Rich's Topping
  (whipped stiff)
1 c. powdered sugar
2 pkg. graham crackers
$^1/_2$ stick oleo
$^1/_2$ c. white sugar
1 can pie filling (of your choice)

Crush graham crackers and mix with melted oleo and white sugar. Put in bottom of 9" x 13" pan. Soften cream cheese and mix with powdered sugar, then add whipped topping. Spread on crumbs. Put pie filling on top when set.

———————— ❖ ————————

To measure solid shortening use water in large measuring cup. Example: to measure 2 cups shortening, put 2 cups water in measuring cup and add shortening enough to bring water to 4 cup line. Drain water.

CHERRY PECAN TORTE
Timothy Alan Miller Grade 2

6 egg whites
$^1/_2$ tsp. cream of tartar
2 c. white sugar
2 c. white cracker crumbs (coarse)

$^3/_4$ c. pecans (chopped)
2 tsp. vanilla
2 c. whipped cream (whipped)
3 c. cherry pie filling

Beat egg whites until foamy, then add cream of tartar and gradually the sugar, beating until stiff peaks. Fold in cracker crumbs, pecans and vanilla; spread in 9" x 13" pan. Bake at 350° for 25 min. Cool completely. Spread whipped cream over top. Spoon pie filling over cream. Chill 1 hr. *Hint: Lite Topping: when using Rich's Topping you can add $^1/_4$ c. water for every $^3/_4$ c. whip.*

BUTTERSCOTCH NUT TORTE
Mrs. Jr. (Barbara) Yoder

$1^1/_2$ c. sugar
$^1/_2$ tsp. almond extract
1 tsp. vanilla
6 eggs (separated)

$^1/_2$ c. nuts
2 c. graham cracker crumbs
1 tsp. baking powder

Beat egg yolks well. Add sugar, baking powder and flavorings; mix well. Beat egg whites until stiff peaks form. Fold into first mixture. Bake (slowly) at 325° until light brown.

SAUCE:

2 c. brown sugar
2 Tbsp. butter
1 tsp. vanilla
pinch of salt
3 pt. boiling water

$^1/_2$ tsp. soda
2 eggs (beaten)
2 c. white sugar
2 c. flour
1 c. water

Boil first 6 ingredients together while you mix eggs, sugar, water and flour. When it first boils, add the rest to thicken (if too thick, add hot water). Layer like a date pudding with **Rich's Topping**. This is enough sauce for 2 tortes.

BANANA CREAM CHEESECAKE

Mrs. William J. Troyer
Mrs. Eli H. Hochstetler

1³/₄ c. graham cracker
  crumbs (about 28 squares)
¹/₄ c. sugar
¹/₂ c. butter
8 oz. cream cheese (softened)

8 oz. whipped topping
4 med. bananas (sliced)
1³/₄ c. cold milk
1 (3.4 oz.) pkg. instant banana
  cream pudding mix

In a small bowl, combine cracker crumbs and sugar; stir in butter; set aside ¹/₂ c. for topping. Press remaining crumb mixture onto bottom and up the sides of a greased 9" spring form pan or 9" sq. baking pan. Bake at 350° for 5–7 min. Cool on wire rack. In mixing bowl beat cream cheese and sugar until smooth. Fold in 2 c. of whip topping. Arrange half of the banana slices in crust; top with half of cream cheese mixture. Repeat layers. In a bowl, beat milk and pudding mix until smooth; fold in remaining whip topping. Pour over cream cheese layer. Sprinkle with reserved crumb mixture. Refrigerate 1–2 hrs. or until set.

LEMON DELIGHT

Mrs. William Schmucker
Mrs. Amos L. Miller

1 stick butter
1 c. flour
¹/₂ c. nuts
8 oz. cream cheese

1 c. powdered sugar
1 c. Rich's Topping
3 c. milk
2 pkg. instant lemon pudding

Mix first 3 ingredients and press into a 9" x 13" pan. Bake at 375° for 15 min. Cool. Mix cream cheese and powdered sugar and fold in whipped Rich's Topping. Spread on cooled crust. Chill 15 min. Beat together milk and pudding, mix until thickened. Pour on top. Chill.

LEMON DELIGHT

Mrs. Paul Whetstone
Mrs. Sam (Wilma) Whetstone

1 c. flour	1 c. powdered sugar
$^1/_2$ c. butter	8 oz. cream cheese (softened)
1 tsp. sugar	2 boxes instant lemon pudding
$^1/_2$ c. nuts	3 c. cold milk
2 c. whipped topping	

Mix well and press in pan: flour, butter, sugar and nuts. Bake at 350° for 15 min. Cool. Mix whipped topping, powdered sugar and cream cheese. Spread on cooled crust. Mix pudding mix and cold milk until right consistency and pour over cream cheese mixture.

———— ❁ ————

Sow radishes thinly into lettuce or carrot rows.
Radishes will come first showing you the row.
Pulling radishes when ready will loosen soil in lettuce row.

———— ❁ ————

Onion skin very thin, mild winter's coming in.
Onion skin thick and tough, coming winter cold and rough.

Favorite Recipes

Ice Cream & Toppings

DAIRY QUEEN ICE CREAM

Mrs. Leroy (Karen) Miller

2 env. Knox gelatin
$^1/_2$ c. cold water
4 c. whole milk
2 c. sugar

2 tsp. vanilla
1 tsp. salt
3 c. cream

Soak gelatin in cold water. Heat whole milk (just hot, not boiling); remove and add gelatin mixture, sugar, vanilla and salt. Cool. Add cream. Chill for 5–6 hrs. before freezing. Makes 1 gal.

COUNTY ICE CREAM

Mrs. Mervin (Katie Fern) Miller

4 eggs
2 c. sugar
5 c. milk
4 c. cream

$4^1/_2$ tsp. vanilla
$^1/_2$ tsp. salt
2 sm. pkgs. instant vanilla
    pudding

Beat eggs for 5 min. Beat in sugar and 1 c. milk until thick. Add rest of milk, cream, vanilla and salt. Sprinkle pudding on top and beat in. This will fill a 6 qt. ice cream freezer. Other flavors pudding mix may be used instead of vanilla if preferred.

ICE CREAM

Mrs. David I. Bontrager

6 c. milk
6 eggs (beaten)
$1^1/_2$ c. brown sugar

$1^1/_2$ c. white sugar
3 rounded Tbsp. flour
pinch of salt

Heat milk, mix together other ingredients; add to milk when milk starts to boil, then heat till it cooks. Add **3 Tbsp. vanilla** and **3 cups cream** before freezing.

ICE CREAM (FOR 6 QT. FREEZER)

Mrs. Naomi Miller

6–7 eggs (beaten very well)   3 c. white sugar
6 Tbsp. flour   3¹/₂ qt. milk
   Heat just to boiling point, take off heat and add:
1 can sweetened condensed   1 qt. cream
  milk
3 Tbsp. vanilla
   Cool. Mix **1 box instant pudding** and add to milk when cold.
Freeze.

ICE CREAM

Mrs. William Schmucker

4¹/₂ qt. milk   3 lg. Tbsp. flour
6 eggs (beaten separate)   1¹/₂ Tbsp. cornstarch
4¹/₂ c. sugar (brown and white)
   Combine 1¹/₂ qt. milk and eggs, heat till hot. Combine the rest
of the ingredients and mix with enough milk to make a paste. Add
to the hot milk and eggs. Cook for 5 min. Remove and add **flavoring of your choice**. Add **milk** to fill 1¹/₂ gal. freezer. Variations: add
vanilla, pecans, chocolate chips or whatever you wish.

HOMEMADE ICE CREAM

Verna Mae Hershberger

Approx. 1 gal. milk   3 heaping Tbsp. flour
3 c. sugar   3 level Tbsp. cornstarch
3 eggs   pinch of salt
   Put milk in big kettle to heat. Mix flour, sugar, cornstarch, eggs
and salt. Add enough milk and cream to moisten. When the milk
reaches the boiling point add the sugar mixture. Stir until the mixture thickens. When thickened remove from fire and add vanilla to
suit your taste. Put through a sieve. Pour into ice cream can, if not
full enough add more milk and stir well. Makes 1¹/₂ gal.

HOMEMADE ICE CREAM   *Mrs. Richard (Helen) Miller*

2$^1/_2$ qt. milk

4 rounded Tbsp. flour (sifted)

1 Tbsp. cornstarch (little more than even)

4 eggs (beaten)

$^3/_4$ c. brown sugar

2$^1/_2$ c. white sugar

Boil together milk, flour, cornstarch, eggs and brown sugar; let cook for a few min.; then add 2$^1/_2$ c. white sugar. Add more milk till thick enough to run through sieve. Add any flavoring you wish. Makes 1$^1/_2$ gal.

BASIC VANILLA ICE CREAM   *Mrs. Mary Kay Graber*

6 eggs (beaten)

2 c. sugar

$^1/_2$ tsp. salt

1 Tbsp. vanilla

4 c. heavy cream

4 c. whole milk

Beat eggs until very thick. Gradually add sugar, beating until thick and light. Add salt, vanilla and cream and beat. Pour into 1 gal. freezer can. Add milk and mix well. Freeze, remove dasher, pack, and let ripen about 2 hrs.

❖

It's easy to read a rain gauge if you put a few drops of food coloring in the tube. Even if the colored water dries up, there is enough residue to help read the next rainfall.

HOMEMADE ICE CREAM

Mrs. Freeman (Lydia Sue) Yoder

2 qt. milk

1 c. sugar

1 rounded Tbsp. cornstarch
4 egg yolks

1 rounded Tbsp. flour

3/4 c. brown sugar
1/2 c. marshmallow cream
1 tsp. vanilla

1/2 tsp. salt
1/4 tsp. maple flavoring

In 6 qt. saucepan mix sugar and milk; bring to a boil. Then add cornstarch, flour and egg yolks mixed with milk to make a gravy. Let boil, then remove from heat; add brown sugar, marshmallow cream and flavorings. Mix till all dissolved, let cool; then before freezing, whip egg whites, add and fill rest of can with milk till top of top paddle. Optional: add **1 c. pecans**, **1/2 tsp. butter pecan flavoring**. Makes 1 gal.

ICE CREAM

Sara Whetstone

8 c. milk
3 c. white sugar
4 Tbsp. flour
1 tsp. salt

8 eggs (well beaten)
3 Tbsp. vanilla
2 pt. cream

Heat milk; mix sugar, flour, salt and eggs. Add to milk and heat to boiling. Add vanilla and cream when cool. Freeze in 1 1/2 gal. freezer.

———— ❁ ————

Newspaper repels moths, which is quite helpful when storing woolen rugs.

ICE CREAM
Mary Sue Yoder

4 eggs
1 c. sugar
1¹/₂ Tbsp. vanilla

2 cans Eagle Brand milk
6 c. milk

Beat eggs 5 min. until light and lemon colored. Add sugar and beat well. Blend in Eagle Brand milk and milk. Freeze in ice cream freezer. Makes 1 gal. ice cream. Variations: May use instant pudding instead of vanilla (butter pecan, vanilla, etc.).

DELICIOUS HOMEMADE ICE CREAM
Velda Kuhns

3 eggs
1 c. sugar
1 can sweetened condensed
  milk
1¹/₂ c. whipped cream
1 box instant vanilla pudding

1 Tbsp. vanilla
pinch of salt
3 c. milk (scalded)
3¹/₂ c. marshmallows (melted
  in 2. c. milk)

Beat eggs until well blended. Add sugar and salt slowly. Continue to mix and add sweetened condensed milk, whipped cream, vanilla and milk. Fill freezer can ³/₄ full. Add more milk if needed. Freeze immediately or refrigerate until freezing. Makes 1 gal.

COOKED ICE CREAM
Mrs. Daniel (Martha) Miller

9 c. boiling milk
1¹/₂ c. brown sugar
¹/₂ c. flour
4 eggs

1 tsp. salt
3 c. milk
2 Tbsp. gelatin

Make thickener with sugar, flour, eggs, salt and the 3 c. milk. Stir into boiling milk and boil a few min. Remove from heat and stir in gelatin that has been soaked in ¹/₂ c. water; cool. Fill freezer to ³/₄ full with milk and freeze.

ICE CREAM

Suvilla Graber

3 boxes instant pudding mix   **3 c. sugar**
  (any flavor)
  Fill 1^1/$_2$ gal. freezer can with **milk**. Beat together and freeze.
1 can Milnot can be added just before freezing.

ORANGE JELLO ICE CREAM

  Beat together:

2 c. sugar   **5 eggs**

  Dissolve:

2 boxes jello in **1 c. boiling water**
  Add this to first mixture. Stir well, then add enough milk to fill 1
gal. freezer.

FAVORITE SHERBET ICE CREAM

Mrs. Freeman E. Yoder
Mrs. Wilbur (Norma) Bontrager

4 sm. boxes or 1^1/$_2$ c. orange   **4 c. water**
  jello   **8 Tbsp. lemon juice**
4 c. (or less) sugar   **10 c. milk**
  Mix water and sugar together. Boil 1 min. When done boiling,
stir in jello and lemon juice. Stir until jello is dissolved. Cool and
add milk. Mixture may look curdled, but will turn out all right
when frozen. Makes 1^1/$_2$ gal. Any flavor jello may be used. Some
flavors require less sugar.

ORANGE SHERBET

Cristine Miller

1 c. water
1/2 c. sugar
3 oz. orange jello
1 Tbsp. lemon juice
2 1/2 c. milk

Mix sugar and water. Bring to boil and boil 1 min. Remove from heat. Add jello and stir till dissolved. Remove from heat. Add jello and stir till well dissolved. Chill. Add lemon juice and milk. Beat well. Freeze 1 hr.; beat again.

ICE CREAM BARS

Mary Esther Yoder
Mrs. Marvin (Ruby) Hochstetler

3 eggs (separated)
1/3 c. powered sugar
1 pt. whipping cream
graham crackers (whole
  or crushed)

Beat yolks and powdered sugar until light and fluffy. Whip egg whites and also cream. Fold all together. Pour into cookie sheet lined with graham crackers on top and freeze.

BUTTERSCOTCH TOPPING

Katie Irene Miller

1 c. brown sugar
2 Tbsp. Karo
1/4 c. milk
3 Tbsp. butter

Pour all ingredients together. Stir until boiling and simmer for 3 min. Good on pancakes and ice cream.

---------- ❖ ----------

Sit down to the table and have a look,
The first complainer is the next meal cook.

CHOCOLATE SYRUP
Mrs. Daniel (Martha) Miller

3 c. sugar
1 c. cocoa
1^1/$_2$ tsp. salt

1^1/$_2$ c. water
^{1}/$_2$ c. Karo
2 Tbsp. vanilla

Mix all together and boil a couple min. This is good on ice cream or for chocolate milk.

RASPBERRY SYRUP (FOR ICE CREAM OR JELLY)
Mrs. Eli Miller

2^1/$_2$ pt. white sugar
1 pt. white Karo

1^1/$_2$ pt. fruit juice

Put all together and cook until syrup stage (222°–223).

HOT CHOCOLATE ICE CREAM TOPPING
Sara Whetstone

1 c. water
1 c. white sugar
3 Tbsp. cocoa

3^1/$_2$ Tbsp. flour
^{1}/$_2$ tsp. salt

Cook together 3 min. Add ^{1}/$_2$ tsp. vanilla.

CHOCOLATE SYRUP
Suvilla Graber

^{1}/$_2$ c. light cream
1 c. white sugar

1 c. white Karo
^{1}/$_2$ c. cocoa

Boil 3 min. Remove from heat. Add:

3 Tbsp. margarine

1 Tbsp. vanilla

Casseroles, Meats & Vegetables

UNDERGROUND HAM CASSEROLE

Inez Yutzy

8 c. ham (cubed and cooked)
4 Tbsp. margarine
1/2 c. onion (chopped)
1 Tbsp. Worcestershire sauce

2 cans cream of chicken or cream of mushroom soup
1/2 tsp. pepper
2 c. Velveeta cheese
1/2 lb. bacon (browned)

Mashed potatoes mixed with sourcream, butter, salt and just enough milk to make it a little thinner. Leave a little thick.

Place cubed ham, onion, pepper, soup, Worcestershire sauce in bottom of casserole dish with 1 c. cheese; then put mashed potatoes on top with remaining cheese and bacon. Bake for 20 min. or till mixture bubbles up the sides.

SEVEN LAYER CASSEROLE

Naomi Sue Shrock

1st   6 c. potatoes (cooked)
2nd   2 cans mushroom soup
3rd   1/4 c. peppers (chopped)
4th   1/2 c. minute rice
5th   hamburger (browned with onion)
6th   1 1/2 pt. pizza sauce
7th   1 lb. mozzarella cheese

Bake at 350° until it's hot all way through.

———— ❖ ————

The underdeveloped bit of property with greatest potential is still between the ears.

CHICKEN AND WIDE NOODLE CASSEROLE

Mrs. Naomi Miller

1 pt. cooked chicken (cubed)
4 qt. wide noodles (cooked in salt water)
2 cans cream of mushroom soup
1 can cream of onion soup
some peas (if desired)
Velveeta cheese (on top)
seasoning salt to taste

Bake for 30 minutes or until hot.

YUM-A-SETTA

Mrs. Eli H. Hochstetler

2 lb. hamburger
salt and pepper to taste
2 Tbsp. brown sugar
$^1/_2$ c. chopped onion
1 can tomato soup
16 oz. pkg. noodles
1 can cream of chicken soup
$^1/_2$ lb. processed cheese (sliced)

Brown hamburger and onions. Add seasonings and tomato soup. Cook noodles; drain. Mix chicken soup with noodles. Layer hamburger, cheese and noodles in casserole. Bake at 350° for $^1/_2$ hr.

CHINESE CASSEROLE

Anna Fern Hochstetler

$1^1/_2$ lb. hamburger (fried)
$1^1/_2$ c. celery (diced)
$^1/_2$ c. onion (chopped)
3 c. water
$^1/_2$ c. rice (uncooked)
1 can cream of mushroom soup
1 can cream of chicken soup
3 Tbsp. soy sauce

Bake at 350° for $1^1/_2$ hrs. Put **chow mein noodles** on top to serve.

———— ❖ ————

Keep a thing seven years and you will find a use for it.

HAMBURGER POTATO CASSEROLE

Freeda Lehman

1¹/₂ lb. hamburger (browned and drained)
  Add: ¹/₂ pkg. taco seasoning
8 med. potatoes (boiled,   1 pt. sour cream
  peeled and shredded)   1 sm. onion (chopped)
4 Tbsp. butter (melted)   1 can cream of mushroom soup
2 c. grated cheese   1 can milk
³/₄ tsp. salt

Put hamburger on bottom of greased cake pan or roaster. Combine all ingredients. Pour potato mixture over hamburger. Mix together 2¹/₂ c. **crushed corn flakes** with ¹/₄ c. **melted butter**. Spread crumbs on top of potatoes. Bake at 350° for 45 min. or till warm all the way through. *May be prepared ahead and refrigerated until ready to use.*

MEAT AND POTATO CASSEROLE

Lydiann Stutzman

2 lb. ground beef   ¹/₄ c. chopped onion
2 eggs (well beaten)   2 tsp. salt
³/₄ c. tomato juice   ¹/₄ tsp. pepper
³/₄ c. Quaker oats (uncooked)

Combine all ingredients thoroughly. Put this on top of **scalloped potatoes** in shallow casserole dish. May add cheese or canned soups to the potatoes, salt and pepper as desired. Bake about 1¹/₄ hrs. at 350°. If a sauce is desired to put on top of meat loaf, mix 2 Tbsp. each of **ketchup, mustard** and **brown sugar**, then spread on top before baking.

---- ❖ ----

Why go out on a limb? That is where the fruit is.

BURRITO CASSEROLE
Laura Yutzy

2 lb. hamburger
2 pkg. taco seasoning
2 cans refried beans
2 cans mushroom soup
2 c. sour cream
10 soft tortilla shells
1 pkg. cheddar cheese
lettuce
tomatoes
onions

Brown hamburger (with onions if you wish). Add taco mix and refried beans; simmer for 5 min. Mix mushroom soup and sour cream together. Put half of this in a 2" x 9" x 13" pan. Put meat mixture and torn tortilla shells in layers, then put remaining soup mixture on top. Add some cheese. Bake for 1 hr. at 325°. Add more cheese and melt. Add lettuce, tomatoes, and onions when you serve, also salsa if you wish.

WET BURRITOES
Loretta Kuhns

1 can cream of mushroom
 soup
1 (16 oz.) sour cream
1 pkg. taco seasoning
$3^1/_2$ lb. hamburger
$3/_4$ c. water
1 can refried beans
8 flour tortillas
1 pkg. mozzarella cheese
1 pkg. sharp Cheddar cheese

Mix together cream of mushroom soup and sour cream—put $^1/_2$ in a cake pan. Fry hamburger. Add taco seasoning, water, and beans. Fill tortillas with hamburger mixture and put in pan. Top with remaining soup and sour cream mixture. Top with cheeses. Bake at 350° till hot. Serve with salsa, lettuce and sour cream.

———— ❖ ————

Those who bring sunshine to the lives of others
cannot keep it from themselves.

CHEESY ENCHILADAS
Mrs. Ervin (Edna) Bontrager

MEAT MIXTURE:

2 lb. hamburger (fried)

1 med. onion (minced)

1 pkg. burrito or taco mix

12 flour tortillas

salt to taste

CHEESE SAUCE:

1 stick oleo

4 Tbsp. flour

3 c. milk

8 oz. Velveeta cheese

8 oz. sour cream

Place meat mixture in tortillas. Roll up and place in greased casserole. Pour cheese sauce over top. Bake at 350° till cheese sauce starts to bubble and turns brown. Remove from oven and top with shredded lettuce and chopped tomatoes. Serve at once.

CHICKEN FAJITAS
Inez Yutzy

$^1/_4$ c. lime juice

1 garlic clove (minced)

1 tsp. chili powder

$^1/_2$ tsp. cumin

2 chicken breast (cut into strips)

1 med. onion (cut into thin wedges)

$^1/_2$ each of yellow, red and green pepper

$^1/_2$ c. salsa

12 flour tortillas

1$^1/_2$ c. shredded cheddar cheese

Combine first 4 ingredients, then add chicken; stir for 15 min. in non-stick pan. Cook onions and chicken for 3 min. or till chicken is no longer pink. Add pepper (cut into strips); sauté for 3–5 min. till crisp and tender. Stir in salsa. Top with cheese; roll in tortilla shells and serve with more salsa. Delicious!

———— ❖ ————

Advice is more acceptable if it doesn't interfere with our plans.

TACO CASSEROLE
Leanna Shrock

1 lb. hamburger
1 sm. onion
¹/₂ tsp. garlic powder
1 env. taco seasoning
1 (8 oz.) can tomato paste

1 c. sour cream
1 c. cottage cheese
2 c. crushed tortillas
8 oz. shredded cheese

In a large skillet brown hamburger, remove from heat and drain off any fat. Add onions, garlic powder and taco seasoning. Mix in tomato sauce; set aside. In a med. bowl mix sour cream and cottage cheese; set aside. Place half the chips in bottom of roaster sprayed with cooking spray. Add meat, then red mixture, then white mixture, then meat again. Repeat layers till roaster is full; then add a layer of chips, then shredded cheese. Bake at 350° for 35 min.

TACO CASSEROLE
Mrs. Freemon (Edna) Mishler

1 lb. ground beef or sausage
1 c. sour cream
²/₃ c. mayonnaise
2 or 3 thin sliced tomatoes
1 c. chopped peppers,
  mushrooms, olives, etc.

2 Tbsp. onion
2 c. Bisquick
1 c. cold water
1 c. shredded cheese
taco seasoning

Preheat oven to 375°. Grease baking dish. Brown beef and drain. Mix sour cream, mayonnaise, cheese and onion (reserve). Mix baking mix and water till soft, pat into pan. Layer beef, tomatoes, and peppers in pan. Spoon sour cream mix over top with **paprika** if desired. Bake till edges of dough are light brown (25–30 min.) Makes 1 (9" x 13") pan. Serve with **lettuce, taco chips** and **taco sauce.**

———— ❖ ————

A fellow who keeps declaring he's no fool usually isn't sure.

IMPOSSIBLE CHEESEBURGER PIE

Mrs. Ezra A. Schrock

2 lbs. hamburger
1 c. onion
$^1/_2$ tsp. pepper
1 tsp. salt
1$^1/_2$ c. Bisquick

3 c. milk
6 eggs
pizza sauce
cheese on top

Brown hamburger and onions; add salt and pepper. Spread this in cake pan. Beat eggs, milk and Bisquick until smooth. Pour over meat and bake at 400° for 30 min. Top with pizza sauce and cheese and bake 5 min.

PIZZA POPOVER

Marilyn Schrock

2 lb. hamburger
1 med. onion (chopped)

1 qt. pizza sauce
1 can cream of mushroom soup

2 c. flour
4 tsp. baking powder
1 tsp. salt

4 Tbsp. vegetable oil
1 c. milk

Brown hamburger and onions; add pizza sauce and soup. Bring to a boil; put in roaster then top with cheese and sprinkle with parsley flakes. Make a dough with the flour and milk ingredients. Put on top of meat mixture. Sprinkle with parsley flakes. Bake until golden brown and a toothpick inserted comes out clean.

---------- ❖ ----------

If you're stung by a bee, apply a slice of onion to the spot and hold it there for a minute or two. It does the trick.

BAKED PIZZA SANDWICH
Mrs. Cristy Eash

1 lb. hamburger
1 pt. pizza sauce
1 tsp. oregano

1 can cream of mushroom soup
$^1/_4$ c. Parmesan cheese
(optional)

2 c. Bisquick
1 egg

$^2/_3$ c. milk
8 oz. cream cheese

Brown and drain hamburger. Stir half of pizza sauce and oregano into meat; heat to boiling. Mix Bisquick, egg, and milk. Measure $^3/_4$ of battter into 9" x 9" pan. Pour remaining pizza sauce over batter, spreading evenly. Put 4 slices cream cheese, the meat mixture, mushroom soup, and remaining cream cheese and batter on top. Sprinkle with Parmesan cheese. Bake uncovered until brown in 400° oven (20–25 min).

PIZZA CASSEROLE
Mrs. (Tobie) Esther Miller

1 lb. ground beef
$^1/_2$ tsp. onion salt
1 can tomato soup
2 c. cooked noodles
1 Tbsp. oregano

$^1/_2$ tsp. garlic salt
1 tsp. salt
$^1/_3$ c. water
$^1/_2$ c. cheese (shredded)

Brown the ground beef. Add other ingredients. Top with cheese. Bake in a 350° oven for 25–30 min.

❖

No more tears when peeling onions if you place them in the deep freeze for 4–5 minutes.

DIFFERENT PIZZA CASSEROLE
Leanna Yutzy

2¹/₂ lb. hamburger
1 sm. onion
¹/₂ c. spagetti
1 qt. pizza sauce
1 c. sour cream
3 c. grated cheese (white or yellow)
1¹/₃ c. flour
2 tsp. baking powder
²/₃ tsp. salt
¹/₂ c. milk
3¹/₂ Tbsp. salad dressing
¹/₄ c. oil

Fry hamburger and onion. Cook spaghetti. Mix flour, baking powder, and salt. Add milk and oil; mix well. Press in bottom of baking dish. Top with hamburger, then spaghetti, then pizza sauce. Mix sour cream, salad dressing and cheese together and put on top. Bake at 350° till top is slightly brown and bubbly.

GERMAN PIZZA
Mrs. Daniel Lee Mishler

2 c. shredded raw potatoes
homemade bologna
8 (or less) eggs
8 slices cheese
1 Tbsp. margarine
salt and pepper

Melt margarine in skillet and add potatoes, salt and pepper to taste. Cover and simmer until done. Slice bologna and arrange on top of potatoes. Beat eggs and pour over top; then cheese. Cover and simmer until done. *Note: Any meat may be used in this quick and easy dish.*

---— ❖ —---

*Add a pinch of baking soda to tomato soup or anything with tomatoes in which you want to add milk or cream.
It will keep it from curdling.*

MEXICAN LASAGNA
Mrs. John Hochstetler

1¹/₂ lb. ground beef
1 Tbsp. chili powder
¹/₄ tsp. garlic powder
¹/₄ tsp. red pepper
1 tsp. salt and pepper
1 c. chopped tomatoes
2 c. sm. curd cottage cheese

2 c. shredded lettuce
3 green onions
1 c. mozzarella cheese
1 egg
1 c. grated Cheddar cheese
1 pt. pizza sauce

Brown ground beef, drain; add seasoning and pizza sauce. Cover bottom and sides of a big cake pan with layer of tortillas. Pour beef mixture over tortillas. Place a layer of tortillas over beef mixture and set aside. Combine cottage cheese and egg. Pour over tortillas. Bake at 350° for 30 min. Remove; sprinkle lettuce, cheese and tomatoes diagonally across casserole.

CLASSIC LASAGNA
Mrs. William Troyer

MEAT SAUCE:

2 lb. ground beef (browned)
3 cloves garlic (minced)
2 (28 oz.) tomatoes (whole)
8 tsp. or 1 can tomatoe paste
2 tsp. sugar

¹/₂ c. parsley
2 tsp. basil leaves
1¹/₂ tsp. salt
1 tsp. oregano
¹/₄ tsp. pepper

16 oz. cream style cottage
    cheese

12 oz. mozzarella cheese

16 oz. lasagna noodles

Cook lasagna as directed on pkg.; drain and rinse with cold water. Layer meat sauce, cottage cheese and mozzarella with lasagna noodles, repeating layers till everything is used up. Sprinkle cheese on top. Bake uncovered at 350° for 45 min. Let stand for 15 min.

SLOPPY JOE

Mrs. Roy E. Miller

2 lb. ground beef (browned
   with onion)
1 can tomato soup

1 (8 oz.) can tomato sauce
2 Tbsp. brown sugar
1 tsp. vinegar

HAMBURGER PIE

Polly Farmwald

5 lb. hamburger
4 med. onions

2 qts. green beans
4 (10³/₄ oz.) tomato soup

In a large skillet brown meat and onions; spoon off fat. Put in 2 (13" x 9" x 2") baking pans. Lightly season each with salt and pepper. Add half the beans and soup to each pan. Mix.

POTATO FLUFF TOPPER:
Cook: **3 lb. potatoes** (mash while hot)

Add: **1 c. milk**   **2 eggs**

Add: ¹/₄ **c. butter**   **1 tsp. salt**

Put on meat mixture and top with **cheese**. Bake at 350° for 30 min. Serves 24.

PIZZA BURGER

Mrs. Freeman J. Yoder

1 lb. hamburger
1 sm. onion
¹/₄ tsp. garlic salt
¹/₄ tsp. oregano leaves

1 c. pizza sauce
1 sm. can mushrooms
cheese
salt and pepper

Fry hamburger, onion, garlic salt and oregano leaves together until hamburger is done. Then add pizza sauce and mushrooms; mix and heat. If the mixture seems too thin you may add a handful of oatmeal, this will thicken it a little. Put cheese on top and cover until cheese is melted; then serve on buns.

BARBEQUED BEEF PATTIES
Polly Farmwald

1¹/₂ lb. ground beef
³/₄ c. oatmeal
¹/₄ tsp. pepper

1¹/₂ tsp. salt
1 c. milk
¹/₄ c. chopped onion

SAUCE:
2 Tbsp. Worcestershire sauce
2 Tbsp. vinegar
1 Tbsp. mustard

4 Tbsp. brown sugar
1 c. catsup
¹/₄ c. water

Mix together sauce, pour over fried patties and bake slowly for 20 min.

DOUBLE BURGERS
Mary Esther Whetstone

1 pkg. white crackers (finely crushed)
2 lb. ground beef
¹/₂ c. ketchup
2 eggs

1 sm. onion
¹/₄ tsp. garlic salt
¹/₄ tsp. pepper
6 slices processed cheese (like American)

Combine first 7 ingredients; mix well. Shape into 12 thin patties and place 6 on baking sheet and top with a slice of cheese. Put other 6 patties on top of cheese and seal edges well. Broil about 5 min. on each side. Makes 6 double burgers.

———— ❖ ————

When making meatloaf, first combine all ingredients except the ground beef. The seasonings will be more evenly distributed this way with little effort.

CHILI SKILLET

Mrs. Edith B. Knepp

1 lb. ground beef
1 c. chopped onion
$1/2$ c. chopped green pepper
1 garlic cloves (minced)
1 c. tomato juice
1 (8 oz.) can red kidney beans (undrained)
4 tsp. chili powder

1 tsp. dried oregano
1 tsp. salt
$1/2$ c. long grain rice (uncooked)
1 c. corn (canned or frozen)
1 c. shredded cheese
$1/2$ c. black olives (sliced) (optional)

In a large skillet cook beef, onion, pepper and garlic until meat is brown and vegetables are tender; drain fat. Add tomato juice, kidney beans, chili powder, oregano, salt and rice; cover and simmer about 25 min. or until rice is tender. Stir in corn and olives; cover and cook 5 more min. Sprinkle with cheese, cover and cook only until cheese melts (about 5 min.). Yield: 4 servings.

HAMBURGERS

Loretta Kuhns

3 lb. hamburger or sausage
$1^1/2$ c. white cracker crumbs
3 eggs
2 tsp. seasoned salt

$1/2$ tsp. paprika
salt
pepper

BARBEQUE SAUCE FOR HAMBURGERS:

$3/4$ c. brown sugar
$1/4$ c. Kraft Hickory Smoke barbeque sauce
Mix well. Put on grill.

$2^1/2$ c. ketchup
$1/2$ tsp. mustard
1 tsp. Worcestershire sauce

———— ❖ ————

To speed up hamburger cooking, poke a hole in their centers when shaping. This causes the center to cook quickly and the holes are gone when the hamburgers are finished cooking.

APPETIZER MEATBALLS

Mrs. Freeman E. Yoder

2 lb. ground beef
1 lb. ground pork (or may use all beef)
2 c. milk
2 c. quick oatmeal
$^1/_2$ tsp. ground pepper

2 tsp. chili powder
$^1/_2$ tsp. garlic powder
2–3 tsp. salt
2 eggs
$^1/_2$ c. chopped onions

SAUCE:
2 c. catsup
$1^1/_2$ c. brown sugar
1 tsp. liquid smoke

$^1/_2$ tsp. garlic powder
$^1/_2$ c. chopped onions

Mix all meatball ingredients together. Shape into small balls. Place in a baking pan in a single layer. Combine sauce ingredients and pour over meatballs. Bake at 350° for 1 hr.

SAUCY MEATBALLS

Viola Bontrager

1 lb. hamburger
$^1/_2$ c. cracker crumbs
$^1/_4$ c. milk
2 Tbsp. chopped onion

$^1/_4$ tsp. salt
$^1/_2$ tsp. Worcestershire sauce
1 egg

SAUCE:
$10^3/_4$ oz. cream of chicken soup
$^1/_3$ c. milk

$^1/_8$ tsp. ground nutmeg

Mix ingredients for meatballs. Shape into $1^1/_2$" balls, brown on both sides in skillet. Combine sauce ingredients. Pour sauce over meatballs. Cover and simmer 20–30 min. Serve with mashed potatoes.

———— ❀ ————

Better burgers: for a juicier hamburger, add cold water to the beef before grilling—$^1/_2$ cup for each pound.

POOR MAN'S STEAK OR BARBECUED MEATBALLS
Mrs. Marvin Yutzy

4 lb. hamburger
4 tsp. salt
1 tsp. pepper
1 tsp. saltless herb seasoning
1 Tbsp. liquid smoke

1 c. chopped onions
1 c. evaporated milk
1 c. milk
2 c. quick oats

For Poor Man's Steak: mix and let set a couple hrs. then form patties and fry or put on grill. When done top with brown gravy and bake until well heated.

For Meatballs: form balls and put on greased cookie sheet single layer and bake for $3/4$ hr. at 350°; then put in casserole and top with the following sauce and heat.

SAUCE:
2 c. catsup
1 c. brown sugar
$1/2$ tsp. liquid smoke

$1/2$ tsp. garlic powder
$1/4$ c. chopped onion or
    1 Tbsp. minced onion

FAVORITE MEAT LOAF
Mrs. Floyd (Loretta) Lehman

$2^1/2$ lb. hamburger
5 eggs
$1/4$ lb. white crackers
    (crushed)

$1/4$ c. diced onion
1 pt. tomato juice
salt and pepper to taste

GLAZE:
$1/2$ c. catsup
1 Tbsp. mustard

4 Tbsp. brown sugar

Mix thoroughly, put in pan and bake 2–$2^1/2$ hrs. at 300°. When nearly done put off juice (if any), and top with glaze. Bake a little longer.

MOCK HAM MEAT LOAF

Mrs. David (Katie) Bontrager

1 lb. hotdogs (ground)
2 lbs. hamburger
2 c. cracker crumbs

2 eggs
$^1/_2$ c. brown sugar

2 Tbsp. vinegar
1 tsp. dry mustard
1 tsp. salt

dash of pepper
$1^1/_2$ c. water

Mix together hotdogs, hamburger, cracker crumbs, eggs and sugar. Dissolve the rest of the ingredients in water and add to meat mixture.

SAUCE:
$^1/_2$ c. catsup
2 Tbsp. brown sugar

1 Tbsp. prepared mustard

Spread over meat loaf and bake at 350° for 1 hr.

MOCK HAM LOAF

Loretta Kuhns

3 lbs. hamburger
$1^1/_2$ pkgs. hotdogs (ground)
2 c. cracker crumbs

2 eggs
2 tsp. salt
$^1/_2$ tsp. pepper

GLAZE:
1 c. brown sugar
1 c. water

2 Tbsp. vinegar
1 tsp. dry mustard

Mix and add $^1/_2$ of glaze with meat. Add remaining glaze on top after it is half done. Remaining glaze may be thickened with cornstarch. Makes 1 cake pan full. Bake at 350° for 1 hr.

———— ❁ ————

Fatigue is the best pillow.

PIZZA LOAF

1½ lb. hamburger
¾ c. oatmeal
1 egg
½ tsp. garlic salt
¼ tsp. pepper
1 c. pizza sauce
½ tsp. onion salt
½ tsp. oregano
1 tsp. salt
8 oz. mozzarella cheese

Mix together all ingredients, except cheese. Put in pan, 3 layers meat and cheese beginning and ending with meat. Bake at 350° for 1½ hrs. or until done.

SCALLOPED POTATOES   *Mary Miller*

8 qt. potatoes (cooked
  peeled and shredded)
5 tsp. salt
black pepper
garlic powder
1 lb. cheese (sliced)
3 cans mushroom soup
1 onion (chopped fine)
½ c. margarine
1–2 qt. milk

Layer potatoes in large roaster, sprinkle each layer with salt, pepper, garlic powder and onion. Add cheese, mushroom soup, and 1½ qt. of milk. Bake at 350°, stirring once or twice and adding additional milk as needed.

CHICKEN DRESSING   *Mrs. Harvey (Marie) Hochstetler*

1 lb. loaf of bread (toasted)
2 c. potatoes (diced and
  boiled)
1 sm. onion (cut up)
1 c. celery (cut up)
1–2 c. cooked chicken (cut up)
½ c. carrots (diced and boiled)
4 eggs
3 c. milk
1 qt. chicken broth

Beat eggs. Add milk and broth and pour over the rest, add salt and pepper to taste. Add milk, water or potato water until liquid comes to top of other ingredients. Bake at 350° until it seems to set. Serves 20 people. Enough for 1 cake pan.

DRESSING
Mrs. Freeman (Lydia Sue) Yoder

13 qt. bowl toasted bread (rounded)
3 qt. potatoes (cooked and diced)
1 pt. onion (diced)
4 c. celery
1 c. carrots (shredded)
2 qt. potato water

2 qt. milk
3–4 qt. chicken broth with meat
12 eggs (beaten)
2 Tbsp. parsley
1 Tbsp. seasoning salt
$^1/_2$ tsp. accent salt
$^1/_2$ c. chicken base
salt and pepper to taste

Bake at 350° for 1$^1/_2$ hrs. Makes 3–4 cake pans full.

CHICKEN CASSEROLE
Mrs. Floyd Bontrager

4 qt. potatoes (cooked)
1 qt. chicken broth
1 qt. chicken pieces
1 qt. water
1 lb. noodles (or enough to thicken casserole)

$^1/_2$ pt. carrots
$^1/_2$ pt. celery (optional)
1 pt. peas
salt
pepper
chicken soup base

Put broth, chicken pieces and water in large kettle. Add noodles once it's boiling, also salt, pepper and soup base. Peel skins off cooked potatoes and put them through Salad Master, then add to noodles and chicken. Add carrots, celery and peas. Simmer for 10 min. to get flavor in potatoes. For a quick and easy meal use all canned ingredients.

———— ❀ ————

Before heating milk rinse pan with cold water.
It helps not to scorch so much.

CHICKEN CASSEROLE

Emma Bontrager
Marietta Miller

2–3 c. chicken (diced and
 cooked)
2 c. marcaroni (uncooked)
2 cans cream of mushroom
 soup

4 hard-cooked eggs (chopped)
2 c. milk or combination of milk
 and chicken broth
$^1/_2$ lb. grated cheese

Mix all ingredients and set overnight in covered baking dish in refrigerator. Bake uncovered at 350° for 1$^1/_2$ hrs.

QUICK AND EASY CHICKEN POT PIE

Leanna Yutzy
Mrs. Glen (Ida Mae) Beechy

1$^1/_2$ c. frozen vegetables
1 c. cooked chicken

1 can cream of chicken soup

BATTER:
1 c. Bisquick
$^1/_2$ c. milk

1 egg

Mix vegetables, chicken and soup. Put in ungreased baking dish. Pour batter over this mixture and bake at 400° for 30 min. or until golden brown and bubbly at the edges.

— ❖ —

When you want to boil eggs crack them very lightly first.
They will peel a lot easier.

— ❖ —

If you were born lucky, even your rooster would lay eggs.

CHICKEN CLUB BRUNCH RING

Mary Sue Yoder

1 c. mayonnaise
2 Tbsp. Dijon mustard
2 Tbsp. fresh parsley (or use dry)
1 Tbsp. onion (finely chopped)
4 slices bacon (crisply cooked and chopped)
1 (10 oz.) can chunk white chicken (drained and flaked)
1 c. (4 oz.) Swiss cheese (shredded and divided)
2 pkg. crescent rolls
1–2 plum tomatoes (thinly sliced)
1 med. red (or green) bell pepper
2 c. shredded lettuce

Preheat oven to 375°. Combine mayonnaise and mustard. Snip parsley, chop onion and add to mayonnaise mixture; mix well. Combine chicken, bacon, $1/4$ c. cheese and $1/3$ c. mayonnaise; mix well. Separate crescent rolls into 16 triangles, arrange in a circle with wide ends overlapping in the center and points toward the outside (3" opening in center). Scoop chicken mixture evenly onto widest end of each triangle. Bring outside points of triangle up over filling and tuck under wide ends of dough at center of ring. Slice tomatoes, cut slices in half. Place 1 tomato half over filling between opening of ring. Bake 20–25 min. or until deep golden brown. Remove from oven; immediately sprinkle with remaining cheese. Cut around pepper, separate halves; remove membranes and seeds. Fill with remaining mayo mixture; place in center of ring. Arrange lettuce around pepper. Cut; serve and enjoy.

❖

Anything that grows under the ground, start off in cold water—potato, beets, carrots and etc. Anything that grows above the ground, start off in boiling water.

CHICKEN AND DUMPLINGS
Polly Farmwald

Use a large kettle with a tight fitting lid. Remove a qt. of chicken meat from bones, add broth and make gravy.

Dumplings: Beat **1 egg, 2 Tbsp. milk**, ¹/₂ **tsp. salt, 3 tsp. baking powder** and enough **flour** to make a good stiff dough. Drop by spoonful into boiling gravy. Place lid on and let covered 10 min. *It is important that the lid be not removed till done.* Remove from heat. Take lid off and serve. Serves 6.

OVERNIGHT MACARONI CASSEROLE
Mary Miller

2 c. uncooked macaroni	¹/₂ **med. onion**
2 c. cooked chicken	¹/₂ **tsp. pepper**
2 cans cream of chicken soup	**3 Tbsp. butter**
2 c. milk	**1 c. grated cheese**
¹/₂ **Tbsp. salt**	

Heat milk and soup; then add seasonings and cheese. Cool. When cool pour over remaining ingredients. Mix and put in a greased casserole. Let set overnight. Next morning bake at 350° for 1 hr.

POPPY SEED CHICKEN
Mrs. Eli (Mary Etta) Miller

4 lbs. boneless chicken
Layer in 13" x 9" pan.

Mix together and pour over chicken:

1 can cream of mushroom soup	**1 c. sour cream**

Mix and spread on top:

¹/₂ **c. oleo (melted)**	**1**¹/₂ **c. Ritz crackers (crushed)**
1 Tbsp. poppy seed	

Bake at 350° for 45 min.

FINGER LICKIN' GOOD CHICKEN

Mrs. Christy Yoder

4 c. corn flakes (crushed)
1 Tbsp. black pepper
3 Tbsp. seasoning salt
1 c. milk
1 tsp. salt

4 c. soda crackers (crushed)
2 tsp. poultry seasoning
1 egg
4–5 lb. chicken

Mix all dry ingredients together. Mix beaten egg with milk. Dip chicken pieces in egg and milk; then roll in dry ingredients. Lay in a greased pan and bake at 350° until well done.

BARBECUED CHICKEN

Laura Yutzy

1 pt. water
1 pt. vinegar
1/4 lb. butter
5 Tbsp. salt

5 Tbsp. Worcestershire sauce
1/2 tsp. garlic salt
1 Tbsp. onion salt
1 Tbsp. pepper

Bring to boiling point and keep hot while saucing. For 5 chickens.

BARBECUED CHICKEN

Mrs. David (Katie) Bontrager

4 Tbsp. catsup
1 Tbsp. lemon juice
2 tsp. Worcestershire sauce
1/2 tsp. prepared mustard

4 Tbsp. brown sugar
1/2 tsp. paprika
5 Tbsp. water
1/2 tsp. chili powder

Heat and blend ingredients thoroughly. Soak chicken pieces in Tender Quick overnight or add 2 tsp. salt to the barbecued mixture. Dip chicken pieces into sauce and place in roaster. Pour remaining sauce over meat; cover. Bake at 350° for 1 1/2 hrs. or until done.

BARBECUED CHICKEN
Mrs. David Eash

1 pt. water
1 Tbsp. garlic
1/2 Tbsp. Worcestershire
  sauce
1 1/2 Tbsp. sugar
1/4 Tbsp. pepper
1/4 lb. butter
2 Tbsp. salt

Heat till butter melts; cool. Soak chicken in brine overnight. Put on grill. This makes very tender chicken.

BARBECUED LIVER
Treva Miller

1 med. onion (chopped)
2 Tbsp. oleo
1/2 lb. liver (cut in 1/2" strips)

In a skillet sauté onion in oleo until golden brown. Add liver. May roll liver in flour and corn (half and half) and sauté until red disappears from liver. Cover and simmer until liver is tender. *Even if don't like liver you will like it this way!*

CHICKEN NUGGETS
Katie Bontrager

1 c. all purpose flour
2 tsp. garlic salt
2 tsp. M.S.G.
1 tsp. black pepper
1 tsp. paprika
1/4 tsp. poultry seasoning
1/2 c. milk
1 egg (lightly beaten)

Combine flour, garlic salt, M.S.G., black pepper, paprika and poultry seasoning in a plastic bag. Shake chicken pieces in seasoned flour. Combine milk and egg. Dip chicken in milk mixture. Shake chicken pieces a 2nd time in seasoned flour to coat evenly.

To deep fat fry: melt Crisco and heat to 365°. Cook chicken pieces for 15–18 min. Drain on paper towel.

BREADED CHICKEN BREASTS *Mrs. Malinda Yutzy*

Roll **chicken breast pieces** first in flour, then dip in **eggs** beaten with a little **milk**. Roll in **crushed cracker crumbs** mixed with **Lawry's salt** and a little **Italian seasoning**. Pan fry in oil 5 min. on each side or until golden browned.

Fish fillets can also be prepared like this, but omit the Italian seasoning. Adjust each ingredient to the amount of breasts or fish you are using.

STROH FISH *Mrs. Ezra (Elsie) Hochstetler*

4 Tbsp. seasoning salt
$^3/_4$ tsp. salt
$^1/_2$ tsp. sage

2 Tbsp. paprika
1 tsp. red pepper
3 c. flour

Dip fish pieces in milk, then in flour mixture. Deep fat fry at 370°.

PORK CHOP SUPREME *Mrs. Kenny (Ruby) Schrock*

6–8 pork chops
$^1/_2$ c. water

1 can cream of chicken soup

DRESSING:
4 c. bread cubes
$^1/_3$ c. celery (chopped)
$^1/_4$ c. butter (melted)
salt and pepper to taste

2 eggs
1 sm. onion (chopped)
2 Tbsp. parsley flakes

Brown pork chops and place in roaster. Make dressing by mixing all dressing ingredients together. Spoon dressing onto pork chops. Dilute soup with water and pour over chops and dressing. Cover and bake in 350° oven for 1 hr.

ZUCCHINI ROUNDS

Mrs. Leroy (Betty) Yoder

$^1/_3$ c. Bisquick
2 eggs

$^1/_2$ c. shredded cheese
2 c. shredded zucchini

Mix first 3 ingredients real well; then add zucchini. Fry in **1 heaping Tbsp. butter.**

ZUCCHINI FRITTERS

Mrs. Marvin Yutzy

1 c. grated zucchini
1 carrot (finely shredded)
2 Tbsp. chopped onion
$^1/_2$ c. flour

$^1/_4$ tsp. Lawry's seasoning salt
$^1/_8$ tsp. Accent salt
$^1/_8$ tsp. each of salt, pepper,
    garlic salt and onion salt

Mix and let set a little. It will thin down some. Drop by big spoonful in frying pan. Yield: about 8–10 fritters.

CORN DOGS

Susan L. Eicher

1 c. cornmeal
1 c. flour
2 Tbsp. sugar
2 tsp. baking powder
$^1/_2$ tsp. salt

1 egg (slightly beaten)
1 c. milk
2 Tbsp. shortening (melted)
1 lb. wieners

Mix cornmeal with flour, sugar, baking powder and salt. Add egg and milk. Blend in melted shortening; mix well. Dip wieners in batter. Fry in deep fat.

❖

What you don't see with your eyes, don't invent with your tongue.

SUPER SPUDS

Aaron David Miller (Grade 6)

14 potatoes
$^1/_2$ c. butter or oleo
1 c. flour
1 tsp. seasoning salt

1 tsp. salt
1 tsp. paprika
1 Tbsp. parsley flakes

Grease 2 cookie sheet pans with stick of butter. Melt remainder in 1 qt. saucepan. Pare and quarter potatoes lengthwise into large bowl. Drain water. Coat melted butter over potatoes; dribble excess onto pans. In small bowl combine dry ingredients; add flour mixture to potatoes. Toss in bowl until evenly coated. Bake at 375° stirring twice or as needed until tender and golden brown. *Potato Pointer: potatoes soaked in water for 20 min. before baking will bake more rapidly.*

PAPRIKA POTATOES

Delilah Yoder

$^1/_2$ c. butter or margarine
$^1/_4$ c. flour
$^1/_4$ c. Parmesan cheese
1 Tbsp. paprika

$^3/_4$ tsp. salt
$^1/_8$ tsp. pepper
6 med. potatoes (quartered lengthwise)

Melt butter in 9" x 13" pan. Combine flour, cheese, paprika, salt, pepper, and garlic salt; set aside. Rinse potatoes under cold water, drain well. Put flour mixture in bag and half of the potatoes. Shake well to coat. Repeat with remaining potatoes. Place single layer in pan. Bake uncovered at 350° for 50–60 min. or until tender, turning once at 30 min.

———————— ❖ ————————

To prevent potatoes from boiling over, add 1 Tbsp. butter.
A butter wrapper laid on top of the potatoes will do the same.

MOJO POTATOES
Mrs. Ezra (Elsie) Hochstetler

4 c. flour
4 c. crushed crackers
3 Tbsp. salt
1 tsp. paprika

2 Tbsp. sugar
$1/4$ c. oil
1 tsp. onion salt

Mix together. Wash **potatoes** and slice. Dip in **milk**, then in flour mixture. Bake at 375° for 1 hr. Melt **butter** and pour over top when done and sprinkle with **Lawry's seasoned salt**.

POTATO PATCHES
Loretta Kuhns

6–8 finely grated potatoes
$1/2$ tsp. paprika
$1^1/2$ tsp. seasoned salt
$1^1/2$ tsp. salt
$1/2$ tsp. pepper

$1^1/2$ tsp. baking powder
3 tsp. sugar
4 Tbsp. flour
3 eggs

Mix all together. Fry in cooking oil.

HUSH PUPPY POTATOES
Mary Miller

6 lg. potatoes
1 tsp. salt (adjust to taste)
4 egg yolks
$1/2$ c. butter or margarine

$1/2$ c. cheese spread or
    shredded Velveeta
$3/4$ c. flour
cracker crumbs

Dice potatoes, add salt; cover with water. Bring to boil, uncover and boil till soft—but not mushy; drain. Put potatoes back on low heat till potatoes are dry. Place potatoes back on low heat till potatoes are dry. Place potatoes in large bowl and mash with wire whip. Add egg yolks, butter and cheese spread and mix well. Fold in flour. Form into ping-pong sized balls and roll in cracker crumbs. Deep fat fry and serve.

NAVY BEANS

Suvilla Graber

4 c. cooked navy beans
  (drained)
3 dabs butter
5 slices cheese
1/2 c. catsup

1 c. cream
1/2 c. brown sugar
2 tsp. mustard
onion, salt and pepper to taste
ham, wieners or bacon

Mix well. Simmer on stove till hot.

SARAH'S BEANS

Mary Esther Whetstone

3 c. cooked navy beans
1 c. (or less) cream
3 dabs butter
1/2 c. catsup
1/2 c. brown sugar

2 tsp. mustard
onion salt and pepper to taste
cheese
ham, bacon or wieners

Mix all together and heat until hot. Takes 5 lbs. dry navy beans (recipe times 8) to fill big roaster or 8 qt. kettle. Half as much cream is enough cream.

THREE BEAN CASSEROLE

Mrs. Marvin Yutzy

8 strips of bacon
2 onions (chopped or cut
  in rings)
1 1/2 tsp. garlic powder
1/2 c. brown sugar
1 tsp. dry powdered mustard
1/4 c. cider vinegar

1 (16 oz.) can dark red kidney
  beans (drained)
1 (16 oz.) can baked beans or
  pork and beans (undrained)
1 (16 oz.) can green lima beans
  (drained)

Fry bacon until crisp. Drain on paper towels. Crumble and set aside. Place onions, garlic powder, mustard, brown sugar and vinegar in large skillet. Cover and cook for 20 min. over med. heat. Combine beans in 3 qt. casserole. Stir in bacon and onion mixture, blending ingredients. Bake covered at 350° for 45 min.

RUSSIAN EGGPLANT

Fanny Mae Bontrager

1 eggplant
1 c. thin sliced onions

2 c. chopped tomatoes

2 Tbsp. flour
2 tsp. salt

$1/4$ tsp. black pepper
1 c. sour cream

Cut up peeled eggplant and boil or steam until barely soft (8 min.); drain. In 9" x 13" pan alternate eggplant, onions and tomatoes. Sprinkle with flour, salt and pepper mixed together. Spoon sour cream over top. Bake at 350° for 45 min.

BREADED CAULIFLOWER

Viola Bontrager

1 med. head cauliflower
1 egg (beaten)
2 Tbsp. flour

$1/2$ tsp. Lawry's seasoned salt
dash of pepper

Separate cauliflower. Cook in covered pan in small amount of water, 4 min; drain. Cool slightly. Beat egg, flour, salt and pepper till smooth. Dip cauliflower in batter. Fry in deep fat heated to 370° for 4 min. or till done.

BROCCOLI AND LIMA BEAN CASSEROLE

Mrs. Edith B. Knepp

1 (10 oz.) pkg. baby lima
  beans
1 (10 oz.) pkg. broccoli
  (chopped)
1 can cream of mushroom
  soup

$1/2$ pkg. Lipton onion soup
1 can sliced water chesnuts
1 c. sour cream
3 Tbsp. butter (melted)
2–3 c. Rice Krispies

Boil together lima beans and broccoli for 10 min.; drain. Add soups, chesnuts and sour cream. Top with butter and Rice Krispies. Bake at 350° for 45 min.

BAKED CUSHAW

Fanny Mae Bontrager

1 qt. peeled, cubed cushaw
   pumpkin (crookneck)
4 wieners
$^1/_2$ stick butter
2 Tbsp. flour
$^1/_2$ c. minced onion

1 tsp. paprika
1 tsp. salt
$^1/_4$ tsp. black pepper
$^1/_2$ tsp. chili powder
$^3/_4$ c. creamy milk

Boil or steam cushaw until soft. Grind wieners and place in 8"
glass baking dish. Melt butter in med. size skillet; stir in flour and
onions. Cover; stir occasionally till onions are clear. Add seasonings and milk. Allow to bubble. Place cushaws in layer over wieners.
Cover with gravy. Bake uncovered at 325° for 20 min.

HUSH PUPPIES

Mrs. Marvin Yutzy

1 c. flour
1 c. cornmeal
4 tsp. baking powder
1 tsp. salt
$^1/_2$ tsp. garlic powder
   (optional)

1 egg
$^2/_3$ c. buttermilk or sweet milk
$^1/_2$ c. onions (finely chopped)

Mix together, drop by teaspoonful in hot fat or oil. Fry, turning
frequently until a golden brown (3–5 min.).

———— ❀ ————

*To make your own tartar sauce for fish, mix relish
with salad dressing, about half and half.*

AUTUMN GARDEN STEW
Fanny Mae Bontrager

1 1/2 c. potatoes (sliced or cubed)
1 c. each sliced or diced carrots, chopped celery, snapped green beans, lima beans
1/2 c. each onions, cabbage, tomatoes
1 c. water
1–2 c. cooked (canned) chicken or beef
2 Tbsp. cornstarch
1/2 Tbsp. salt
1 Tbsp. cheese powder
1/8 tsp. black pepper or basil

Bring to a boil in heavy pan with tight fitting lid and hold on vegetables and water. Low flame 15 min. or until vegetables are done. Add meat and rest of ingredients, making paste of cornstarch with some water. Mix well and bring to boil. Remove from heat and hold 10–15 min. covered, to blend flavors.

BAKED CABBAGE
Mrs. Marvin Yutzy

1 med. head of cabbage
1 Tbsp. sugar
2 Tbsp. flour
1 c. cream or evaporated milk
salt and pepper to taste
2 or 3 slices of bacon

Shred cabbage and place in buttered casserole. Mix sugar, flour, and cream thoroughly, add salt and pepper. Pour over cabbage, place slices of bacon on top. Bake at 350° until cabbage is tender. May also add cheese. You can put cabbage in a saucepan and bring to boil until almost tender and then drain and put in casserole and add some sauce.

Remember this: very little is needed to make a happy life.

SUPER SUMMER SAVORY STIR-FRY

Fanny Mae Bontrager

2 c. zucchini (thinly sliced or shredded)
$1/2$ c. onions (chopped)
$1/2$ c. celery (thinly sliced)
$1/2$ c. cabbage (shredded)
$1/2$ c. frozen peas
$1/2$ c. green beans (chopped fine)
$1/2$ c. broccoli (chopped)
$1/2$ c. thin sliced sweet pepper
hot corn oil
seasoning
1 c. cubed cheese, ham or pork (if meat is used have hot)

Choose several vegetables to go with the zucchini. Heat oil in skillet. Use one tablespoon oil per 2 cups vegetables. Fry at least 10 min. stirring frequently. Season with salt, pepper and seasoned salt. Stir in cheese or meat. Serve immediately.

CASSEROLE SAUCE MIX

Mrs. Marvin Yutzy

2 c. nonfat dry milk
$3/4$ c. cornstarch
$1/4$ c. chicken base
2 Tbsp. dried onion flakes
1 tsp. dried thyme
1 tsp. dried basil
$1/2$ tsp. pepper

Combine all ingredients and store in airtight container. To substitute for 1 can of condensed soup, mix $1/3$ c. of the dry mix with $1^1/4$ c. water in a saucepan. Cook and stir until thickened. Add fresh or canned mushrooms to sauce if desired.

———— ❁ ————

In youth we learn; in age we understand.

CHILI CORN BREAD CASSEROLE

Fanny Mae Bontrager

1/4 c. onions (chopped)
1 pt. canned hamburger
  (or 1 lb. raw)
1 c. water

1 c. spaghettti sauce
1 c. cooked pinto beans
1/2 c. mushrooms (canned)

BATTER:

1 c. cornmeal
1 c. flour
4 tsp. baking powder
1/4 c. sugar

1 egg
1/4 tsp. salt
1/4 c. soft shortening or oil
1 c. milk

Heat onions with hamburger in skillet, add spaghetti sauce, beans and mushrooms and allow to heat while mixing corn bread batter. Spread batter in equivalent of 9" x 13" cake loaf pan. Add water to hamburger mixture and spoon over corn bread. Bake 45 min. in moderate oven. Top with grated cheese. Serve with cole slaw.

HAMBURGER BROWN RICE CASSEROLE

Fanny Mae Bontrager

1 lb. brown rice
5 c. water

3–4 lbs. hamburger
1 can cream of celery soup

Put rice and water in 4 qt. roasting pan. Cover and place in 350° oven. Fry 16 hamburger patties. Drain and arrange over rice which is cooking. Add soup. Bake a total of 1 hr. Serves 16.

A smile is understood by all languages.

TATOR TOT CASSEROLE
Loretta Kuhns

4 lbs. hamburger
1 pkg. taco seasoning
4 lbs. frozen vegetables
2 pkgs. tator tots
Velveeta cheese
1 can cream of mushroom soup
2 c. milk

Fry hamburger with taco seasoning. Add mushroom soup and milk and a couple slices cheese, salt and pepper. Put in large casserole, put vegetables on meat, add a layer of cheese slices. Put tator tots on top. Bake at 350° 1^1/$_2$–2 hrs.

HAMBURGER DINNER
Mary Miller

2 lb. hamburger
salt
pepper
8 oz. cream cheese
^{1}/$_2$ c. catsup
^{1}/$_4$ c. milk
1 can cream of mushroom soup
   (optional)
biscuits (any recipe)

Brown hamburger and onions, season with salt and pepper. Add cream cheese, catsup, milk and cream of mushroom if desired. Place in casserole or cake pan, top with biscuits. Bake at 350° till biscuits are browned.

DUTCH AND GRAVY
Mrs. Mervin C. Miller

3 Tbsp. flour
3 eggs
1^1/$_2$ c. milk

Put flour in a bowl, then eggs; add milk stirring slowly. Put on a frying pan; stir every once in a while.

GRAVY:

1 pt. tomato juice
1 pt. water
^{1}/$_2$ c. flour
water

Put tomato juice and 1 pt. water together and heat to boiling point; then put together your thickening of flour and water, stir into tomato juice. Gravy is good to eat with white crackers. A simple and quick supper. Serves about 4 people.

Recipe Exchange

I didn't have potatoes, so I substitued rice,
I didn't have paprika, so I used another spice.
I didn't have tomato sauce, so I used tomato paste,
A whole can—not a half can—I don't believe in waste.
A friend gave me the recipe,
She said you couldn't beat it.
There must be something wrong with her—
I couldn't even eat it.

—*Author Unknown*

Soups, Salads & Dressings

CHILI SOUP

Mrs. Harley H. Lambright

2 lbs. ground beef
3 med. onions
1 qt. chili beans

2 qt. water
1 qt. tomato juice
1 tsp. chili powder

Fry hamburger with salt, pepper and onions. Chop hamburger with food chopper and add to other juice. Heat and serve.

CHILI SOUP

Mrs. David Eash

10–12 lbs. hamburger
12 qt. tomato juice
3 qt. red kidney beans or
 chili beans
1 qt. onions (fry with meat)
4 Tbsp. chili powder
$^1/_2$ tsp. red pepper (may use
 black)

1 pkg. taco seasoning
1 c. pickle relish
salt and pepper to taste
2 c. brown sugar
2 c. clear jel
1 qt. water

Fry meat with onions; drain. Stir in rest of ingredients. Just before it boils add brown sugar, clear jel and water. Stir these 3 together first. May add Chili-O-Mix and omit taco seasoning. Make it to suit your taste.

CHILI SOUP

Velda Kuhns

2 lbs. hamburger
1 med. onion
1 qt. tomato juice
1 qt. water

1 can chili beans
2 tsp. salt
1 Tbsp. chili powder
$^3/_4$ c. brown sugar

Fry hamburger and onions. Heat and serve with crackers. Makes a good meal.

———— ❖ ————

When making soup remember the maxim: "Soup boiled is soup spoiled." The soup should be cooked gently and evenly.

CHILI SOUP
Mrs. John Hochstetler

6 qt. tomato juice
4 lbs. meat (browned with
   3 or 4 chopped onions)
salt to taste

1 tsp. red pepper
5 Tbsp. chili powder
1 c. brown sugar

Mix all together in large pot and heat to serving temperature.

CHILI SOUP TO CAN
Mrs. Daniel (Martha) Miller

6 qt. tomato juice
6 qt. water
3 qt. browned hamburger
$1^1/_2$ c. onions
3 Tbsp. dry celery leaves

$^1/_3$ c. salt
1 tsp. black pepper
3 c. brown sugar
2 Tbsp. chili powder

In 6 qt. kettle thicken 3 qt. juice with 2 cups Permo Flo and some water. Cook 3–4 min. Brown hamburger with onions. Heat rest of juice and water then mix everything together. Put in jars and pressure process 10 lbs. for 30 min. Yield: 14 qt.

TACO SOUP
Mrs. Ezra (Elsie) Hochstetler
Mrs. David (Marlene) Miller

1 lb. ground beef
1 sm. onion
$1^1/_2$ qt. tomato juice
1 pkg. ($^1/_4$ c.) taco seasoning
1 pt. corn

15 oz. can chili beans
$^1/_4$ c. sugar (optional)
cheddar cheese
sour cream
corn chips

Brown beef and onion together. Add tomato juice, seasoning, sugar, corn and chili beans; cook all together. Serve over corn chips, sprinkle with grated cheese. Then add a spoonful of sour cream.

CHILLY DAY STEW
Mary Esther Whetstone

1 lg. carrot
2 onions
1 qt. potatoes (peeled
  and chunked)

2 Tbsp. rice
2 Tbsp. macaroni
1 tsp. salt
1 pt. cream or butter and milk

Into a kettle of boiling water chip carrot. While it is cooking, clean and chop onions and prepare potatoes and add to stew. Add rice, macaroni, 1 tsp. salt and enough water to cover. Cook slowly until tender. When ready to serve add cream or substitute butter and milk. Mix thoroughly, but do not boil again. Serve with crackers or toast.

CHUNKY BEEF SOUP
Lydia Mae Bontrager
Treva Miller

2¹/₂ gal. water
³/₄ c. beef base
2 qt. beef broth
¹/₂ c. butter
4 qt. tomato juice
1³/₄ c. sugar
¹/₄ c. salt
4 qt. carrots (chopped)

2 qt. green beans
3 qt. peas
4 qt. potatoes (chopped)
2 qt. flour
8 lbs. hamburger
2 lg. onions
salt and pepper

Heat till boiling: water, beef base, and broth, butter, tomato juice, sugar and salt. Add to mixture 2 scant qt. flour; add enough water to thicken soup. Fry hamburger with salt, pepper, and onions. Mix to soup. Cook vegetables separately then add to mixture. Cold pack 2 hrs., or pressure cook 1 hr. at 10 lbs. pressure. Makes 30 qt.

———— ❖ ————

If the soup tastes very salty, a raw piece of potato placed in the pot will absorb the salt.

———— ❖ ————

Scissors are a great convenience for cutting celery and herbs.

CABBAGE AND BEEF SOUP

Ervin Jay Miller

2 lb. lean ground beef
1 tsp. garlic salt
$^1/_4$ tsp. pepper
4 celery stalks (chopped)
1 med. head cabbage
(chopped)
2 (16 oz.) cans kidney beans
(undrained)
2 qt. tomato juice
2 qt. stew tomatoes
2 Tbsp. beef base (optional)
chopped fresh parsley

In 6 qt. kettle brown beef. Add all remaining ingredients. Bring to boil. Reduce heat and simmer, covered, 1 hr. Garnish with parsley. Yield: 6 qt.

TURKEY CHOWDER SOUP

Andrew Ray Miller (Grade 8)

2 turkey wings or 2–3 c.
turkey meat plus 4 c.
water or broth
2 tsp. salt
1 med. onion (chopped)
1 c. carrots (diced)
1 c. celery (chopped)
1 c. potatoes (chopped)
6 Tbsp. flour
2 c. milk
4 Tbsp. butter
1 c. cheese (shredded)
salt and pepper to taste

Place turkey wings in 3 qt. saucepan and cover with water. Add salt and onion. Bring to boil. Simmer for $2^1/_2$ hrs. or until done. Remove meat; cut into small pieces. Save broth equal to 4 c. water, add water if necessary. Add vegetables to broth water; cook approx. 20 min. Blend milk into flour until smooth. Stir into broth/vegetable mixture along with butter. Cook over med. heat stirring constantly until thick. Season with salt and pepper to taste. Add meat and cheese when soup is done cooking. Makes approx. 13 cups.

❀

Veggie how tos: tomatoes can be frozen if you plan to stew them or use them for cooking. When boiling corn, add sugar instead of salt. Salt toughens the corn.

TUNA-VEGETABLE CHOWDER

Mrs. John (Edith) Hochstetler

2 c. cauliflower   1 c. celery (diced)
1 c. carrots (diced)

Cook till tender, then add milk and heat to almost boiling again. Season with **celery salt, black pepper, soup base, spike or veg. salt.** Thicken a little. Add **1 or 2 cans tuna,** or to suit your taste. Add enough **Velveeta cheese** to color it a bit. Serve with **crackers.**

CREAM OF BROCCOLI AND CHEESE SOUP

Mrs. Eli H. Hochstetler

2 c. celery (chopped)   2 c. whole milk
1 c. onion (finely chopped)   1 can cream of chicken soup
2 c. broccoli (chopped) $1/2$ tsp. salt
1 c. cottage cheese $1/8$ tsp. white pepper

Cook celery, onion and broccoli in small amount of water. Whip up cottage cheese with egg beater, slowly add milk and continue beating. Add soup; blend; add to undrained vegetables. Season as desired. Heat to serving temperature. Do not boil.

CAULIFLOWER SALAD

Emma Bontrager

1 head lettuce $1/2$ c. onion (chopped)
1 head cauliflower   1 lb. fried bacon

2 c. salad dressing $1/2$ c. Parmesan cheese
$1/2$ c. sugar

CAULIFLOWER SALAD
Mrs. Naomi Miller

1 lg. head cauliflower
6 slices bacon (diced and fried)

1 sm. head broccoli
2 c. shredded Cheddar cheese

DRESSING:
1 c. sour cream
1 c. salad dressing

$^1/_2$ c. sugar
1 tsp. salt

Pull apart cauliflower and broccoli in small bits. Add bacon and cheese. Pour sauce over all and mix. This can be fixed the day before but do not add sauce until ready to serve.

BROCCOLI SALAD

$^1/_2$ head cauliflower
2 bunches broccoli
1 pepper

$^1/_2$ med. onion
$^1/_2$ c. County Line cheese (diced)

DRESSING:
1 c. sour cream
1 c. salad dressing

$^1/_2$ c. sugar
$^1/_2$ tsp. salt

SALAD
Polly Farmwald

2 bunches broccoli
1 head cauliflower

County Line cheese

DRESSING:
1 c. sour cream
1 c. salad dressing
$^1/_2$ c. sugar

1 tsp. salt
1 tsp. celery seed (optional)

Chop vegetables, cube cheese and toss. Mix dressing ingredients and stir. Chill and serve.

COLD SLAW

Marietta Miller
Sarah Yoder

1 head cabbage
1 head broccoli
1 sm. onion
2 med. carrots

1 pepper
1¹/₂ lb. fried bacon
8 oz. shredded cheese

SAUCE:
2 c. salad dressing
1 c. sugar
1 tsp. salt

1 tsp. vinegar
2 tsp. celery seed

SEVEN LAYER SALAD

Mrs. William J. Troyer

1 head lettuce (diced)
¹/₂ c. celery (diced)
¹/₄ c. onion (diced)
¹/₂ c. green peppers (diced)
1 can peas

2 c. salad dressing
2 Tbsp. brown sugar
¹/₂ c. grated Colby cheese
bacon (fried and crumbled)

Layer first 6 ingredients in salad bowl, sprinkle brown sugar over; cover; let stand overnight or 6 hrs. Before serving, sprinkle with cheese and bacon.

PEA SALAD

Leanna Shrock

1 med. head lettuce (cut up)
1 lb. crisply fried bacon
   (broken)
1 pt. frozen peas (thawed)

1 pt. salad dressing
1 c. shredded Swiss cheese
onion (chopped)

Mix peas, bacon bits, eggs, onions and salad dressing. Spread on top of lettuce and sprinkle with cheese.

TACO SALAD
Lillian Mast

1/2 c. salad oil
1/2 c. vinegar
1 1/2 c. sugar
1/2 c. ketchup
1/2 tsp. celery salt
1/2 tsp. paprika
1/8 tsp. black pepper
1 sm. onion

1 head lettuce
1 c. grated cheese
3 tomatoes
1 lb. hamburger
1 pkg. Doritos
green peppers
radishes

For the dressing, combine the first 7 ingredients and stir over low heat until sugar is melted. Cool. Brown onion and hamburger together. In a Fix 'n Mix bowl add the remaining ingredients, plus the hamburger and onion. Just before serving, add the Doritos and dressing and toss all together.

TACO SALAD
Catherine Bontrager

1 lb. hamburger (fried and cooled slightly)
1 lg. tomato (chopped)
1 med. onion (cut fine)
1 med. can kidney beans (drained)

1/2 lb. cheese (grated)
1 head lettuce (torn in pieces)
8 oz. pkg. taco flavored corn chips

Mix together then add Mexican dressing.

DRESSING:

1 med. onion (finely chopped)
1 c. sugar
1 tsp. salt
1/2 tsp. pepper

1 tsp. celery seed
3 tsp. prepared mustard
1/3 c. vinegar
1 c. oil
2 Tbsp. salad dressing

3 batches equal 1 Fix 'n Mix bowl full.

HILLBILLY CORN BREAD SALAD

Mrs. Katie Hochstetler

1 pan corn bread
3–4 c. pinto beans (drain
  some of them)
1 lg. onion

2 c. tomatoes
2 lbs. bacon (browned, drained
  and crumbled)
cucumbers

DRESSING:
2 c. mayonnaise

1 c. pickle juice

Break corn bread into small pieces and put in a pan. Pour the beans over bread, then add peppers, onions, tomatoes, bacon, then cucumbers (not canned pickles). Pour dressing on top. Wait 15–20 min. to serve!

PICKLED RED BEET SALAD

Fanny Mae Bontrager

1 pt. canned pickled red
  beets (drained and diced)
1 hard cooked egg (chopped)
$^1/_4$ c. chopped onions (green
  if available)

$^1/_2$ c. dry wagon wheel pasta
  (cooked and cooled)
$^1/_3$ c. mayonnaise
1 tsp. prepared mustard
$^1/_4$–$^1/_2$ tsp. seasoned salt to taste

Combine all ingredients in bowl and mix thoroughly. May be served immediately.

———— ❖ ————

Peel onions under water or in a draft to prevent "crying".

POTATO SALAD

Mary Miller
Mrs. Elmer Hochstetler

12 c. cooked potatoes
12 eggs
1^1/$_2$ c. celery (chopped)
1^1/$_2$ c. onions (chopped)
3 c. salad dressing

3 Tbsp. vinegar
3 Tbsp. mustard
4 tsp. salt
^{1}/$_2$ c. milk
1–2 c. sugar

Cook potatoes and eggs. Peel and chill. Put through Salad Master; add celery and onions. Mix remaining ingredients in separate bowl, then pour over potatoes and stir only enough to mix. Best when mixed the day before. Yield: 3 qt.

OVERNIGHT POTATO SALAD

Mrs. Amos Beechy

12 c. shredded potatoes
  (6 qt. kettle full, cooked)
12 hard-boiled eggs
  (shredded)
1^1/$_2$ c. celery

3 c. Miracle Whip salad dressing
3 Tbsp. mustard
3 Tbsp. cider vinegar
4 tsp. salt
2 c. sugar

Mix and let stand overnight. Makes a Fix 'n Mix bowl ^{3}/$_4$ full.

———— ❖ ————

If your hands smell from handling onions or fish, rub
toothpaste on them and wash with soap. The smell is gone.

———— ❖ ————

Keep your words soft and sweet, you never know when
you'll have to eat them.

POTATO SALAD

Mrs. Perry A. Bontrager

12 c. potatoes
1/2 med. onion (chopped)
2 c. celery (diced)

12 hard-boiled eggs
3 c. cooked macaroni (with salt)
1 c. shredded carrots (optional)

DRESSING:
3 c. salad dressing
6 Tbsp. mustard
2 tsp. salt

2¹/₂ c. white sugar
¹/₄ c. vinegar
¹/₂ c. canned milk (optional)

Cook potatoes and put through Salad Master, (important to shred rather than cube). Mix all together and chill. Best when mixed a day before serving. Makes about 1 gal. or fills Tupperware Fix 'n Mix bowl. Handy recipe to use to take to funerals.

EGG SALAD (FOR CHURCH)

Mrs. Paul Whetstone

10 doz. eggs (hard-boiled)
¹/₂ gal. potatoes (cooked)
1 qt. onions (chopped)

2 qt. celery (cut fine)
5 lb. hot dogs or bologna

Put egg, potatoes and meat through Salad Master. Add onions and celery and enough salad dressing for right spreading consistency. Add mustard, salt and sugar to taste.

EGG SALAD (FOR CHURCH)

Malinda Yutzy

15 doz. eggs (hard-boiled)
6 lbs. wieners
3 qt. pickles (chopped)

6 med. onions (chopped)
2¹/₂–3 qt. mayonnnaise
mustard and salt to taste

Put eggs and wieners through Salad Master. Add rest of ingredients and mix well. A little pickle juice may be added.

POPPY SEED DRESSING

Mrs. Perry A. Bontrager

1 c. Miracle Whip or salad
  dressing
$^1/_3$ c. vegetable oil
1 c. sugar
$^1/_4$ c. vinegar

1 onion (grated)
1 tsp. salt
$1^1/_2$ c. sour cream
2 tsp. poppy seed

Mix well and keep refrigerated.

FRENCH DRESSING

Mrs. Naomi Miller
Mrs. Sam (Wilma) Whetstone

2 c. Miracle Whip
2 c. (or less) sugar
$^1/_4$ c. vinegar
$^1/_2$ c. catsup
2 tsp. mustard

1–2 tsp. paprika
$^1/_2$ tsp. salt
4 tsp. water
$^1/_2$ c. cooking oil

Mix well and store in cool place. Makes more than 1 qt.

FRENCH DRESSING

Mrs. Edith B. Knepp

2 c. salad oil
2 c. sugar
1 c. vinegar

1 c. catsup
1 Tbsp. salt
1 lg. onion (grated)

Mix thoroughly. Store in airtight jar in refrigerator.

FRENCH DRESSING

Mrs. Perry A. Bontrager

1 scant c. sugar
$^1/_3$ c. catsup
1 tsp. salt

1 c. vegetable oil
$^1/_4$ scant c. vinegar
1 tsp. Worcestershire sauce

Mix well and store in refrigerator. Keep some in fridge during summer and use on fresh garden salads.

FRENCH DRESSING
Katie Irene Miller

2 c. Miracle Whip salad
  dressing
1 c. sugar
2 Tbsp. vinegar
$^1/_4$ c. cooking oil

1 Tbsp. mustard
$^1/_2$ tsp. salt and pepper
1 tsp. paprika
very little garlic

Mix all together. Best if put in the refrigerator 1 hr. before using.

COLE SLAW DRESSING
Ruby Yutzy

1 c. salad dressing (such as
  Miracle Whip)
$^1/_2$ c. sugar
1 tsp. garlic powder

1 tsp. salt
1 tsp. celery seed
2 tsp. vinegar

Blend well, then mix into shredded cabbage. Let set 1–2 hrs. before serving.

TACO SALAD DRESSING
Mrs. Roy E. Miller

1 c. sugar
1 c. oil

$^1/_2$ c. vinegar
$^1/_2$ c. catsup

Mix all ingredients until blended. Enough for 1 (3 qt.) bowl of salad.

POTATO SALAD DRESSING
Emma Bontrager

$^3/_4$ c. sugar
1 c. salad dressing
2 Tbsp. vinegar

2 tsp. prepared mustard
$^1/_2$ tsp. celery seed

THOUSAND ISLAND DRESSING

Mrs. Eli H. Hochstetler

3/4 c. plain nonfat yogurt
3 Tbsp. chili sauce
1 Tbsp. sweet pickle relish

artificial sweetner equivalent to
3/4 tsp. sugar

In a small bowl whisk together all ingredients. Refrigerate until serving. Yield: 1 cup.

BANANA SPLIT SALAD

Mrs. Eli H. Hochstetler

8 oz. cream cheese (softened)
1/2 c. sugar
1 (20 oz.) can crushed
   pineapple (drained)
1 (10 oz.) pkg. frozen sliced
   strawberries in syrup
   (thawed)

2 med. firm bananas (chopped)
1 (12 oz.) carton whipped
   topping
1 c. chopped walnuts

In a large mixing bowl, beat the cream cheese and sugar. Stir in pineapple, strawberries and bananas. Fold in the whipped topping and walnuts. Pour onto an oiled 13" x 9" x 2" dish. Cover and freeze until firm at least 3 hrs. Remove from the freezer 30 min. before serving. Yield: 12–15 servings.

COTTAGE CHEESE SALAD

Mrs. Glen (Ida Mae) Beechy

1 lb. marshmallows
1/2 c. milk
8 oz. cream cheese
1 (#2) can crushed pineapple (drained)

1 c. cream (whipped)
1 qt. cottage cheese

Put marshmallows and milk into top of double boiler. Heat till melted, add cream cheese, stir till cream cheese is melted, cool; then add drained crushed pineapple and whipped cream, cottage cheese. Put in bowl to set.

COOL LIME SALAD

6 c. crushed pineapple 24 oz. cottage cheese
1¹/₂ c. lime gelatin 3 c. whipped topping

 In 3 qt. kettle bring pineapple to boil. Remove from heat and stir in gelatin until dissolved. Cool to room temperature. Stir in cottage cheese and whipped topping. Chill until set. Makes 12 cups.

FRUIT SALAD *Mrs. Glen (Ida Mae) Beechy*

2 c. water ¹/₂ c. cream
2 c. sugar 2 tsp. vinegar
2 Tbsp. cornstarch 2 tsp. vanilla
¹/₂ tsp. salt

 Mix water and sugar. Heat to boiling. Mix remaining ingredients and add to the sugar water. Bring to boil; boil till it thickens. Cool. Add these fruits: **apples, pineapples, grapes and bananas.**

CREAM CHEESE SALAD *Mrs. Glen (Ida Mae) Beechy*

8 oz. cream cheese 2 c. hot water
³/₄ c. jello 2 c. whipped topping

 Whip jello and cream cheese together. Add hot water. Let cool. Add whipped topping.

———— ❖ ————

A young mind is like gelatin. The idea is to put in lots of good stuff before it sets.

FRUIT SALAD

1 c. pineapple	3 c. honeydew melon
3 c. watermelon	2 c. strawberries
3 c. cantaloupe	2 c. bananas
1 c. red seedless grapes	

Clean and cut everything into bite size pieces. Mix altogether adding strawberries and bananas last.

SUNSHINE SALAD   *Mrs. Wilbur (Norma) Bontrager*

16 oz. sour cream	16 oz. cottage cheese
1¹/₂ c. Rich's topping	20 oz. crushed pineapple
(whipped)	3 oz. jello (any flavor)

Mix together and chill.

THREE LAYER SALAD   *Mrs. Katie Hochstetler*

1st **2 (3 oz.) boxes jello (lemon and lime is good)**
  3³/₄ c. hot water
  1 c. drained, crushed pineapple
Let stand till firm.

2nd **8 oz. cream cheese**
  1 c. cream (whipped and sweetened)
Whip together and spread on top of first layer.

3rd **1 c. sugar**
  2 Tbsp. flour
  2 eggs
  1 c. pineapple juice
Cook till thick, put on top when ready to serve.

PINEAPPLE COOL WHIP SALAD
Viola Bontrager

In large bowl mix:

1 c. sugar | 1 lg. can crushed pineapple

In saucepan:

6 Tbsp. cold water | 1 pkg. Knox gelatin

Bring to a boil and pour over sugar and pineapple. Stir. Let set in refrigerator till slightly set.

Prepare:

2 lg. carrots (finely shredded) | 1 c. cottage cheese
1 c. celery (chopped) | 1 c. nuts
1 lg. container Cool Whip | 1$^1/_2$ c. mayonnaise

Mix with mixture in bowl; let set.

DRY JELLO SALAD
Mrs. Sherman (LuElla) Miller

1 (3oz.) box lime jello | 2 c. whipped topping
1 pt. cottage cheese | $^1/_2$ c. English walnuts (chopped)
1 c. crushed pineapple
(drained)

Pour dry jello over cottage cheese, pineapple, whipped topping and nuts. Stir well and chill for 2–3 hrs. This is also good with orange or grape jello.

---- ❖ ----

Never put a cover on anything that is cooked in milk unless you want to spend hours in cleaning the stove when it boils over.

GRAPE SALAD

Mary H. Hochstetler
Leanna Yutzy

4 lbs. red seedless grapes
   (halved, if desired)
8 oz. cream cheese
8 oz. sour cream

8 oz. Cool Whip
1 1/2 c. powdered sugar
1 tsp. lemon juice

   Wash grapes and drain well. Mix rest of ingredients except grapes and mix well. Add grapes and enjoy! Oranges, apples, peaches or sliced fresh strawberries can also be used instead of grapes.

CABBAGE COTTAGE CHEESE SALAD

Fanny Mae Bontrager

6 oz. lime gelatin
6 oz. lemon gelatin
4 c. boiling water
3 c. crushed pineapple
   (undrained)

1 1/2 c. mayonnaise
4 c. shredded cabbage
24 oz. cottage cheese

   Dissolve gelatins in boiling water. Cool. Combine pineapple, mayonnaise, cabbage and cottage cheese. Add cold gelatin. Blend. Refrigerate until ready to serve.

APPLE SALAD

Mrs. David (Marlene) Miller

2 c. water
2 Tbsp. vinegar
1 c. white sugar
   Cook together then add:
3 or 4 apples (red and yellow
   with the peelings)
celery

1/3 c. flour
vanilla

pineapple tidbits
shredded cheese
marshmallows

APPLE SALAD WITH COOKED DRESSING

Mary H. Hochstetler

1 egg (beaten)
1 c. sugar
1 pt. water
2 Tbsp. vinegar

2 rounded Tbsp. flour or
    clear jel
1 tsp. vanilla
2 Tbsp. butter

Mix together and cook until thickened. Cool completely. Fill 3 qt. bowl with **diced apples, celery, nuts, marshmallows, bananas, pineapple** and **seedless** or **seeded red grapes.** Hard cheese bits may be added. If preferred, leave some apples unpeeled for a more colorful salad. Pour dressing over fruit and mix.

VEGETABLE PIZZA DOUGH

Mrs. Leroy (Betty) Yoder

2 c. flour
1 Tbsp. sugar
3 tsp. baking powder

1 tsp. salt
$^1/_2$ c. shortening
$^3/_4$ c. milk

Mix and bake at 350° for 10–15 min. Makes 1 cookie sheet.

VEGETABLE PIZZA CRUST

Betty Yoder

2 eggs
1$^1/_4$ c. sugar
$^3/_4$ c. lard
$^3/_4$ c. milk

$^3/_4$ tsp. sda
1$^1/_2$ tsp. baking powder
2$^3/_4$ c. flour

FILLING:

8 oz. cream cheese
2 c. salad dressing

1 pkg. dry Ranch dressing

Bake at 350°. Makes 2 cookie sheets. Put filling on top of crust. Then put any kind of raw vegetables, cheese or dry meat on you prefer.

VEGETABLE PIZZA

Katie Bontrager

2 c. flour
2 tsp. baking powder
1/2 tsp. salt
4 Tbsp. butter

4 Tbsp. shortening
2 eggs (beaten)
4 Tbsp. milk

Make a stiff dough with the above ingredients. Pat into bottom of pan or cookie sheet. Bake at 350°. Cool.

Mix thoroughly and spread on crust:

11 oz. cream cheese
1 pkg. Hidden Valley Ranch seasoning
1/2 c. Miracle Whip

Top with your favorite vegetables: **head lettuce, cauliflower, carrots**, etc., and **shredded cheese.**

VEGETABLE PIZZA

Mrs. Perry Schrock

2 tubes crescent rolls or
pizza crust
2 (8 oz.) pkgs. cream cheese
and cottage cheese

1 lg. pkg. Hidden Valley Ranch
dressing mix
1/2 pt. cream

Mix all together. Put on top of crust; then add **vegetables, cheese, meats, cauliflower, radishes, lettuce, celery** and **carrots.**

———— ❖ ————

*If you want to be happy
Healthy and gay—
Eat a good meal at
the beginning of the day.*

VEGETABLE PIZZA

Anthony Jay Miller (Grade 8)

CRUST:

1 pkg. (1 Tbsp.) yeast

1 Tbsp. sugar

3 eggs

$^1/_2$ c. sugar

$^1/_2$ c. shortening or butter

$^1/_2$ tsp. salt

5 c. flour

In a small bowl dissolve yeast and sugar in water. In Fix 'n Mix bowl beat eggs, add sugar, shortening and salt. Add yeast water then flour. Stir and knead well. To use immediately, roll $^1/_2$ of dough as thin as you can work with. Place in 15" x 10" x 1" pan. Let rise for 1 hr. Use remaining dough for another pizza crust or butterhorns.

$^1/_2$ of butterhorn recipe or 2 (8 oz.) tubes crescent rolls may be used instead of the above crust recipe. For butterhorns: roll dough in 12" circle, cut 16 wedges, roll up starting with wide end. Let rise 3–4 hrs. or double in size. Bake both at 400° for 15 min. or until golden brown. This dough can be put together and stored in refrigerator to rise overnight, covered.

DRESSING:

1 c. salad dressing or mayonnaise

8 oz. cream cheese (softened) (cottage cheese, sour cream, or another $^1/_2$ c. salad dressing works also)

1 Tbsp. sour cream and onion powder

3 c. mixed, chopped vegetables (green peppers, broccoli, cauliflower, onions, celery, carrots)

1 c. shredded cheese

In a small bowl vigorously stir three dressing ingredients. Spread over cooled crust. Top with vegetables of your choice. Sprinkle with cheese. Press slightly. Cover and chill for 1 hr. Cut into squares. Yield: 20 squares.

————— ❖ —————

A man will follow your footsteps more than your advice.

Favorite Recipes

_____

_____

_____

_____

_____

_____

_____

_____

_____

_____

_____

_____

_____

_____

_____

_____

_____

_____

_____

_____

Harvest Home

Potatoes rumbling into bins
At the end of the day;
Corn cribs bulging with the yield
Mows stuffed full of hay . . .

Pumpkins in a golden heap,
Future pie galore;
Butternuts spread out to dry
On the barn board floor . . .

Rows of pickles, jams and jellies
Stores in cellars now;
Apples, red and juicy ripe
On the waiting bough.

Sudden gusts of wind that put
A thousand leaves on wing;
As autumn harvest now fulfill
The promises of spring.
—Author Unknown

Canning & Freezing

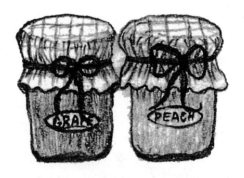

CATSUP BEST

Mrs. Perry (Melinda) Lambright

2 gal. thick tomato juice
2¹/₂ c. vinegar

1 Tbsp. pickling spice mix
2 lg. onions

8 c. sugar
8 Tbsp. clear jel
¹/₂ tsp. cloves

¹/₂ tsp. cinnamon
7 Tbsp. salt

Boil together first 4 ingredients until onions are soft. Put through sieve; put back on stove and boil 1 hr. Mix the rest of ingredients together in a bowl and moisten with water, then add to the juice. Boil 10–15 min. more. Put in jars and seal.

MOM'S KETCHUP

Ida Lambright

4 qt. tomato juice
1 pt. vinegar
2 c. sugar
1 Tbsp. salt
¹/₂ tsp. red pepper

1 Tbsp. mustard
1 Tbsp. cloves
1 Tbsp. cinnamon
1 Tbsp. allspice

Tie cloves, cinnamon and allspice in a bag. Boil 2 hrs. Thicken with **clear jel or Perma Flo** (¹/₂ c. or more) and cook 15 min. more. Put in bottles or jars and seal.

---- ❖ ----

The really happy person can enjoy the scenery when he has to take a detour.

CATSUP
Mrs. Jonas Yoder

4 qt. cooked and strained
   tomatoes
2 Tbsp. salt
3 c. white sugar
2 c. vinegar
1 Tbsp. cinnamon

$^1/_2$ tsp. nutmeg
$^1/_2$ tsp. red pepper
1 tsp. allspice
$^1/_2$ tsp. ground cloves
$^1/_2$ tsp. ground mustard

TOMATO JUICE
Mrs. Jonas Yoder

7 qt. tomato juice
1 c. sugar
3 Tbsp. salt

3 tsp. celery salt
1 tsp. onion salt
1 tsp. garlic salt

   Heat to boiling point and seal hot.

SALSA (MILD)
Lydia Mae Bontrager
Esther E. Eash

6 hot peppers
10 green peppers
14 lb. tomatoes
$2^1/_2$ lb. onions
1 c. vinegar
$^1/_4$ c. sugar

$^1/_4$ c. salt
3 cloves garlic
2 Tbsp. chili powder
2 tsp. oregano
$1^1/_2$ tsp. cumin (optional)

   Cook peppers, tomatoes, onions and garlic till done. Then put through strainer. Cook all ingredients together until hot. Add $^1/_2$–1 cups clear jel or cornstarch mixed with 1 cup water. Makes $1^1/_2$ gal. Put in jars. Cold pack 20 min. For medium salsa add 12 hot peppers. For hot salsa add 24 hot peppers.

SPAGHETTI SAUCE

Fanny Mae Bontrager

1 gal. tomato puree	2 cloves garlic
1 c. sugar	1 c. sweet peppers
3 Tbsp. salt	2 hot peppers
1 tsp. black pepper	$1/2$ c. clear jel
1 tsp. dry oregano	1 c. cold water
1 c. olive oil	$1^1/_4$ c. onion

Quarter tomatoes to fill 2 six qt. stockpots. Cook. Let set 5 min. Drain off clear liquid. Strain and measure juice. Add sugar, salt, pepper and oregano. Chop very fine: onion, garlic and peppers. Cook till soft in the olive oil. Add to tomatoes. Cook 15 min. Can and seal. Steam seal jars 10 min. Yield: 10 pt.

TACO SAUCE

Mrs. Floyd (Loretta) Lehman

20 lg. tomatoes	3 Tbsp. sugar
4 lg. onions	2 Tbsp. salt
4 carrots (chopped)	1 tsp. pepper
3 green peppers (chopped)	3 Tbsp. basil
5 hot peppers (chopped)	1 tsp. cumin
$1/2$ c. parsley	ReaLemon juice

Skin and chop tomatoes. Bring all ingredients to boil except lemon juice. Simmer until mixture is desired consistency. Pour into clean sterilized jars adding lemon juice (1 Tbsp. per pt.). Stir gently. Cold pack for $2^1/_2$ hrs.

❖

If you know that God's hand is in everything,
you can leave everything in God's hand.

PIZZA SAUCE

Wilma Beechy

6 qt. tomato pulp
3 med. onions
2 Tbsp. dried parsley
1 c. cooking oil
1 pkg. Chili-O-Mix seasoning

4 or 5 cloves garlic
1/8 tsp. red pepper
2 Tbsp. Italian spice
1/2 Tbsp. rosemary leaves

Cook onion, garlic and parsley together with small amount of tomatoes put through food mill. Mix altogether. Simmer 1 1/2–2 hrs. Makes 10 pt. Can be made without Chili-O-Mix.

PIZZA SAUCE

Mrs. William Schmucker

1/2 bu. tomatoes
2–3 garlic bulbs
3 lb. onions

4 peppers
1 pt. vegetable oil

Cook all together and put through strainer. Then add:

1 Tbsp. basil
1 Tbsp. oregano
1 1/2 c. sugar

1/2 c. salt
clear jel or cornstarch
(to thicken)

Simmer all together till it comes to a boil. Put in jars and cold pack 15–20 min. or can open kettle.

———— ❀ ————

The only thing that sat its way to success was a hen.

PORK AND BEANS

Mrs. Mervin (Ella) Schrock
Mrs. Glen Hershberger

8 lb. dry beans
$1^1/_2$ lb. bacon
$^1/_3$ c. salt
4 qt. tomato juice
3 c. white sugar
26 oz. ketchup

4 c. brown sugar
$^1/_2$ tsp. black pepper
1 tsp. cinnamon
1 tsp. dry mustard
4 Tbsp. cornstarch
1 lg. onion (chopped)

Soak beans overnight in water, drain and cook till soft in fresh water; drain. Add the rest of the ingredients. Can be used right away or can be canned. Cold pack $1^3/_4$ hrs. or pressure 40 min. at 10 lbs.

PORK AND BEANS (TO CAN) *Mrs. Perry A. Bontrager*

8 lb. dry beans
5 c. brown sugar
$^1/_2$ c. salt
2 onions (chopped fine)
2 c. celery (diced)
1 Tbsp. prepared mustard
5 qt. tomato juice

28 oz. bottle ketchup
2 Tbsp. Worcestershire sauce
2 tsp. chili powder
1 tsp. pepper
2 lb. ham or weiners (diced)
 (or meat of your choice)

Soak beans overnight. Cook till nearly done. Drain and mix all together. Cold pack $1^1/_2$–2 hrs. or pressure at 10 lbs. for 20 min.

———————— ❖ ————————

Add some vinegar to your water when you cold pack.
Then your cans will not need to be washed off.

PORK AND BEANS

Mrs. Glen (Alma) Whetstone

8 lb. dry soup beans
$1^1/_2$ lb. bacon (fried)
$^1/_3$ c. salt
3 c. water
3 c. white sugar
4 qt. tomato juice

4 c. brown sugar
$^1/_2$ tsp. red pepper
1 tsp. mustard
1 tsp. cinnamon
1 lg. onion (chopped)
$1^1/_2$ bottle ketchup

Soak beans overnight or until puffed up. Then cook till tender. Pour off water and put rest of ingredients in and mix. Put in cans and cold pack 3 hrs., or pressure at 10 lbs. for 30 min. Cut up onions and bacon and fry before mixing. Add grease and all to the mixture. Makes 15–16 qt.

BEAN AND BACON SOUP

10 lb. navy beans
2 stalks celery (chopped)
3 med. onions (chopped)
red pepper
salt and all purpose
  seasoning salt

2 lb. bacon or ham
1 qt. carrots (cut fine)
brown sugar

Soak beans overnight then cook. When beans are half tender add rest of ingredients and cook till tender. Then add some brown sugar. Put hot in cans and pressure cook at 10 lbs. for 45 min. Tomato juice may be added. Makes 14 qt.

———— ❖ ————

*Bibles that are coming apart usually belong to
people who are not.*

CHICKEN BOLOGNA (TO CAN)

Mrs. Sam (Wilma) Whetstone
Mrs. Mary Kay Graber

30 lb. chicken meat   1 lb. Tender Quick

Grind 2 times. Let stand 24 hrs, then add:

4 Tbsp. (or less) black pepper   2 Tbsp. chicken soup base
1/2 c. white sugar   1 1/2 lb. white crackers
2 tsp. salt petre   3 Tbsp. liquid smoke
2 tsp. garlic salt   3 qt. water

Soak cracker crumbs in water for a while then it will mix easier. Mix well, put in jars and cold pack, or pressure can it.

CHICKEN BOLOGNA   *Mrs. Floyd Bontrager*

40 lb. chicken meat (cut off the bones)

Add: 1 lb. Tender Quick

Grind twice. First through course blade then through fine blade. Add:

1 tsp. black pepper   1/2 c. sugar
2 tsp. salt petre (optional) 2 tsp. garlic
4 heaping tsp. chicken
  soup base

Mix in:

2 lb. fine cracker crumbs (white)

Then add:

3 Tbsp. liquid smoke with 1 gal. water

Mix well! Cold pack 2 hrs. or 20 min. at 10 lb. pressure. Can be frozen too.

———— ❖ ————

Sorrow looks back, worry looks around and faith looks up.

CHICKEN BOLOGNA

Loretta Kuhns
Mrs. William A. Miller

30 lb. meat | 1 lb. Tender Quick

Grind twice. Let set 24 hrs. Then add:

1 oz. black pepper
$1/2$ c. sugar
2 tsp. salt petre
2 tsp. garlic powder

4 heaping Tbsp. soup base
2 lb. crackers (finely crushed)
3 Tbsp. liquid smoke
3 qt. water

Mix well. Cold pack 2 hrs. or freeze. 1 gal. water can be used instead of 3 qt. This works for turkey bologna also.

CHICKEN BOLOGNA

Mrs. Tobie E. Miller

50 lb. raw meat
$3/4$ lb. Tender Quick
$1/2$ c. salt (not iodized)
1 c. brown sugar
1 Tbsp. coriander
1 Tbsp. dry mustard

1 Tbsp. garlic salt
4–5 Tbsp. liquid smoke
1 Tbsp. black pepper
1 Tbsp. Lawry's 17 seasoning
1 qt. water
$2^1/2$ long packs saltine crackers

Mix Tender Quick with meat and grind twice. Add rest of ingredients with meat. Work in well, pack into jars. Let set 2 days to cure. On third day process 3 hrs. in boiling water bath or pressure cook $1^1/2$ hrs. at 10 lbs. *Note: This recipe uses less Tender Quick and is delicious.*

———— ❖ ————

*Cleaning house while children are growing is like
shoveling snow while it is snowing.*

CHICKEN OR TURKEY BOLOGNA

Mrs. Ora Mast

25 lb. fresh meat	2 tsp. salt petre
1 lb. Tender Quick	2 tsp. garlic powder
1 oz. black pepper	3 Tbsp. liquid smoke
1/2 c. sugar	

Cut meat from bones (uncooked). Add Tender Quick to meat, grind twice. Let stand 24 hrs. Add the above ingredients. Mix well and process as hamburger or bologna.

BOLOGNA (WHEN BUTCHERING)

Mrs. Alvin (Wilma) Beechy

40 lb. ground beef	1 tsp. salt petre
10 lb. pork or sausage	1 Tbsp. garlic
1 lb. Tender Quick	8 lb. cold water
2 oz. coriander powder	5 Tbsp. liquid smoke
1 Tbsp. black pepper	1 tsp. mace

In large tub mix all the meat and other ingredients well. Let cure 24 hours; then grind again. Put in cans and cold pack 3 hrs. or pressure cook at 10 lb. for 30 minutes.

BEEF BOLOGNA

Vera Mae Miller

40 lb. beef (ground)	5 Tbsp. liquid smoke
10 lb. pork (ground)	2 Tbsp. chicken soup base
2 lb. Tender Quick	1 c. brown sugar
1 Tbsp. black pepper	3 qt. water
1 Tbsp. garlic salt	

Mix well. Put in jars. Pressure at 10 lbs. for 30 min.

———— ❖ ————

Life is 10% how you make it and 90% how you take it!

HOMEMADE SALAMI
Polly Farmwald

4^1/$_2$ lb. unsalted ground
  beef
1^3/$_4$ c. water
4 tsp. liquid smoke

1 tsp. onion powder
^{1}/$_2$ tsp. garlic powder
2 tsp. mustard seeds
5 Tbsp. Morton Tender Quick

Mix together. Shape into rolls and wrap in aluminum foil (shiny side out). Keep in fridge for 2–3 days. Then poke holes in tin foil. Put on broiler pan and bake 1 hr. in 350° oven. Take out of tin foil right away. Can be frozen. This is good warm or cold.

CANNED MEAT LOAF
Mary H. Hochstetler

15 lb. ground beef
^{1}/$_2$ c. salt
4 slices bread
36 crackers (little squares)

1 c. oatmeal
3 c. water, milk or tomato juice
4 eggs

Mix well and pack in jars. Chopped onion may be added if desired. Boil 3 hrs. or 10 lb. pressure for 90 min. Note: If meat is seasoned already add only ^{1}/$_4$ c. plain salt or seasoned salt.

SAUSAGE MIX
Mrs. Ora Mast

5 oz. black pepper
32 oz. salt

20 oz. brown sugar

Mix altogether. Use 9 oz. of this mixture to every 20 lbs. of sausage. Add **2 oz. mustard powder, 1 oz. sage** and **5 oz. Tender Quick** to each 100 lb. of meat. Mix altogether, grind, and put in casings. Smoke for one hr. then can or freeze.

——————— ❀ ———————

A man with ambition can do more with a rusty screwdriver than a loafer with a shop full of tools.

SAUSAGE SEASONING FOR CANNING

Mrs. Amos L. Miller

60 lb. ground pork
2 c. salt
2 Tbsp. dry mustard
1 Tbsp. red pepper

2 c. brown sugar
1 Tbsp. black pepper
6 Tbsp. liquid smoke

SAUSAGE (50# MEAT)

Lydia Mae Bontrager

$^1/_2$ c. fine table salt
$^1/_2$ c. Tender Quick
1 Tbsp. accent
3 Tbsp. black pepper
1 Tbsp. red pepper

2 Tbsp. salt petre
$^1/_3$ c. liquid smoke
5 Tbsp. Lawry's seasoned salt
2 Tbsp. sage
$^3/_4$ Tbsp. mace

Mix well. Freeze or can. Pressure cook 90 min. at 15 lb. pressure.

SAUSAGE (60# MEAT)

Lydia Mae Bontrager

1 Tbsp. coriander
1 Tbsp. red pepper
2 Tbsp. garlic powder
1 Tbsp. mustard
2 Tbsp. black pepper
12 oz. (1$^1/_2$ c.) salt

1 Tbsp. chili powder
2 tsp. ginger
$^1/_3$ c. liquid smoke
1 Tbsp. fennel seed
1 Tbsp. accent

Mix well. Freeze or can. Pressure cook 90 min. at 15 lbs. pressure.

———— ❖ ————

*Stop wishing for things you complain you have not
and start making the best of all you've got.*

BRINE FOR BEEF STEAKS
Christina Miller

1 c. salt   1 gal. water
1 c. brown sugar

Heat until clear, then put 1 cup in a quart jar and fill with fresh steak. Process 30 minutes at 15 lbs. pressure in pressure cooker.

BRINE FOR CURING MEAT
Mrs. Daniel (Martha) Miller

2¹/₂ gal. water   1 c. soy sauce
2 c. Tender Quick   ¹/₂ c. liquid smoke
2 c. salt   2 c. brown sugar

This works real well for spare ribs, ham or bacon. Soak 3–4 hrs. depending on how thick slices you have.

CURE HAMS AND BACON
Mrs. Paul Whetstone

1 c. Tender Quick   1¹/₂ c. water
1¹/₂ c. sugar cure (Mortons) ¹/₂– ³/₄ c. liquid smoke

Cut your whole side bacon in fourths to fit in 5 gal. bucket. Fix brine and soak in cool place 5–6 days; rinse. Freeze and slice when halfway thawed.

SMOKED HAM AND BACON
Mrs. Floyd Bontrager

2¹/₂ gal. water   Approx. 4 oz. liquid smoke
2 lb. Tender Quick

Put liquid in crocks, flat plastic tubs or pails. Then put meat in. Put plate with weight on top to hold meat under water mixture. Let ham chunks cure 10 days and bacon only 4 days. Stir every day. Rinse ham chunks 3 times after it is cured before using it. Cold pack 1 hr. without adding liquid. May also freeze.

BARBEQUE BEEF

Wilma O. Schrock

1 gal. meat (use what
  was left on bones)
1$^1/_2$ bottle catsup
2$^1/_2$ qt. tomato juice

1 bunch celery (chopped)
4 onions (cut up)
salt to taste
2 c. brown sugar

Mix all together. Put in cans and cold pack 1$^1/_2$ hrs.

CANNED SLOPPY JOE (FOR 6 QT. BONE MEAT)

Ruth Ann Shrock

2 onions
2 c. brown sugar
4 c. water
4 c. catsup

4 tsp. salt
4 tsp. celery salt
4 tsp. mustard
6 Tbsp. Worcestershire sauce

Pressure cook at 15 lb. for 10 min.

SLOPPY JOES

Treva Miller

20 lbs. hamburger
4 c. onion (chopped)
6 c. celery (chopped)
2 c. brown sugar
6 c. quick oats
1 c. mustard

1 c. vinegar
$^1/_2$ c. white sugar
$^1/_2$ c. Worcestershire sauce
2 Tbsp. salt
1 gal. ketchup

Put meat in large kettle or saucepan. Stir until browned, do not fry. Pour off all juice, cook celery and onions together in pressure cooker and cook at 10 lbs. pressure for 20 min. Use potato masher and mash celery and onions; add to meat. Add remaining ingredients and mix well. Chill and freeze.

MINCE FOR PIE

Mrs. David Bontrager

6 lb. ground beef
4 lbs. raisins (cooked)
4 qt. applesauce
2 qt. grape juice
4 c. brown sugar

2 Tbsp. allspice
1 Tbsp. cinnamon
3 tsp. cloves
4 tsp. salt

Stir altogether. Put in jars and cold pack 2^1/$_2$ hrs.

APPLE PIE FILLING

Mrs. Freeman Schmucker

2 qt. water
4^1/$_2$ scant c. sugar
1^1/$_4$ c. clear jel
1 tsp. salt

3 tsp. cinnamon
3 Tbsp. lemon juice
2 qt. plus 2^1/$_2$ c. shoe string
apples

Bring 2 qt. water and sugar to a boil in an 8 qt. kettle. Mix clear jel with 2^1/$_2$ c. water to make a smooth paste; slowly add to boiling water stirring constantly. After mixtures thickens, add salt, cinnamon, and lemon juice. Fold in apples. Makes enough filling for 6 double crusts. Bake at 425° for 25 min. Cold pack 15 min.

STRAWBERRIES (TO CAN)

Fanny Mae Bontrager

3 c. sugar
3 Tbsp. cornstarch or
Perma Flo

2^1/$_2$ c. cold water
4 qt. strawberries (cleaned)

In 6 qt. pan combine sugar, cornstarch and cold water. Bring to boil and cook till clear. Add berries, may be sliced or chopped. Bring to a thorough boil. Can berries and seal jars. Place jars in steamer and steam 15 min. Yield: 4 qt.

FREEZER CORN

Wilma Miller
Emma Bontrager

4 qt. cut corn **4 heaping tsp. salt**
1 qt. water **³/₄ c. sugar**

Cook lightly for 10 min. then set pot in cold water and cool right away. Put liquid and all in containers and freeze.

TO FREEZE CORN

Mrs. Paul Whetstone

4 qt. corn **4 tsp. salt**
¹/₄ c. sugar **1¹/₂ pt. water**

Cut corn from cob. Boil corn, sugar, salt, and water for 5 min. Stir to keep from sticking. Place kettle in sink of cold water to cool. Then pack the cooked corn in freezer boxes. Use brine to cover corn. Do not drain.

HOMINY

Mrs. Andrew (Carrie) Hochstetler

1 gal. corn **salt**
8 heaping tsp. soda

Soak corn in 2 gal. water with soda for 15 hrs. Cook 4 hrs. or until hulls come off easily when rubbed between hands in cold water. You may have to add hot water while cooking and stir often to keep from sticking to bottom. Wash in several waters then cook again until soft. At this stage if you are canning it, leave 2" space in cans. Add 1 tsp. salt per qt. Process for ¹/₂ hr. at 10 lb. pressure or cold pack 1 hr.

———— ❖ ————

Swallow your pride occasionally, it's non-fattening.

PICKLED BEETS

Mrs. Andrew (Carrie) Hochstetler

6 qt. sm. beets
4 c. sugar
3 c. vinegar
1^1/$_2$ c. water
2 Tbsp. salt

Cook beets. Put hot in jars. Pour boiling liquid over them. Cold pack 10–15 min.

PICKLED BEETS

Mrs. Raymond (Malinda) Yutzy

8 qt. med. sized red beets
1^1/$_2$ c. vinegar
2 pt. beet juice (water from boiled beets)
1 Tbsp. salt
4 c. sugar
^{1}/$_4$ tsp. celery seed

Scrub and clean beets well. Cook in 8 qt. kettle till just tender. Do not overcook. Peel skin off beets. Cover with towel to retain color. Cut up beets to desired size. Bring to boil, vinegar, beet juice, salt, sugar and celery seed. Boil several min. Pack beets in jars and fill with boiling mixture. Turn lids on tight and set upside down to seal. These will have a nice red color.

RED BEETS

Loretta Kuhns

4 c. white sugar
1 qt. beet juice
2 tsp. cinnamon
2 c. vinegar
1 Tbps. salt

Wash and boil beets till tender. Peel, slice and fill cans. Cook juice till sugar is dissolved; pour into cans. Boil cans 10 mins.

GARLIC DILL PICKLES
Mrs. Raymond (Malinda) Yutzy

3 c. sugar	2 Tbsp. salt
2 c. water	3 or 4 garlic buds to each qt.
2 c. vinegar	2 heads dill to each qt.

Soak sliced pickles in salt water 1 hr. Drain. Bring to a boil: water, vinegar and salt. Add sliced pickles and stir until they change color, then ladle into jars. Put flats on jars temporarily to keep pickles hot. Add sugar to the vinegar mixture and bring to a good boil. Pour boiling mixture over pickles. Turn rings on tight. Set jars upside down to seal. Do not cold pack. Makes crispy pickles.

GARLIC DILL PICKLES
Mary Esther Yoder
Mrs. Eli Miller

2 c. vinegar	2 Tbsp. (or less) salt
2 c. water	2 (per qt.) garlic buds
3 c. sugar	2 (per qt.) heads dill

Put a bulb on the bottom of the can and 1 head dill. Fill can with cucumbers and put 2 garlic bulbs and 2 heads dill on the top. Heat other ingredients and fill cans. Cold pack till boiling. Remove cans right away. Approx. for 4 qt. liquid.

GARLIC DILL PICKLES
Mrs. Andrew (Carrie) Hochstetler

sliced cucumbers	6 c. water
2 heads and stems dill	4 Tbsp. salt
8–12 garlic buds	6 c. sugar
2 c. vinegar	

Into 2 qt. can put cucumbers, dill and garlic buds. Boil together: water, vinegar, salt and sugar. Pour over cucumbers. Cold pack. Bring just to a boiling point. Do not cook. Makes 7–8 qt.

DILL PICKLES
Mrs. Paul Whetstone

3 c. white sugar 1 c. white vinegar
2 c. water 2 Tbsp. salt
Put **dill** and **garlic** in your cans with pickles. Add liquid.

REFRIGERATOR PICKLES
Sarah Yoder

onions 2 tsp. salt
pickles $^1/_2$ tsp. celery seed
$^3/_4$ c. sugar $^1/_2$ tsp. mustard seed
$^3/_4$ c. vinegar $^1/_4$ tsp. tumeric powder

Slice layer of onions in bottom of 2 qt. jar. Fill jar with sliced pickles. Make brine with remaining ingredients. Heat to simmer. Pour over pickles while hot. Cool and refrigerate. Shake jar several times. Will keep for weeks.

FREEZER PICKLES
Mrs. Perry A. Bontrager

25 med. cucumbers 2 qt. water
   (sliced thin) $^1/_2$ c. salt
10 med. onions (sliced)

Soak all together 48 hrs. in refrigerator. Drain; add **3 c. vinegar** and **9 c. sugar**. Mix and freeze.

———— ❖ ————

Beat the high living cost; diet to prevent food shortage; take long walks to save your gasoline. Your doctor will think this is good for your health, therefore you can also beat him out of the high cost of being sick!

FREEZER PICKLES
Mrs. Harley H. Lambright

2 qt. pickles (sliced thin)
2 sm. onions (sliced thin)
2 Tbsp. salt
1$^1/_2$ c. white sugar
$^1/_2$ c. vinegar
1 c. water
$^1/_2$ tsp. celery seed

Place pickles, onions and salt in bowl. Cover with water and let set 2–3 hrs. Drain well. Boil together until clear: sugar, vinegar, water and celery seed. Cool, then mix with pickles. Put in freezer containers and freeze.

PICKLE RELISH
Emma Bontrager

1 gal. pickles (ground and soaked in salt water)
1 pt. onions
$^1/_4$ c. salt
6 c. sugar
3 tsp. mustard seed
3 tsp. celery seed
2 tsp. tumeric
2 c. vinegar

Put in cans. Cold pack.

BAR-B-QUE RELISH
Mary Esther Whetstone

1 peck green tomatoes
6 lg. onions
6 green peppers (sweet)
6 red peppers (sweet)
2 qt. water
1 c. vinegar
$^1/_2$ c. salt
1 scant pt. vinegar
4 c. white sugar
1 Tbsp. white mustard seeds
1 Tbsp. celery seeds
1 tsp. cinnamon
1 tsp. tumeric

Grind tomatoes, onions and peppers. Add water, 1 c. vinegar and salt. Cook together 20 min. then drain well. Mix together and add to drained vegetables: 1 pt. vinegar, sugar, seeds, cinnamon and tumeric. Bring to boil and seal in hot jars.

FRESH TOMATO RELISH
Marvin and Ruby Hochstetler

4 tomatoes (coarsely
  chopped)
1 c. green peppers (chopped)
2 tsp. sugar
1 tsp. celery seed

2 med. onions (sliced)
4 Tbsp. vinegar
1 tsp. salt
$^1/_4$ tsp. black pepper

Combine tomatoes, onions and green peppers. Stir together vinegar, sugar, salt, celery seed and pepper. Stir into tomato mixture and chill thoroughly. Keep refrigerated. Drain before serving.

PEPPER RELISH
Mrs. Daniel (Martha) Miller

1 doz. sweet peppers
2 doz. sweet banana peppers
3 hot peppers
$2^1/_2$ c. onions

3 c. vinegar
3 c. sugar
2 Tbsp. mustard seed
5 Tbsp. salt

Chop or grind peppers and onions. Combine with other ingredients. Boil 30 min. Thicken with $^3/_4$–1 c. Perma-Flo. Cook 10 min. longer. Pack in hot jars, water bath 10 min.

CANNED PEPPERS
Mrs. Amos Yoder

green and/or red peppers
2 qt. white vinegar
1 qt. water

2 c. sugar
1 Tbsp. salt
corn oil

Cut peppers in pieces and pack in canning jars. Combine vinegar, sugar, water and salt; boil a few min. Fill jars until peppers are almost covered. Add 1 Tbsp. oil to each qt. Cold pack 5 min.

Candies, Jams & Jellies

COCONUT BON BONS
Lydia Sue Yoder

4 lbs. unsweetened med.
  coconut
2 cans sweetened
  condensed milk

1 qt. Karo (more or less to form
  nice balls)
1 tsp. coconut flavor
2 tsp. vanilla

Mix ingredients together and form into balls; let cool till firm; dip in white chocolate coating. While making balls rinse hands to avoid stickiness.

COCONUT BON BONS
Ruby Mullet

3 (8 oz.) pkgs. cream cheese
3 tsp. vanilla
6 tsp. coconut flavoring

4 lbs. powdered sugar
2 lbs. unsweetened coconut
$1^1/_2$ tsp. salt

Have cream cheese room temperature. Work in salt, vanilla and coconut flavoring. Mix well. In a bowl mix powdered sugar and coconut together; then add to cream cheese; roll and cool. Dip in chocolate.

VALLEY TAFFY
Mrs. Ora Mast
Mrs. Amos Beechy

2 pt. sugar
1 pt. light corn syrup
1 pt. cream

$^1/_2$ c. water
1 Tbsp. unflavored gelatine
1 Tbsp. paraffin (optional)

Put all together except gelatine dissolved in water. Bring to a boil and boil 15 min. Then add gelatine and continue to boil till 250°. Put on buttered cookie sheets and cool. When cool, two people help each other take it in their hands and pull till it turns white. Cut in bite size pieces and wrap in wax paper. Delicious!

PEANUT RIPPLE DIVINITY
Mrs. William Schmucker

3 c. granulated sugar
1/2 c. water
1/2 c. light corn syrup
2 egg whites
1 tsp. vanilla extract
1/2 c. peanut butter chips
1/2 c. roasted peanuts
(chopped)

Combine sugar, water and syrup in 3 qt. saucepan; cook over low heat, stirring constantly until sugar dissolves. Cook over high heat, without stirring, until mixture reaches hard ball stage (260°). Have egg whites at room temperature; beat in large mixing bowl until stiff peaks form. Pour hot sugar mixture in a very thin stream over egg whites while beating at high speed. Add vanilla and continue beating until mixture holds its shape (5–7 min.). Stir in remaining ingredients. Drop by teaspoonful onto waxed paper. Let stand until firm. Makes about 3 1/2 doz. Variations: substitute peanut butter chips and peanuts for pecans and butterscotch chips.

DIVINITY FUDGE
Christina Miller

3 c. sugar
1/2 c. light syrup
1/2 c. cold water
2 egg whites
1 tsp. vanilla
nut meats (optional)

Place sugar, syrup and water in a pan over low heat. Stir only until sugar is dissolved, then cook until a little tried in cold water forms a soft ball. Beat egg whites until stiff, continue beating and pour 1/2 the syrup slowly over the beaten egg whites, beating all the time. Continue beating. Meanwhile, cook the remaining 1/2 of the syrup until it forms a hard ball when tried in cold water and cracks when it hits the side of the cup. Now add this syrup gradually to the egg mixture beating all the time. Add vanilla and beat until mixture is thick enough to pour in pans.

❁

Music soothes a troubled soul.

AMISH FUDGE

24 soda crackers (rolled fine)   1 tsp. vanilla
nuts (optional)   2 c. sugar
1 pkg. chocolate bits $^2/_3$ c. milk

Boil together sugar and milk 3–5 min. at a full rolling boil. Then pour over cracker crumbs, chocolate bits and vanilla, which have been put in a bowl. Mix well and pour into a previously buttered pan as this sets up very fast.

PEANUT BUTTER FUDGE   *Mrs. Ray (Malinda) Yutzy*

2 c. sugar   1 c. peanut butter
$^1/_2$ c. milk

In heavy saucepan boil sugar and milk to soft ball. Take off heat and add peanut butter. Pour into buttered pan.

HEAVENLY HASH   *Susan L. Eicher*

1 lb. white chocolate   1 c. mini marshmallows
1 c. Cap'n Crunch cereal   roasted peanuts or walnuts
1 c. Rice Krispies

Melt chocolate and mix rest of ingredients in with chocolate. Drop by teaspoon on wax paper.

---------- ❖ ----------

Results? Why man, I have gotten a lot of results. I know 50,000 things that won't work.

—*Thomas A. Edison*

CHOCOLATE SCOTCHEROOS

Mrs. Mervin (Ella) Schrock

1 c. light Karo
1 c. Flavorite sugar
1 c. Jiffy peanut butter
6 c. Kellogg's Rice Krispies cereal

1 pkg. Hershey's semi-sweet chocolate chips
1 c. Hershey's butterscotch chips
vegetable spray

Place corn syrup and sugar into large saucepan. Cook over med. heat, stirring frequently, until sugar dissolves and mixture begins to boil. Remove from heat. Stir in peanut butter. Mix well. Add Kellogg's Rice Krispies cereal. Stir until well coated. Press mixture into 13" x 9" x 2" pan coated with cooking spray; set aside. Melt chocolate and butterscotch morsels together in small saucepan over low heat, stirring constantly. Spread evenly over cereal mixture. Let stand until firm. Cut into 2" x 1" bars when cool. Yield: 48 bars.

FROSTY CHOW

Elizabeth Kay Miller (Age 6 months)

1 lb. white chocolate (melted)
1 bag (14.5) crispy M & Ms
1 c. nuts (optional)
2 c. Cheerios
4 c. Chex (rice or corn)
4 c. pretzel sticks

In double boiler melt white chocolate. Butter 4 cookie pans and a large bowl. Measure remaining ingredients into bowl. Do not mix yet. Pour melted white chocolate over top. Blend everything thoroughly. Spread onto pans. Chill; cut into large pieces to store. Makes 5 qt. pail full.

———— ❖ ————

Those who truly wish to sing can always find a song.

COW PIES

2 c. milk chocolate chips
1 Tbsp. shortening
$^1/_2$ c. raisins
$^1/_2$ slivered almonds (chopped)

In double boiler over simmering water, melt chocolate chips and shortening, stirring until smooth. Remove from heat. Stir in raisins and almonds. Drop by tablespoonful onto waxed paper. Chill. Yield: 2 doz.

CINNAMON CANDY
Freeda Lehman

$2^1/_2$ c. granulated sugar
1 c. light Karo
1 c. cold water
red food coloring
$^1/_4$ tsp. oil of cinnamon

Cook together sugar, Karo and water to soft or hard crack (290°). Remove from heat and immediately add food coloring and cinnamon oil. Pour into buttered 9" x 13" x 2" pans. Cut as soon as cool enough to handle. Roll each piece into a little ball.

PEPPERMINT CANDY
Mrs. Ervin (Edna) Bontrager

1 (13 oz.) can marshmallow creme
3 rounded Tbsp. Crisco
$1^1/_4$ box powdered sugar (sifted)
$^3/_4$ tsp. peppermint flavoring

Mix and let stand overnight. Dip in melted chocolate.

❖

The best angle from which to approach any problem is the "try" angle.

TRUFFLES
Vera Mae Yoder

1$^1/_2$ lb. chocolate   1$^1/_2$ tsp. vanilla
$^2/_3$ c. light cream

Melt chocolate; stir until smooth. Meanwhile heat cream to scalding. Remove and cool to 130°; add warm cream to melted chocolate all at once. Beat until smooth, add vanilla, mix well and cool. When cool beat till light and fluffy. Let stand in refrigerator till firm. Roll in small balls. Can dip in white or chocolate dipping. *Variation: roll in coffee, cocoa and powdered sugar ($^1/_3$ c. each for 2 batches).*

PEANUT LOG
Loretta Kuhns

1 c. sugar   1 c. salted peanuts
1 c. Karo   3 c. Rice Krispies
1 c. peanut butter   3 c. Cheerios

Heat first 3 ingredients till melted. Pour over cereals and nuts; mix well. Put in buttered cake pan.

CARAMELS
Ruby Yutzy

2 c. white sugar   1 c. heavy cream
1 c. brown sugar   1 c. milk
1 c. light corn syrup   1 c. butter

Cook all ingredients together slowly. Stir occasionally. Cook to firm ball (248°). Remove from heat. Add 1 tsp. vanilla. Pour into greased pan. When firm turn onto cutting board. Cut into small pieces and wrap in plastic wrap. Pecans may be added with the vanilla. Also good dipped in chocolate.

———— ❖ ————

A lot of people can talk; saying something is more difficult.

MELT IN MOUTH CARAMEL
Freeda Lehman

1 c. butter or oleo
1 lb. brown sugar
pinch of salt
1 c. light Karo

1 can sweetened condensed
 milk
1 tsp. vanilla

Melt butter in heavy saucepan; add brown sugar and salt. Mix well; add Karo and mix well. Blend and bring to boil. Stir constantly till 240°. Pour into buttered 9" x 13" pan. Cool. Cut in pieces and wrap in waxed paper.

SALTED PEANUT CHEW CANDY
Mrs. Mervin (Ella) Schrock

1 pkg. yellow cake mix
$^1/_3$ c. softened oleo

1 egg
3 c. sm. marshmallows

TOPPING:

$^2/_3$ c. corn syrup
$^1/_4$ c. oleo
2 tsp. vanilla

10 oz. pkg. peanut butter chips
2 c. Rice Krispies
2 c. salted peanuts

Mix cake mix, oleo and egg until crumbly and press in bottom of 13" x 9" pan. Bake at 350° for 12–18 min. or until light brown. Remove from oven and immediately sprinkle with marshmallows. Return to oven and bake until marshmallows just begin to puff. Cool. Meanwhile in large saucepan combine corn syrup, oleo and chips. Heat just until chips are melted and mixture is smooth, stirring constantly. Remove from heat and stir in cereal and peanuts. Immediately spread warm topping over the marshmallows. Cool until firm. Cut into bars. Store in covered container. Yield: 48 bars.

Don't you love doing what you're good at?

CASHEW CRUNCH
Mary Esther Yoder

1 c. butter
1 c. white sugar

1 1/2 c. raw cashews
2 Tbsp. water

   Mix and cook till thick and turns light or brown or until it smokes a little. Cook in a large, heavy frying pan, stirring all the time. Put on buttered cookie sheet.

SEA FOAM CANDY
LaVerda Yoder

3 c. sugar
1 c. Karo
3/4 c. water

2 egg whites
1 tsp. vanilla
1 c. nutmeats

   Boil together sugar, Karo and water till firm ball stage (250°). Beat egg whites then add hot mixture slowly to whites. Add vanilla and nutmeats. Whip till sugar dissolves. This takes quite awhile.

PEANUT BUTTER PUFFS
Mrs. Fernandis Graber

36 lg. marshmallows
8 oz. melting chocolate
1/4 c. honey

1/2 c. chunky peanut butter
1 tsp. vanilla
2 Tbsp. butter or margarine

   Line 8" sq. pan with aluminum foil. Cover bottom with marshmallows, tightly packed. Melt chocolate over low heat. Stir in honey, peanut butter, vanilla and butter or margarine. Blend well. Spread over and between marshmallows. Chill and remove from pans. Cut in pieces. Makes about 4 doz. pieces. Store in refrigerator.

---------------- ❖ ----------------

What dainty morsels rumors are. They are eaten
with great relish. Proverbs 18:8.

RICE KRISPY CANDY
Mrs. Mary Kay Graber

5 c. Rice Krispies
1/3 c. butter

2 doz. (or more) marshmallows

Melt butter and marshmallows then add Rice Krispies; pour into well greased pan. Cool.

BUCKEYES
Susan L. Eicher

1 lb. peanut butter
1 1/2 lb. powdered sugar
1 c. oleo

1 (12 oz.) pkg. chocolate chips
1/2 stick paraffin

Mix peanut butter and powdered sugar like pie dough, then add oleo. Roll in balls and chill thoroughly. Melt chocolate chips and paraffin. Dip balls in chocolate.

GRANDMA'S CHOCOLATE DROPS
Miss Rebekah Miller

1/3 c. butter or margarine
   (softened)
1/3 c. light Karo

1/2 tsp. salt
1 tsp. vanilla
3 1/2 c. powdered sugar

Blend butter, Karo, salt and vanilla in large bowl. Add powdered sugar all at once. Mix with spoon then knead with hands till well blended and smooth. Shape into balls or patties. Chill and dip in melted chocolate. This is also good when adding peppermint for mint patties.

❖

Never let the opportunity to say a kind word pass.

BABY RUTH CANDY BARS
Mrs. Leroy (Karen) Miller

1 c. white sugar
1 c. white syrup
1½ c. peanut butter

1 Tbsp. marshmallow creme
1 c. peanuts or nuts
4 c. Rice Krispies

Bring to a boil: white sugar and syrup; remove immediately and add: peanut butter, marshmallow creme and peanuts; stir well. Then add Rice Krispies and press into pan; cut into bars before too cold and hard. Dip bars in chocolate.

PRALINES
Mrs. John (Edith) Hochstetler

2 c. sugar
1 c. buttermilk
1 tsp. soda

pinch of salt
2 Tbsp. butter
2 c. pecan halves

Combine first 4 ingredients. Cook over high heat to 210°, stir frequently. Add butter and pecans. Cook to 230°; stir frequently. Remove from heat. Cool a few min. Beat until thick and creamy. Immediately drop by teaspoonfuls onto waxed paper.

JELLO JELLY
Loretta Kuhns

3 c. water
1 box Sure-Jell

4½ c. sugar
1 lg. box jello

Cook water and Sure-Jell to rolling boil and add sugar and jello. Pour in cans and seal.

PEACH JELLY
Mary Esther Whetstone

Cook peelings and stones of peaches in enough water to cover for 10 min. Drain, take juice and make same as raspberry jelly using the recipe on the Sure-Jell box, or the recipes on the paper inside the box.

BEET JELLY

Mrs. William (Luella) Schrock

6 c. beet juice
$^1/_2$ c. lemon juice
2 pkgs. Sure-Jell

8 c. sugar
6 oz. ($^3/_4$ c.) raspberry jello

Bring to a hard boil: beet juice, lemon juice and Sure-Jell. Add sugar and jello. Boil 6 min. Put in jars and seal. Makes 2$^1/_2$ qt.

QUICK APPLE BUTTER

4 qt. unsweetened apple-
  sauce
5 c. sugar (use less if
  applesauce is sweetened)

2 Tbsp. cinnamon
2 tsp. allspice
1 tsp. cloves
$^1/_2$ c. red hots (optional)

Combine all ingredients in 8 qt. kettle. Bring to boil over med.– low heat. Stirring occasionally, simmer until thick (about 30 min.). To process put apple butter in jars, boil water for 10 min.

HOMEMADE APPLE BUTTER

Leanna Yutzy

6 qt. applesauce
2 c. brown sugar
2 c. white sugar

2 c. Karo
1 tsp. cinnamon

Bake in roaster or baking dish at 400° till it bubbles then reduce heat to 300° and simmer approx. 2 hrs. Stir frequently.

PEACH MARMALADE

Mary Esther Whetstone

5 c. peaches (sliced)
1 sm. can crushed pineapple

7 c. (or less) sugar
1 lg. box orange jello

Cook together peaches, pineapple and sugar for 15 min. Add jello. Cook until dissolved. Pour into jars and seal or pariffin may be used. This is a good way to use up overripe peaches.

ZUCCHINI APRICOT JAM

Mrs. Christy Yoder
Esther E. Eash

6 c. zucchini (peeled, seeded and grated)
6 c. sugar
2 Tbsp. lemon juice
1 (20 oz.) can crushed pineapple (well drained)

2 (6 oz.) pkgs. apricot jello
$^1/_4$ tsp. pineapple flavoring (optional)

Add 1 cup water to zucchini. Boil 6 min. Add sugar, lemon juice and pineapple. Cook 6 more min. Add apricot jello and cook 6 min. more. Seal in jars.

ZUCCHINI JAM

Mrs. Daniel (Martha) Miller

5 c. shredded zucchini
$^1/_2$ c. water

4 c. sugar

Boil together 5 min. Remove from heat and stir in 2 small boxes strawberry jello. Put in hot jars and seal.

1-2-3-4 RASPBERRY JAM

Mary Esther Whetstone

1 c. water
2 c. red raspberries
3 c. chipped apples (Northern Spy are good)
4 c. white sugar

Cook for 10 min. Put in jars and seal.

---------- ❀ ----------

*Happiness is like jam; you can't even spread a
little without getting some on yourself.*

RHUBARB JAM

Mrs. David (Marlene) Miller
Mrs. Sam (Wilma) Whetstone

4 c. rhubarb (diced)
4 c. white sugar

1 sm. can crushed pineapple
3 oz. box cherry gelatin

Cook rhubarb and sugar 12 min. Add pineapple and cook 3 more min. Add jello. Put in jars and seal.

PINEAPPLE JAM

Mrs. Amos Beechy

5 c. crushed pineapple
$^1/_2$ c. water

4 c. granulated sugar

Mix together and boil 5 min. Remove from heat and stir in **1 large box orange jello**. Add marshmallow cream when cold, if desired.

RHUBARB STRAWBERRY PINEAPPLE JAM

Mary Esther Whetstone

4 c. rhubarb (cut in $^1/_2$"
  pieces)
4 c. sugar

$9^1/_2$ oz. can crushed pineapple
3 oz. pkg. strawberry jello

Mix rhubarb and sugar and allow to stand overnight. Boil 12 min. at rolling boil. Add pineapple and simmer 3 more min. Take off heat, add jello, and stir until dissolved. Pour into hot jars and seal.

———— ❖ ————

Waitress: Wanna roll with your coffee?
Man: No, I'd rather just drink it.

Favorite Recipes

Popping Corn

And there they sat a-popping corn
John Styles and Susan Cutter
John Styles as fat as an ox
And Susan fat as butter.

And there they sat and shelled the corn
And raked and stirred the fire
And talked of different kinds of corn
And hitched their chairs up higher.

Then Susan, she the popper shook
Then John he shook the popper
Till both their faces grew as red
As saucepans made of copper.

And then they shelled and popped and ate
All kinds of fun a-poking
While he haw-hawed at her remarks
And she laughed at his joking.

And still they popped and still they ate
John's mouth was like a hopper
And stirred the fire and sprinkled salt
And shook and shook the popper.

The clock struck nine—the clock struck ten
And still the corn kept popping
It struck eleven and then struck twelve
And still no sign of stopping.

And John he ate and Sue she thought
The corn did pop and patter
Till John cried out, "The corn's afire
Why, Susan, what's the matter?"

Said she, "John Styles, it's one o'clock
You'll die of indigestion
I'm sick of all this popping corn—
Why don't you pop the question?"

—Author Unknown

Dips &
Snacks

FRUIT DIP

Loretta Kuhns

8 oz. cream cheese
1 c. brown sugar

8 oz. Cool Whip
1 tsp. vanilla or maple flavoring

Mix and dip apples, oranges, grapes or bananas.

FRUIT DIP

Mrs. Freeman (Lydia Sue) Yoder

8 oz. cream cheese
1 c. brown sugar

1 tsp. vanilla

Mix.

APPLE DIP

Mrs. Leroy (Karen) Miller
Mrs. Sherman (LuElla) Miller

8 oz. cream cheese
1 can sweetened condensed milk

Cook condensed milk in can for 1 hr. Soften cream cheese and mix together while milk is still warm.

CHEESE DIP

Mrs. Perry A. Bontrager

2 lbs. cheese (Velveeta is
best, others work too)
2 (8 oz.) pkgs. cream cheese
1 tsp. Lawry's seasoning salt

$^1/_2$ tsp. garlic salt
2 pkgs. slender sliced ham
several drops liquid smoke
parsley (optional)

Soften cheese and cream cheese. Add rest of ingredients and mix well.

---- ❁ ----

A bad day makes good days even better.

CHIP DIP
LeAnna Shrock

8 oz. cream cheese
2 Tbsp. Worcestershire sauce
1 Tbsp. onion salt
1 pkg. ham (cut up)

Mix all together. Top with parsley leaves.

CHIP DIP
Emma Bontrager

8 oz. cream cheese
1 can chili (with or without
   beans)
grated cheese

Layer in glass pie pan. Bake at 350° until heated. Serve hot with tortilla chips.

PIZZA DIP
Delilah Yoder

8 oz. cream cheese
1 tsp. oregano
$^1/_8$ tsp. red pepper
$^1/_2$ c. sour cream
$^1/_8$ tsp. garlic

Mix together and put in the bottom of a 9" pan. Next day layer the following:

$^1/_2$ c. pizza sauce
$^1/_2$ c. pepperoni (chopped
   fine)
$^1/_2$ c. green pepper
   (chopped)
$^1/_2$ c. onion (chopped)
$^1/_2$ c. mozzarella cheese
   (shredded)

Bake 10 min. at 350° then put cheese on top and bake 5 min. longer. Serve warm with crackers.

———— ❖ ————

Blessed is the one who is too busy to worry in the daytime and too sleepy to worry at night.

CHEESE BALL

Mrs. Ervin (Edna) Bontrager

8 oz. cream cheese
6 oz. bacon cheese
1/4 tsp. garlic salt
1/4 tsp. onion salt
1/4 tsp. celery salt or
  Lawry's seasoned salt

1–2 tsp. Worcestershire sauce
1 pkg. dried beef (cut up)
1 tsp. minced onion (optional)

Form into ball. Roll in parsley flakes and nuts if you wish.

CHEESE BALL

Vera Miller

8 oz. cream cheese
1 lb. Velveeta cheese
  (or other)
2 tsp. Worcestershire sauce

dash of seasoned salt
pinch of garlic salt
1 sm. onion (chopped)
1 pkg. dried ham or beef

Cream together cheeses and mix rest of ingredients. Garnish with parsley. If desired add slivered almonds.

SOFT PRETZELS

Mrs. Ervin (Edna) Bontrager
Mrs. Leroy (Betty) Yoder

2 Tbsp. yeast
1 1/2 c. warm water
3/4 tsp. salt

2 heaping tsp. brown sugar
4 1/2 c. bread flour

Mix well. Roll and shape. Dip in soda water solution of **1 1/2 c. hot water** and **2 Tbsp. soda**. Butter pans heavily. Bake at 450° until brown as you would for bread. Dip in melted butter and sprinkle with salt. Very good to dip them in cheese sauce.

---------------- ❖ ----------------

How beautiful the stars on a dark night.

SOFT PRETZELS
Emma Bontrager

3 pkgs. yeast
2¹/₄ c. warm water
1 tsp. sugar

6³/₄ c. flour
¹/₂ c. lukewarm water
4 tsp. soda

Mix yeast, warm water and sugar. Let rise until foamy then add: flour. Knead. Let rise 15 min. Mix lukewarm water and soda; set aside. Shape dough, dip in soda water and place on greased cookie sheet. Sprinkle with salt. Let rise, then bake at 350° for 15 min. Brush with butter. Serve with cheese sauce.

SOFT PRETZELS
Delilah Yoder
Mrs. Ezra (Elsie) Hochstetler

¹/₃ c. brown sugar
1 Tbsp. yeast (instant)

1¹/₂ c. warm water
5 c. flour

Mix together the first 3 ingredients and let stand 5 min. Then add the flour; stir until dough no longer sticks to bowl. Let rise ¹/₂ hr. Pinch off a piece and roll out into pretzel shape. Dip into bowl with 1 c. hot water and 1 tsp. soda mixed together. Place on greased cookie sheet. Sprinkle with course pretzel salt. Let rise 15 min.–¹/₂ hr. Bake at 450° for 10 min. or until golden brown. Brush with butter. Serve with cheese sauce dip.

SOFT PRETZELS
Mrs. Amos Yoder

2 c. warm water
2 Tbsp. yeast
¹/₄ c. butter
¹/₂ c. brown sugar

2 tsp. salt
2¹/₂ c. whole wheat flour
4 c. white flour

Knead thoroughly and let rise for ¹/₂ hr. in a warm place. Divide dough into 24 pieces. Roll and shape into pretzels and place on a well greased cookie sheet. Bake at 450° for 10–15 min. or until well browned. Dip into melted butter and sprinkle with pretzel salt. Serve with cheese sauce or salsa.

GARLIC BREAD STICKS
Mary Esther Yoder

1 rounded Tbsp. sugar
1 Tbsp. dry yeast
1 tsp. salt

1 Tbsp. shortening
1$^1/_4$ c. water (very warm)
4 c. flour

Mix together and let them rise. Roll out to long thin strips and let them rise to double in size. Bake them at 400° for 20 min. When done sprinkle with garlic powder and parsley flakes.

PIZZA BREADSTICKS
Mrs. Katie Fern Miller

$^1/_2$ c. milk
$^1/_3$ c. sugar
$^1/_2$ c. butter (softened)
$^1/_2$ tsp. salt

1 pkg. active dry yeast
$^1/_2$ c. warm water
1 egg (lightly beaten)
3$^1/_2$ c. all purpose flour

Scald milk; add butter, sugar and salt. Dissolve yeast in warm water. Let stand 5 min.; add to milk mixture. Add egg and flour until well blended. Cover and let rise in warm place for 45 min. Put half of dough on floured surface and roll out to 10" x 14". Cut dough in half lengthwise. On one half spread 3 Tbsp. spicy salsa, sprinkle with Parmesan cheese and oregano. Top with other half of rolled out dough. Cut strips width-wise every $^1/_2$". Twist strips as you place them on greased cookie sheets. Repeat with last half of dough. Bake at 350° for 15 min. or until slightly brown.

SNACK STICK
Mrs. Edith B. Knepp

1 or 2 kinds cheese
grapes
pineapple

apples
oranges

Cut cheese, apples and oranges in bite size pieces. Thread on wooden skewers. Enjoy.

TORTILLA ROLL-UPS

Mrs. Harvey (Marie) Hochstetler

8 oz. cream cheese
8 oz. sour cream
$^1/_4$ c. pepper (chopped)
$^1/_2$ c. onions (chopped)
1 c. cheese (shredded)

dash of garlic powder
$^1/_4$ tsp. sour cream and onion
   powder
$^1/_4$ tsp. Lawry's seasoned salt
cubed ham

Mix all ingredients except ham and spread on **tortilla shells.** Add cubed ham to taste and roll up shells. Chill for several hrs. Slice and serve with salsa.

CHEESE WAFERS

Susan L. Eicher

2 sticks oleo
2 c. flour
8 oz. sharp cheese (grated)

$^1/_2$ tsp. pepper
$^1/_2$ tsp. salt
2 c. Rice Krispies

Cut oleo into flour; mix in cheese, pepper and salt. Fold in Rice Krispies and mix thoroughly. Roll into rolls and refrigerate. Slice to a medium thickness and bake at 350° for 15 min. Sticks can be frozen and baked as needed.

MUSTARD PRETZELS

Lydia Mae Bontrager

1 pkg. Hidden Valley Ranch
   dressing mix
$1^1/_2$ c. salad oil
1 tsp. garlic

$1^1/_2$ tsp. dill (weed or seed)
$^3/_4$ tsp. lemon pepper
3 Tbsp. dry mustard

Mix all these ingredients in a large bowl. Add **pretzels** and toss till all covered. Put on cookie sheets. Bake at 200° or 250° till they are dry. Add Accent if desired.

RANCH PRETZELS

Laura Yoder

$^1/_2$ c. cooking oil
$^1/_2$ tsp. lemon pepper
$^1/_2$ tsp. dill weed
$^1/_2$ tsp. garlic powder
1 pkg. Ranch dressing mix
2 lbs. pretzels

Mix together first 5 ingredients; then pour over pretzels. Bake at 300° for 15–20 min. Stir once in awhile.

HIDDEN VALLEY RANCH PRETZELS

Freeda Lehman

$^1/_2$ c. oil
1 pkg. Hidden Valley Ranch
  dressing mix
1 lg. pkg. mini twist pretzels

Mix oil and dressing mix and pour over pretzels. Bake at 250° for 20 min. Stir as for party mix.

RANCH PRETZELS

Anita Kuhns

2 Tbsp. dill weed (optional)
1 c. oil
1 pkg. Ranch dressing mix
2 (24 oz.) bags pretzels

Mix together first 3 ingredients; pour over pretzels. Bake at 325° for 1 hr., stirring every 10 min.

PARTY SNACK

Ida Sue Hershberger

2 c. Cheerios
2 c. Kix
2 c. sm. pretzels
2 c. Rice Chex
2 c. Wheat Chex
2 c. salted peanuts
2 c. mixed nuts
$^1/_2$ c. butter
$^1/_2$ tsp. garlic salt
1 tsp. Worcestershire sauce

Mix butter and add seasoning. Cool 5 min. Pour over mixed cereals. Bake 1 hr. stirring every 5 min., in a 250° oven.

PARTY MIX

Mrs. Raymond Yutzy

6 c. Wheat Chex
6 c. Corn Chex
5 c. sm. pretzels
4 c. Cheerios
1 sm. bag cheese twists
1 box bugles

1 c. butter
2 tsp. Worcestershire sauce
1 tsp. garlic salt
1 tsp. Lawry's seasoned salt
1 tsp. celery salt

Mix Chex, pretzels and Cheerios in a large bowl. Melt butter and add seasonings. Pour over mixture in bowl. Toss until well coated. Toast in 250° oven for 1 hr. stirring every 10–15 min. Nuts may be added. Add cheese twists and bugles as soon as it is done toasting. Mix well to get flavor to everything. Do not add bugles and cheese twists while toasting as they scorch too easily and leave a bad taste.

CARAMEL CORN

Mrs. Eli Miller
James Howard Miller (Age 3)

7 qt. popped corn
2 c. brown sugar
1 stick oleo
1/2 c. light Karo

1 tsp. salt
1 tsp. vanilla
1/2 tsp. soda

In 2 qt. saucepan put oleo, sugar, Karo, and salt. Bring to a low boil, stirring constantly for 5 min. Watch cooking time limit. Burns easily. Remove from heat; add vanilla and soda; stir rapidly. Immediately pour over popped corn in a 13 qt. greased bowl. Mix well. Spoon into large roaster bottom and top or cake pans and place in oven for 10 hr. at 250°. Stir every 20 min.

———————— ❖ ————————

Money can't be used to buy one necessity of the soul.

CINNAMON BEARS
Mary Miller

$^1/_2$ c. margarine or butter (melted)
$^1/_2$ c. sugar

1 Tbsp. cinnamon
4–6 slices bread

Take two bowls; in one bowl a put melted butter and in the other put cinnamon and sugar. Cut bread into squares and dip the bread in the butter then in the cinnamon and sugar.

CARAMEL APPLES
Vera Miller

40–50 apples
2 lbs. peanuts (crushed)

10 (14 oz.) bags or 8 lbs. caramels

Wash apples then dry on a towel. Insert stick into each apple. In double boiler melt caramels and add 2 Tbsp. water for every 14 oz. bag caramels. Butter pan so caramel will not scorch. Dip apples in caramel, scrape off excess; dip in crushed peanuts and place on cupcake paper. This makes a nice treat to take to school.

MINTED WALNUTS
Mrs. John Hochstetler

$^1/_4$ c. light Karo syrup
1 c. sugar
$^1/_2$ c. water

1 tsp. essence of peppermint
3 c. walnut halves

Combine first three ingredients in saucepan. Cook over med. heat, stirring constantly until mixture boils. Boil to a soft boil stage. Remove from heat. Quickly add peppermint and marshmallows. Stir until dissolved. Add nuts. Stir until well coated. Pour onto waxed paper. Separate nuts while still warm. Let set for a day or 2 until they are no longer sticky.

FINGER JELLO
Mrs. David (Katie) Bontrager

2 Tbsp. unflavored gelatin $5^1/_3$ c. boiling water
$1^1/_3$ c. fruit flavored gelatin

In large bowl mix unflavored and flavored gelatin together. Add boiling water. Stir until completely dissolved. Fills a big Tupperware mold.

FINGER JELLO
Mrs. Lester A. Beachy

2 lg. boxes jello   5 c. boiling water
5 env. Knox gelatin

or

3 sm. boxes jello   4 c. boiling water
4 env. Knox gelatin

Stir and mix jello and Knox gelatin together before adding water.

JELLO JIGGLERS
Lynda Ruth Miller (Age 6)

3 Tbsp. unflavored Knox   4 c. boiling water
  gelatin
$1^1/_2$ c. gelatin flavor of your
  choice

Blend dry ingredients, then add hot water. Pour into pan. Chill until firm, about 4 hrs. Cut with cookie cutters. Cube remaining gelatin. Variations: Omit 1 c. water after jello is dissolved then either add: 1 c. fruit juice, melted ice cream, applesauce plus 2 Tbsp. red hots dissolved beforehand, fruit tidbits, or whatever you wish.

————— ❖ —————

Time will reveal everything.

WIGGLY PUMPKINS

Mary Miller
Freeda Lehman

2 (6 oz.) pkgs. orange gelatin 1 (3.4 oz.) pkg. instant vanilla
$2^1/_2$ c. boiling water　　　　　pudding
1 c. cold milk

　Dissolve gelatin in water. Set aside 30 min. Whisk milk and pudding until smooth. Quickly pour into gelatin. Whisk until well blended. Pour into oiled pan (13" x 9"). Chill until firm. Cut into any shapes.

POPSICLES

Loretta Kuhns

1 c. boiling water　　　　　3 c. cold water
1 sm. box ($^1/_3$ c.) jello　　　1 pkg. Kool-Aid
$^1/_2$ c. sugar

　Dissolve jello in boiling water. Mix well. Add rest of ingredients. Put in sm. containers with popsicle sticks. Place in freezer.

———— ❖ ————

If you pay attention when you are corrected
you are wise. Proverbs 15:31.

———— ❖ ————

A quiet life gives sweet delight.

Favorite Recipes

Playing House

A boy of three, a girl of four,
Were playing house one day.
They played that they were man and wife,
And they were going away.
They knocked upon the neighbor's door,
The little girl bowed low,
This is my husband, I'm his wife,
We're visiting you know.
"Come in, come in," the lady said,
"And take yourself a seat,
I'll bring you both some lemonade
And something good to eat."
She gave them each a big tall glass
A cookie on a plate,
She offered them a second cup
Of frosty lemonade.
"Oh, no thank you," the wee lass said.
As she took the small boy's hands,
"We really have to go now,
My husband wet his pants."

—Author Unknown

Beverages & Miscellaneous

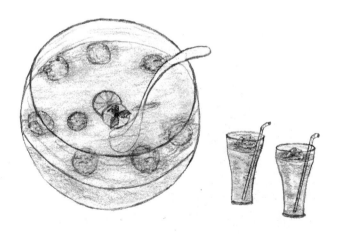

FRUIT SLUSH

Mrs. Naomi Miller

8 Tbsp. ReaLemon juice or 4 lemons	4 oranges
$^3/_4$ c. pineapple juice	4 bananas
1 c. grapes	4 c. water
2 c. sugar	2 apples
$^1/_2$ can crushed pineapple	2 kiwi

Chop everything up as small as you want it and mix together. Put in containers and freeze. Takes around 24 hrs. before it's frozen hard enough to serve. Fill glasses $^3/_4$ full with slush and fill up with 7-up or Sprite to serve. Very good!

SLUSH

Betty Yoder

2 c. sugar	6–8 bananas (sliced)
1 (12 oz.) can frozen orange juice concentrate	1 (20 oz.) can crushed pineapple
3 c. boiling water	8 oz. ($2^1/_2$ c.) 7-up

Dissolve sugar in boiling water. Add orange juice concentrate, bananas and pineapple until orange juice is dissolved. Stir in 7-up then pour into large container or several containers and freeze. Thaw approx. 1 hr. or until slushy before serving. Variation: Add fresh sliced peaches or seedless grapes.

SLUSH

Mrs. Edith B. Knepp

1 (6 oz.) pkg. jello	2 qt. cold water
2 c. sugar	1 (46 oz.) can pineapple juice
1 qt. boiling water	

Mix all together and freeze. When ready to use, open and add a 3 or 2 liter bottle Sprite.

GRAPE WINE
Leanna Shrock

20 lb. grapes   **1½ gal. hot water**
10 lb. sugar

Wash the grapes and put in a crock all together. Then let stand 4 days and put it through a cloth and put in jugs. Don't seal, let it work out on top and keep it filled up with water or wine. Put balloons on top for about 2 weeks, then put on caps and store in cellar.

GRAPE JUICE
Mrs. Perry A. Bontrager

Put **2 c. grapes** and **1 c. sugar** in a qt. can. Fill with **water**. Cold pack 10 min. Put in 3 c. grapes per qt. When you open to use, drain juice into pitcher and add about ½ qt. water, more or less to taste.

RHUBARB DRINK
Mrs. Enos Hilty
Mary Sue Yoder

4 lbs. rhubarb   **4 qt. water**

Boil until soft. Drain and add:

2–3 c. sugar   **6 oz. orange juice**
1 c. pineapple juice

Put in jars and can or keep juice boiling and put in jars and seal. 7-up can be added when ready to use.

---------- ❖ ----------

Are we not all a part of nature?

FROZEN GARDEN TEA CONCENTRATE

Emma Bontrager

1 qt. water
1 c. sugar

2 c. fresh tea leaves

Bring water and sugar to boil. Add tea leaves and bring to a boil again. Steep 10 min. Strain; cool; freeze. Enough for 1 gal. of drink.

EGGNOG

Edna Fern Schrock

1^1/$_2$ qt. milk
6 eggs

^{1}/$_2$ c. sugar
1 Tbsp. vanilla

Beat eggs and add rest of ingredients.

OLD FASHIONED LEMONADE

Mrs. David (Katie) Bontrager

Boil for 5 min.:

2 c. sugar

1 c. water

Remove from heat and stir in:

1 c. squeezed lemon juice

Cool and refrigerate. To serve stir 2 Tbsp. syrup into **1 c. water**.

SHERBET PUNCH

Loretta Kuhns

16 c. 7-up or Lemon Lime
soda
^{3}/$_4$ c. grapefruit juice

1 qt. lemon sherbet
1 qt. lime sherbet

Put chilled pop and juice in punch bowl. Spoon in sherbet, let stand 15 min. Stir gently before serving. Very refreshing. Also good with orange and pineapple sherbet.

PUNCH

Lydia Mae Bontrager

6 pkgs. cherry Kool-Aid
6 pkgs. strawberry Kool-Aid
12 c. sugar
11 qt. water
   Mix well.

3 (12 oz.) frozen orange juice
3 (12 oz.) frozen lemonade
2 (2 liter) 7-up or gingerale

HOT CHOCOLATE MIX

Mrs. Harley H. Lambright

4 c. instant dry milk
1 c. coffee creamer
2 scant c. powdered sugar

1 (1 lb. 14 oz.) container
Nestle's Quick

Mix all together. Makes 1 gal mix. Put $1/4$ c. mix in 8 oz. cup; fill with boiling water.

HOT CHOCOLATE MIX

Wilma Miller

2 lbs. Nestlé Quik
2 lbs. powdered sugar

2 lbs. dry milk
8 oz. creamer

Mix altogether $1/4$ c. mix to 1 c. hot water.

PEDIALYTE PEP

4 c. water
1 Tbsp. sugar

$1/4$ tsp. salt
jello

Bring water to boil. Add sugar and salt. Remove from heat. Add jello to taste. This is for a person/child who is sick with fever and/or isn't able to keep food down. A drink doctors have recommended for said ailment and works well. Very cost efficient.

WHOOPING COUGH SYRUP

Emma Hochstetler

Take **1 lemon** (sliced thin) and add:

$^1/_2$ pt. flax seed oil	**1 qt. water**

Simmer for 4 hrs. Do not boil! Strain while hot, add **2 oz. honey.** If there is less than a pint of mixture, add enough water to make a pint.

Dose: 1 Tbsp. 3 times a day and an additional dose after each severe coughing. This remedy has not been known to fail a case being affected in 4–5 days if given when child first whoops. Keep in a cold place; it spoils easily! Also good for chest colds.

HOMEMADE YOGURT

Esther E. Eash

1 gal. skim milk	**1 c. sugar**
1 heaping Tbsp. unflavored gelatin (dissolved in $^1/_2$ c. water)	**1 c. plain yogurt**
	$^1/_2$ c. flavored gelatin (lemon, lime, orange, etc.)

Heat milk to 180°–190°. Cool to about 115°. Add the unflavored gelatin (dissolved in water), sugar, yogurt and flavored gelatin. Whip it up real good with egg beater, then put lid on and set in oven with just pilot light for 8 hrs. or overnight. Whip it up again when done and put in jars and refrigerate overnight or until thoroughly chilled.

───── ❖ ─────

We do not know one millionth of one percent about anything.

—*Thomas Edison*

───── ❖ ─────

More time is what we want, but where does it go?

YOGURT

Mrs. Daniel (Martha) Miller

2 qt. milk
2 Tbsp. yogurt
$^1/_2$ c. sugar
1 pkg. plain gelatin
vanilla to taste

Heat milk to 190°. Add gelatin which has been dissolved in a little water. Cool to 130°. Mix yogurt and sugar together until smooth then add to milk. Pour into jars and set in 80° water for 8 hrs. May set it on your warm cookstove shelf. Chill and it's ready to eat. Save 2 Tbsp. for your next batch.

YOGURT

Treva Miller

1 gal. milk
2 Tbsp. gelatin
$^1/_2$ c. water
2 Tbsp. vanilla
4 Tbsp. plain yogurt
1$^1/_2$ c. white sugar

Heat milk to 190°. While heating, soak gelatin in water, add to milk when it reaches 190°, then cool to 130°. Then add vanilla, plain yogurt, and white sugar. Beat until smooth. Cover and put in oven with pilot on (or anywhere it's warm) overnight or 7–8 hrs. Honey or maple syrup can be used instead of sugar. Any fruits or pie fillings can be added to yogurt.

EAGLE BRAND MILK

Mrs. Daniel (Martha) Miller

Boil together **1 part sugar** and **2 parts milk** until thickened, (225° or jelly on candy thermometer). Put this in double boiler and cook until caramelized; works for fixing pineapple rings.

❖

Computers can figure out anything except the things that just don't add up.

DIRECTIONS TO SPROUT SEEDS, BEANS OR GRAINS

Mrs. Daniel (Martha) Miller

1. Take a 2 qt. jar and pour 3–4 Tbsp. seeds or 1 c. beans or grains.
2. Pour 1 pt. lukewarm water over the seeds or 1 qt. over the beans or grains.
3. Put sprouting lids on the jars and let them soak about 7 hrs. or overnight.
4. Every morning and evening rinse them off thoroughly with room temperature water, then let them drain 3–10 min. in your sink with lid on and jar upside down, a little slanted.
5. Next, turn jar around and around so as to get the seeds or grains to cling to the sides of the jar (beans won't cling).
6. Set the jars in a bowl (a 5 qt. ice cream pail works great) in a slanted upside down position.
7. Set in a dark place between rinsing times for the first 3 days. We set ours in the cabinet, but it shouldn't be too warm or they will wither and die. Keep on rinsing every day until ready to eat.

Note: if you want healthy looking houseplants, water them with the water your seeds were soaked in. It's full of goodies for you and your plants.

MARINATED CARROTS

Anna Fern Hochstetler

3 lbs. carrots	1 tsp. salt
1 can tomato soup	1/2 pepper
1 c. sugar	1 tsp. dry mustard
1/2 c. oil	1 onion (sliced)
1/3 c. vinegar	1 green pepper (sliced thin)

Peel and slice carrots in 1/2" pieces. Cook just till tender and drain. Whip next 7 ingredients till well blended. Combine carrots, onion rings and pepper slices and pour dressing over all. They keep in refrigerator for several weeks.

MARINATED CARROTS
Fanny Mae Bontrager

5 c. carrots (sliced and cooked)
1 med. onion (thinly sliced in rings)
1 sm. green pepper (thinly sliced in rings)
1 (10$^1/_2$ oz.) can tomato soup
$^1/_2$ c. salad oil
1 c. sugar
$^3/_4$ c. vinegar
1 tsp. prepared mustard
1 tsp. Worcestershire sauce

Mix vegetables. Blend remaining ingredients. Pour over vegetables. Cover and marinate 12 hrs. Keeps 2 weeks. Sauce may be used again.

SWEET AND SOUR SAUCE

2 c. water (divided)
$^1/_4$ c. oil
1$^1/_2$ c. corn syrup
$^3/_4$ c. vinegar
2 tsp. paprika
$^1/_4$ tsp. ginger
$^1/_4$ tsp. turmeric
3 tsp. salt
1 tsp. soy sauce
$^1/_2$ c. white sugar
3 Tbsp. cornstarch
pinch of onion salt

In 2 qt. saucepan heat 1 $^1/_2$ c. water, oil, corn syrup, vinegar, paprika, ginger, turmeric, salt and soy sauce. In shaker put $^1/_2$ c. water, sugar and cornstarch until well blended. Slowly pour into simmering liquid. Chill. Use this sauce to dip chicken nuggets.

BARBECUE SAUCE FOR 10 CHICKENS
Mrs. Eli (Mary Etta) Miller

1 qt. water
$^1/_2$ tsp. black pepper
$^1/_2$ c. salt
$^1/_2$ oz. Worcestershire sauce
$^1/_2$ lb. butter

Apply with a dish mop or pastry brush after each turning.

CHICKEN BARBECUE SAUCE
Mrs. Roy E. Miller

$1^1/_2$ c. water
$1^1/_2$ c. vinegar
$2^2/_3$ Tbsp. salt
$3/_4$ Tbsp. pepper
$1/_2$ stick butter

1 tsp. garlic salt
$1^1/_2$ Tbsp. Worcestershire sauce
$1/_3$ onion (diced)
a little sugar

Simmer then brush on chicken as you grill them. Enough for 3 chickens.

CHICKEN BRINE FOR GRILLING
Delilah Yoder

1 gal. water
1 c. Tender Quick
$1/_2$ c. Worcestershire sauce

1 c. brown sugar
$1/_8$ c. soy sauce
$1/_2$ tsp. black pepper

Mix all together. Let chicken soak for 3 days before grilling.

BRINE TO SOAK TURKEY
Mrs. Roy E. Miller

$1/_2$ c. Tender Quick   1 gal. water

Make brine with Tender Quick and water and immerse turkey into the brine. Let soak $2^1/_2$ days. When ready to bake turkey, rub with $1/_2$ stick oleo mixed with **2–3 Tbsp. liquid smoke.** Bake for several hrs.

———— ❖ ————

Wash hands with cold water and soap to remove smells!
Hot water opens pores and lets the smell into the skin.

FRENCH FRY BATTER (FOR ONIONS RINGS AND CHICKEN PIECES)
Mrs. William (Luella) Schrock

1 c. flour (sifted)
1 tsp. salt
1 tsp. paprika
1 tsp. baking powder
1 Tbsp. sugar
1 c. milk

Mix dry ingredients, add milk and beat until smooth. Dip pieces of chicken or onion rings in batter and fry in fat heated to 365°. For chicken cook meaty pieces first then fry 13 min.

DEEP FAT FRY MIX
Mrs. Jr. (Barbara) Yoder

1 c. flour
1 heaping Tbsp. seasoned
  salt
1$^1/_2$ tsp. salt
1 egg
a little milk

Dip in flour mix first, then in egg mix, then back in flour mix again.

FISH OF STROH BATTER
Mrs. David (Marlene) Miller

4 Tbsp. Durkee seasoned salt
2 Tbsp. paprika
$^3/_4$ tsp. salt
$^1/_2$ tsp. sage
1 tsp. red pepper
3 c. flour

Mix all dry ingredients well. Beat together:

2 eggs
1 c. milk

❖

To remove fish odor from hands, utensils, and dish cloths, use one teaspoon baking soda to a quart of water.

TARTAR SAUCE

Mrs. David (Marlene) Miller

1 c. mayonnaise
1/4 c. milk

1/4 c. sugar
2 Tbsp. sweet pickle relish

EXTENDER FOR MAKING REDUCED FAT MAYONNAISE

Fanny Mae Bontrager

1 qt. water
1/4 c. sugar
1/2 Tbsp. salt
3/4 c. Perma Flo or clear jel

1 c. water
1/2 c. vinegar
1/2 Tbsp. prepared mustard
4 Tbsp. lemon gelatin powder

Bring to boil water, sugar and salt. Make paste of starch and water. Add to boiling water. Stir constantly while mixture comes to boil and thickens. Remove from heat. Add vinegar, mustard and jello. Stir till ingredients are well blended. Keep stirring until you are sure jello is completely dissolved. Cool. Mix with 1 qt. mayonnaise. Refrigerate.

HOMEMADE BISQUICK

Mrs. Alvin (Wilma) Beechy

9 c. flour (sifted)
1/3 c. baking powder
1 Tbsp. salt
2 tsp. cream of tartar

4 Tbsp. sugar
1 c. nonfat dry milk
2 c. shortening

Sift together dry ingredients 3 times. Cut in shortening until it looks like coarse cornmeal. Store in covered airtight container. Note: To measure: lightly pile into cup and level. Do not pack. This dough can be used for biscuits and pizza dough and cornbread.

BISQUICK MIX

Mrs. Wilbur (Norma) Bontrager

10 c. flour
5 Tbsp. baking powder
2^1/$_2$ tsp. salt
1^2/$_3$ c. shortening

Mix all together till crumbly. Store in airtight container. Measure out amount needed and add milk till right consistency. Use for biscuits, pizza crust or whatever you wish.

TACO SHELLS

Mrs. Floyd (Loretta) Lehman

^{1}/$_2$ tsp. Tabasco sauce
2 c. milk
^{3}/$_4$ c. cornstarch
4 Tbsp. butter (melted)
4 eggs
1 tsp. salt
1^1/$_2$ c. cornmeal

Mix all together. Fry in a well greased pan. About ^{1}/$_2$ c. for 1 shell. Use a hot pan. Serves 8.

QUICK HOMEMADE NOODLES

Mrs. David (Katie) Borntrager

2 c. egg yolks + 3 more yolks
1^1/$_2$ c. boiling water
4 lb. pastry flour (scant)

Take a Tupperware Fix 'n Mix bowl and put on scales. Put in flour until it shows 4 lbs. Set aside. Beat egg yolks. Add boiling water and beat until frothy. Dump into flour mixture and stir until well mixed. Let stand for 15 min. Flour your working surface lightly and knead until done. Proceed as usual.

TEN MINUTE NOODLE DOUGH
Wilma Miller

2 c. egg yolks
1¹/₂ c. boiling water
1 Tbsp. salt (optional)

Put enough pastry flour in Fix 'n Mix bowl, so that bowl and flour weigh 4 lbs. Beat egg yolks, water and salt together till foamy. Don't let water and egg yolks set, beat at once. Add flour and stir with large fork till you can't stir anymore, then knead with hands till you have a ball. No need to have flour worked all through dough. If this is too sticky add some flour and put lid on and let set for 10 min. Then knead again. The rest of flour will disappear in a hurry. Do not mix 2 batches in 1 hitch.

PERFECT PEANUT BUTTER

7 (1 lb. 2 oz.) jars peanut butter (plain or crunchy)
3 c. butter
3 c. brown sugar
1¹/₂ gal. marshmallow topping
3 c. light Karo or maple syrup
4¹/₂ c. hot water

In 3 qt. saucepan melt butter and dissolve brown sugar. Meanwhile in 13 qt. bowl, combine peanut butter, marshmallow topping, and Karo. Rinse sticky jars with the hot water and store in jars until just before serving if using crunchy peanut butter, otherwise the peanuts absorb water. Add water immediately for plain peanut butter.

❖
---

*1 tablespoon cornstarch equals 2 tablespoons
flour for thickening gravies.*

PEANUT BUTTER

Mrs. Freeman E. Yoder

8–10 lb. peanut butter
2 gal. marshmallow topping
2 lbs. oleo (softened)
4 c. Karo (white)
6 c. brown sugar
4 c. hot water

Mix together in a large mixing bowl. Dissolve the brown sugar in the hot water. Mixture will thicken after setting. If too thick when ready to use, may add a little more water.

ANDERSON SAUCE

Mrs. Lester A. Beechy

2 c. brown sugar
1 c. cream
$^1/_2$ gal. light Karo

Boil sugar and cream until soft ball stage. Take off stove and slowly add Karo. If you use white sugar, use dark Karo.

CHEESE SPREAD FOR CHURCH

Mrs. Perry A. Bontrager

1 (2 lb.) box cheese
1 can Milnot evaporated milk
$^1/_3$ stick oleo
$1^1/_3$ c. milk

Heat milk to boiling point. Add rest of ingredients. Heat and stir until melted. Set kettle in boiling hot water then it will not scorch so easily. 5 batches for a large church.

ZESTY CHEESE SPREAD

6 (2 lb.) boxes cheese
1 c. oleo
4 qt. milk (divided)
12 Tbsp. flour

2 scant tsp. salt (optional)
2 tsp. Worcestershire sauce
2 tsp. garlic salt

Use oleo wrappers to grease bottom and sides of large roaster. Place oleo and cheese in roaster to melt at 250° oven. Heat 3½ qt. milk in 6 qt. kettle. Make paste with remaining 2 c. milk and flour. Pour paste through sieve then slowly add to hot milk, stirring constantly until it thickens slightly. When it simmers remove from heat. Add salt and sauce. Combine white sauce mixture and melted cheese in 13 qt. bowl. Makes approx. 10 qt. This has a nice thick spreading consistency when cooled. Add more scalded milk if you want it thinner.

CHEESE WHIZ

Mrs. John Hochstetler
Mrs. David I. Bontrager

3 (2 lb.) boxes cheese
½ c. butter

2 c. milk
3¼ c. cream

Melt cheese in double boiler; then add butter, milk and cream. Scald milk and cream before adding cheese.

CHEESE WHIZ

Mrs. Amos L. Miller

2 c. cream or evaporated
   milk
2 c. milk

4 lbs. processed cheese
1 stick oleo (melted)

Heat milk and cream until a skin forms on top. Gradually add slices of cheese and allow to melt. Keep well stirred. Add oleo. After starting to add cheese, mixture may be transferred into a roaster and placed in oven. May also be left in pan and placed on an inverted iron skillet on stove to continue adding cheese, to keep from scorching or boiling, yet hot enough to melt the cheese.

SPREADING CHEESE

Mary Miller

3 gal. thick milk
1¹/₂ tsp. soda

¹/₂ c. margarine
1 c. hot cream

Scald milk and let set 20 min. Drain off whey. Wash curds in salt water and drain. Put soda in curds and let set 1¹/₂ hrs. Melt curds and margarine in skillet; curds will dissolve. Add hot cream.

CHEESE SAUCE

Mrs. Lester A. Beechy

2 Tbsp. butter
2 Tbsp. flour
¹/₂ tsp. salt
1¹/₂ c. milk

¹/₂ lb. cheese
1 can cream of mushroom soup
 (optional)

Melt butter in saucepan. Add salt and flour and stir. Add milk slowly. Add cheese and heat until cheese melts and bubbles. Add cream of mushroom soup if desired.

CHEESE SAUCE (FOR HAYSTACKS)

Mary Miller

1¹/₂ c. butter
1¹/₂ c. flour
1 Tbsp. salt
¹/₂ Tbsp. pepper

3 qt. milk
1 Tbsp. prepared mustard
3 c. shredded cheese

Melt butter and heat with milk. Heat ¹/₂ of milk to boiling. Mix flour, salt and pepper. Gradually add remaining ¹/₂ of milk. Stir mixture into boiling milk. Bring to boil. Boil gently for 1 min. Remove from heat and add cheese and mustard.

GUNK

Mary Esther Yoder

2 c. Elmer's glue
1¹/₂ c. water
2 tsp. 20 Mule Team borax

1 c. water
few drops of food color

Measure glue and 1¹/₂ c. water into a bowl and mix. In a second bowl dissolve borax and 1 c. water; add coloring. Add to glue mixture. Stir. This is a fun thing for children to play with. Keep refrigerated.

PLAY DOUGH

Christina Miller

2 c. flour
3 Tbsp. vegetable oil
4 tsp. cream of tartar

2 c. water
1 c. salt
food coloring

Mix all these ingredients together in a pan. Cook over med. heat until mixture starts boiling or forms a ball (about 2–3 min.). Remove from heat and cool enough to handle. Knead dough like bread until smooth and supple.

PLAY DOUGH

Mrs. Freeman Schmucker

2 c. flour
1 c. salt
2 tsp. cream of tartar

2 c. cold water
2 Tbsp. vegetable oil

Mix all dry ingredients. Add water, oil and food coloring. Cook till sticking to sides of pan. Knead till smooth.

---- ❖ ----

One dog barks at something, the rest bark at him.

PLAY DOUGH
Mrs. Ezra A. Schrock

2 c. pastry flour
$^1/_2$ c. salt
1 Tbsp. alum

1 Tbsp. liquid shortening
$^1/_2$ c. cornstarch

Mix together then bring 2 c. water to a boil, add food coloring then pour over flour mixture and stir. It will be lumpy, knead thoroughly as soon as possible or cool enough. Keep in airtight container when not in use.

DOUGH IT YOURSELF
LaVerda Yoder

1 c. salt
2 c. flour

1 c. water

Mix together salt and flour, adding water a little at a time. Knead 7–10 min. Roll dough $^1/_4$" thick. Cut shapes with cookie cutters, or knife; attach separate pieces by moistening with water. Bake at 325° for 30 min. or until hard. Varnish when cool. Can be painted with acrylic paints. Fun for children! They will break!

BABY WIPES
Mrs. David (Katie) Bontrager

2 c. boiling water
3 Tbsp. Baby Bath

1 Tbsp. baby oil

Cut **1 roll Bounty paper towels** in half. Remove center cardboard. Place upright in airtight container and pour solution over it. Cover tight. Ready to use in 1 hr. These wipes can be pulled up like store bought ones.

---- ❖ ----

When men retire they go to pieces,
women just go on cooking.

HOMEMADE BABY WIPES
Mrs. Mervin C. Miller

Cut **Bounty paper towels** into fourths, (use only Bounty brand). Fold up and put into sq. Tupperware. Mix:

1 c. water

2 capsful rubbing alcohol

2 squirts baby bath

Pour over towels. Put on seal and turn upside down until absorbed.

MAGIC GARDEN
Edna Fern Schrock
Mrs. Freeman (Lydia Sue) Yoder

6 Tbsp. liquid bluing

6 Tbsp. water

6 Tbsp. salt

1 Tbsp. ammonia

Mix all together and pour over a lump of coal, piece of rock or clinkers in a deep dish or a fish bowl. Add four different colors of **food coloring** at different places. Set aside and watch it grow.

CRUMBLY HOMEMADE SOAP
Lydia Mae Bontrager

Mix in plastic pail in order given:

10 c. water

9 c. melted lard (not hot or tallow)

$^1/_2$ c. ammonia

$^1/_2$ c. borax

$^1/_2$ c. white sugar

1 can lye (1$^1/_4$ c. bulk lye)

Sprinkle lye in last (very important); stir. Let set for 5–10 min., stir again—stir frequently the first 1$^1/_2$ hrs. Thereafter every hr. the rest of the day. Make sure there is no liquid at the bottom or you might have to stir it the next day. Let set in the pail a few days, then cover soap or put in a tight container to prevent drying out. The mixture may look separated at first, but it will eventually absorb and be beautiful and crumbly by stirring. For best results only 1 patch per pail. After a few days it is okay to put together in a 5 gal. pail and seal to cure.

GRANULATED SOAP

Mrs. David Bontrager

1 can lye **³/₄ c. borax**
3 qt. water (preferably rain) **4 lbs. melted lard**

Dissolve lye in water. Add borax, then add to lard. Stir slowly for 10–15 min. Then stir off and on for 24–36 hrs. Use only crocks or enamel containers to put your lye water in.

❁

Doctor: "I see your coughing's better this morning."
Patient: "Why not? I've been practicing all night."

Equivalent Measures

Dash or speck =	less than $1/8$ tsp.
3 tsp. =	1 Tbsp.
4 Tbsp. =	$1/4$ c.
$5^1/_3$ Tbsp. =	$1/3$ c.
8 Tbsp. =	$1/2$ c.
$10^2/_3$ Tbsp. =	$2/3$ c.
12 Tbsp. =	$3/4$ c.
16 Tbsp. =	1 c.
2 c. =	1 pt.
4 c. =	1 qt.
4 qt. =	1 gal.
8 oz. =	1 c.
4 oz. =	$1/4$ lb.
16 oz. =	1 lb.

Household Hints

• To mix bulk jello: $1/3$ c. jello, 1 c. boiling water and 1 c. cold water.

• For any stained Sunday clothes, fix cold water and Swipe and soak clothes for 5 min. or overnight. No need to rub every spot. It's safe on colors and very seldom the spot doesn't come out. This is simpler than spraying etc.

• If you get burned, apply toothpaste and you'll get relief.

• Hairspray takes out ink marks in clothing.

• To clean the lime and water spot buildup around sink faucets, place a paper towel on top and saturate with vinegar. Let set 10–15 min.

• Japanese Beetle Trap: Open a can of fruit cocktail and let it sit in the sun for about a week to allow it to ferment. Then set in on bricks or wood blocks in a light-colored pail. Fill the pail with water to just below the top of can and put it about 25 feet from the plants you want to protect. The beetles, attracted to the sweet and potent bait, will fall into the water and drown. If rain dilutes the fruit cocktail you'll have to start over.

• If you have trouble with diaper rash: put 1 cup vinegar in tub of last rinse water which is $1/2$ full. Soak diapers 10–15 min. The rash will disappear in a few days. You must soak them.

• Keep sewing needles in plastic bag with a piece of chalk to keep from rusting.

• To clean suede shoes rub with white vinegar. Brush with stiff brush when dry.

• When setting out early tomato plants—when they get a good size, take off cuttings and put in water and in a few days you'll have more plants.

• Window cleaner for spray bottle: mix 1 part alcohol and 2 parts water.

• Zippers not working on boots: run a lead pencil over zipper when closed.

• Use vinegar as a conditioner. Fill glass $1/4$ full with vinegar then fill rest up with warm water. Pour on head and rub in, then rinse as usual. Leaves hair smoother and no tangly hair! Save yourself frustrations and your children tears while you comb! Another plus: lice aren't fond of vinegar.

• Add a little salt to applesauce, takes less sugar and brings out a richer flavor.

• To soften brown sugar lumps: put lumps in a jar with a piece of moist paper towel under the lid or heat in oven for several minutes.

Index

COOKIES, BROWNIES & BARS

354

ICE CREAM & TOPPINGS